Justified?

ROB PIOTTER

outskirts press

Outskirts Press, Inc.
http://www.outskirtspress.com

ISBN: 978-1-9772-5826-7

Cover illustration by John F. Welsh

PRINTED IN THE UNITED STATES OF AMERICA

Thank you for taking the time to read my book. I'd like to let you know that this is a work of fiction. Names, characters, businesses, places and events are the product of the author's imagination, as is the story itself. Any resemblance to actual persons, living or dead, or actual events is purely coincidental. Any public agencies, institutions or historical figures mentioned in the story, serve as a backdrop to the characters and their actions, which are entirely imaginary.

To my Creative Muse
You've Always Been In My Mind…

Acknowledgments

I'd like to thank my beautiful wife, Vivian, for your encouragement and support over the years. For believing in my talents and endeavors, I cherish you.

Mom & Dad, I thank you from the bottom of my heart for all you do. Another woman gave birth to me, you gave me LIFE and taught me the true meaning of family. I can't imagine where I would be without you. All that you've done means the world to me.

To my best friend, Jeannie, thank you for always being there in my crazy life!

Special Thanks to John F. Welsh for his masterful watercolor painting, "In The Tuileries, Paris 1956," which ultimately became the cover artwork for this novel. R.I.P. My friend.

To my Editor, Lissa Land. Thank you for helping make this a reality.

For all of you that helped me get where I am today, there are too many names to mention, you know who you are... Thank you!

Chapter One

September 1961

"Faster!" Charlene yelled, adrenaline coursing through her veins, her long strawberry blonde hair flying straight out behind her. Kneeling on the front seat of Kyle's baby blue and white convertible, holding on to the windshield, she had never felt more alive.

Side by side, the last 100 yards to the finish line, engines screaming, tires squealing as each driver pushed their cars to the limit. In the last second, Kyle pulled out in front of the souped-up Camaro, shutting it down as they crossed the designated finish line. The teen cussed through gritted teeth, slamming his hands down on the steering wheel. He knew that he'd been beaten.

"That was a close race!" Charlene laughed, catching her breath and looking over her shoulder as Kyle got out and walked over to the Camaro. Rolling down his window the driver swore under his breath, and with an unsportsmanlike attitude, he thrust out a wad of bills.

"Next time, we'll race for pinks! I could sell your car in the Motor City for a few hundred bucks!" Kyle taunted, pocketing his winnings as he got into his car. Responding with a one-finger wave and spraying gravel across the highway, the disappointed youth sped past them, disappearing around the bend.

Sitting next to Kyle, racing along the twisting mile stretch of shoreline highway between Harbor Cove and Vickers Point, never got old for them. Kyle enjoyed winning road races against local teens with Charlene riding shotgun. Her exuberance and lust for excitement enthralled him. He'd never known a woman quite like Charlene, so carefree and crazily impetuous. It was electrifying.

"You're my good luck charm, Doll! Let's go grab a burger at Smilin' Joe's." Kyle grinned, pulling Charlene closer.

Smilin' Joe's Diner, owned by Joe Walker, became their favorite hangout when they first met. It was a chance meeting. Kyle was on his way back to Detroit when he stopped for coffee and a slice of apple pie at the diner. Well-known for miles around, Joe's Diner had become the place to eat ever since Joe cleverly posted three signs along the highway. The first in the row; *Eat at Joe's.* The second; *Best Burgers and Malts in the State.* The third sign read *Smilin' Joe's Diner, Exit Now.* All led to the bustling Michigan shoreline tourist town of Harbor Cove.

Smilin' Joe, a short and stocky Italian, greeted every patron personally with a wide, toothy grin. Walking from table to table, Joe would ask how their meal was. He was constantly chit-chatting with his customers. No one was a stranger.

Charlene lived two blocks from the diner. She often stopped

by on Wednesday evenings after going to St. Matthew's. A tight-knit, cozy and comfortable community church, it was located at the corner of State and Monroe Streets. She helped lead the youth group and assisted the pastor with the bookkeeping and other secretarial duties. Pastor Mike, a kind, older gentleman in his 70s, saw potential in Charlene. He recognized that she was bright and encouraged her to succeed. The trusted mentor gave her important responsibilities within the church quite often. Most Sunday mornings found Charlene attending the service and enjoying Pastor Mike's sermon. He lovingly spoke to his congregation whom he warmly referred to as his flock. On Wednesday evenings, after finishing the activities with the kids, Charlene would type up Paster Mike's notes for the coming Sunday's sermon. Not considering herself religious, she still managed to find solitude in her faith. Faith in creating her own destiny…

Charlene slipped on her tennis shoes and walked down the well-worn path toward the diner. The familiar trail was overgrown with fragrant alfalfa and wild sunflowers. Joe had hung Old Glory proudly just to the side of the front door and it waved lazily in a mild breeze coming in off the lake.

Charlene noticed a stunning baby blue and white convertible in the parking lot. Sleek and shiny, with fat white-walled tires, it demanded one to look and appreciate her beauty as she sat gleaming in the last remnants of an orange and gold sunset. Charlene ran her fingers along the highly polished surface. It was cool to the touch. She smiled as she kicked off her tennis shoes at the door and slipped on a pair of dark blue high heels. As she entered the diner, her best friend and Joe's head waitress, Alice, greeted her with a hug.

"Wow! Don't you look sharp tonight?" Charlene never went anywhere without dressing to impress. She beamed at Alice's compliment.

"Do you like it?" Charlene spun around showing off the tight-fitting blue dress. It was smartly cut in the latest fashion according to her glamor magazines. Her long strawberry blonde hair cascaded down her back while a couple of curly locks escaped down her front. Charlene's eyes danced with their usual excitement.

"I love it!" Alice replied then added, "Where did you get those heels? They add at least three inches. Now you're almost as tall as me!"

"These heels? Oh, they came with the dress." Charlene smiled coyly and added, "Whose convertible out front?"

Alice laughed and nodded toward a gentleman at a corner table. "His, I think."

Charlene walked to the corner booth with no apprehension whatsoever. "Nice car. Hi, I'm Charlene Strypher," she said, offering her hand.

He took her hand in his, "Kyle Edwards. It's a pleasure to meet you." Taken aback by this beauty that stood before him, he looked her up and down and smiled appreciatively. His eyes lingered an extra moment and then looked towards the plate glass window. "I'm glad you like my car. Ain't she swell?" Still holding her hand, longer than he realized, he let go and pulled out the chair next to his. "Would you care to join me?"

Charlene smiled, "Thank you. I'd love to."

As she sat down, she looked at him through dazzling hazel eyes. They were perfectly lined in coal black and accented by long, thick eyelashes. She was grateful for Merilee's Traveling Cosmetics as they taught her almost everything she knew about makeup.

Sipping his coffee, Kyle hid a smile behind his cup. Cutting an impressive figure, he had dark wavey hair, piercing blue-gray eyes and a finely chiseled face. His square jaw was punctuated with A Devil's Dimple that made him strikingly irresistible.

"Are you just getting off work, Kyle Edwards?" Charlene questioned.

"Yes. Well..., kind of." He took a drag from his cigarette and continued. "I had a meeting up this way. I'm just heading back to the city. Thought I'd stop for a bite. What brings you in this evening?"

"I got off a couple of hours ago. I'm a bookkeeper, but I'm taking classes to become an executive secretary."

Almost an hour passed with friendly conversation and she learned that Kyle was from Flint, a good hour and a half drive west and that he worked for Detroit Motors. The company divided his talents between Flint and Detroit. They put him up in a furnished apartment on the outskirts of the city. Kyle told her it was mostly to avoid the long commute when he worked the week at the Detroit plant.

"My place isn't far from here. It's just about 40 minutes away or so. Can I offer you a nightcap?" Kyle asked as they walked up to the counter.

Alice gave Charlene a knowing glance as she rang up the ticket at the till.

Hesitating and looking at the clock above the cash register that read 9:00 p.m., Charlene answered, "Not tonight, I'm afraid. I've got to get up early. I also work as a nanny during the day. Maybe another time?"

"Wow! You've got a lot on your plate. Bookkeeper, nanny and student? Busy girl!" Kyle exclaimed.

"Hey..." Charlene shrugged. "It's a man's world. I'm just trying to make my own way."

"Well, sure, another time. Can I drop you off somewhere? I noticed you came up from that way and I could save you walking back in the dark."

"That would be nice. Thank you." Charlene smiled and grabbed her tennis shoes on the way out.

Kyle opened the passenger door and Charlene slid onto the white leather seat. He couldn't help but notice his heart racing as he closed the door behind her. Going around the other side, Kyle got in and Charlene snuggled up next to him. He fired up the engine. A deep throaty roar erupted from the dual exhaust and the wheels squealed in protest as he added a bit too much throttle pulling onto the blacktop. "Where to?" Kyle asked.

Charlene pointed, "Just around the corner to the end of the block. It's the second house on the left."

Pulling alongside the curb, Kyle let the engine idle. Elvis Presley's "Are You Lonesome Tonight" came on the radio as Kyle looked over.

"I enjoyed meeting you, Charlene. You are one beautiful lady and I hope to see you again."

"I'm always at Joe's on Wednesday nights," Charlene replied. "Could we meet up there next week around 8 o'clock?"

"Joe's it is. Let's call it a date, okay?" Kyle asked.

Walking around the front of the car, he opened Charlene's door and offered his hand.

"A date it is. I'll see you then and thanks for the lift." Charlene gave him a brilliant smile and took his hand again as he gently pulled her out of the front seat. Unbeknownst to him, Kyle Edwards had instantly become Charlene's knight in shining armor.

She watched as he drove off with a wave and disappeared around the corner. Once he was out of sight, Charlene walked down the sidewalk, around the corner to the end of the next block where she entered Alice's house.

Chapter Two

Alice Brooks was a lovely young woman. She was tall and thin with dark chocolate brown eyes accented by a slender face and long dark brown hair hanging limply down her back. Nothing remarkable about her, more of a plain Jane, she blended in with her surroundings. Despite her rather average appearance, she still had an undeniable grace about her. Although her friends often thought her to be a bit too reserved, Alice had a love for life that was contagious, to say the least.

Head waitress at Joe's Diner for a year, she lived in a modest house with an attached garage on Mulberry Street owned by her mother, Florence. Florence Brooks owned an upscale fashion boutique in Detroit. She occasionally came home to Harbor Cove when she had the urge to visit her daughter. Otherwise, she wined and dined with the elite class in the city. After all, her daughter could take care of herself.

Alice was content with the arrangement. She enjoyed the freedom of living by herself. Of course, she didn't have to work. Her mother could easily help her financially.

Nevertheless, she enjoyed making her own money and embraced the responsibility. Growing up with Florence for a mother taught her early on what a determined woman could do if she put her mind to it.

It was almost midnight when Alice got home from her shift at Joe's. Charlene was stretched out on the sofa and watching an episode of The Twilight Zone. She looked up, "Another long night?"

"Yes, as usual. With the movie getting out at 10:00, it seems everyone decides to come down for a late-night treat. The tips were good so I can't complain." Alice kicked off her shoes and picked up Charlene's legs. She dropped down on the sofa, exhausted.

"You're staying, right?" Alice asked, stifling a yawn.

"Yes," Charlene replied. She sat up, crossing her legs, asking, "so, what do you think about Kyle? Isn't he a dream boat? I love his car!"

Eyebrows raising in amazement, Alice cautioned, "slow down! You just met this guy. Besides, he looks quite a bit older."

"With age comes the experience I love and he's obviously well off. He wants to see me again!" Charlene giggled impishly. "I told him next Wednesday night at Joe's." She winked. "We'll see where it goes from there."

Alice just shook her head. She knew her best friend better than her best friend knew herself. Once Charlene made up her mind, there was no changing it. She was bound and determined to fill the emptiness in her life by running and loving blind. Jumping from relationship to relationship often resulted in her clouded judgment. Fortunately, Alice was always there to pick up the pieces when things didn't work out as Charlene had planned.

"I'm heading to bed. You coming?" Alice took Charlene's hand and together they trudged up the stairs. Alice was out the minute her head hit the pillow. Across the hall, Charlene stared up at the ceiling looking past the darkness to next Wednesday night. Already, she longed for Kyle's caress. In Charlene's mind, the first time almost always predicted how the relationship would play out. Alice told her there was much more to it than just sex. Charlene knew she was right but she needed the physical attention, too. The attraction was definitely there. This time would be different. She wanted more. She wanted it all.

Rolling over on her side, she looked out the window and focused on the brightest star in the midnight sky. She made a wish, said a little prayer and drifted off to sleep.

The 6:30 alarm sounded and Charlene knocked it off the nightstand in an effort to silence the maddening contraption. It clattered on the hardwood floor, spinning out of control. She got out of bed and silenced the annoying object. She dressed and made her way downstairs to the welcoming aroma of coffee brewing. Pouring a cup, she added cream and sugar then scribbled a note to Alice.

"*Headed out. You know where I'll be. Have a wonderful day, sleepy head! Love you!*" Closing the door lightly behind her, Charlene walked a block and a half to the second red brick house from the corner.

"Good morning, JoAnn. I'm here."

Standing in front of the floor-length mirror, putting in her earrings and fussing with her hair, JoAnn offered up a thin smile.

"Good morning." she clipped. "Make sure the girls are up and get them ready for school. Feed them breakfast and get them to the bus stop on time. Oh! And be a dear and pack their lunches." Turning, JoAnn picked up her purse and walked down the foyer, high heels clicking on the tile as she went. "Gotta go," she recited robotically.

Morning after morning, day after day, this was the routine Charlene was used to.

Completely devoid of emotion, it's what JoAnn expected of her. She saw it as a fair exchange for room, board and a small stipend. She worked Monday through Friday until the parents got home, leaving her weekends free to do as she pleased. In this upper-middle-class family, both parents worked to make a living. JoAnn was a teller at Harbor Cove's Savings and Loan and her husband, Sam, worked on the assembly line at Detroit Motors. He would leave early and take a shuttle into Detroit. He often arrived home late depending on the shifts. Charlene was responsible for nine-year-old Mildred and six-year-old Suzanne.

The girls got along okay. Mildred, who preferred to be called Millie, was blessed with sharp blue eyes and curly auburn hair. A little on the heavier side, with a devilish rebellious streak, she enjoyed pushing Charlene's buttons. She learned to stop when Charlene threatened to tell her father that Millie had been unruly. Sam was downright mean when it came to discipline so the girls cowered when there was the looming fear of punishment. Knowing this, Charlene would never go through with the threat.

Petite with smiling hazel eyes and blonde ringlets of her own, little Suzanne, Suzi Q, had Charlene wrapped around her little finger. Charlene often thought that, if one day, she ever had a little girl, that girl would be just like Suzanne. "Time to get up you two!" Charlene called out as she climbed the stairs. "Let's get dressed and ready for school." Both children were sound asleep in dreamland, making it challenging for Charlene to get them going. She gently shook them awake. Millie stretched and yawned then made her way to the bathroom.

"Come on, Suzi Q. Time to get up."

Charlene picked her up and gave her a little tickle. In no time, she was giggling. "Can we have pancakes for breakfast?" Suzi asked.

"I think I can whip up a batch. Only if you get ready quickly. No lollygagging."

"Deal!" Suzi slid down and ran over to her dresser.

"See you downstairs for breakfast!" Charlene called out towards the bathroom making sure Millie heard her.

Kids were dressed, breakfast was served and lunches were packed. "Off to the bus stop, girls. We don't want to be late."

Millie fussed, "I wish it were the weekend. I hate school!"

"Me, too. It will be here soon enough. Just a couple more days. Now, come on. Let's go."

The children climbed aboard the school bus and Charlene waved at Suzi Q who was smiling from the front seat window. Always happy, this little girl was Charlene's saving grace. She knew she would miss her dearly when it was time to move on. The clock was ticking. That time for Charlene would be sooner rather than later. She hoped.

Chapter Three

"It's finally Wednesday!" Charlene exclaimed. "What am I going wear tonight?"

Alice laughed at Charlene's excitement. "I'm sure you'll find something in Mom's wardrobe. Don't overdo it, though. After all, it is a Wednesday night. Save the major flair for the weekend." Alice and Charlene lived for the weekends. During the day, it was fun in the sun along the Lake Huron shoreline, sunbathing on the beach without a care in the world. Evenings were reserved for letting their hair down and unwinding in the limited nightlife of Harbor Cove. One of their favorite things to do was raid Florence's closet and dress to the nines for a night out on the town. They usually ended up at Vic's, the one and only hot spot in Harbor Cove. Charlene was certain she would go insane without this temporary escape from reality and the weekly mundane life that held her captive.

Charlene shrugged, "Okay. I guess I could dress a little more casually. Maybe I can take Kyle on a tour of our little town and do some hiking along the beach up to Vickers Point."

Alice nodded and encouraged, "There you go. Sounds like fun."

Charlene settled on a pair of tight blue jeans with a white sleeveless top. When reaching for her bra she stopped, deciding to go braless. Her nipples hardened as the soft silky material brushed against her skin. Looking in the mirror with an appreciation for her seductiveness, she caught a glimpse of the past. Lost in the moment, she stiffened.

"There you go again, dressing up like a Hussy!" He railed. Charlene knew better than to reply. Doing so might result in a backhand, blackening an eye. She felt the burning in her cheeks as he roughly rubbed the makeup off her face with a dry cloth.

Alice glanced across the room, watching the scene unfold. She knew instantly what was happening as Charlene began to shake with deadpan eyes staring back from the mirror.

"Charlene, are you okay?" Alice called out. No response.

Breaking her trance and then exhaling a long breath she didn't realize she'd been holding, Charlene nodded. "Yeah. I'm okay. It's just…" she stopped mid-sentence, choking back a sob.

"I know." Alice walked over and gently embraced her. "No crying now. Your makeup will run." Both girls began laughing as calm settled around them. Charlene applied cherry red lipstick as Alice retrieved a stunning set of pearls from her mom's jewelry chest.

"Careful with these. They're real," Alice playfully warned as she fastened the back hasp.

Pulling her strawberry blonde hair back in a ponytail and tying it with a red bow, Charlene did one last touch-up and slipped on a pair of white sandals. She smiled, "God, I look so much younger than usual. Time to go have some fun!"

Alice reached out lightly grasping her shoulders and made eye contact, "Please be careful tonight. I worry about you. I mean, you don't know this guy. Take it slow. Promise me?"

Charlene sighed and offered her pinky, "I pinky swear."

Alice smiled and gripped the digit with her own. "I'll be home after work and no staying out all night."

Sarcastically, Charlene replied, "Okay, Mom. I didn't realize I had a curfew." Alice gave her the look, "You know what I mean. I want you to be safe. Love you."

"Love you too, and don't worry," Charlene called over her shoulder, grabbing a red cardigan sweater on the way out and slipping it on. Although it was still the end of summer, the evenings were getting chilly.

Glancing at her watch, it was almost 6 p.m. when she entered Saint Matthew's sanctuary. As she walked to a large room in the back used for youth group meetings, Pastor Mike greeted her with his usual, warm smile. "Good evening, Charlene."

"Good evening, I was wondering, a friend invited me to hang out down at Joe's this evening. Would it be okay if I left right after youth group?"

Pastor Mike nodded, "Well then, let's get the kids together. Since you have another engagement, we'll not worry about reworking my Sunday sermon. I think I've got it down and hopefully, it has God's stamp of approval."

Charlene led the youth group, twelve kids ranging from eight to fourteen, with the evening prayer and scripture study. Afterward, they shared an open discussion about the lesson and chatted about how everyone's week had gone.

"How does one last picnic and hike along Vickers Point sound?" Charlene questioned. "When should we do it?"

Everyone nodded in approval as Pastor Mike suggested, "We could plan for Sunday, October 7^{th,} after our morning Church Service. The fall leaves on the maple trees should be colorful and, hopefully, the weather will hold out." Again, everyone agreed and talked casually among themselves.

Writing it down on the chalkboard, October 7th, Charlene announced. "Okay. The date is set so please plan to attend. Bring a covered dish for the picnic if you'd like. We'll plan more next Wednesday night."

After closing with a prayer, Pastor Mike led everyone out. Charlene brought up the rear of the group. Pastor Mike stopped her.

"Have fun tonight, My Child. As always, be responsible."

Knowing what he meant, Charlene smiled. "I will, Pastor Mike. See you Sunday."

With her heart beating wildly with anticipation, Charlene quickened her pace. She took the shortcut through the abandoned lot to Smilin' Joes Diner. Parked at the end of the line, gleaming and inviting once again, the baby blue and white convertible seemed to beckon her. The sunset reflected pink hues off the paint. Charlene glanced at her reflection. She exhaled a deep breath and entered the diner. Alice greeted her at the door. "Table for two?" she teased. Kyle was just returning to the corner booth after dropping a quarter in the jukebox.

The first selection of three, "The Way You Look Tonight," by The Letterman, crooned through the speakers.

Charlene offered up a brilliant smile as she walked toward him.

Kyle stood up, "Hello, Pretty Lady!" Stepping back and allowing Charlene to slip into the booth, Kyle smiled. He was dressed in dark blue slacks, brown leather wingtips and a buttery yellow golf shirt. He sported a navy-blue sweater tied neatly around his neck. One might assume he was a college professor. Charlene thought he looked dashing and he couldn't stop smiling, awestruck by Charlene's captivating beauty.

"Is it hot in here?" Charlene questioned slyly. Removing her sweater and feeling the immediate coolness through her thin top, her nipples hardened. She smiled coyly when she caught Kyle stealing an appreciative glance. Charlene felt a pooling of warmth between her thighs as she discerned the lust that burned in Kyle's eyes. Her thoughts further fueled her desire.

Interrupting the sizzling moment, Alice brought over a pitcher of ice water and menus.

Opting for the dinner special, shrimp baskets with fries and Cokes, they talked easily about the past week and planned the rest of the evening together.

"If you're game, I'd like to take you on a tour of Harbor Cove. It's rather pretty at night, especially along Vickers Point." Charlene suggested.

"Sounds good. I hear there's a golf course on the outskirts of town."

"That's right. The Bay Nine. It's just this side of the Starlight Drive-In. I think it opens at 10." Charlene then added, "Maybe we can catch a flick at the Starlight some evening?"

Kyle grinned broadly. "Definitely. We'll plan that for a weekend. Maybe on a Saturday night." Charlene loved where the conversation was going. Kyle was planning on more dates and suggested weekends. She would begin to see more of him. "Stand By Me", by Ben E. King, began. It was on the way up to the number one chart spot.

After dinner, Alice returned with the check.

"I haven't formally introduced you. This is my best friend and roommate, Alice."

Rising from his seat, he offered his hand, "Kyle Edwards. A pleasure to meet you."

Alice shook his hand with a firm grip. Their eyes locked for a moment. In her stare, he saw flashes of an unspoken warning. "Likewise," she managed.

Smiling nonchalantly, Kyle gave Alice›s hand a brief squeeze. Letting go, he sat back down next to Charlene. Curious, Alice asked, "So, what will you two be doing this evening?"

"We're thinking about a tour. Maybe stroll along the beach, up to Vickers Point."

Kyle added, "I'd like to check out your golf course, too. I've got my clubs in the trunk."

Alice studied Kyle. He was fit and trim. She could see him as a golfer. Upon further observation, she saw no wedding ring. Instead, a thick gold pinky ring, with a diamond flashing in the fading sunlight, adorned his left hand. He appeared well-to-do, owned a fantastic car and was gainfully employed, too. He was well-mannered and jovial. Still, there was something that didn't quite sit right with her. Maybe it was his age. Up close, she thought he might be in his mid to later thirties. Ruggedly handsome, she couldn't help but notice his receding hairline and crow's feet at the edges of his eyes. Alice knew Charlene had no concern for his age, preferring older men. Alice was hesitant. Trying not to stereotype Kyle, she still felt an uneasiness that sent up warning flags. She would do her best to respect Charlene's choices. For now.

"We'd better get going. There's a lot to see," Charlene announced.

"A pleasure meeting you, Alice. I'm sure we'll see one another again." Kyle smiled as he opened his billfold and lay a $20 bill on the table. "Keep the change."

As the striking couple walked away, Alice called out after them, "Have fun, you two! Be safe and, Charlene, I'll leave the porch light on for you!"

Del Shannon›s "Little Runaway" echoed through the diner as Charlene and Kyle made their way out. At the door, Alice waved as they got in Kyle's convertible. Charlene's smile was radiant. Watching her snuggle up next to Kyle, Alice fought off feelings of helplessness, premature loss and quite frankly, cold fear.

Kyle was doing everything right. Charlene could see the golden key to her hope chest right in front of her. Everything; the two-story house, large front yard, white picket fence, 2.5 kids and the manicured poodle. From financial stability to, most importantly, her husband's approval, it made her believe she would be his number one, too.

Knowing Charlene›s reasons for dating older men, it was what she was looking for in Kyle that truly worried Alice. She feared this knight in shining amour might end up being a rogue in disguise. For Charlene's sake, she hoped she was wrong.

Chapter Four

After leaving Smilin' Joes Diner, Kyle pulled onto Main Street and passed through the business district of Harbor Cove. Acting as a tour guide and pointing out favorite stores, Charlene directed Kyle to the city's center. A large park with a fountain and a bronze statue of a mariner gazing across Lake Huron came into view.

"Sometimes I come here to eat lunch. Right there, next to the flower beds." She pointed to a park bench facing the fountain.

"Very nice. Who is the statue?"

"That would be John Vickers. He's responsible for saving many lives during the Great Storm of 1913."

Charlene led Kyle to a beautiful bronze plaque that read; "At the north end of Harbor Cove lies Vickers Point. A narrow peninsula jutting off at a 45-degree angle for a half mile into Lake Huron, a slight curve towards the shoreline and creating a protected cove, Harbor Cove is complete with a sandy beach and calm warm water for swimming. Past the jetty rocks, at the end of the peninsula, rising over 100 feet, Vickers Point Lighthouse graces the skyline, standing proud since her creation in 1890. John Vickers, an old sea captain, and his wife Mary became the caretakers and were well known for their heroic acts, guiding ships through severe storms. Married in 1893, John and Mary were about to celebrate their 20th wedding anniversary when the great storm of 1913 hit. Later referred to as the Big Blow or Whitewater Fury, a blizzard with hurricane-force winds bore down on Lake Superior, Lake Michigan, Lake Eire and Lake Huron. It wreaked unprecedented havoc for three days and three nights. November 9th through November 11th. In her wake, causalities were in the hundreds along The Great Lakes shorelines. Boats and crews were cast into oblivion. John, Mary and their 13-year-old son, John Jr., fought valiantly against insurmountable conditions. They kept fires burning and searched for survivors among the wreckage. John and his son floated the lifeboat while Mary kept the lighthouse beacon lit. In the end, they discovered the lighthouse in shambles and Mary was nowhere to be found. Having searched for days, and never locating her, they determined she had been carried away by the storm.

With help from the Department of Commerce and the Bureau of Lighthouses, John Vickers rebuilt the lighthouse and continued manning it with his son. The lighthouse became automated in 1931."

Turning to Kyle, Charlene recalled, "John Vickers died five years after he lost Mary, some say of a broken heart. The ghost stories spring up every November when a cold wind howls mournfully along the point. Locals whisper amongst themselves, telling tales of the flickering light from a lantern seen late at night. Many believe it's the ghost of John Vickers, searching for his Mary along the shoreline and out past the jetty rocks. As you can tell this story has been repeated so many times over the years, I guess I sound like a museum tour guide". Charlene laughed, then continued, "John Jr. went on to further develop Vickers Point. He purchased the land along the peninsula and built log cabins for vacationers. There are twenty-one in all. John finished his project by building a dining and social dance club at the entrance to the point, simply calling it Vic's. His club, log cabins and historical tours of the lighthouse help to keep Harbor Cove on the map."

"Vic's, at the entrance to the point, right?" Kyle questioned. "That's where we had our meeting. It was in one of the rooms just off the bar. Think it was called the Elbow Room. We played some billiards afterward. I was impressed with the high-quality tables. It's quite the place."

Charlene smiled, "Yes, it is. John Jr. tends the bar on the weekends. He's a nice guy. I'll have to introduce you sometime. So, do you want to head on over to Vickers Point? We could walk along the beach."

"Sounds beautiful," Kyle replied as he drove around the park and back onto Main Street. He couldn't refuse opening his convertible up and she responded. He pushed the speed past 80mph. "Careful." Charlene laughed. "My Uncle Frank is the Chief of Police here. He loves giving tickets to speeders along this stretch of highway."

Kyle slowed, pulling onto Vickers Point Road. He parked a few hundred feet adjacent to the beach. Quaint little log cabins lay nestled in the cedars along the point. Flames from a few campfires danced and flickered, casting shadows in the trees and offering the faint scent of wood smoke. The sun was beginning to disappear into the lake. Exploding hues of red, yellow and orange danced within the whisps of clouds in the evening sky. They created a breathtaking masterpiece. Walking along the beach, they skipped stones.

"So, did you grow up here in Harbor Cove?" Kyle asked.

"Yes. I've been here all my life. I think I'm ready to move on to bigger things, though."

"Like what? I mean, don't you like it here? It's so peaceful and there's a lot to be said for small towns. Usually, they're friendly and safe places to live."

"I agree but, I want more than this town has to offer. I'd like to be a full-time secretary in the city and get away from being a caretaker. Don't get me wrong. I love kids but, taking care of someone else's can be a bit much. Yes, I'm ready to move on." Charlene pitched another flat stone across the calm water, watching it skip along the surface. "One, two, three, four, five, six! Beat that!" She exclaimed.

Accepting the challenge, Kyle searched for the perfect skipper. He found a stone to his liking and chucked it across the water's mirrored surface.

"One, two, three, four, five, six." He counted. The stone was running out of momentum. Kyle coaxed, "Come on!" Then seven, just as it disappeared below the surface. "Seven!" Kyle shouted.

As they walked further along the beach, feeling ever more comfortable, Charlene brushed her fingers against Kyle's in a silent invitation. Kyle responded by gently caressing her palm, entwining his fingers with hers.

"If you move away from here, won't you be missed?"

"Maybe by Alice and my uncle, but that's about it."

"How about your parents?"

Charlene hesitated, "My parents are dead."

Kyle felt the mood beginning to change as Charlene became silent. He pulled her close.

Knowing she might bristle at what he needed to tell her next, he rushed to explain, "There's been a change in plans. I won't be able to come up here to see you on Wednesdays anymore due to my job in Detroit."

Charlene began to shake her head, eyes moistening. Before she could reply, Kyle pressed his finger to her lips and smiled.

"I'd like to come up on the weekends and spend time with you. How does that sound?" Kyle asked, his blue-gray eyes staring into Charlene's.

Smiling and blinking back happy tears, she whispered, "I'd really like that."

"How about this Saturday?" Kyle grinned. "Hope that's not too soon?"

"Yes!" Charlene cried, smiling and throwing her arms around his neck and trying to contain her happiness. Kyle leaned in and Charlene met him with their first kiss. Gentle at first, then hungry and passionate. They bordered on losing control. Charlene could feel his hardness pressing against her. Before things got any further out of hand, she slowed their kiss. Charlene buried her head into Kyle's shoulder. She wanted him badly but, not there on the beach. There was no privacy. The first time had to be special.

Kyle took Charlene's hint and they walked silently back to his convertible, savoring the moment.

"The night is cooling off. Let's put the top up and go check out the Bay Nine." Kyle suggested.

Just past the Harbor Cove business district, he turned onto Westmore Road. The Starlight Drive-In could be scen in the distance. It was tucked against a shadowed pine forest.

"Turn here." Charlene pointed as they passed under a wrought iron arch, dimly lit by a spotlight. Bay Nine Golf Club was neatly stenciled across the front. The parking lot was dark, as was the clubhouse.

Charlene stared bewildered at Kyle, "I told you it doesn't open till 10 a.m."

Kyle grinned mischievously, "Yup! This way, we can check it out without having anyone bother us. Come on, let's go."

Kyle drove over the curb and onto the edge of the golf course, pointing his headlights across the green. He stopped the car, got out and pulled out his golf bag.

"You're crazy!" Charlene exclaimed. "We're going to get caught."

Kyle laughed and removed a ball from his bag. He held it in front of the headlight for a few moments and it began to glow a bright florescent green.

Charlene stared in awe, "How on earth?" she questioned.

"Just a little invention of mine." Teeing it up, he drove the ball hard and watched it float down the fairway. It was a sight all its own.

"Night golfing. What a concept!" Kyle called out laughing. Charlene just shook her head in amazement.

"Ever golfed?" Kyle asked.

"No. Wanna give me a lesson?" Charlene teased.

"Come here." He retrieved another ball from his bag

and held it to the headlight. Then, after placing the ball, he handed her a club. "Let me help you set up your stance." Guiding her in front of him, Kyle put his arms around her. He could smell her perfume, the sweet essence of lilac. He breathed in deeply, intoxicated by her scent as he pulled her closer. Charlene looked over her shoulder and held his smoldering gaze with her own.

"Like this?" She smiled devilishly. As she deepened her stance against him, she could again feel his passions rising against her backside. Kyle stifled a groan.

Regaining his senses, he showed her how to grip the club, whispering in her ear, "Yes. Like that. Now, give it a try. Hit the glowing ball down the fairway and follow through with your swing." Stepping back, Kyle watched in anticipation. Charlene hesitated only a moment and then swung with all her might. Making contact with the ball, she sliced it to the right and sent it on an arc along the edge of the fairway.

"Fantastic! You just might be a natural." Kyle shouted. Charlene curtsied and laughed.

"We'd better get out of here," Kyle noticed car headlights exiting the Starlight. Returning his golf bag to the trunk, he opened the passenger door for Charlene. He got in after her and pushed the pedal to the floor. The car skidded onto the highway.

"That was an adventure!" Charlene exclaimed. As they reached her neighborhood, Charlene directed Kyle to Alice's house. It was just past midnight when he parked alongside the curb. "As promised, Alice left the porchlight on for me." Charlene giggled, "She's such a mom."

Kyle got out of the car and opened Charlene›s door.

Offering his hand and escorting her up the walk, they stood beneath the glowing yellow bulb. Kyle leaned in and their lips met. Gently at first then, the spark ignited into a flame with tongues searching. Her heart beat wildly and she could feel the heat rising between her thighs. She moaned and Kyle thought he would lose his mind. Reluctantly, slowing their kiss and catching her breath, Charlene ever so slightly pulled away.

"Saturday night," she whispered.

"Yes." Kyle cleared his throat. "Should I pick you up here? Say, 6 o'clock? We could go have dinner at Vic's. Perhaps dance the night away?"

"That would be lovely," Charlene fished out a ballpoint pen from her purse and took Kyle's hand. "Let me give you my telephone number. Mulberry 68321," she wrote the digits on his palm. "If anything changes, please call me."

"Will do. See you soon." Charlene watched Kyle swagger back to his car. Her lust grew as heat once again began building in her core. He looked over his shoulder with a Cheshire grin as he caught her brazenly admiring his nicely shaped ass. He was thankful that he still found time to work out.

Chapter Five

"So, how was your date?" Alice asked. She leaned against the sink and sipped her coffee, her tone reserved.

"It was amazing!" Charlene replied as Alice poured her a cup and handed it to her.

"What time did you get in?"

"A little after midnight, I think." Charlene smiled wickedly.

Alice listened as she recounted the evening. In her excitement, Charlene began to ramble.

"Slow down. Breathe," Alice crooned.

Not realizing how she was going on, Charlene grinned, "I know! But I can't help it. Kyle was, is amazing!" She fairly sang.

"When are you going to see him again?" Alice asked.

"He told me we can't see each other on Wednesday nights anymore because of his work." Charlene mocked a pout, watching Alice.

"Oh, really? So… was it a one-night thing or what?

Having Alice's full attention, Charlene could no longer contain her excitement.

"He wants to spend the weekends with me! He's picking me up here this Saturday night at 6. We're going out to dinner at Vic's then dancing afterward!"

Alice set down her coffee cup. "Here? He's picking you up here? Why not at Smiling Joe's? Charlene, we talked about this. Until you are totally sure about a guy, he's not supposed to..." Stopping mid-sentence, Alice shook her head. "Things are going awful fast. Please. Be careful. I can't put my finger on it, but something doesn't seem on the level with Kyle."

Charlene's eyes flashed, "Would you quit being so damn protective? I can take care of myself. You're just jealous!"

"I Am Not! Relax. I'm just looking out for you, Charlene." Alice attempted.

"Are, too! I've finally found the One. I've been searching for and you can't handle it!"

Charlene was on a roll and not backing down. She blurted out, "You're so damn worried that you're going to end up being all alone here in this big house when Kyle takes me away from here!" "Alone! Look who's talking. It seems like you're the one who is afraid of being alone. You change boyfriends more than I change clothes. Sometimes I wonder who the lucky guy will be this week. Besides, I have Walter. And eventually, we'll be together. We've been dating steady for over a year!" Alice answered defensively.

Charlene laughed sarcastically, "When was the last time you saw Walter? It's been at least a month. Right?"

"We went out for dinner three weeks ago. With Walter living and working near my mom, we don't get to see each other as often as we'd like. But I've known him much longer than you've known Kyle."

"At least my Kyle is making an effort to see me every week, can't say that for your Walter, can you?"

Alice laughed, "Ever think why Kyle is so anxious to see you? He's after one thing, Charlene. I mean, a pretty girl like you? Do I have to spell it out? Get your head out of the clouds before you get hit by an airplane!"

The silence became deafening as the girls glared at each other. Charlene had made up her mind and, as usual, Alice knew there was no changing it or even reasoning with her. Still, she had to try.

"I'm not sure how many more times I can pick you up when your world begins to unravel, Charlene. Please, take it slow with Kyle and learn more about him," Alice pleaded, then questioned, "Do you even know if he has someone else? Maybe back home? Didn't you say he was from Flint and commuted for his work?"

Charlene extended her hand, palm out. "Stop it, Alice! I appreciate that you care so much, but like I said, I can take care of myself. Stay out of it!" After dumping the rest of her coffee down the sink, she slammed the cup hard onto the counter.

Alice winced and reached for Charlene, attempting to embrace her in a hug. Fighting back the tears burning the corner of her eyes, she begged, "I'm sorry, let's not argue anymore."

Charlene jerked free, "Not now. Just let me cool down. I've got to go. I'm late." Letting the screen door slam behind her she pressed forward. Through the tears streaming down her face, Charlene replied, "I'm sorry, too."

Thursday, Alice worked her shift at Smilin' Joe's. Returning home that evening, hoping her friend had cooled off and maybe come to her senses, even just a little, Alice worried.

The note on the kitchen table was brief. "Alice, staying a couple of nights at JoAnn's. See you Saturday. Love You, Charlene."

Being their first fight of this magnitude, Alice figured it was probably best that Charlene spent a couple of nights away. Also, she needed a break from the drama and stress of it all. She thought, "Maybe JoAnn might offer some advice to Charlene that would be helpful. Then again, maybe not."

Saturday morning Alice, still in her pink robe, heard the front door open. Glancing up from the paper, expecting Charlene, her jaw dropped.

"Good morning, Darling!" Florence Brooks all but sang as she entered the room dressed in a bright yellow sundress and black floppy hat with a matching yellow bow. Such an ensemble might be gaudy to some but Florence carried it with elegance and grace. With short auburn red hair, a power cut and bright red lipstick, she stood out, shining above the rest. In her surprise, Alice almost spilled her coffee as she rushed to fold the newspaper and stand up.

"Mom! When did you get back in town?" Alice asked, and knowing her mother loved compliments, she added, "You look amazing, as always."

"Oh, this? Why, thank you. It's comfortable and still in style even though it's the end of the season. We'll be rolling out the new Holiday line next week. I'll have to make sure I bring up the latest pieces for you and Charlene to try on. By the way, where is Charlene?" Florence questioned, looking towards the living room.

"She's not here yet. We had a bit of a disagreement and she's spent the past couple of nights at JoAnn's. I figure she'll be here later today." Alice explained.

"Disagreement?" Florence questioned with eyebrows furrowed. "JoAnn's? Really!? It must have been quite the disagreement. Charlene hardly ever spends the nights there anymore. Hell, she practically lives here. You two have always been inseparable."

"I know, Mom, but Charlene's changing. I mean, she's so desperate to find who she calls, The One. I'm worried. She is always on the defense whenever I try to talk with her and it's been getting worse since she met this new guy, Kyle. I don't think she realizes what she's getting herself into this time. He's so much older than Charlene and I get a really bad vibe whenever I'm around him. On the surface, he appears to be Mr. Right, but something about him scares me."

Florence sighed, "You have a big heart, Alice. However, you can't beat yourself up trying to be there for Charlene whenever she makes a lousy choice and gets hurt. She will eventually learn. Unfortunately for her, it will probably be the hard way. Maybe the time has come for you girls to take a break from each other."

Alice shrugged, "Maybe you're right."

"You can always come to the city with me for a while," Florence suggested.

"What about my job at the diner? I'd hate to leave Joe hanging and he's been so good to me."

"There are other jobs. Much better than a diner. I could set you up. You'd be working in no time. I have so many connections. Besides, you'd be closer to Walter. I do like him.

He has a great job that pays well. He appears to have a good head on his shoulders, too." Florence praised.

"I like it here. I'm comfortable. But, you're probably right. I would be closer to Walter. A new job? Can I think about it?" Alice questioned nervously.

"Sure, but don't wait too long. This is your life, Alice. Staying here in Harbor Cove is just existing. There is no future in this tiny tourist town. It's time to step up and make something happen. You'll watch the world go by, and before you know it, you won't leave here, ever. God forbid you end up like that cat lady down the street. She must have at least 20 cats!" Both Florence and Alice began laughing and found solace in a mother-daughter hug.

At arm's length, Florence looked at her daughter, "Let's have brunch at Vic's and afterward we can go down to Betty's for manicures and have your hair styled. My treat!"

"Sounds like fun. Let me get dressed and we can get out of here!" Alice always enjoyed spending the day with her mother. Living miles apart, they didn't get much quality time together.

Chapter Six

Arriving at Vic's shortly after 11 a.m., a pretty blonde hostess led them to a table to the side of the entrance. A good number of locals and tourists were going through the buffet line. While deciding what they wanted for brunch, Alice looked up and surveyed the guests in the dining room. To her right, she could see the bar. Wiping the bar down and washing glasses, John Vickers went about his daily routine, getting ready for the lunch rush.

"Good morning. Whom do I talk to about renting a cabin on the point?" Alice recognized the voice. It was Kyle.

"Well, that would be me," John replied. "Being the end of the season, I've got a few cabins available. How long will you need it? I can rent you one by the night, week or month."

"Just for the night. For now, anyways," Kyle replied.

John studied Kyle, "You were here last weekend, right? Had that meeting in the Elbow Room and shot some billiards?"

"Yes. I liked your place and the view so much I thought I'd come back this weekend and rent a cabin, grab some much-needed R&R," Kyle replied.

John pulled a key from beneath the bar, "Cabin 7 is available, tucked back in the trees a bit, plenty of privacy. It's a kitchenette, bedroom, and bath with a clawfoot tub for soaking and has a nice stone fireplace. Outside there's a firepit, fully stocked with kindling and a path down to the water. It's $15.00 a night. Check-out is at noon."

"I'll take it," Kyle replied, signing the ledger and laying a $20.00 bill on the bar.

Handing him the key and his change, John asked. "What are you drinking? I'll buy."

"Maybe later. When I get back from checking out the town, I might drive a few balls down the fairway at The Bay 9."

"Sounds like a plan. Catch you later on." John went back to cleaning the glasses.

Looking up from her menu and following Alice's gaze towards the bar, Florence questioned, "Know him?"

Alice was so engrossed in her eves dropping that she jumped at her mother's comment. "Yes!" she whispered fiercely. "That's him. That's Kyle!"

Florence starred. "Charlene's Kyle? Well, well, well… He does look a bit older. Dresses well and appears well to do. What's not to like?" Florence said coyly, smiling.

"Mom! Keep it down. He might hear you." Alice replied rather harshly.

"In a pinch, I'd consider a go with him. After all, he is closer to my age." Florence teased, knowing it would raise Alice's dander.

Rolling her eyes and shaking her head, Alice replied somewhat disgusted, "You would." She continued to whisper,

"I heard Kyle renting a cabin for the night. He's picking up Charlene at 6 o'clock. Should I tell her what he's obviously planning?"

Florence shook her head, "No, Alice. It's none of your business. Charlene is a big girl and can take care of herself. I really think you should come with me. You need a weekend, away from the drama, with Walter."

After brunch, Florence and Alice enjoyed an afternoon of pampering at Betty's Hair Salon.

"I need to head back, Dearest." Florence said hugging Alice then adding, "give what I said some serious thought. It would be a great opportunity for you. We'll talk soon. Love you."

"I will and, I Love you, too," Alice replied and watched her mother exit the drive. Turning, she entered the house. Glancing at the clock above the kitchen sink, she read 4:30 p.m.

Heading up the staircase, Alice called out. "Charlene, I'm home. Are you here?" As she entered the bedroom, she saw Charlene sitting in front of the maple vanity, applying eyeliner.

"Yes. I'm here. I want my eyes to draw Kyle's attention tonight. What do you think?" Charlene questioned. Winking at Alice in the mirror, she applied the rest of her makeup and finished with lipstick. Then, dabbing her favorite lilac perfume at the nape of her neck and on her wrists, she gushed, "Everything needs to be perfect tonight!"

Alice decided she would be there, as always, for Charlene and replied, smiling, "You look ravishing, Charlene. I'm sure Kyle will be amazed." She almost told Charlene she'd seen

Kyle at Vic's but thought better of it. Their disagreement had all been forgiven and forgotten and Charlene behaved as if nothing had ever happened.

"Help me pick out my dress for tonight?" Charlene asked. Standing in her white silk slip, she went through the outfits hanging in the closet. Alice helped, holding dresses up in front of Charlene as she checked them out in the floor-length mirror.

"I love this ruby red cocktail dress. The velvet feels so sexy." Charlene hugged the dress to her body. Then, putting it on, she raised her hair as Alice zipped the back. A ruby necklace with matching earrings was the perfect accent for the outfit. Alice helped her fasten the clasp as Charlene put in the earrings. Standing back from the mirror, Charlene smiled. The dress fit like a glove, accentuating every curve. She spun around, nodding approvingly, grateful that she was still the same size as Florence. She draped a creamy, ivory lace shawl over her shoulders and pulled on her gloves. Then, grabbing a matching satin clutch, Charlene paced, watching the clock tick away the final minutes.

The doorbell rang promptly at 6 o'clock. Alice walked down the stairs, opened the door and escorted Kyle into the foyer. Dressed smartly in a grey suit with a black tie, Kyle removed his coordinating fedora. "Hello Alice. Is Charlene ready?" he asked with that devastating grin.

Alice had to admit that Kyle looked rather handsome.

"I'll let Charlene know you are here," she said, leaving Kyle standing just inside the door.

She climbed the stairs and entered the bedroom. "Kyle is here."

With one last look in the mirror, Charlene fussed with her hair. Smiling a radiant smile, she turned and walked down the stairs, feeling like she was floating on air.

Watching her descent, Kyle was indeed awestruck at the enchantress before him. "You are lovely."

"You don't look so bad yourself," Charlene replied, giving Kyle a brief hug and light kiss on the cheek, careful not to leave lipstick behind.

Kyle offered his arm, "Shall we go? Don't want to be late for our dinner reservation at Vic's."

Charlene smiled, encircling her arm in his, "Certainly." Turning towards Alice, "Don't wait up for us. We'll probably close Vic's down. I hear John has an amazing band booked for tonight!"

"Have fun. Um… I'll leave the porch light on for you." Alice choked out, closing the door behind them. She felt the cold fingers of dread encircle her heart as she whispered a silent prayer for her friend.

Chapter Seven

The sun began to set earlier as the summer season faded away into fall. Brilliant colors danced in the clouds above the lake and added a unique ambiance to Vic's dinner club. When building his resort, John Vickers gave special attention to every detail, including the positioning of his dinner club. He was banking on the picturesque shoreline, the lake and all its splendor to bring tourists and locals in again and again.

Kyle reserved a table for two in the back of the dining room overlooking the lake. The view did not disappoint. The big orange ball sank ever so slowly into Lake Huron's shimmering deep blue water, showcasing Vickers Point Lighthouse at its center, a dark silhouette.

Their waiter brought them the evening's dinner menu. Upon returning, Kyle ordered for them. "We'll have the New York strip steaks, please. My companion will have her steak medium and I'll have mine medium rare. We'd like baked potato, butter, sour cream and green beans. To drink, a glass of Merlot for the lady and I'll have whiskey, neat. Make it a double."

"Excellent, Sir." The waiter nodded.

Holding hands across the table, they watched the setting sun as the waiter bought their drinks.

"A toast to a wonderful evening together and most of all to you and your beauty." Kyle smiled, raising his rock glass.

Charlene blushed, raising her glass, "Thank you, Kyle, you're so sweet."

Sipping the Merlot, a bit too fast in her nervousness, she grimaced. Feeling the warm liquid settle, however, she began to relax. "How has the rest of your week been?" Charlene asked.

"Very nice, thank you. I arrived back in town early this morning and played a round of golf. Nice little course." Lighting a cigarette and taking a sip of his whiskey, he added, "How was your week?"

Charlene gazed out the window, seeing Kyle's reflection in the glass as he listened attentively.

"Nothing too exciting, JoAnn, the woman I nanny for, took me to Betty's Salon this morning where we had our hair and nails done. Aside from that, it was a pretty normal week, nothing too exciting."

"Well done, Miss Betty!"

The waiter brought their meal and set Charlene's plate down in front of her, followed by Kyles. "Will there be anything else? Perhaps another cocktail?"

"Yes, please. Top the lady's glass off and I'll take another whiskey." Kyle instructed.

Charlene placed the linen napkin across her lap and began cutting her steak. Reaching for the ketchup bottle, Kyle stared in amazement as Charlene opened the cap.

"Ketchup? Really?" Kyle blurted, trying not to laugh.

"What? I like ketchup on my steak. Is that a problem?" Charlene asked, giggling.

"No, I'm just a bit surprised. I've never seen anyone put ketchup on a steak before." Kyle replied, grinning from ear to ear.

Charlene shrugged, "Well, maybe you should try it. You might find you like it." After setting the bottle down, she dipped a piece of the steak in the ketchup and smiled. Before Kyle realized what she was doing, Charlene held the ketchup-glazed steak inches from his lips. "Taste it," Charlene teased, "Trying something new adds excitement to life. Even little things."

Kyle opened his mouth, taking the bite in and savoring it as he chewed. "Hmm… Not bad. But, I think I'll pass. Kind of takes away the natural flavor."

"Okay. As they say, to each his own," Charlene replied, grinning.

Finishing their meal with easy conversation, Charlene studied Kyle. She had grown very fond of him in the past month. Checking off the boxes on her mental list of pros and cons, she discovered very few were left unchecked. Secretly fantasizing how the rest of the night would progress, her thoughts were interrupted. From the stage across the dance floor, John Vickers tapped the microphone.

"Ladies and Gentlemen, please welcome our entertainment for your dancing pleasure. Up from the Motor City, Mike Wheeler and The Motor City Cruisers!" As the lights came up, John stepped down clapping and bowing to the band and his guests.

"Thank you, John!" Mike called out from the stage.

"We're going to open up with a hit song that's climbing the charts by the Marcels! "Boom Chicka Boom, Boom Chicka Boom Boom, Blue, Blue Moon." The Motor City Wheelers chimed in on their cover of the doo-wap remake. Guests packed the dance floor. Charlene was grateful she took dance lessons a year prior as Kyle was an excellent dancer. The band played through the night and Kyle and Charlene danced to almost every song. Sweating, and nearly worn out, Charlene called out just as the band began playing Bill Haley and the Comets hit, Rock Around the Clock.

"Let's take a breather, maybe go outside and catch some air!" Charlene brushed the hair back from her eyes.

"Okay, better get your shawl. It might be a bit chilly," Kyle suggested.

He returned with her shawl and clutch and they stepped out the back door. Charlene removed her heels and walked along the beach in her bare feet. Hand in hand, they strolled as waves gently lapped at the shore. A full moon reflected white ripples across the water.

"It's been a wonderful night and I've had such a grand time!" Charlene leaned into Kyle.

He smiled, pulling her closer. Glancing at his watch in the moonlight, he suggested "The night is still young. It's only 11:30. I've got a little surprise." Kyle led Charlene from the water's edge, up a path, to cabin #7. He reached into his pocket and pulled out a key, then opened the door with a brilliant smile.

Feeling her heart pounding loud in her chest, Charlene feared he might just hear it. The full moon cast a soft glow across the room, settling on a vase with a dozen red roses. Walking over, Charlene buried her face into them, breathing in their sweet aroma. "Are these for me?" Charlene asked, knowing they were.

"Yes. They are, but they don't even compare to you." Kyle replied, reaching for her.

He pulled her close. The first kiss, a question. The second kiss, an eager answer. And with the third, Kyle deepened the kiss. Charlene kept pace with his escalating desire.

Her mind reeling and fighting back her inhabitations, she threw caution to the wind. Kyle ran his hands across her breasts, kissing her neck. Hands searching further, he began lifting her dress, fingers probing. Charlene moaned, surrendering herself to him. Again, she felt his hardness rubbing against her. Lifting her into his arms, Kyle carried her to the bedroom.

Trembling as Kyle unzipped her dress, feeling it slide to the floor, she allowed Kyle to remove the rest of her clothing.

Watching Charlene as he undressed her, Kyle thought to himself, this time, patience had paid off. He would soon have his beautiful prize.

Standing naked before him, she returned the favor and slowly undressed Kyle, eyeing his lower extremities. She turned and lay on the bed then, reached for his hand. Taking it, he pulled her to the edge. Kyle knelt down and began kissing her thighs, across her belly then between her legs. Charlene arched her back in ecstasy, amazed at how quickly she came. Kissing his way back up to her breasts, suckling her soft pink erect nipples, then kissing her fully on the mouth, he slowly entered her. Charlene gasped for a second, eyes wide. She winced and pursed her lips at the pain as he filled her. Feeling her tightness, Kyle understood the need to be gentle. Charlene relaxed as he quickened his pace. She met him with unbridled passion. Kyle smiled, his blue-grey eyes gazing into Charlene's, watching him as he slid in and out of her. Lost in the moment, Charlene cried out as he brought forth the woman in her. Following his lead into different positions, they loved on through the night. When Kyle could hold back no longer, he emptied himself inside her. They lay wrapped in each other's arms, tangled in damp, sweaty sheets, breathing heavily as the heady aroma of their passion filled their senses.

An hour passed and they drifted off to sleep, spent from the exhaustion of their lovemaking. Rolling over, Charlene sleepily glanced at the alarm clock on the bedside table, then focused on the softly glowing hands. It read 1:45 a.m. "Kyle, wake up! We've got to get going. I need to get home!" Charlene insisted. Untangling herself from the sheets and getting up, she gathered her clothes.

Kyle stirred and groaned. "What's your hurry? Come back to bed." Kyle begged.

"I'm sorry. Even though I told Alice not to wait up, I know she won't go to sleep till I get in. I'm trying to avoid another blowout with her. Tonight, was perfect. We can plan for an all-nighter next time." Charlene winked, reassuring him.

"Okay, let me get dressed, and I'll take you back to Alice's." Kyle got up and turned on the bedside lamp. Watching longingly as Charlene began to dress, Kyle cleared his throat. Looking over, glancing at his naked body and rising manhood, Charlene smiled, fighting the urge to climb back into bed.

Arriving at Alice's 20 minutes later, they stood once again beneath the yellow bulb. One more porch light kiss and Charlene reluctantly pulled away.

"See you next Saturday?" Kyle questioned.

"Yes, for sure. Hey, how about we take in a show at the Starlight? I think Breakfast at Tiffany's with Audrey Hepburn is showing. I love her."

"Then it's a date. What time shall I pick you up?"

"How about 5:30? Should we grab a bite at Joe's beforehand?" Charlene asked.

"That sounds good. I can't wait to see you again." Kyle grinned.

"Can't wait." Charlene agreed and waved as he pulled onto the street.

Watching Kyle drive away and looking skyward, Charlene found the brightest star. Claiming it as her own, she whispered, "Thank you."

Chapter Eight

"Good morning, sleepy head. Are we heading to the beach today?" Alice asked as Charlene made her way groggily down the stairs, heading for the coffee pot.

"Coffee first." Charlene firmly stated. Taking a long sip and inhaling the aroma, she stifled a yawn.

"Long night?" Alice asked knowingly.

"Yes, but I won't kiss and tell." Charlene smiled devilishly.

Shrugging it off, "Whatever. So, are we going to the beach?" Alice asked again.

"Since I overslept and missed going to church, I guess so. Let me finish my coffee and then I'll get dressed."

Alice thought to herself, girl, you might need more than church if you continue down the path you are on. Keeping what she knew about Kyle reserving the cabin to herself, Alice opted to just enjoy the day. Besides, she knew Charlene all too well. She couldn't *not* kiss and tell. It was only a matter of time before her friend revealed all her secrets.

Arriving a little after 1:00 that afternoon, Alice and Charlene laid their beach towels out on the sand. A clear blue sky greeted them with the sun smiling down.

Applying suntan lotion to each other's backs and legs they laid down on their bellies, absorbing the rays. This would more than likely be the last time sunbathing this season. The end of September ushered cooler winds off the water. John Vickers had taken down the volleyball nets in preparation for fall weather. There were already fewer tourists along the beach as many snowbirds were starting to head south.

Charlene lay with her head pointing away from the glare of the water. From there, she could see it. Tucked back in the trees, Cabin 7. Just under 12 hours had passed since she lie in Kyles' embrace, sweat trickling down between her breasts, tangled in the aftermath of their lovemaking. Charlene could feel the warmth growing in her loins as she reminisced. With the waves lapping at the shoreline lazily, the heat of the sun on her back and sweet memories in her heart, she smiled drifting off into dreamland.

She was lying on her belly, naked. The room was sweltering as sweat trickled down her back. Her hair was tangled and sticking to her face. Kyle had just taken her for the second time. She could smell him all over her and feel his seed slipping down her inner thighs. Total blissful exhaustion filled her. Kyle had awakened her insatiable desire for sex and she couldn't get enough of him. Reaching over, wanting more, expecting Kyle to be lying next to her, she found the bed empty. Thinking he must have gone to the bathroom to clean up, she closed her eyes, still smiling and breathing deeply.

The unmistakable hiss of leather clearing belt loops halted her fantasy. Staring wide-eyed, a scream caught in her throat, she saw him coming fast through the floor-length mirror. In seconds he was upon her. Leather made contact with her exposed buttocks. "You Slut!" The man bellowed. Charlene screamed from the pain as the belt came down upon her again and again. The smack on bare skin echoed off the walls, ringing in her ears. He held her down, smothering her into her pillow. She struggled to break free. On the verge of unconsciousness, Charlene broke through the nightmare, falling into Alice's arms.

Cradling and rocking her, Alice whispered, "It's okay," knowing the nightmare all too well that held her friend captive. Still gasping and shaking, tears streaming down her face, then looking over her shoulder, Charlene reached back, pulling down her bikini bottom and searching for the invisible welts. She could still feel the sting from the strikes. Shuddering and melting into Alice, Charlene sobbed uncontrollably. Minutes passed, and soothing her, Alice continued rocking Charlene in her arms, repeating, "Shh… it's okay. Everything is okay. It was just a bad dream."The dreams and nightmares had become more frequent in the past month. Alice could hear Charlene tossing and turning in her sleep, sometimes crying out. Guilt-ridden and born from a haunted past, Charlene was spiraling. She was lost in an uncontrollable dive into oblivion.

Back at the house, the girls cuddled on the sofa and watched television. The Andy Griffith Show was one of their favorites, followed by Bonanza and Gunsmoke. Munching on pizza and sipping cokes, they lazed the rest of Sunday away.

Alice carefully broached the incident at the beach. "Charlene, maybe you should go back and talk to your therapist. Please, hear me out before you say no." Alice continued, "you told me that talking about it with Molly has helped in the past. Keeping it bottled up inside can't be good. Please give her a call. Even though it's been a while since your last visit, I'm sure she would be able to schedule a session."

Charlene withdrew into herself as she often did after one of her nightmares, especially after one this bad. Staring blankly at the television she slowly and slightly nodded her head in agreement. She realized that it was getting harder to spring back like nothing ever happened.

Monday morning, Charlene called Dr. Molly Williston. "Hello, Mrs. Williston. It's Charlene Strypher. Yes, I know, it's been a while. Would you be able to schedule a time for me to come in and speak with you? This afternoon at 2'oclock. Yes, I'll be there. Thank you." Charlene hung up the receiver. Alice gave her a reassuring hug, "I'm proud of you, I'm sure Molly will be able to help, just give her a chance." Charlene offered a weak smile and nodded. "Let's hope so."

Inside Dr. Williston's office, dimly lit with a relaxing scent of lavender, Charlene took a deep breath and closed her eyes, listening to the steady tick, tick, tick of the clock on the wall. She relaxed into the comfortable leather chair focusing on the soothing voice of her therapist.

"That's good. Just relax... Feel yourself settle into the chair. Now, breathe in slowly, hold for just a beat and, let it out. Good, Charlene. That's very good." It had taken Dr.

Molly Williston several months and many sessions to get to this point. This particular case was hard. When the abuse was primarily emotional, it was so hard to prove. Molly knew this young lady had many dark secrets locked away and she hoped to discover the truth in this session. "Today, Charlene, I would like to talk about your father, you've referred to him as *"The Man."* The doctor watched her young charge visibly tense. "We will walk through this together. I will keep you safe. Do you understand, Charlene?"

"Yes," came a strangled reply. The color had drained from Charlene's face and she had become rigid. "Okay. I'm ready." She said through clenched teeth that chattered. "Go back with me now," the doctor began in her soothing voice. "I would like you to take me to that Christmas Eve. Can you tell me what happened that night, Charlene?" That quick, Charlene was back in her old childhood home. She was thirteen and getting ready for her first boy/girl party. She was so excited! Alice would be here any minute with her mom, Florence, to pick her up. Dressed in a beautiful Christmas red dress her mother had purchased for her, Charlene felt like a princess. In her bedroom, she did just one more twirl in front of the mirror to see the bell skirt of her dress fan out. Then, she made a decision. She wasn't supposed to wear makeup but sometimes, her mother would let her try a dusting of rouge. Her mind was made up. She tip-toed from her bedroom at the end of the hall to her parent's room. Everyone was downstairs and she would be super quick. She would dab on the blush and a coat of lip gloss and be out of the house before her father ever saw her. He was undoubtedly already halfway through with tonight's amber addiction. The drinking was getting worse. Many nights, one could find him alone in his den, brooding. He would rant and rave about battles already fought with comrades that had already died. The war sent a very different man home than Charlene knew as a small child. As she stood before her mother's vanity and applied the gloss, the door slowly creaked open. Past her reflection in the mirror, Charlene watched her father walk into the room. She froze. Her heart sank and she started to tremble, hiding the lip gloss in the palm of her hand. As he stood and stared at his daughter, realization finally dawned. His blank expression mangled into one of rage. Before Charlene could take another breath, he started toward her. "Where in the Hell do you think you are going looking like that? You look just like the little slut you are! Streetwalkers wear red dresses, not children! But you're not an innocent girl, are you? You're a hussy! Nothing but a dirty little slut!" Spittle coated the edges of his twisted mouth and he was struggling to catch his breath after the tirade. It didn't stop him, though. The attack continued, covering the distance between them and grabbing a dry facial cloth from his wife's makeup table. Not gently, grabbing Charlene by the hair with one hand, and with the other, roughly swiped at the embellishments on his daughter's face. Struggling free she ran to her bedroom where she cowered in a corner, waiting. Ranting he went downstairs. Angry words were exchanged with his wife. When Alice arrived, her mom told her that Charlene wasn't feeling well and wouldn't be able to make it to the dance.

It had been years since that Christmas eve, but time had a way of keeping it present in Charlene's mind. The memory, intermingling with snide remarks from her father, drove Charlene down a path of depression, self-destruction and pure defiance. Dr. Williston prescribed medication for Charlene but the side effects caused her to have mood swings, fogginess and weight gain. She would stop taking the medication and "*The Man*," would reappear in her life. Taunting her from the deepest recesses of her mind and driving her over the edge.

Dr. Williston escorted Charlene out of the office to her front receptionist, asking the assistant to schedule the next appointment. Writing out a new prescription, she reminded with a stern voice, "Take your meds, Charlene. We'll work together at our next session and further discuss how you are handling things." She pocketed the prescription with no intention of filling it, didn't like the way it make her feel. Besides, she didn't honestly believe that she needed medication. She wasn't crazy. It was easier to deny her fragile state than to face the heart of the matter. In the end, it was always the same. Charlene would be fine, until the next time…

Chapter Nine

"This is your weather forecast for the southeast region, including Port Sanilac, Harbor Cove, and the shoreline up into Michigan's thumb area. Better break out your umbrellas and raincoats, folks! The first week of October will be very wet and cold. With daily thunderstorms, sometimes severe high winds, possible..."

Charlene clicked off the countertop radio. "I hate this time of year," Charlene complained, digging out her raincoat from the hall closet. Her mood was as gloomy as the threatening dark grey clouds rolling in off the lake. Thunder rumbling in the distance just added to her angst.

"Quit being so glum. It is fall, after all, and warm weather can't last forever." Alice chided and then laughed at her rhyme.

"Not funny, Alice. You know, I can deal with a little rain now and then. It's the cold I truly hate. Someday I want to live somewhere warm and leave this godforsaken town behind." Charlene grumbled.

"Have a wonderful day, Dear. See you tonight when you get home." Alice teased.

Charlene huffed, saying something barely audible and sounding like eff this, under her breath she walked out the front door into the early morning rain. Faking a smile to hide her mood, she met JoAnn just as she was getting ready to walk out the front door.

"Oh! There you are. I was wondering if you were going to make it on time." JoAnn commented sarcastically.

"It's cold and raining and I'm here. You don't have to fret," Charlene replied while coolly removing her raincoat and hanging it on the hall tree.

"I'm not fretting. I simply don't want to be late for work," JoAnn fired back defensively. "Anyway, nothing out of the ordinary here. Girls are already up and getting ready for school. You can fix them breakfast and pack lunches. Make sure they wear their rain gear. See you later today."

"Okay," Charlene replied, closing the door behind JoAnn. She leaned against it and sighed, thinking to herself, hang in there. It won't be much longer before she would make her great escape from this mundane existence. Banking everything on life with Kyle, this was Charlene's way out of Harbor Cove.

By Wednesday, she was stir-crazy and longing for the coming weekend. The fall storm raged on in its fury raining all day, every day, and into the night. That evening, after JoAnn and Sam had returned from work, Charlene grabbed her umbrella. Bracing herself against the wind and rain, she fought her way to St. Mathews for her youth group meeting. She ran through the entrance into the sanctuary. Pastor Mike pushed the door closed against the howling wind and rain and greeted her. "Well, hello Charlene. I missed you this past Sunday. How are you, My Child?"

Brushing back locks of wet hair from her eyes, she smiled weakly. "Besides being soaked, I'm fine."

"I see. Do you want to talk about it?" Pastor Mike offered, knowing what *fine* meant whenever Charlene used the word.

Hesitating, Charlene chose her words carefully. In no way was she going to discuss anything concerning Kyle or her nightmare, especially the one she had on the beach.

"I guess I'm just worried about this coming Sunday. I mean, look at the weather. It's raining cats and dogs out there. The weekend forecast doesn't appear promising for our picnic and hike along Vickers Point, either. The kids will be so disappointed."

"Well, if the weather is bad, we can plan something else. How about spending the afternoon bowling? We have enough funds in the youth entertainment coffer to cover that. Don't we?" Pastor Mike questioned.

"Yes. I believe we do." Charlene smiled, grateful for the escape that changing the subject provided. "It's settled. We'll make that our contingency plan. Although, with the way the week's been, it will more than likely be bowling." Charlene commented.

"So, is there anything else you'd like to talk about?"

Charlene chose her words carefully and searched for an out before the conversation became more uncomfortable. She saw it instantly. David, a scrawny pre-teen about 11 years old, was aiming at one of the other kids with the basketball.

"David, you know better. Be careful with that basketball. Don't hit anyone. You know the rules. This isn't dodgeball!" She scolded.

"Yes, Miss Strypher. I'm sorry, Miss Strypher," David recited, holding the ball tightly to his chest and looking down at the floor.

"Okay gang, let's gather round and get started." Pastor Mike called out.

"David, please lead everyone with our opening prayer," Charlene instructed.

"Yes, Ma'am. Please God, bless our gathering together and guide us this evening as we discuss your Word. Oh, and please let the weekend be clear and sunny for our picnic and hike. Amen!"

"Amen!" Everyone replied in unison. As the group discussed their upcoming picnic and hike along Vickers point, the idea of bowling as a backup was well supported by everyone if the weather was rainy. Charlene wrote on the chalkboard, Next Sunday, October 7th. Meet outside Vic's after our church service at 12:30 for our picnic and hike. We'll meet at Lakeside Lanes if it's raining.

After playing a few more games of half-court basketball, Pastor Mike closed with a prayer and escorted everyone out of the sanctuary. The rain had stopped and, walking down the sidewalk towards Smilin' Joe's, Charlene called out, waving to Pastor Mike. "See you Sunday!"

Due to the gloomy weather, Smilin' Joe's was void of patrons. Alice busied herself with filling salt and pepper shakers.

"Looks like it's been a slow night," Charlene noted as she walked in, eyeing the empty booths.

Alice grimaced, "Yes. A very slow night. Joe might even let me off early if it doesn't pick up." Looking up, she asked, "How was your night?"

"Same old thing, nothing special," Charlene remarked.

"So, how was your date with Kyle?" Alice questioned.

"As I said, I won't kiss and tell." Charlene laughed. "Honestly, we had a great time and I'll leave it at that. I'm looking forward to this weekend. We're planning to see Breakfast at Tiffany's it's showing at the Starlight. I hope it doesn't rain. How about you? Any plans for the weekend?"

Alice paused, "Well, Mom is picking me up Friday and taking me to see her new place in the city. She's been wanting to show me around. We'll have a long weekend together. Lately, she's been hinting for me to move down there with her."

Turning, Charlene stared out the window as the rain splashed harder and harder against the pane. Alice watched her closely, waiting for her response.

Forcing a smile, there was a slight catch in her voice, "Wow! That's cool. I guess… I mean, I'd miss you, but then on the bright side, you'd be closer to Walter. You plan to see him this weekend, right?" Charlene questioned.

"Of course, we're going out for dinner Saturday night. I spoke with him right after Mom called last night." Alice answered.

"So, when do you think you'll be back?" Charlene asked.

"Mom will probably bring me home sometime Sunday afternoon. I'm sure she'll have to be back at work Monday morning and Joe will have my new schedule up at work." Alice replied.

"Well, I guess I'll see you then. We can compare notes," Charlene winked. "Oh, and depending on the weather Sunday, we'll either have our last picnic and hike for the youth group or go bowling at the Lakeside. Either way, it will be a busy afternoon." Charlene smiled.

Joe walked out of the kitchen wiping his hands on a towel. He began ringing out the cash till. "Hey, Charlene. How goes it? Alice, I think we're gonna go ahead and close for the night. With this storm picking up, I doubt we'll have anybody else coming in."

"See? I told you." Alice whispered, untying her apron. She hung it behind the counter. "I've finished everything on the evening checklist. Is there anything else you need me to do?"

"Nope. That's about it. Have fun this weekend, but not too much fun! That goes for you too, Charlene." Joe laughed.

"Now, Joe. What could you possibly mean?" Charlene bantered back. Joe just shook his finger at her, smiling his toothy grin.

Chapter Ten

"Are you ready to go, Alice?" Florence hugged her daughter then, holding her at arm's length, brown eyes dancing, she went on excitedly. "We are going to have so much fun this weekend! First, the Holiday Fashion Gala tonight at The Plaza. My partner and I have come up with some fantastic pieces! You will have to pick one for your date with Walter Saturday night. I've also scheduled our Saturday morning at Mimi's Salon down on Colfax. With a new outfit and Mimi working her magic, Walter won't know what hit him. You'll be dazzling!" Florence beamed.

"I'm looking forward to it. We'd better get going." Alice laughed. She was always amazed at how much energy her mom had.

"Yes! We'd better. We'll try to beat the traffic downtown." Florence said, locking the front door to the house. Tossing her daughter's overnight bag into the back seat of her red Jag, Florence climbed in and pulled the door shut. She put on her seat belt and dropping the clutch, she sped out of the driveway, skillfully shifting into high speed within a quarter of a mile. The "*Welcome to Harbor Cove*" sign disappeared in the rear-view mirror. An hour later, they arrived at Florence's new home in an upscale neighborhood on the east side. A two-story brownstone with a large, well-manicured front yard lay before them.

"It's beautiful, Mom!" Alice stared in awe.

"Wait until you see the backyard. You're going to love the pool. Come with me!" She could hardly contain herself.

Alice followed her mom down the walk alongside the house, then through the back gate. Inside, a large sunken pool with glistening deep blue water looked cool and inviting. Alice removed a sandal and dipped her toe in, testing the water. It was welcomingly warm.

Florence sighed. "You'd better take advantage of the water this weekend. I'll be having my pool boy drain it for the season come next Monday. I'm not ready for cold weather."

"Hope you have a spare swimsuit. I didn't pack mine," Alice replied.

Florence grinned, "No worries! You don't need one. You can just skinny dip."

"Oh my God, Mom! Really?" Alice shook her head in amazement at her mother.

"Yes, Dear! Really! I do have a privacy fence. The neighbors can't see in and my gardener won't be here till next week." Florence laughed, then added, "Although, he is rather cute and he gives a great massage!"

Rolling her eyes, Alice replied, "I'll bet he does." Still shaking her head, she laughed.

"Come on inside. I'll give you the grand tour," Florence said leading Alice by the hand and unlocking the back patio door. It opened into a large kitchen and from there, they passed through the dining room and into the formal living room. Rare art adorned the walls and it was, indeed, a dream home. Alice hadn't realized how well her mother was doing with her design company. Until now. Across the formal living room, watching the crystal chandelier sparkling in the sunlight, sending rainbows of elegance dancing everywhere, Alice stared in awe. A large grandfather clock stood stately against the far wall next to a mahogany china cabinet. She could hear the rhythmic tick-tock, as the pendulum swung back and forth. Her eyes settled on a shiny black baby grand piano. It was positioned off the center of the room. Alice ran her fingers along the keyboard, scaling up to the middle C and striking the key. A deep, rich tone resonated through the room.

"Wow! Mom, this is very, very nice! I'm so proud of you. It looks like you made it to the big time. There's so much to take in!" Alice rambled.

"Why, thank you. I've worked hard to build this life and I'm proud of it, too. I have Sophia to thank, among other clients, that have taken my fashion designs seriously. You know, there's almost too much room for one person. Come upstairs. I'll show you what I mean." Florence climbed the spiral staircase and Alice followed. "There are three large bedrooms upstairs with full walk-in closets and dressing rooms. At the end of the hall is the master bath, complete with an oversized sunken tub." Florence pointed as they reached the top of the stairs. "My bedroom is on the left. You can sleep in this bedroom here on the right. Whenever we have company, they stay in the third bedroom across the hall. I'm sure you'll find everything you need and if not, we'll go shopping!" Florence exclaimed.

Alice opened the bedroom door and a much larger version of her bedroom in Harbor Cove greeted her. Lying down on the queen-sized mahogany sleigh bed, she snuggled into the maroon plush comforter, smiling. Alice got up and entered the walk-in closet and dressing room. Rows of elegant dresses and outfits, in every style and color imaginable, left her in stunned silence.

Finding her voice, Alice turned, "I feel like Cinderella! It's going to take me an hour to select an outfit for my date with Walter!"

"By the time we're done, Cinderella won't hold a candle to you. However, the task at hand right now is to get us ready for tonight's Gala at The Plaza Hotel! I'll leave you to pick out an evening gown to your liking." Florence turned and walked across the hall to her bedroom. She returned 30 minutes later wearing an elegant white chiffon evening gown with a halter-style neckline designed to accentuate her breasts, the back opening down to her tailbone. Black lace adorned one side along the front, cascading down to an open slit exposing her long legs as she walked. Black, 3" heels clicked along the hardwood floor. She added the finishing touches; black lace gloves, a black headpiece adorned with pearls and a diamond necklace with matching dangling earrings. Applying her signature red lipstick, she asked.

"What do you think, My Dear?"

"Maybe a bit much?" Alice replied carefully, eyeing her mother's ample breasts and the slit up the side of her dress, exposing her leg.

"Nonsense! Maybe I'm a bit ahead of my time but, I'm

combining flair with fashion! This is becoming all the rage in New York and L.A."

Alice knew that her mother knew what she was doing. It was evident when one looked around. She smiled, supporting her mom. "You do look ravishing!" Alice praised.

"What have you chosen for tonight?" Florence asked.

"I'm not sure. I just can't decide." She held up an emerald satin floor-length evening gown. "I like this one."

"Oh, yes! That will look beautiful on you, especially with my cream-colored teardrop pearl earrings and necklace." She continued, "I'm sure there is a matching green shawl and heels that go with it. Add the emerald headpiece and you'll have the perfect ensemble."

Alice smiled approvingly, "Yes. I'll go with this one." Removing her clothes and slipping into the gown, she lifted her dark hair, "Zip me, please."

Florence zipped the gown and turned her daughter to face her, "You look beautiful." Thinking to herself, tomorrow night, we'll pick out an outfit that accentuates the more positive attributes of her daughter's figure, just enough to catch Walter's eye.

An hour later, both ladies left the house and arrived at The Plaza Hotel shortly before 8 p.m. The valet opened the door for Florence and then Alice. Arm in arm, they walked the red carpet. The doorman smiled slightly tipping his hat as they entered the Plaza Hotel. Inside the foyer, the concierge, a dignified middle age man with graying hair, greeted them. "Ms. Brooks! So nice to see you again! And who is this ravishing young lady?" Reaching out to take Alice's hand and giving it a brief kiss, he smiled.

"Thank you, George. May I introduce you to my daughter, Alice. She's spending the weekend with me."

"So nice to meet you, Alice. Your mother is an amazing designer and we are always honored when she has an event here at The Plaza." George commented.

"Pleasure meeting you also," Alice smiled, curtseying slightly.

"Thank you again, George. Now, we must be going to make sure my models are ready for the runway!"

"Very well, Madame." George bowed as Florence led Alice away to the back of the hotel. Entering a large conference room, complete with dressing areas, stage and lighted runway, Alice watched in bewilderment as the gala event unfolded before her.

Cameramen, Buyers, Socialites and Fashion Magazine reporters all lined up on both sides of the runway as they waited for the show to begin. The room was humming with excitement.

"Okay. Alice, it's time. Wow! I didn't expect this event to bring out this many people." Florence whispered in a rare moment of humility. She kissed her daughter on the cheek then stepped behind the curtain to the dressing rooms. The lights went down, and a single spotlight focused on center stage. Florence stepped into the harsh white light and everyone applauded. They quieted as she began to speak, "Ladies and Gentlemen, I bring you our new Winter Collection!" Florence was indeed in her element, and the night was hers. Smiling brightly, she introduced each beautifully dressed model. They strolled down the runway, showing off her breathtaking creations. Bulbs flashed and reporters took notes while buyers made their selections.

The show was a huge success. Afterward, Florence and her crew celebrated with champagne toasts. The evening wound down and everyone exited The Plaza. George bid them farewell as the valet pulled up with her Jag. Tipping him handsomely, Florence and Alice drove off into the night.

Saturday, heavy clouds still hung over the city threatening rain. After a light breakfast, Florence and Alice drove to Mimi's for their morning at the spa. "Hello Florence! This must be your daughter, Alice," Mimi welcomed.

"Good morning, Mimi. Yes. This is Alice and we're here for you to do your magic. Her boyfriend, Walter, is picking her up tonight at 6. We hope to catch his eye, if you know what I mean." Florence winked.

"Oh, Mom, quit! You're embarrassing me." Alice blushed.

"Don't fret, Hon. I'll make you so beautiful that your man won't know what hit him!" Mimi smiled reassuringly.

Mimi thumbed through a hairstyle magazine and handing it to Alice, suggested a new hairdo.

"Oh, I don't know. I'm pretty happy with my hair the way it is." Alice reasoned.

"Your hair has been the same for the past couple of years, Sweetie. Why don't you try something new?" Florence coaxed.

"Okay, I'll have a look." Alice opened the magazine to a random page. Staring back at her was Natalie Wood with a complete photo layout and an article about her film career thus far. The article focused on her back-to-back upcoming films, Splendor in The Grass and West Side Story. Both were set for release on the silver screen in October. Natalie, pictured in a conservative, flipped bob hairstyle for the photo shoot, caught Alice's eye.

"Can you do this?" Alice pointed.

"Yes, I can. That would look wonderful on you!" Mimi confirmed.

After an hour of Mimi's undivided attention, Alice turned to face the mirror. Studying her reflection, Alice turned her head from side to side. Slowly, a wide grin spread across her face.

Even Florence was awestruck and taking Alice's hand she said, "I always knew you were beautiful but this is amazing! I think you should work for my company. My business will boom with a Natalie Wood lookalike modeling for me!"

Everyone celebrated in agreement as Alice stood, giving the mirror one last look of approval. "Yes. Walter WILL be surprised."

Chapter Eleven

Meanwhile, back in Harbor Cove, Charlene went about her day, planning. She checked the clock above the kitchen sink for the third time in the past hour. Thinking to herself, 2 o'clock, Kyle will be here in four hours. With Alice gone until sometime tomorrow evening, Charlene decided she would have dinner ready when he walked through the door. After all, it was hard to tell the last time he'd had a home-cooked meal. Scanning various cookbooks, Charlene found a recipe for a chicken casserole that looked relatively easy and shouldn't take too long to prepare, maybe an hour. She found most of the ingredients she needed in the cupboard; spices, wide egg noodles, a can of cream of chicken soup and there was butter and milk in the fridge. Realizing she needed just a few more items, Charlene went for her coat. Under heavy-laden, dark clouds, she walked hurriedly, with an umbrella in hand, over to Stan's Grocery Store. Fortunately, it was only a block past St. Matthews and only a few sprinkles dotted the sidewalk, so far. There, she purchased fresh chicken breasts and some potatoes for a side dish. For dessert, she picked out a fresh apple pie from the bakery.

Once back at Alice's, she showered and dressed, choosing a cute, light blue and yellow paisley shirt dress that buttoned down the font. She tied her hair up in a ponytail with a matching blue ribbon. Another glance at the clock. It was almost 4:00. Smiling, Charlene thought, "Kyle will be here in 2 hours! I better get busy. Everything has to be perfect!" Charlene set the dining table while the casserole and potatoes were baking. Finding a white tablecloth, napkins, fine crystal from Florence's buffet and red tapered candles, she set a bottle of white wine on ice. The wine, a Chardonnay, she found in the liquor cabinet. Everything was coming together nicely. She removed and mashed the potatoes and turned the temperature down so the casserole would stay warm without burning.

Eyeing the clock again, she read 5:50. Charlene gave one last look at the dining room table. She dimmed the lights and lit the candles. Her heart pounded in her chest and Charlene felt flush. Realizing it was a bit warm, she opened the kitchen window just a smidge. Rain began pelting the window panes in earnest, dampening her mood. Thunder grumbled in the distance as the sky darkened and the wind began to blow harder off the lake. Charlene waited impatiently for Kyle's knock. 6:00 p.m. passed with just the sound of rain on the roof. At 6:30, Charlene began to feel a twinge of panic. He was just running a bit late, she told herself and checked the casserole. The candles began flickering wildly while casting menacing shadows on the walls. 7:00 o'clock... Cold fear began to overwhelm her. Where was Kyle? Insecure and panicked thoughts ate at the fringes of her psyche...

The man was standing there, ghostly and terrifying, just beyond her peripheral vision, sneering, "Did you really think he was coming back? Silly girl. He got what he wanted from you and moved on! Just look at yourself. You're not good enough for him. Worthless slut! Sure, you're a good lay. I'll bet he really enjoyed himself! By now, he's moved on and is banging someone else while you're left here looking like the fool you are!"

Trying desperately to regain control, Charlene shouted back at her tormentor. "Go Away, Leave Me Alone!" Almost instantly, she heard Alice's voice over the man's taunts, soothing her subconscious. Breathe in, hold it. Now, let it out slowly. And again. You're okay... Charlene worked to steady her breathing, then remembered the casserole. Upon inspection, she saw it was getting dry and the potatoes were, too. She wasn't okay. This was not okay. Nothing was okay! Tears were flowing freely down her cheeks. Shaking, she grabbed the wine bottle, removed the cork and filled a wine glass to the brim. She took a long drink while staring blankly and unbelievingly at the door. Had he stood her up? No phone call? Despair turned to anger and just as she was about to throw her glass, she heard him knocking. Running to the door, Charlene flung it open. In front of her, rain-soaked and smiling, stood Kyle. "Hi Honey! I'm sorry I'm so late. I had a flat tire on the way here," he apologized. "Aren't you going to invite me in?"

Pulling Kyle through the door, she threw her arms around his neck, "I was so worried!" she cried.

Kyle looked across the room at the half-burned candles

and the glistening crystal. He could smell the faint aroma of a burnt dinner coming from the kitchen.

"Awe… you've made me dinner. I am so sorry I'm late. Please, forgive me." Kyle pleaded.

Charlene wiped the tears from her eyes, "I'm afraid it's ruined. It's probably too dried out to eat."

Kyle smiled, "That's okay. I'm only hungry for you." Pulling Charlene's chin up, he kissed her lips tenderly. At that moment, all was forgiven. In between kisses, Charlene realized Kyle was soaked to the skin. While he was removing his suit jacket and tossing it on a chair, she could smell his essence mingling with the damp clothing. She unbuttoned his dress shirt while he began unfastening her dress. While leaning against the dining room table, the crystal place settings shook and clattered as passion erupted between them. Blowing out the candles, Kyle carefully pushed the entire tablecloth and dinnerware toward the center of the table. Lifting her, he set her down on the tabletop. Hands searched as he removed her dress, fingers trailing across her bare breasts and further down. Charlene moaned with pleasure as his fingers caressed her. She whispered in his ear, "the bedroom…" In one graceful swoop he picked her up and she kissed his neck as he pushed open the door to Florence's bedroom. Charlene had hoped they would find themselves there and placed candles all around the room. Teasingly, holding Kyle at arms-length, she whispered seductively, "Wait. You've gotta wait just a bit longer. Let me light these candles."

Laughing and chasing each other around the room and finally crashing down on the bed, they hastily removed the remainder of one another's clothing and discarded the pieces on the floor. Outside, the storm matched them in intensity and thunder shook the atmosphere. Lightning flashed, momentarily bathing their naked bodies in harsh bluish-white light. Across the bed, a large floor-length mirror reflected the candles, doubling the count and adding to the soft glow in the room. Rolling Charlene over onto her belly Kyle pulled her haunches up and slid himself inside, taking her from behind. For a second, just a second, Charlene braced herself allowing a small cry to slip from her lips. Grabbing her ponytail, Kyle pulled her head up and thrust himself in deeper. Staring into the mirror, half expecting *The Man* from her nightmares to step through with his belt hissing through the air, Charlene tensed for a moment then relaxed. No man was stepping through the mirror. Instead, it was her lover in the reflection. Watching him take her, the look of pure satisfaction on his face, Charlene smiled defiantly into the mirror. She knew *the man* in her nightmares would never be able to touch her again as long as she had her Kyle. Watching him as he quickened the pace of his thrusts, clinging to the edge of the mattress, she screamed out in euphoric pleasure. Feeling him swell inside of her, she reached climax just as he did. She had never had a lover as… skilled, as Kyle.

Lying in one other's arms, they finally surrendered to exhaustion. Dozing, they listened to the rain on the roof and the rumble of thunder echoing off the lake. Somewhere in the night, they found themselves cuddled back under the covers and Kyle took her again. Slowly, this time, gently and lovingly.

Afterward, Charlene lay in the protective circle of his arms. "I love this." She whispered.

"Me, too." He whispered back as he drifted off to sleep. Charlene listened to his rhythmic breathing.

"I love you," she whispered, happy to say it, even if Kyle's only response was light snoring. The low rolling thunder, lightning and lightly falling rain lulled Charlene to sleep shortly after. Content and secure, she dreamed of her fairy tale life with Kyle.

Early Sunday morning, the sun filtered through the blinds chasing away the darkness.

The alarm clock read 6:45. Charlene stretched, looking over at her still-sleeping Kyle and smiled. She felt amazing. Everything was right in her world. Carefully sliding out of bed, so as not to wake Kyle, she stepped down. Her foot landed on an object that slightly made her lose her balance. Catching herself and looking down, she spied Kyle's billfold. Realizing it must have fallen out of his pants pocket while they were undressing each other, she smiled. Picking up the wallet, she put on Florence's robe and walked into the dining room. Dreaming her name would soon match his she said aloud, "Charlene Elizabeth Edwards," giddy with how it sounded. She opened his billfold, curious to see his driver's license picture. As Kyle's face looked back at her, she froze. It was unmistakably Kyle, but the name was NOT. Charlene questioned aloud as she read, Jacob Lawrence MacDonald? The address was not in Detroit, but in Washington D.C.? Parallel to the license was a government identification card. On top, in bold black letters, Central Intelligence Agency? Jacob Lawrence MacDonald, Agent SO 003, District of

Columbia, Washington D.C.? Charlene shook her head in disbelief almost dropping the billfold. Shakily, she turned to the next slot. There was a picture of a woman dressed all in white, smiling and sitting in the front seat of Kyle's baby blue convertible. Dumbfounded, Charlene felt lightheaded and the room began to spin. Closing her eyes, she breathed deeply, steadying herself. Doing her best to control the anger welling up inside her and failing miserably, she stalked back into the bedroom. Kyle stirred in bed, opening his eyes. He sat up, leaning against the headboard.

"Hey Babe, Good morning." He smiled.

"Good morning, my ass!" Charlene yelled, hot tears welling up in her eyes. Before Kyle could answer, she chucked his billfold at his head, "Who the hell are you? Who is Jacob MacDonald? And who the hell is this woman sitting in the front seat of *our* convertible?"

He stared at her in disbelief. "You went through my billfold?" He questioned defensively.

"Not intentionally. It was lying on the floor and I stepped on it so I picked it up. I saw your driver's license, the government I.D. and the picture. Don't you dare make this about my invading your privacy!" Charlene cried with her voice shaking.

"Okay, calm down. You're right. Can we talk about this like two civilized adults?" He pleaded.

Charlene slowly nodded her head and crossed her arms, eyes blazing.

"Okay. My name is actually Jacob MacDonald. I am a C.I.A. agent. I use Kyle Edwards as my undercover name. I can't tell you much more about it. Very few people know anything at all. Please understand. I cannot have my cover blown and it's already been compromised.

"So, you don't work for Detroit Motors?" Charlene asked, completely mesmerized.

"Yes… and no. It's hard to explain. Call it an alias created for me by the government."

"What about the woman?" Charlene questioned, afraid of his answer.

Kyle sighed, "She's my wife, Ava. We've been married for the past 13 years. I assure you, it's a passionless marriage."

What Charlene feared the worst had just become her reality. "You Bastard. If it's such a passionless marriage, why not just divorce her?"

"It's complicated. I can't go into it right now. Besides, you're making this much more difficult than it has to be. I mean, we're having fun, right? I love being with you and spending time together. You mean more than you know." Kyle reassured her.

Standing silent, Charlene glared hard at him, then continued her rant, "Let me get this straight. You're only in it for fun. What am I, just a great piece of ass? Getting some on the side since you're not getting it at home? Unbelievable!"

Kyle attempted to rally, "Come on, Charlene," he pleaded.

Charlene raised her hand to him, palm out, "Don't even!" Turning, she stormed back into the dining room. Sitting down at the table, she eyed the bottle of wine in the ice bucket, now floating in cool water. Removing the cork, she took a long drink, almost choking on the wine as it burned down her throat. Wanting off the emotional rollercoaster, Charlene tried to reason through all Kyle had told her. Questioning; herself, was I as much at fault as he? After all, I never did ask if he was married. I assumed he wasn't. There was no ring on the left hand. Surely, that should have been enough. Right? The truth was, she didn't want to know. She didn't care. Charlene had fallen in love and believed it was real for the first time in her life. Maybe she could love Kyle the way he needed and he would leave what's her name, Ava? Charlene took another swallow of the fortifying liquid somehow it calmed her, taking the edge off. Continuing to ponder her dilemma, she embraced the romance of his secret life. A C.I.A. agent? How exciting that must be!

Kyle peaked around the door frame then walked in and sat down at the table next to her.

"Hey. Got a glass for me?"

Charlene looked over, shaking the empty bottle, she smirked, "Nope."

"So, are we okay?" Kyle questioned, carefully.

Charlene tipped the bottle over on the table watching it roll into the crumpled tablecloth. Still fending off the last of her anger, she wanted to answer, "Hell no!" Instead, in her alcoholic haze, she replied, "We will be. I think." She continued, "Dammit! I love you and I don't want us to end like this." Charlene looked into his eyes, searching for the love she so desired.

Not looking away, he smiled, "It doesn't have to end. We can keep loving each other whenever we're able to get together. You drive me crazy. In a good way!"

Charlene sighed, "Okay, I'll be here for you but I've never been good at sharing. I get jealous easily and friends say I'm high-maintenance. So, bear with me on all of this. It's a lot to take in and it will take some time to adjust."

"I understand. There will be plenty of time and I'll be there for you in every way possible. If you need anything, all you have to do is ask."

"So, what do I call you? Mr. C.I.A., Kyle, Jacob?" Charlene asked, failing to hide the sarcasm in her voice.

"It's your choice, but I prefer Kyle. I only use Jacob for intelligence work. Speaking of which, I need to tell you a couple of things." Making direct eye contact with Charlene, he continued in an austere tone, "First and foremost, you can't tell anyone, and I do mean anyone, about my secret identity. If you do, the higher-ups will take drastic measures. Do you understand?"

Charlene slowly nodded, feeling a chill running down her spine and along her arms.

"Good. Secondly, I'll be gone for possibly a couple of months. I have to travel out of the country on government business. Things are heating up in…" Kyle stopped abruptly, shaking his head. "I can't tell you. It's top secret. Please understand."

Charlene hesitated, "Okay. Just so I don't go crazy here, you have to promise to call me or at least write to me whenever you can. I'll worry about you."

"I'll do my best. I can call when I'm stateside. When I'm out of the country, it will be a bit more challenging. It may even appear that I've fallen off the map but don't be too concerned. I always resurface. I've been doing this for a long time and I'm well-trained, I'm always careful and in control." Nodding to reassure her he changed the subject. "Now, how about some breakfast? I'm starving. You made me work up quite an appetite last night." Kyle winked.

"Ditto!" Charlene exclaimed, standing up, laughing, still a bit uneasy. "I'll brew some coffee, and we have fresh-made apple pie. Well, it was fresh last night." She cut a large slice and placed it on a plate in front of him.

"That will work for an appetizer." Kyle grinned, pulling her back down on his lap and embracing her in a hug. Secretly thanking his lucky stars that he hadn't lost her and at the same time, cursing himself for being so irresponsible.

A large thunderhead followed by chain lighting burned through the atmosphere leaving the smell of ozone drifting through the kitchen window. The heavens opened and a torrent of rain began to fall. "Wow! That's quite some storm building," Kyle noticed as he devoured the pie.

"Yes, I'm so tired of it. Just when you think it's done, the weather goes crazy." Then Charlene remembered the youth group had bowling planned for 12:30 that afternoon. Charlene checked the clock above the sink. It read, 11:10. She'd missed attending church again and Pastor Mike would likely question her absence. Using the excuse of sleeping in wasn't too far away from the truth.

"The youth group I help with has a bowling party at Lakeside Lanes this afternoon. I've committed to making sure it goes smoothly. It's at 12:30. We could have breakfast at Smilin' Joe's beforehand if you don't mind dropping me off. It'll only be a couple of hours."

"That sounds good. I can drop you off afterward. However, I should probably get going back to the city to pack for my trip. I've got a 6 p.m. flight out of Willow Run Airfield."

"Where will you go from there?"

Kyle pursed his lips, shaking his head, "Sorry, Honey. That's all I can tell you."

Charlene nodded, "This will take some getting used to. I want to understand."

Kyle smiled, offering reassurance, "Trust me, things will all work out. We'll be okay.

This is my crazy life and you're a part of it now. Let's go get some breakfast."

Smilin' Joe's wasn't as packed with people as it usually was on Sunday mornings. The rain had once again put a damper on business. With Alice gone for the weekend, it was only Joe and one other waitress taking care of his customers. "Table for two? Right over here." Joe led them to a corner booth and handed the couple menus as they sat down.

Remembering her manners, Charlene made the introduction, "Good morning, Joe. This is my…, this is Kyle. Kyle Edwards." That man stood and shook Joe's hand.

Joe smiled his usual toothy grin, "Pleasure to meet you. You've been in before with Charlene, right?"

"That's right," Kyle replied.

"I think Alice mentioned you're not from around here. What brings you up from the city?" Joe inquired casually with his usual chit-chat conversation.

"I had a business meeting at Vic's last month and met Charlene here at your diner on the way back to the city," Kyle replied.

"Business meeting? What sort of business?"

"Well...," Kyle hesitated and started thinking that Joe was much too inquisitive for just casual small talk. "I work at Detroit Motors. My boss enjoys Vic's Resort and conducts meetings out of the Elbow Room. It's a nice getaway from the city."

Joe nodded, "I see. So, what kind of work do you do?"

As Charlene observed the conversation, she noticed the uneasiness in Kyle.

"What's the breakfast special, Joe?" Charlene inserted, attempting to dispel the growing tension.

"Oh! That would be biscuits and sausage gravy with a side of eggs and toast."

Joe answered, still eyeing Kyle.

"We'll have that," Kyle stated, annoyed.

"How do you like your eggs, Charlene?" Joe asked.

"Over easy, with wheat toast, please."

"Make mine the same, and two coffees," Kyle added gruffly, handing the menus back to the nosey proprietor.

"Will do." Joe headed back to the kitchen.

"Good thinking, Doll. By asking what was on special, you stopped old Joe from digging too deep into my business," Kyle complimented.

"No problem. Joe was just being Joe. He's curious about everyone's business, especially when they aren't local."

Kyle sighed, "You're probably right. I'm just a bit jumpy. This is the first time anyone has known about my active status in years." The special agent was kicking himself for his carelessness. How could he have been so stupid?

Reaching for Kyle's hand, Charlene attempted to dispel his fears, "It's our secret. I won't tell anyone. You can trust me. I promise. Maybe I can even help you in some small way with all this."

She had no idea! "I'll keep that in mind," Kyle hedged, offering too quick a smile. He was sure that would never happen, too risky.

Joe returned with their coffee and filled their cups. He left the carafe on the table. "I'll be back with your breakfast here in a jiff."

Each lost in thought, they ate in silence. Charlene wanted to ask more about his wife, Ava but thought better of it. Why upend the mood again? They had salvaged the relationship and she believed that was a good thing. Charlene remembered hearing once that true love never runs smoothly. Smiling to herself she thought, if that's true, we're on the right track to a long and lasting relationship. Although everything wasn't exactly "right" with her world, she did have faith that someday she would be Mrs. Kyle Edwards, aka Mrs. Jacob MacDonald, the wife of a special agent. Charlene was content…, for now anyway.

"Well. That certainly hit the spot!" Kyle exclaimed as he lit a cigarette and took a long drag. He leaned back against the booth and closed his eyes for a moment.

"You're not tired, are you?" Charlene asked jokingly.

Opening one eye, Kyle grinned, "Not at all. I have plenty of energy but I don't think you have the time unless you're okay with being late."

Charlene laughed, "Hmm… Lakeside Lanes is about 10 minutes away and it's almost noon. That's a tricky proposition. I'm already in hot water with Pastor Mike for missing two Sunday services in a row. Better not be late for this bowling event. He'll need my help."

Acting hurt, Kyle crushed out his cigarette. "Okay then. I guess we'd better get you over to the bowling alley." It was 12:10 when Kyle pulled into Lakeside Lanes and parked at the end of the lot.

Staring out at the entrance, Charlene's eyes went misty. "I'm sorry for our fight and how I acted," she began quietly as she turned to face him.

Kyle pressed his fingers to her lips, "Hush. We're past all that. No need to hash it out all over again. We've forgiven each other. Right?"

Charlene nodded, "Yes, we have. We'll move forward. Please try to keep in touch while you're gone. If you are at an address where you can receive mail, send me a postcard. Better yet, write me a letter. I'll write to you every day." Uncertain tears began trickling down her cheeks. Kyle wiped them away.

"Hey, there. This isn't goodbye forever. It's just for now. Time will fly, you'll see. I'll be back before you know it." He kissed away another tear. Charlene took a deep breath and pulled herself together as she exited the car.

"I'll miss you," Kyle called out as he started the engine.

"I'll miss you more," Charlene replied, adding. "Please be safe and call me!"

"I'll try," Kyle replied as he backed out of the parking spot.

Watching him drive away, Charlene waved and called out, "I Love You!" Her words were swept away by the wind.

At the Lakeside, Charlene noticed the two end lanes were reserved for the youth group. Most of the kids had arrived and were putting on their borrowed shoes or picking out colorful bowling balls. Pastor Mike met Charlene at the top of the steps, visibly relieved. "There you are! I missed you again at service this morning and thought you might not make it. Are you well?" The beloved mentor seemed to be looking for signs of distress as he peered at her through concerned eyes.

"I'm sorry. I…, I overslept," Charlene replied, tripping over the lie and feeling a guilty blush rise in her cheeks.

"You look flushed, My Child. Are you feeling all right?" Fatherly consideration flowed from his eyes as he reached out to feel her forehead.

"I'll be fine, really. I'm just tired. I didn't sleep well last night." Charlene smiled sheepishly thinking, "I'm *going to hell for this*."

"Well, if you need to go home and rest, that's okay. I can manage here." Pastor Mike offered.

"That's okay. Really, I'm fine." Charlene then called out, "Come on kids! Let's bowl!" Two hours later, they wrapped up the bowling party and the parents arrived to pick up their children. Ruth McGuire, a neighbor who lived a couple of houses down from Alice, was picking up her daughter, Louise. She noticed Charlene putting on her raincoat and the lack of any other vehicles outside and greeted her.

"Hello Charlene. Can I give you a lift? It's still raining."

"That would be wonderful. Thank you, Mrs. McGuire." Charlene was very, very grateful. She had been working up the nerve to dash out into the storm.

Pastor Mike caught up with Charlene as they were leaving. "I'll be at the parsonage if you need anything. Please feel free to drop by. Oh! And catch up on your sleep," he suggested, then added, "We don't need you getting worn down and sick in all this damp weather."

Charlene smiled. "Will do. I'll see you Wednesday evening." She was grateful for this one man in her life that really cared about her. Then she thought, wait! Now there are two men!

Ruth escorted Louise and Charlene out to her car and they drove the 10 minutes back to their neighborhood. On the way, Ruth questioned her young neighbor. She responded with tales of everyday mundane life. She finished by sharing how she wanted to move to the city and become a secretary. Dropping her off in front of Alice's, Ruth wished her well in all her endeavors.

Charlene waved and turned to unlock the door. Once inside, she looked around the kitchen and dining room. "Time to clean everything up before Alice gets home," she thought aloud.

Charlene started with the kitchen, washing the dishes and wiping down the counter. Cutting a piece of the apple pie, taking a bite, then staring blankly out the kitchen window. Charlene missed Kyle already. Never had she been so taken by a man. Bringing herself back into the moment, she finished the pie and began cleaning the dining area. Afterward, Charlene walked into the bedroom. Lying down on the bed, she buried her head in the pillow. Breathing in deeply, Charlene could still smell Kyle. Staring into the floor-length mirror, she could see him and the look of pure pleasure on his face as he took her to the edge of ecstasy. Suddenly, it was *The Man* in Kyle's place, staring back at her, smiling smugly. Charlene rushed over and turned the mirror hard against the wall, almost shattering it, "Not today!" She shouted.

Chapter Twelve

On the way home from Mimi's salon, Florence stopped at her boutique. She picked a royal-blue silk, form-fitting evening dress from her collection that accentuated the hourglass waistline look.

She found the matching jacket and handed the ensemble to Alice.

"You always look good in blue," Florence said, adding, "There are some heels that will go perfectly with the dress over on the shelf."

Alice retrieved the shoes, smiling and grateful that her mother had such an eye for knowing what would look dazzling on her. She held the dress up and admired it in the mirror. "Thanks, Mom. Walter will love this on me."

"Well, go try it on," Florence coaxed. Alice stepped out of the dressing room, smoothing the silk dress and twirling around.

"Simply magnificent!" Florence exclaimed proudly.

At the house, Florence helped Alice finish getting ready for her date. After professionally applying makeup, Florence brought out a single string of pearls from a dark walnut box.

"These belonged to your Great-Grandmother, Catherine. They are over 100 years old.

You know Alice, we should have your ears pierced. I have a beautiful set of pearl earrings that would go with this necklace. For now, we'll use these clip-ons."

Alice put them on. "Maybe we can get my ears pierced next time I'm here when we have more time." She replied.

"I'll hold you to that. We can get them done at Mimi's salon," Florence said, smiling.

Alice put on a mauve lipstick, stood, and stepped back, checking herself in the mirror. Smiling approvingly, she loved the transformation.

"I can't believe it. Who is this looking back at me?" Alice questioned.

Florence beamed, "It's you, my Dear! And you look absolutely marvelous!" She was still amazed at how her daughter resembled Natalie Wood.

"Walter will be here soon. Do you know where he will be taking you on your date?" Florence asked.

"No idea. Walter just said it was someplace special. I love how he spoils me!" Alice remarked excitedly.

Waiting patiently, Alice sat down at the baby grand piano, fingers lightly pressing the keys as she began playing a song from memory, Fur Elise, by Beethoven.

Slowly at first, then increasing the tempo, Florence stood beside her, eyes closed, feeling the music fill the room. As Alice finished, Florence coaxed her to play another selection. "It's so nice to hear you play again. Please play another."

Just then, the doorbell rang, "It's Walter!" Florence

exclaimed, walking over to the door. She turned and smiled at her daughter.

Alice appeared calm but her heart was racing and her hands began to feel clammy.

Florence opened the door, and there stood Walter. Leading defensive lineman on the Harbor Cove Pirates football team in high school two years prior, Walter was tall and lean 6'2" and about 230 pounds, all muscle and short, light brown wavey hair with gentle smiling brown eyes. Dressed in a navy-blue suit, a maroon tie, a white dress shirt, navy blue slacks and black wingtip shoes, Walter projected an air of dignified trust. In his hand, he held a bouquet of red roses.

"Good evening, Mrs. Brooks." Walter greeted her, and Florence leaned in, kissing him on the cheek.

"Good evening, Walter. You sure look spiffy tonight! Let me take those roses and put them in a vase of water." She remarked. Walking down the hall with roses in hand and Walter following, she entered the front room. Stepping aside, she watched Walter as he stopped when he saw Alice standing before him. He stood, frozen in place, staring in stunned silence.

"Aren't you going to say something?" Alice questioned shyly.

"You... I... My God you are gorgeous! I love what you've done with your hair and your dress. You look amazing. I've missed you so very much!" Walter replied, meeting her in the middle of the room and embracing her.

"I've missed you, too, and you look pretty darn good yourself," Alice remarked.

As Walter stood admiring Alice, Florence positioned the

crystal vase of roses on the top of the baby grand. They reflected brightly on the polished black surface. Florence had gotten her camera out, "How about a picture of you two? Right here next to the piano. It's been a while since I've been able to get a photo of you together. Move in a bit closer," Florence commented, making sure the roses were in the picture. Alice and Walter blinked from the bright flash.

"Oh darn, that was my last bulb," Florence complained, searching through her camera bag.

Alice smiled, "That's okay, Mom. We need to get going anyway, right Walter?" Alice offered up a questioning smile, slightly nodding her head towards the door.

On cue, Walter replied, "That's right, Alice, we need to get going so we're not late for dinner at Mon Chéri's."

"Mon Chéri's? Wow, that's quite the place. You have wonderful taste, Walter," Florence complimented.

"Thank you, Mrs. Brooks." Walter smiled.

"Have a wonderful evening." Florence followed them down the hall, smiled, and waved as they got into Walter's sedan.

Walter had made dinner reservations for 7:30. He accounted for Saturday night traffic in downtown Detroit being rather busy. His insight was correct. They pulled into the parking lot with only 10 minutes to spare. The sun was in the final stages of setting, coloring the Detroit skyline with streaks of orange, yellow, and red amongst the few remaining wisps of clouds.

"Reservations for Greensboro, table for two," Walter stated to the hostess. Checking the reservation sheet, she nodded and led them to a table next to the stone fireplace, where a small fire crackled, adding an ambiance to the setting. Walter pulled out the chair for Alice, then walked around the table and sat down.

Candlelight danced in the dimly lit room, and the waiter brought menus and glasses of water. Each ordering filet mignon medium rare with baked potatoes and asparagus, Walter added a bottle of Pinot Noir with their dinner. The waiter brought the wine, removed the cork, and filled their glasses. A single musician played "Unchained Melody" on his saxophone from a corner stage. Taking Alice's hand, Walter smiled, "I'm so happy you are here with me tonight."

"Me too," Alice replied, squeezing his hand gently, smiling.

"So, how are things in Harbor Cove?" Walter asked.

"Same ole, same ole. My job at Smilin' Joe's is going well. Charlene is the same as usual. She has met some guy that she thinks is Mr. Right. Yes, again. Mother is urging me to move to the city and live with her. She keeps telling me that I have no future in Harbor Cove.

She's probably right. However, I've gotten used to being on my own. It seems it's been years since I've lived with her. Not sure how that will go over, and I'd have to find a new job." Alice sighed.

"I'm sure you'd be able to find a new job, but it could get interesting, living with your mother after all this time. It might only be a temporary thing. On the plus side, you'd be closer to me, and we'd have more time together," Walter offered, smiling.

"Yes, that would be nice," Alice remarked as the waiter brought them their dinner. The steaks were so tender they could cut them with a butter knife. They enjoyed the rest of their dinner, sipping their wine and enjoying the saxophone music. After a few slow dances, Walter whispered, "Let's get out of here."

He paid the bill, and they stepped out into a clear, cool evening. The full moon shone brightly, punching a hole through the night and pushing the clouds out of the way, allowing stars to glisten like diamonds on black velvet. It was becoming the perfect evening. Alice leaned in, and Walter kissed her tenderly, running his fingers through her hair, breathing her in.

"Come on. I've got a special place to show you." Walter urged. They drove further into the city ending up in front of a rather large building, which stood majestically before them. Alice looked skyward, eyes scanning up the walls to the top where a tall spire glowed, emitting a soft yellow light.

"What is this place, and what are we doing here?" Alice asked curiously.

"Come on, follow me." Walter grinned as he retrieved a set of keys from his jacket. Unlocking the door, he pulled her through, then locked it behind them.

"Please explain," Alice asked, pulling on his sleeve.

"All right, this is The Guardian building. We're in the heart of the downtown financial district. My father offered me a position with his company last month. Their offices are located here on the 27th floor. I'll be helping out with accounting. The pay is much better than what I was making at Detroit Motors, and best of all, I get to use my mind instead of my back. I've always had a talent for numbers, and now here I am." Walter declared excitedly.

"I'm so proud of you!" Alice exclaimed, hugging him.

"Let's take the elevator to the observation platform. The view is breathtaking!"

They entered the elevator. Walter took out his keys and turned a small lock next to an unmarked white button, he pushed it and in no time the door opened onto the observation deck. Under the starlit sky, Alice took in the spectacular view, flashing and twinkling city lights as far as the eye could see, mingling with hundreds of headlights from automobiles going in all directions.

"Oh my God, it's just like you said, breathtaking!" Alice whispered.

Walter smiled, then knelt down on one knee, taking her hand. He removed a small black box from his jacket pocket. "Alice Brooks, we've known each other for as long as I can remember, and we've been dating for over a year. I want to spend the rest of my life with you. Will you marry me and do me the honor of being my wife?" Walter asked, opening the box, and smiling. The diamond ring sparkled brilliantly in the glow from the spire. Alice covered her mouth with her hand. Happy tears welled up in her eyes.

"Yes, I will marry you. I would love to be your wife!" Placing the ring on her finger, Walter stood up and kissed her, "I love you."

Returning his kiss, Alice whispered, "I love you, always have, always will." She looked at her ring appreciatively, touching the diamond ever so lovingly, whispering softly, "Mrs. Alice Greensboro." Moments later, holding each other and staring out over the city lights, Walter looked into her eyes. "We're going to have a great life together."

"That we are. We have so much planning to do! Wait until Mom finds out," she fairly moaned. "She's going to be overjoyed!" Alice laughed.

"I can see it now. Your mother won't be able to contain herself! She'll want to plan the wedding of the century."

Alice hesitated, "Walter when I was growing up, I dreamed of a fairy tale wedding. I mean, what little girl doesn't? But now that I'm older, well, I really don't want a big fancy shindig. How about you? Would you be okay with that? Just a small church ceremony with family and a few friends in attendance? Maybe just an informal dinner afterward in the church basement?"

Walter smiled, "That sounds wonderful. I've never been one for a big splash, either.

Now getting your mother to agree with that, Mmm, that's going to be a challenge."

"Agreed, but I think she'll eventually come down to earth on all of it and see it our way, hopefully." Looking up at the night sky, Alice shivered, "I'd love to stay here the rest of the night, but we'd better get going. Besides, it's getting a bit chilly." Walter removed his suit jacket and draped it over Alice's shoulders. She smiled, thinking to herself, "I have the perfect gentleman. How could I have gotten so lucky?"

They arrived back at the house a little past midnight. Walter walked Alice to the door.

"Will I see you later today before you go back to Harbor Cove?"

"You can count on it! Let's plan for brunch." Alice suggested.

"Where would you like to meet?" Walter asked.

"You pick, surprise me! Oh, I'm sure Mom will want to come along. I hope you're ready. She's going to be a handful!" Alice teased.

"Bring it on love. I'm sure I can handle it." Walter grinned. Embracing her, he kissed her passionately, leaving her breathless.

"See you in about 12 hours." Walter put his hands in his pockets and strolled to his sedan with a slight swagger to his step. Then he looked over his shoulder, and with a radiant smile, he called out, "I Love You, Alice Brooks!"

Alice giggled, "You're a nut. I Love You, too! Drive safe and see you soon." She watched him drive away. She opened the door and stepped into the foyer.

"So, how was your date?" Florence questioned from the front room. She was sitting on the sofa, a glass of wine in her hand, legs propped up on the ottoman, watching some late-night show on the television.

Alice walked in and smiled, almost unable to control her excitement. She held her left hand out to her mother.

Florence gasped, almost dropping her wine glass as she sat up and kicked the ottoman out of her way. It was true; she could hardly contain herself.

"Oh my God! Alice, this is amazing!" Florence beamed and embraced her daughter. "Congratulations, soon-to-be, Mrs. Greensboro!" Taking her hand, admiring the diamond ring, "Walter has such good taste. You are so blessed!"

"Thanks, Mom. Walter is pretty special. He took me completely by surprise." Alice wiped tears of joy from her eyes as she recounted the evening and Walter's proposal on the observation deck of The Guardian office building.

"The Cathedral of Finance, that's what they call it, one of the most interesting art deco buildings in the downtown financial district," Florence remarked. Tipping her head slightly, she asked, "How did you get in and up to the observation deck? That building had to be closed for the night."

"Well, Walter surprised me again. It seems his father hired him to work in the accounting department. They have their offices there. He has the keys to the building, Mom!"

"Wow, that had to be a financial boost compared to his working at the Detroit Motor Plant! He'll definitely be able to support you." Florence continued, "We need to get to planning your wedding! I'm so excited. My only daughter is getting married!"

"Mom, Walter, and I want a small wedding. Nothing too elaborate," Alice stated.

"Nonsense, you only get married once, Alice! It's got to be amazing, memorable, and exciting." Florence argued.

"Mom, I know this is a disappointment for you not being able to throw the wedding of the century, but this is what Walter and I want. Please be supportive of our decision."

"Okay, you're right. It's your wedding, but please allow me to help with it. I promise I won't go overboard."

"That will work. Walter is dropping by to take us to brunch around 1:30 this afternoon. I doubt I can sleep, but it's been a long weekend. We should turn in." Alice suggested.

"Yes, a long and exciting weekend!" Florence replied, giving her daughter another hug, "I'm so happy for you, my dear!"

Alice lay awake staring into the darkness, thinking, "I wish Dad could have been here for this." She choked back the overwhelming need to cry, thinking about the loss of her father almost five years ago in a horrific car accident on his way home from work. Her emotions had been running high all evening, and she didn't want to end the happy rush of emotions on a sad note. Forcing a smile, Alice knew her father was looking down on her and that he would approve of her marriage to Walter. With this thought, she drifted off peacefully, sleeping undisturbed until the morning sun greeted her.

Out back, she heard splashing. Alice grabbed her robe and stepped outside on the landing next to the pool. There, her mother was swimming laps, naked.

"Join me, Darling! The water is wonderfully warm and refreshing!" Florence splashed Alice laughing.

"Mom, quit! Oh my God! You weren't kidding about swimming naked?" Alice blurted.

"Oh, don't be a prude, Alice! No one can see in, I assure you. Now drop the robe and get in here!" Florence urged.

Still amazed at her mother's carefreeness and how she could easily cast away her inhibitions, she shrugged. "I guess when in Rome…" Her robe dropped and crumpled around her ankles, exposing her naked body. Alice dove into the pool's deep end, swimming under the surface to the other side. Upon rising above the water, she heard her mother laughing exuberantly!

"See, what did I tell you? Isn't this grand? I'm so glad you've joined me. Like I said yesterday, sadly, this will be the last time swimming this year."

Together, mother and daughter enjoyed their swim under a bright blue sky and the warmth of the sun. They were splashing about, carefree, and loving every minute of it. Alice was happy she had thrown caution to the wind. The water felt fantastic against her naked body as she swam laps with her mother. Without a doubt, Alice knew she would savor this particular moment in time, just her mother and her making a very unusual memory.

By the time they finished their swim, got out and toweled off, showered, then dressed, it was almost 1 p.m. "Walter will be here soon," Florence stated, primping in the mirror, adding the final touches to an exquisite attempt at her youthfulness. Sometimes she could pass as Alice's sister, not mother. This was one of those times.

Smiling, Alice replied, "You look beautiful, Mom."

Florence looked at her daughter, "And you, my dear, look radiant, a blushing bride-to-be!"

Alice picked a bright yellow sundress from her mother's extensive wardrobe. Accented by her tan skin from summer sunbathing at Vickers Point, she looked terrific.

Alice styled her hair similar to the way it was the night before, knowing how much Walter enjoyed her new look.

Promptly at 1:30, Walter rang the doorbell. Florence opened the door, embracing him in a hug.

"Congratulations Walter! I am so happy for the two of you!"

"Thank you, Mrs. Brooks," Walter replied.

"Soon, you'll have to stop referring to me as Mrs. Brooks and call me Mom!" Florence exclaimed.

Alice walked over, putting her arms around them in a group hug. Walter kissed Alice on the cheek, "Right you are, Mom." He replied, grinning at Alice.

"Shall we get going to brunch," Florence suggested, then added, "I'll follow you two in my Jag so I can take Alice back to Harbor Cove after we eat."

Florence followed Walter and Alice to Marcel's Bistro, just off the downtown financial district. Known for its numerous selections of crepes, it was akin to Smilin' Joe's diner regarding the layout. Long and narrow with shiny stainless-steel counters, green-backed chairs with gold-flecked Formica tables, and large black and white checked tile. "I suggest any of the crepes, as they are Marcel's specialty. There are so many different selections. I come here in the mornings on the way to work sometimes. Everyone at the office loves it when I bring a carton." Walter stated.

"Crepes it is," both Florence and Alice replied in unison. From breakfast crepes, dinner crepes, and dessert crepes. the selection was almost overwhelming. Alice counted the lines on the menu, coming up with at least 20 different choices, not to mention the nearly unlimited possibilities on the build-your-own crepe menu. Finally settling on breakfast crepes and splitting a couple of dessert crepes, they placed their order.

"That was delightful. I'll have to remember this place for my clients," Florence stated. Alice agreed, and Walter smiled satisfactorily at selecting an excellent bistro for their brunch. Checking the diner clock it read, 3:30. Alice commented regretfully. "I'm sorry, Love, we should probably get back to Harbor Cove."

Florence grabbed the bill before Walter could stop her, "I'll catch this one. It's my treat."

Walter and Alice went through the door and out to

Florence's Jag as she paid the bill. Leaning up against it, they shared a tender kiss.

"I'll see you this coming weekend. Hopefully, I can get down here on Friday after Mom gets off work," Alice stated, gazing into Walter's smiling brown eyes.

"If your mom can't bring you down for some reason, I'll come up to Harbor cover and get you. I'll call you, and we'll make it happen. Give it some thought as to what you'd like to do next weekend." Walter grinned.

Alice blushed slightly, and thoughts of making love entered her mind. "Oh, I'm sure we'll think of something to do," Alice replied.

Florence interrupted their playful conversation, "Better get going. It's 3:30 p.m. There will more than likely be traffic coming back to the city."

One last kiss and Walter waved goodbye. Alice waved back as Florence pulled onto the highway driving back to Harbor Cove.

Chapter Thirteen

Sunday, October 8th, 1961. C.I.A. Headquarters, Langley. Director Stephen Marshall sat at the end of the mahogany conference table. Jacob walked into the room, stood at attention, and saluted.

"At ease, Major. Bring me up to speed, Jacob. How did the meeting go at Vic's last month?" Director Marshall asked.

"Same as always, John was very accommodating. He set us up in the Elbow Room, a closed-door meeting. The five of us were there and our strategic plans were set into motion. Four, Five, Six, and Seven have all been briefed and are ready. We'll fly out at 1800 hours."

Tapping a pencil on the table, The Director questioned. "Think there will be any trouble locating the package?"

Jacob pursed his lips, "It could take a bit. They'll hide the cell in some ungodly terrain, but when we do, we'll drop in, gather the intel and make our way to the extraction point."

Director Marshall nodded, "Be careful, watch your 6. You're a few men down." Director Marshall hung his head. "Damn shame that we lost Number Two on the last mission the way we did. I know it was his poor judgment to break away from the team and step off the path even if it was just for a second. What the hell was he thinking? Damn land mine. How did it go undetected in that quadrant? Still…" The Director's voice trailed off.

"Yes, Sir," Jacob replied, realizing there was nothing else he could say that hadn't been said.

Director Marshall stood exhaling deeply, "Okay, on with you, and Godspeed. Oh, tell Ava hello, and give her a hug for me. I assume you'll see her before you leave?"

"Yes, Director, I hope to," Jacob replied.

"You'd better get going then. You don't have much time. I'll see you when you get back from a successful mission."

"Definitely and I'll keep you posted on our progress." Jacob saluted, excusing himself.

Getting into his black sedan that waited just outside the office, Jacob showed his I.D. to the guard and exited onto F Street. Ten minutes later, he pulled into his driveway and Ava was getting up from the front porch swing.

"Hello Jacob! I've missed you. I'm so glad to see you've made it back home safe. How much time do we have?" Ava questioned, knowing it wouldn't be long before he was gone again.

"Hello Dear. Sorry, just here to check in, pick up a few things, and I'm off with the boys on another wonderful excursion," Jacob remarked sarcastically and smiled.

"Come on inside. Tell me about your trip." Ava invited, taking him by the hand and leading him through the front door of their Victorian mansion.

Closing the door behind them, Ava put her arms around her husband and kissed him lightly on the lips. "I've missed you, so tell me how things are in the exciting world of the C.I.A.?"

Jacob laughed and shook his head, playfully smacking her squarely on the butt.

"You know I'm not supposed to share intel."

"Okay, I know. At least you can tell me how things went in Detroit. Did you get to meet up with Four through Seven?" Ava asked.

"Yes, it was good to see all of them again. We met at Vic's in the quaint little town of Harbor Cove. It's about 40 miles from The Refuge, by the Blue Water Bridge. We were able to plan out our next mission, which, by the way, is beginning sooner than I'd like. I need to get to the airport, wheels up at 1800 hours, and that gives me about 15 minutes to gather up the rest of my things." He grabbed a black leather duffle bag stuffing it with clothes and other essentials.

Ava leaned against the door frame, "So, how long will you be gone this time?"

"Not sure, as usual. All depends on how things go. It might only be a month, might be two. I hope to be back by Thanksgiving. I'll have Director Marshall keep you posted. We should be able to stay in contact with him through our secure channels at basecamp." Ava walked over and embraced Jacob.

"You know, I've grown quite fond of you, Jacob MacDonald. So, you'd better keep your head low, pay attention and bring yourself back home in one piece, intel and everything else intact, you hear?" Ava remarked.

"I've grown rather fond of you too, my Darling, and I shall be careful. Most importantly, how have you been feeling lately?"

"I've been better. The new treatments seem to be working. We'll just have to wait and see."

He sighed, "Hopefully you'll get to feeling better." Jacob did his best to hide his fears from Ava and how concerned he actually was. He'd been losing sleep worrying about her to the point where he was off his game, sometimes not thinking straight. In his line of work that could render drastic and possibly unintended consequences. Jacob kissed her fervently, and the years melted away for a second.

"I do love you," Ava whispered.

"Love you too. I'll see you when I get back," he smiled, turned, and walked out the door. A hard rain began to fall and lightning cut across the darkening sky. Jacob cursed under his breath,

"Another storm. It seems terrible weather follows me wherever I go!"

Married on Christmas Eve in 1948, thirteen years had taken their toll on Jacob and Ava's relationship. The ups and downs of an uncertain life, riddled with secrecy, often stretched the boundaries of their marriage. Still, through it all, an understanding remained. Jacob would *always* be there for Ava. No matter what.

Jacob reflected on June 1st, 1942. On that day, fresh out of high school, Jacob Lawrence MacDonald was drafted into the United States Armed Forces. He proceeded through the basic training, and by the end of the month, his superiors noticed his proficiency and attention to detail.

Selected for an intense, three-week, Office of Strategic Services (OSS) training program, Jacob excelled. There, he grasped code-breaking like it was second nature. An elite team of seven men, sanctioned to infiltrate the enemy on foreign soil, gathered intel. Whatever it took to succeed in their missions. It was code-named, Phoenix. Colonel William "Bill" Gray, "Number One," led the group. In his mid-50s, Colonel Gray was by far the most seasoned, well-trained soldier. With a no-nonsense way about him, he earned the respect of men above and below his rank. Colonel Gray, watchful over his men, noticed significant potential in codebreaker, Jacob MacDonald. He thought to himself, this 19-year-old, "Kid from Detroit," has just what it takes to really become something. The truth was, Jacob reminded William Gray of himself at that age. By the end of '42, Colonel Gray made Jacob MacDonald "Number Three" in his elite force. Number Two was Charles, "Charlie," Prescott. In his 30's, he was a mountain of a man, quick on his feet and deadly when he needed to be. Prescott was Gray's, right-hand man. The team operated as one and continued to succeed in their missions over Germany throughout the year and into 1944. By the fall of that year, William Gray and Jacob MacDonald became close friends. One evening, after their camp had just been shelled and the dust settled, Bill dug out his billfold.

"This is a picture of my wife, Ava." Bill handed the faded photograph to Jacob.

Jacob studied it, then handed it back, "Very pretty."

"Yes, she is," Bill smiled." With our missions becoming so intense, I'd like you to promise me that if something ever goes wrong, you'll look after my Ava and take care of her if I don't make it back."

Jacob nodded, "I will, but don't talk about something going wrong. Besides, you're too damn ornery to die anyway."

Both men laughed, and it seemed funny to Jacob until Bill handed him a letter.

"I'm serious. Give this to Ava if something ever happens. I've written her an introduction to you. Jacob, you're my best friend, and I'd feel more at ease knowing you will take care of Ava."

Jacob pocketed the letter. He nodded and smiled, "I promise."

The shelling continued and the men hunkered down in the trench. Being fired upon and returning fire into the darkness, bullets whizzed by. Then, one found its mark, buried deep in the chest of Colonel William Gray. Jacob caught him as he collapsed, watching the light fade from Bill's eyes. He uttered his last word in a final gasp, "Ava."

Germany surrendered on May 8th, 1945. WW2 with Europe ended. Phoenix continued to infiltrate the foreign soil of Japan under the command of Number Two, Major Charles, "Charlie," Prescott, until the announcement of Japan's surrender on September 2nd, 1945. With the war over, President Truman disbanded the OSS on September 20th, 1945.

After the military funeral at Arlington, Jacob approached Bill's widow as she was standing alone at the gravesite. Ava was dressed in black. She was tall, almost 6' with an air of sophistication. Turning, she questioned. "Yes? May I help you?"

"Hello, Mrs. Gray? My name is Jacob MacDonald. I served under your husband in Germany. We were friends." Jacob pulled the letter from his jacket breast pocket and handed it to her.

"Bill asked me to give this to you."

Ava took the letter and opened it reading it silently to herself.

November 3rd, 1944

My Dearest Ava,

If you are reading this letter, I guess I never made it back. I want to introduce my closest friend, Jacob Lawrence MacDonald. He's promised to take care of you and be there for you as a friend. Mind you, he's just a kid from Detroit, a little cocky at times, but his heart is in the right place. He's a good, honorable man.

You know I will always love you, and if there is a heaven, I'll be looking down on you.

Please take care. I've loved the life I had with you.

Always and forever,
Love,
William

Ava's eyes went misty as she folded the letter holding it to her breast along with the triangled United States flag. She offered her black-gloved hand.

"A pleasure to meet you, Jacob."

In the months to come, their friendship grew. Jacob rented a house only minutes from Ava Gray's Victorian Mansion and found a job working as a die setter. Always a phone call away, Jacob would help with things that needed fixing; leaky faucets, squeaky hinges on doors and helping tend the grounds. He was happy doing so, biding his time, always looking for a better job, leading to a better life. Two years drifted by and their friendship flourished, loving each other in their own special way. They'd become very close.

In September 1947 Jacob answered the phone thinking and hoping it was Ava.

"Hello?" Jacob answered.

"Is this the kid from Detroit?" A gruff voice questioned.

Jacob grinned, "Hello Number 2, Dammit Charlie, how the hell are you?"

"I could tell ya, but then I'd have to kill ya." Charlie laughed.

"So, have you been waiting by the phone for my call?" He asked jokingly.

"Well, not exactly, but what's up?"

"Are you ready to go back to work? It seems the powers that be must have missed us. They've created something called the Central Intelligence Agency. They're probably not as cool as we were in our OSS days, but then who knows? There appears to be a lot of red tape, but I'm certain we can cut through all that. I'll get ahold of the rest of the men. Are you in?"

Jacob could hardly believe what he was hearing. "Damn right I am!" He exclaimed.

"Ok. Meet me at 0800 hours at Langley's front office. Use your old I.D. at the gate. They'll be expecting you."

With their service and military experience, Number Two

through Seven were reinstated and Phoenix began her flight once again.

On New Year's Eve, 1948, Jacob and Ava they had a military wedding on base, officiated by then-1st Lieutenant Stephen Marshall.

Chapter Fourteen

Charlene continued to straighten up after her night with Kyle. The house was coming back together and by 4:00 p.m. it was spotless. She finished changing the sheets on the bed and turned the floor-length mirror around so it sat properly in its place. Grateful that she hadn't broken it against the wall. Charlene gathered the candles. All but burnt stubs remained along with their holders. She surveyed the room. Nothing was left but the memory, bittersweet as it may have been. Refusing to look at her reflection in the mirror, she walked back into the dining room closing the door behind her. The telephone rang at 4:25 p.m.

"Hello, Brook's residence. This is Charlene." Static rattled across the line, mixed with an eerie distant silence.

"Hey Babe, it's Kyle. I wanted to give you a call before I...," static cracked through the receiver.

"You're breaking up... Kyle, where are you?" Charlene asked, plugging her other ear, trying to decipher his words as they faded in and out of the interference.

"Sorry! There's one heck of a storm brewing here. I'm at the airport, I... flight to..." static proceeded to eclipse their call.

"I'm flying out on a transcontinental flight this...," Seconds ticked by as more static danced across the line.

Charlene called out, afraid she might lose him, "I love you and I miss you!"

More unrelenting interference squealed and whistled in the receiver. Then, she thought she heard him, faint and distant. "I...," followed by inaudible crackling and one last word, fading off into oblivion, "You." The line went dead. Charlene clicked the receiver lever a couple of times. There was nothing but silence. Then a dial tone buzzed in her ear. Heart racking against her ribcage and replaying the conversation over in her mind, she questioned herself. What was he trying to say? Was it, "I love you, too?" Charlene decided it was close enough. Kyle called! He actually called! He does love me! She smiled, telling herself that everything was going to be okay.

Charlene heard Florence and Alice pulling into the drive shortly after 7 p.m. She opened the door, putting on a perfect, plastic grin as she greeted them.

"There you are. So happy to see you!" Charlene hugged Alice and then Florence.

"Good to see you, too. How was your weekend?" Florence questioned, looking around the house as she entered. Mentally noting that everything seemed to be in place, nice and clean, it looked like Charlene hadn't even spent the weekend there. The tea kettle began to whistle and Charlene took the pot off the burner, "I made us some hot water for tea." She commented.

"Thank you, Charlene, but I can't stay long. I need to get back to the city. Busy day tomorrow. Mondays always are."

Florence stated, already making her way down the hall to the door.

Charlene was used to Florence's exit strategies, chalking it up to her not approving of her wild lifestyle. It wasn't her wild lifestyle that concerned Florence. It was her poor life choices she feared would rub off on Alice.

"Okay, drive safe. We'll see you again," Charlene called out after her.

Alice hugged her mother, "Love you, and thank you for a wonderful weekend!"

Florence smiled, "Love you too, my Dear. I look forward to seeing you again next weekend. I'll try to get off Friday so we can spend more time together. I'll call you mid-week to confirm." "Thanks, Mom, I'll be looking forward to it," Alice replied as Florence closed the front door behind her.

"I'll take a cup of tea," Alice commented as she sat down at the kitchen table.

Charlene grabbed a cup from the cupboard and poured hot water over a tea bag.

"Two weekends in a row with your mother, what gives? Florence only comes down about once a month to check on things."

"I guess you're right but we just had such a wonderful weekend together that we decided to have another," Alice replied, sipping her tea.

"There's something you're not telling me. Come on, spill it." Charlene squinted questioningly.

"Okay, I have some news." Alice began. Charlene smiled, thinking, "I bet my news is bigger than yours." She waited patiently, "Go on," Charlene coaxed.

Placing her left hand on the table, "Walter asked me to marry him!" Both girls screamed in excitement!

"Oh my God! Alice, this is crazy! And you said, "yes?" Well, of course, you did. You're wearing his diamond! What a beautiful ring." She held Alice's hand, closely examining the sparkling stone.

"I've never seen one of these close up. Hey, maybe we can have a double wedding if I can get Kyle to talk marriage." Charlene commented excitedly.

Alice laughed, "Take it easy. Walter and I are looking at having a small church wedding, just relatives and close friends."

"Well, that's no fun," Charlene grumbled, then added, "I'm just teasing, it's your wedding and I understand. What does your mother have to say about it?"

Alice smiled, "She's on board, not really happy about it as she always wanted to throw a gala event for me when I got married. But she agrees it is my wedding."

Charlene nodded. "Wow, you're getting married. So how did Walter pop the question?"

Alice recounted their evening together and how Walter took her up to the observation deck of The Guardian building. "The evening was perfect! More than I could have ever hoped for. He really surprised me." Alice was radiant with happiness.

"Wait a minute. What is The Guardian building?" Charlene asked.

"It's one of the tallest financial buildings in Detroit. Walter surprised me when he pulled out the keys and unlocked the front doors. His father hired him to work at his company in the accounting department on the 27th floor. We took the elevator to the observation deck. The view over the city was breathtaking! He popped the question right there on the deck, got down on one knee, the works!" Alice exclaimed.

"I'm so happy for you! Although, I'm a little jealous. I wish it were me." Alice noticed a touch of sadness in Charlene's voice.

"Don't worry. It will happen for you when the time is right." Opting not to disclose her plan to move down to the city in a matter of weeks, Alice hedged, "How was your weekend with Kyle? Did you go see "Breakfast at Tiffany's" at the Starlight?"

"No, it rained so hard all night that I doubt they even showed the movie," Charlene replied.

Alice frowned, "So, what did you do?" She realized too late that she shouldn't have asked.

Charlene smiled coyly, "We had fun just spending time together." She recounted the evening, telling Alice how Kyle had a flat tire and arrived late. How, in turn, the dinner she prepared was ruined. She started to tell more, then stopped when she remembered her promise to Kyle that she was not to disclose his secret identity to anyone. There was no way was she going to tell Alice about Ava.

"Go on, what else?" Alice asked, genuinely interested.

"Well, we had fun the rest of the weekend." Charlene smiled. Alice knew what "fun" meant and didn't press the conversation further. Charlene continued, "Kyle had to fly out on business early this morning and says he'll be gone till the middle of next month. He dropped me off at the

Lakeside where I helped Pastor Mike with the youth group's bowling party."

"Lakeside Lanes is a good distance from here. How did you get home?" Alice asked, then added, "Hope you didn't have to walk all that way back in the rain."

"No, Ruth McGuire, who lives just down the block a couple of houses, offered to drive me back here. She's nice like that. Always watching out for her neighbors."

"Agreed, I like her. Glad to know she was there for you."

"After I returned, I cleaned up the rest of the place, and here you are. That's about it." Charlene shrugged.

"Kyle will be gone for a month and a half? That's a bummer," Alice commented.

"Oh, I'll be all right. Time will fly by. There's plenty to do. I've got Mildred and Suzy Q to care for and I need to continue improving my typing skills and stenography. Then, there's helping out with the youth group and I have you."

Thinking it was the right time, Alice broke in. "Charlene, I have some other news. It's important. I'm going to give Smilin' Joe a two weeks' notice. After that, I'm moving to the city to be closer to Walter. I'll be staying with Mom in her new house."

Charlene stared at her. It was a lot to take in. Trying not to be too dramatic, she measured her response, "Two weeks, that's not much time. Are you sure? I mean, living with your mother under the same roof?" Charlene questioned, choking back uncertain tears.

Alice hugged Charlene. "I'm sure I can make it all work out. Mom's right. There's no real future for me here in Harbor Cove. I'm getting married. Time to start a new life with my husband." Still hugging Charlene, she soothed her fears, "We'll still come down to visit you. It'll be just like old times."

Charlene nodded stepping away, "Don't worry about me. I'll be fine."

"Sure, you will," Alice knew her meaning of fine. "Freaked Out, Insecure, Neurotic, and Emotional." Both girls laughed, although it really wasn't a laughing matter.

Charlene swallowed hard, wiping a tear from her eyes. "I hope you don't mind me staying at your place now and then while you're gone?"

"That would be great. Besides, Mom will be reassured that someone is watching the place," Alice replied.

Then, just like that, Charlene straightened and regained her composure. "Well, what are we going to do for dinner? I feel like pizza. Let's call Luigi's and have one delivered."

Alice picked up the telephone and looked up the number dialing it. "Yes, a large, everything on it except mushrooms and anchovies. Yes, we'll take extra cheese. Thirty minutes will work. Thank you!" Alice cradled the receiver. Charlene turned on the television. "Leave it to Beaver" lit up the screen. Retrieving two cokes from the fridge, Alice looked down and noticed the empty wine bottle in the trash. Sitting down next to Charlene, she made light of it.

"I see you found the bottle of chardonnay."

Charlene rushed to explain, "I pretty much drank that myself," not elaborating on the actual reason why. Instead, she went on about how scared she was that Kyle wasn't showing up and how she almost shattered her wine glass against the door.

Alice listened intently, knowing Charlene needed to open up and get things off her chest. She also believed that Charlene was holding something else back that was of great importance.

Charlene hesitated. Then, whispered, through gritted teeth, "The man showed his ugly face again. I turned the mirror against the wall. I damn near broke the thing!"

"Where, the upstairs mirror?"

"No," Charlene replied, unable to stop herself, noticing too late that she had slipped up.

Alice's eyes narrowed as the realization hit her, "If not the upstairs mirror, it had to be down here, in Mom's bedroom. Oh my God, you didn't!"

Charlene broke down, sobbing uncontrollably and trying desperately to recover, "*The Man* was also in my mind, telling me I wasn't good enough for Kyle. He was so mean, insisting Kyle had his fun with me and was out banging someone else while I stood there like a fool in waiting."

Alice stifled her anger knowing how devastated Charlene was.

"Come here," Alice pulled her in for a hug. "It's okay. You're allowing him to get to you. Let it all go. You're safe. He can't touch you here unless you let him. You've got to believe that." Alice urged more gently.

"I'll try." Charlene stammered.

"Now, breathe in, hold it, and let it out slowly. Again," Alice repeated soothingly.

She did as Alice instructed, eventually bringing her sobbing back under control. Exhausted, Charlene lay down on the sofa, closed her eyes and fell into a deep sleep. Covering her up with a quilt, Alice pondered aloud, "What on earth am I going to do with you?"

The doorbell rang. It was the driver from Luigi's. Opening the door, Alice paid him, then setting the pizza on the kitchen table, she closed the door behind her. Opening the box, she took out a couple of pieces for a late-night snack. Then, shrugging, Alice put the box in the fridge, "Looks like it will be cold pizza for breakfast Charlene." Alice took her plate upstairs to her bedroom.

Alice got up Monday morning at 7 a.m. and checked on Charlene, she was still sleeping. Being the good friend she was, Alice dialed JoAnn's telephone number.

"Hello JoAnn, it's Alice. Charlene isn't feeling very well today. I don't think she'll be able to make it over."

"Put her on the phone," JoAnn requested.

"I'm afraid she's still sleeping. She had a long night." Alice rushed to explain, "she's sick. I don't know. Maybe it was something she ate." Alice winced at telling JoAnn a white lie.

"Okay, tell her to get to feeling better. Hopefully, she can come by this afternoon for the girls, at least, until I get home. Thanks for the heads up."

"I will, and you're welcome." Alice cradled the receiver. Climbing the stairs, she went back to bed, sleeping soundly until 10, when she was jolted awake by a commotion downstairs.

"I overslept!" Charlene yelled, scrambling to get ready.

Alice ran into the hall shouting down the stairs, "Relax, it's okay. I called JoAnn and told her that you weren't feeling well and wouldn't be there this morning."

Charlene exhaled in relief, calming herself. She sat back down on the sofa, "Thanks for covering for me."

"Not a problem," Alice replied, walking down the stairs. "I, correction, we need coffee,"

After setting the coffee pot to brew, Alice opened the fridge and took out the pizza box. She dropped it on the kitchen table, laughing. "Breakfast is served."

Charlene joined her, munched on pizza, drank coffee and talked. Alice was genuinely concerned about Charlene's overall demeanor. Her moodiness, vagueness in detail and overall secrecy regarding Kyle had begun to build a wall between them.

"Talk to me, Charlene. I can't help if you don't want to share. You can't keep it bottled up inside of you. I know you too well. You're hiding something, and it will eat you alive if you don't open up." Alice coaxed.

"I can't," Charlene replied, shaking her head.

Taking her hand, "Can't what?" Alice pleaded.

"I can't tell you anything about Kyle. I promised him I wouldn't tell anyone. It's all so complicated. Please just let it go. I'll be fine. Don't look at me like that! Let's change the subject. Tell me more about you and Walter. What are your plans for your wedding? Have you set a date?"

Alice just shook her head and knew Charlene was done with sharing anything else regarding her mysterious Kyle. Eventually, it would all be disclosed. Alice feared she wouldn't be around to help pick up the pieces when everything came crashing down.

"No, we haven't set a date. Hopefully, we'll be able to do that this coming weekend. There's so much to do, starting with putting in my notice with Joe. I need to get ready for work," Alice replied.

At the diner, Alice gave Joe her two weeks' notice. Although he wasn't happy about losing Alice, he was delighted for her.

"Let me see that rock!" Joe exclaimed. Alice held out her hand.

"She's a beauty, just like you, young lady. We're gonna miss you here at the diner." Joe appeared to choke back a tear.

"Whenever I visit, I promise to stop by," Alice assured him.

Joe smiled sadly, then shrugged, "Once young people leave here and move on with their lives, they hardly ever come back. That's just the way things are, Alice. Regardless, I wish you the best!"

By Wednesday, Alice felt like time was dragging its heels. The days seemed to creep by. She longed for the coming weekend. Alice lost all interest in Harbor Cove, focusing instead on what her new life would be like in the city. Looking for a job worried Alice and she contemplated asking her mother if she needed help at her boutique. Another thought crossed her mind, Christmas is coming. I'm sure I can find a job at a department store as a clerk. Waiting tables at a restaurant didn't even cross Alice's mind.

After a day that seemed to last forever, Charlene returned to Alice's. Wednesday wasn't over yet. She promised Pastor Mike she'd be there to help with the youth group. Starting to get ready, she fell prey to self-pity. She paced back and forth throughout the house, dreading the coming weekend. Walter would be there to pick up Alice. They would go on their date and leave her alone with just her thoughts. She missed Kyle, caught up in the memories and feeling so many emotions hitting her from all directions. First, she was angry at Kyle and his secrecy. Then, elated that he had telephoned. Jealously reared its ugly head when Ava entered her mind, and finally, *The Man* lurking just beyond her peripheral vision, gloating.

Charlene fell on the bed, and panic invaded her subconscious. She began screaming into her pillow. It hadn't even been a week without Kyle. Like a drug she was addicted to, Charlene already needed her fix. Remembering Alice's breathing exercises helped her calm down. She forced herself to think about something else but other worries encroached upon her mind. Charlene hadn't realized how much she depended on Alice. They'd been together almost every day for the past three years and they were best friends. When it came down to it, Charlene honestly didn't know how she would function without her. Sure, she would busy herself with her schooling and helping Pastor Mike and JoAnn. But she wouldn't have much of a social life. From somewhere deep inside she heard herself say, "Get a grip. It's not all bad! Stop with the pity party already. Focus, there's still hope. Kye IS coming back. I've just got to be patient." It was a coping mechanism deep in her heart, call it a personal pep talk, that spurred Charlene into action. She pulled herself together, dried her eyes, touched up her makeup and curled her hair. Staring at herself in the mirror, she stood straight, speaking to her reflection,

"Hang in there, Charlene, you can do this! Think positive. Be positive."

Upon arriving at Saint Matthew's, Pastor Mike greeted Charlene, as always, with a smile.

"Welcome, my child. I'm so happy to see you! I trust all is well with you. Did you enjoy our bowling party?

"Very much so. The weather didn't cooperate with our hiking plans, so it was a good thing we decided on our bowling party. I think everyone enjoyed it." Charlene commented.

"Me too. Let's gather the kids up, and we'll get this evening underway." Pastor Mike suggested.

After evening prayer and bible discussion, the kids all shared their excitement about how they enjoyed the bowling party and also excited for the Halloween trick-or-treat trail weekend. Harbor Cove downtown merchants banded together every Halloween, handing out candy to all the children making sure to do it on Saturday morning, depending on when October 31st fell.

"Halloween falls on a Tuesday this year, so the merchants are planning the trick-or-treat trail for the Saturday before, I believe that's the 28th. Oh, we'll have a Harvest Party here on Wednesday the 25th," Pastor Mike announced.

"Everyone needs to start thinking about what they want to dress up as and write down what you want to bring for our party." Charlene commented as she wrote, "Harvest Party October 25th and Trick-or-Treat trail October 28th," on the blackboard.

Excitement erupted as the children talked about their costume ideas among the group. After closing prayer, Pastor Mike escorted the children out. Charlene hung back inside the sanctuary.

"Would you like me to type up your Sunday sermon?" Charlene asked as Pastor Mike closed the door.

"Yes. I would greatly appreciate it. I'll get my notes from the parsonage."

Charlene stepped into the church office and sat down at the desk. She loaded paper into the typewriter and Pastor Mike handed her his notes.

"The sermon this Sunday is about temptation," Pastor Mike began. "How to deal with and avoid the pitfalls of temptations that Satan puts in our path."

Charlene felt the heat rising under her collar as she listened to Pastor Mike and transposed his notes. It didn't take her long to type them up. Grateful that she could type over 50 wpm.

"Here you go, Pastor Mike, your notes are all done. Is there anything else you need me to do?" Charlene asked.

"No, I think that's about it. I am a bit concerned about you, Charlene. How are things going with you lately?"

Charlene sighed, "Things are going as good as they can be, I guess. So much has been happening. It seems I can't keep up with everything anymore."

"Please tell me more, child. May I be of any help? You know I am always here for you to offer guidance. Life can be hard for a young adult. Sometimes choices can seem impossible, and there are consequences for your earthly and heavenly actions. It's comforting knowing that we are forgiven through believing in our Lord and Savior. All we have to do is pray, Charlene."

She smiled, "Thank you, Pastor Mike but, I'm fine. I guess I just have to slow down and look at the big picture. I'll keep you in mind if I need to seriously talk things through."

Pastor Mike stared at Charlene, thinking there was that word *fine* again.

"Well, if there isn't anything else, we'll call it an evening. Go with God, my child. Remember, I'm here if you need anything."

She nodded, "Thanks again. I'll see you Sunday morning."

The evenings were beginning to cool down, and Charlene pulled her shawl closer around her shoulders as she walked to Smilin' Joe's Diner. Joe was ringing out the register when Charlene walked in.

"Hello, Charlene. Alice is in the back and we're about to close up for the evening. With Summer fading away, it looks like she's taken the tourists with her. The only good thing is since things are slowing down, I won't have to hire another waitress to take Alice's place when she moves to the big city. We are sure gonna miss her here at the diner." Joe remarked sadly.

"I'm gonna miss her too, so much I won't know what to do," Charlene replied.

"Oh, quit it, you two! It's not like I'm leaving your lives forever," Alice exclaimed as she approached the front of the diner.

"It's just tough adjusting to change, especially when it hits you from out of the blue," Charlene commented.

"You knew this day would come. Eventually, it's just a bit sooner than any of us expected. Please, be happy for me," Alice laughed.

"We are. You've just been a big part of our lives. It's hard to let go. You've been like a daughter to me!" Joe embraced her in a hug.

"Thanks, Joe. That means a lot." Alice fought off the emotion welling up in her eyes.

Charlene felt a brief twinge of envy then shrugged it off.

After the hug, Joe escorted the girls out, turned off the lights, and locked up for the night.

The phone was ringing as Alice and Charlene entered the house. It was a race to the phone. Alice got to it first.

"Hello, Brooks residence, Alice speaking."

"Hello Beautiful!"

"Oh, Walter, it's so nice to hear your voice! What time are you coming to get me this Friday?"

"Well, it's going to have to be Saturday. I'm hoping to be there around noon. Dad has me slaving away at some reports that he wants to be completed for an 8 a.m. meeting on Monday. I'm sure I can get them done. How're things going on your end?"

"All is well here. I gave Joe my two weeks' notice."

"How did he take the news?"

"He's a bit sad that I'm leaving but happy for us. Otherwise, he thinks of me as his daughter."

"That's good, and Charlene, how's she taking it?"

"Pretty much the same, it will take some adjusting for her but I'm hoping she'll adapt to the change."

"Let's hope so. Depending on the weather, maybe we can drive along the shoreline this weekend. What do you think? Or do you have something else you'd like to do?"

"Well, we can wait and see when you get here. Maybe we can catch a movie at the Starlight. I think they might close for the season this weekend."

"Okay, maybe we can do both. Catch dinner at Vic's too?"

"No worries, whatever we do, I'll be happy as long as we're together. I love you."

"Love you too, Sweetheart. See you this coming Saturday."

As Alice hung up the receiver, Charlene was walking down the stairs.

"Walter will be here Saturday around noon," Alice said. She couldn't stop smiling.

"I heard," Charlene remarked, then added, "Yes, I was eavesdropping on the upstairs line."

"Charlene!" Alice exclaimed, chasing her up the stairs, laughing.

"Hey, I just want to live vicariously through you!" Charlene teased.

"Yeah, right, you're just nosey," Alice remarked, giggling.

The phone rang again twenty minutes later. Charlene took the call.

Finding out it was Florence, she handed the phone to Alice and walked upstairs to her bedroom.

"Hi, Mom. How are things going?"

"Hello Darling. Everything is going well here. I've been so busy promoting my holiday line that I'm afraid I won't be able to make it down this weekend. I'm sorry."

"That's okay, Mom. Walter is driving down to pick me up at noon on Saturday."

"Oh, that's wonderful. You two have a great time. Fill me in on all the details when you get here. I'll be at my fashion boutique."

"We might stay in this area for the weekend, drive north along the shoreline or take in the last flick at the Starlight. They close for the season this weekend."

"Okay, that works too, have fun. We'll plan to get you moved down here the next weekend.

I've already cleared the whole day off my calendar on the 21st. Nothing scheduled except helping you."

"I'm looking forward to it, Mom. Thanks for calling, Love you."

"Love you too, bye."

Alice hung up the receiver, headed upstairs, and turned in for the night.

Chapter Fifteen

"Since I'll be moving next weekend, there's a good chance this will be my last night to go out in Harbor Cove. I've gotten ahold of Julie from the diner and Claudia from the salon to join us for a night out on the town. Girls' night out to celebrate my engagement, are you in? We can get all dolled up and cut a rug at Vic's." Alice remarked invitingly.

"Sounds good. Count me in! It's Friday night, and Vic's should be hopping. Hope he has a good band." Charlene replied, running up the stairs with Alice close behind to their dressing room. By 8:30 p.m., both girls were dressed to the nines in risqué evening gowns with slits up the side revealing their legs. Maybe a bit eccentric for Harbor Cove nightlife, but neither gave it much thought. Alice chose her favorite navy blue, and Charlene opted for crimson. Both gowns matched except for the color designed by Florence and her staff. They admired their final results after helping each other with their hair and makeup.

"I love what you've done with your hairstyle. You do look like Natalie Wood!" Charlene complimented.

"I'm still self-conscious when people do a doubletake when they see me, but Walter loves it." Alice grinned.

"Nonsense, why not take advantage of your look? Maybe you can sign autographs. Wouldn't that be a hoot!" Charlene suggested, and both girls broke out laughing.

"With your beehive hairstyle, you could pass for Audrey Hepburn, especially if we got you some dark sunglasses!" Alice exclaimed, now wiping tears from the corner of her eyes from laughing so hard.

"Cool! Look out, Harbor Cove, the movie stars are in town and are showing up at Vic's. So, get out your autograph books!" Charlene strutted across the bedroom with her hand on her hip.

The doorbell rang, and they headed downstairs. When Alice opened the door, Claudia and Julie stood on the step, surprised.

"Wow, you two look amazing!" Claudia applauded as Julie whistled a catcall.

"You Chicks don't look too bad yourselves," Alice said admiringly.

"Groovy," Charlene added.

The four of them got in Claudia's car, and they drove to Vic's, talking nonstop about Alice's engagement and plans for her future.

They arrived a little after 9:00 p.m., and Vic's was already hopping as Charlene had hoped. Mike Wheeler and The Motor City Cruisers were back at Vic's, packing the dance floor. The girls danced the night away, catching the attention of every single guy in the place.

John watched with a careful eye from behind the bar.

As directed by Alice, whenever a drink was bought for the girls by some guy hoping to get lucky, he would slightly water it down. He'd done this on several occasions to keep the girls safe, diluting the alcohol content just enough for a light buzz but not enough to significantly blur their judgment. John saw it as a win-win situation. No one knew the difference. It was almost midnight when John learned that Alice was engaged. He got up on the bandstand and made the announcement.

"Ladies and Gentlemen! Let me congratulate Alice Brooks on her engagement to Walter Greensboro, the Harbor Cove Pirate's leading defensive lineman in 1959! I understand Walter will be back in town next weekend to sweep Alice off her feet and move her to the big city! Best Wishes, Alice!"

The spotlight landed on Alice, she curtsied, "Thank You!"

John stepped off the stage and held his hand out to Alice, "May I have this dance?"

He nodded toward the bandstand, and Mike Wheeler began to sing, "Take Good Care of My Baby," by Bobby Vee, the band joined in as the dance floor filled up. Blending right into the next song, "Only You," by The Platters, John escorted Alice off the dance floor and bowed, offering his hand to Charlene, "Now, it's your turn!"

Charlene graciously accepted, and he embraced her as they danced to the center of the floor.

"So how goes it, Charlene?" John asked.

"Great! You have an awesome band tonight. I'm glad you were able to bring them back again!"

John smiled, "Yes, they're pretty good. I noticed you had

a great time when you were here last." He hesitated. Let me see if I remember correctly. His name was, Carl, no Kyle, right?"

Charlene replied, "Yes, that's right, Kyle. Do you know him?"

"Yes, we have a history together. I know Kyle from another time quite a few years back. I need to be honest, Charlene. Are you sure you know what you're doing? I hear things, especially behind the bar, people talk, and I listen if you know what I mean."

"Do tell. You're sounding a bit cynical, John," Charlene remarked. "Not that I give a damn, but what are people saying?" She questioned.

"Well, I'm not one to spread rumors, but what I'm hearing might give you a bad reputation and more than you can handle. Be careful with him. He's not whom he seems. I can't go into details here tonight, but if you want to talk more, drop by sometime this coming week." John spun her around at the song's end, bowing with a smile.

"Thank you, John. I'll be in touch." Charlene let go of his hand, turned, and walked to the ladies' room. Alice caught up with her.

"Is everything okay? You look a little flustered."

"I'm fine. I just need to pee and powder my nose."

"I'll join you, are you sure that you're, okay? I watched you talking with John. Did he say something that caught you off guard?" Alice questioned.

"Well, he mentioned seeing me and Kyle dancing here last month and that people are talking, whatever that means. He offered to tell me more if I come in sometime next week."

Alice frowned, "Maybe you should drop by and see what John says. He might know something beneficial to you."

"Oh, I plan to. Vic's and Harbor Cove are such rumor mills. You can't do anything without someone blowing it way out of proportion!" Charlene replied angrily, then added, "You're so lucky you found a way out of this damn place!"

"Calm down, Charlene. Things will work out. Just breathe," Alice replied soothingly, worried that Charlene was on the verge of a breakdown.

Charlene left the ladies' room and decided to step outside for some air. She walked along the boardwalk ending up behind Vic's. An outer storage building loomed in the shadows. Charlene spied the back of a car, thinking nothing of it. She almost missed the blue and white convertible tucked under the tarp. One corner was exposed, shining in the moonlight. Running across a small driveway, she looked around, making sure no one was watching, and lifted the tarp higher. It was indeed Kyle's convertible. Charlene pondered, "What was it doing here? Why not at the Willow Run Airfield? Keeping it here made no sense. Harbor Cove was north of Detroit. Unless… Alice was right. John knew something." Charlene pulled the tarp over the corner and cut back across the driveway onto the boardwalk. Back inside Vic's, Alice walked up. "Everything okay?"

"Sure, just had to get some air. I'm fine now." Charlene faked a smile.

"Well, it looks like Julie left with Bud Harper. They took off in his car.

Claudia is hanging all over Skip Rogers there in the corner. It looks like you and I are the only two who won't be getting lucky tonight," Alice laughed.

"Heck, that's fine with me. Things are already complicated enough."

The evening was winding down. Alice and Charlene walked over to Claudia and Skip.

"Hey, you two, maybe we should call it a night," Alice suggested.

"I don't think I can stand, let alone drive!" Claudia grinned crazily, adding, "I'm hammered," as she clung to Skip trying to remain upright. Skip let out a blech, "Me too, but let's get the fuck out of here. I can drive."

"Oh no, you can't, Skip. Please give me your keys. We can drive you home," Alice urged, holding her hand out. Skip reluctantly handed her his keys. Alice tossed them across the bar to John. "They're to Skip's truck. He's not going to be needing them tonight." John nodded.

"Charlene, help me. Skip's gotta weigh close to 175 lbs. Can you get your arm around him and help him out to Claudia's car? I'll get Claudia."

After getting Claudia and Skip into the back seat, Alice took Claudia's keys and started the car. Charlene climbed into the passenger side.

"How are we going to do this?" Charlene asked.

"Well, it looks like they're both pretty much passed out. I think I know where Skip lives, so we can maybe drop him off at his place." Alice suggested. Claudia can spend the night with us and leave when she gets up."

"Sounds like a plan. Let's hope my Uncle Frank isn't out

tonight. That's all we'd need to have the cops pull us over. I'd never hear the end of it." Charlene stated.

"Don't worry, I'll drive safe and a few miles under the speed limit," Alice replied as she started the car.

Fifteen minutes later, they pulled into Skip Roger's driveway off lakeshore road. "Come on, Skip, we're here at your place." Charlene urged, half pulling him out of the back seat, putting her arm around him as they staggered to the door.

"Let me help," Alice offered.

"I got him," Charlene insisted.

"But I don't wanna go to bed alone. I want Claudia." Skip, mumbled incoherently.

"Sorry, Skip. She's passed out in the back seat. She's going home with Alice and me."

They got to the front door and unlocked it. Charlene helped him through the door and over to his sofa. Skip clung to her, pulling her down as he fell on top of her. The next thing she knew, Skip had his hand between her legs, pulling down her panties. The other hand was tearing the gown off her shoulder and exposing her breast.

"Dammit, Skip, I'm not Claudia. You're fucking drunk. Quit it!" Charlene screamed, pushing him off.

"You'll do," Skip muttered with an evil grin. Undoing his pants, Skip pulled Charlene's gown over her head and held her down. In seconds he was inside her, thrusting deeper and deeper. She could smell the whiskey on his breath, panting harder with each shove. Charlene screamed, thrashing about, arms flailing. She caught him hard with her fist, a blind right cross, square on the nose, sending him sprawling to the floor, blood spewing across his face. Skip yelled, "You Bitch!"

Holding his nose in his hands, face contorted while he lay writhing on the floor. Charlene pulled her gown back into place and noticed that he ripped the material at the shoulder. She got up and kicked him with all her might, hard in the ribs, feeling the bones cracking beneath the blow.

He let out a deep, mournful groan grasping his side. Charlene kicked him once more for good measure and Skip screamed in pain.

"You ripped my gown, you fucking asshole," Charlene shouted, then ran out the door.

"What took you so long?" Alice called out. Then, her jaw dropped. Charlene's hair was a mess, falling across her eyes. The torn gown hung off her left shoulder, exposing her breast and her right hand was bloody and swollen. She was visibly shaken.

"Oh my God! He raped you!" Alice cried out.

"He was drunk and wanted me to be Claudia. It happened so fast I couldn't stop him. He was so strong. The son of a bitch tore my gown. Let's just go!" Charlene screamed.

"Do you need to go to the hospital? We've got to report this to the police, Charlene!" Alice exclaimed. She fired up the engine and accelerated, wheels spitting gravel across the driveway. "What's going on?" Claudia called out through slurred speech, trying to pull herself upright in the back seat as Alice negotiated a curve along the highway past Vickers Point.

"You're fucking boyfriend raped Charlene!" Alice yelled.

It took a minute for it to sink in. Claudia smelled of strong whiskey and not the whiskey served at Vic's. Skip was known to carry his own bottle of 100-proof hooch.

"Wait a minute, are you saying Skip rapped you?" Claudia stammered in her alcoholic haze.

"Yes, he did. He raped me," Charlene replied coldly.

"He wouldn't do that! You must have led him on or something," Claudia smirked.

In a flash, Charlene backhanded Claudia, sending her back into the seat. Her head hit the window with enough force to crack the glass. "Fuck you!" Charlene screamed.

Claudia slumped down in the seat, silent, eyes glazed. Alice slammed on the brakes and slid to the side of the road stopping the car. Getting out, she opened Claudia's door. There was a lump forming on the back of her skull. Alice lightly slapped Claudia's face hoping to bring her around, but there was no response. Alice looked over at Charlene, fearing the worst. Then, Claudia stirred, tried to focus, reached up, and held the back of her head.

"Ouch!" Claudia exclaimed.

"You'll be all right. It's just a bump, maybe a concussion. Just relax." Alice held Claudia for a second, then made sure she was sitting upright.

"What the hell happened?" Claudia mumbled, rubbing her head tenderly.

Alice looked at Charlene, "I, um, swerved to miss a deer. You hit your head on the window."

"Where's Skip?" she questioned.

"We dropped him off at his place. He was really drunk," Alice replied, eyeing Charlene, all the while, praying silently that she wouldn't say anything. Charlene remained quiet, biting her lip, desperately trying to control her anger.

"Where are you taking me?" Claudia asked, holding her head.

"I'd take you to your place, but with that bump on your head you should come home with us so I can make sure you're okay. You can drive home in the morning after you sober up."

Ten minutes later, they pulled into Alice's drive. Alice got out and helped Claudia out of the car and into the house. Charlene followed. Inside, she poured herself a glass of water, standing at the sink, she stared outside into the darkness.

"We'll need to get some ice on that lump," Alice suggested, setting Claudia down at the dining room table. She found a plastic bag in a drawer and filled it with ice from the freezer.

"Here, put this on the back of your head. Sit up with your head against the cushion here on this chair." Alice directed.

Claudia complied, "Thanks Alice, God, my head hurts."

Alice thought to herself, "You had it coming." She then directed her attention toward Charlene.

"How are you doing? Do you need to go to the hospital or the police station?" Alice asked.

Charlene shook her head no. "Think about it, Alice. No one will believe me. They'll write it off as alcohol abuse, and it will be my word against his. In the end, they'll paint me as the Slut that asked for it. What's the use? God, I hate this town!" Charlene grimaced.

Alice was at a loss for words, and she knew Charlene was right, unfortunately.

"What about your Uncle Frank? He's the Chief of Police. Wouldn't he be able to help?"

"Get real, Alice, that would be all I need. Talk about persecution. You might as well stone me in the street. My family is the last people I'd want to know about this." Charlene laughed bitterly.

"At the very least, let's get you cleaned up. I'll draw a bath. Come with me."

Upstairs in the bathroom, Charlene undressed. Alice turned on the water and filled the tub, adding a bubble bath. She inspected Charlene's body. Physically, all Alice could see was that her shoulder rendered an ugly purple and black bruise, and her right hand remained slightly swollen. The blood was from the contact with Skip's nose, which she washed off with a facecloth. Alice couldn't fathom the damage to Charlene's mental state.

Charlene settled into the tub, the warm water comforted her body and the bubble bath washed away his filth and sickening whiskey scent. There was mild discomfort from when he entered her including pain in her shoulder and hand. Her body ached from the struggle. Staring blankly at the tile wall, Charlene spoke bitterly with malice in her voice.

"That bastard will think twice next time he messes with a woman. I broke his ribs on the way out, kicking them as hard as I could. I felt them crack under the blow. He groaned, and I kicked him again for good measure. That made him scream. I should have stomped on his nuts! I'm sure I broke his nose too." Charlene rubbed her shoulder.

"He was so drunk I doubt he'll remember anything. He'll probably figure he got into one of those fights he's always getting into." Alice remarked.

Charlene described in detail what and how fast it all

happened. "I doubt he got off. Hell, I'm surprised he got it up at all, as drunk as he was," Charlene stated disgustedly.

Alice shook her head, "I wish there were some way for you to report this and not be ridiculed."

"Well, there isn't, and life goes on. I've just got to figure out a way I can get out of this town. I'm almost finished with my secretary classes. Then I can apply to those prestigious firms in Detroit as a professional business secretary with the diploma to prove it. I need to get my head around stenography. Damn shorthand, there's so much to remember. I'm good at typing, over 60 wpm, and once I get the shorthand down better, I'll have dictation mastered. I've made up my mind to succeed at this and leave this town." Charlene looked up at Alice with a slight smile.

"I'm proud of you, Charlene. Despite it all, you're going make it happen, I know it."

Alice smiled warmly, stroking Charlene's long strawberry-blonde hair, untangling it as she did so.

It was almost 4 a.m. when Alice turned off the last light in the house. She checked on Claudia's head. The swelling had gone down considerably. Alice put her up in Florence's bedroom, and Claudia was fast asleep before she even crawled under the covers. Together Alice and Charlene walked upstairs. Worried about Charlene's state of mind and what she had gone through, Alice took Charlene's hand and led her into her room. In bed, Alice wrapped her arms around her, whispering soothingly that everything would be okay until Charlene relaxed and surrendered to the sandman. Only then, did Alice drift off to sleep, snuggled up to her best friend.

11 a.m., Alice yawned and looked over at Charlene. Charlene opened her eyes; she was inches from Alice's face. Giving her a quick kiss on the cheek, Alice smiled, "Good Morning, Sleepy Head. It's time to get up and start the day." Charlene stared at her for a second, then rolled over, faking sleep.

"I don't want to get up. If I do, this is the last morning we'll ever have like this and it will never happen again. I'm so going to miss this." Charlene whispered.

"Never say never, my Dear. Now, come on. Let's fix breakfast and see how Claudia feels. I bet she's got one monster of a headache."

"Okay. Fine. I'll get up."

"Promise you won't make a scene with Claudia?" Alice asked, holding out her pinky.

Charlene hooked her pinky around Alice's. "I promise. As long as she doesn't talk trash. If she does, all bets are off."

Downstairs, Claudia sat at the kitchen table holding a cold cloth to her forehead.

"I've got the headache from hell!" Claudia complained. "Got some aspirin?" She asked.

"It's no wonder. You were incredibly intoxicated," Alice said, handing her two pills and a glass of water.

"I know. Skip is always pushing that skunk piss on me that he calls moonshine. Guess I need to learn to say no and mean it. By the way, did you say you swerved to miss a deer last night on the way home?"

Alice hesitated, "Yes, and that's how you hit your head on the back door window. How is the back of your head? Alice asked, adding, "I bet it hurts."

"I can't decide what hurts more, the front or the back." Claudia tried to laugh then winced at the pain. Alice and Charlene exchanged troubled glances.

"Wait a minute, just before I hit my head, I remember..." Claudia's voice trailed off.

"Oh, something about Charlene's hand maybe hitting my face." Claudia tipped her head slightly, looking puzzled.

"That was Charlene reaching out, trying to catch you when I swerved," Alice reassured her.

"Yeah, sorry I missed catching you," Charlene added, hoping like hell she wouldn't remember the conversation prior to her hitting her head.

Claudia shrugged, "Maybe that was it. Everything is so foggy. Anyway, my dogs and cats are probably going nuts, wondering when I'm coming home to feed them. It's time for me to get going."

"Are you sure you're okay to drive?" Alice asked.

"Yeah, it's just a headache. The aspirin is kicking in already and I don't have far to go," Claudia replied as she got into her car and pulled out of the driveway.

"That was a close one," Alice blew out a long breath.

"Yes, it was." Reiterating, "let's just hope Claudia doesn't remember what transpired before she hit her head. Although, the Bitch did deserve it." Charlene remarked flatly.

Alice prepared coffee and pulled a box of cornflakes out of the cupboard, "Hope this will work. I don't have the energy to make anything else."

"I'm not hungry anyway. The coffee will be enough," Charlene said, looking out the kitchen window and seeing nothing but dread under a hazy mid-October sky.

Chapter Sixteen

Walter checked his wristwatch, almost 11 a.m. He hurriedly finished the last financial report and put it in the manilla folder.

"Here you go. The report you've been waiting for." Walter handed the folder to his father, Jeremy Greensboro, C.E.O of Greensboro Financial.

"Thanks, Walter, I knew you'd come through. Now, you'd better get going to Harbor Cove. You don't want to keep your fiancé' waiting. When does Alice move down here?"

"Next weekend. We've got a lot of planning that we hope to accomplish over the next couple of days."

"Keep me posted. I'll see you Monday morning, 8 a.m. sharp. I'll have you sit with the board in this meeting. It will be good for you to see the company's inner workings." Jeremy patted Walter on the back as he led him to the elevator.

"Thanks, I'm looking forward to it. I'll see you Monday."

Walter pulled into Alice's driveway at 12:30 p.m. "Sorry I'm late. The weekend traffic on the way up was a bit congested."

Alice kissed him, "No problem. Charlene and I are just hanging out."

"Hey Charlene, long time. How are things going?" Walter hugged her, and Charlene tensed when he squeezed her. He felt her reaction and stepped back, eyes questioning.

"Sorry I'm so tense. I slipped and fell, just a bit sore. It's no big deal." Charlene gingerly rubbed her shoulder and looked away.

"Slipped and fell?" Walter questioned.

Alice changed the subject, "Hey, it's 12:30. How about the three of us go down to Smilin' Joe's for lunch? Joe wants to congratulate us on our engagement."

"That sounds good to me, I haven't had one of Joe's burgers in a while, and I'm starving."

"You're always starving, you nut!" Alice commented, eyeing Charlene and giving her a little nod toward the door.

"Yeah, sure, I could eat," Charlene remarked, following Alice and Walter out the door.

Joe was fairly busy with the lunch rush and he motioned them to a booth next to the jukebox. A group of teens had just finished up. The table needed clearing. Alice fought off the urge to grab a bus tray and help out. Julie beat her to it, clearing the dishes and wiping down the table.

"Hey, good to see you, Walter. Welcome back to Harbor Cove." Julie directed her attention to Alice and Charlene, "That was quite the party last night at Vic's. I've still got a hangover. I wonder how Claudia faired. She was really trashed."

Julie handed out menus, and Alice explained to Walter that they had a girls' night out at Vic's to celebrate her engagement.

"It wasn't anything too crazy. Just the four of us; Julie, Claudia, Charlene and me.

The band was good." Alice commented.

"Yes, we had a really good time." Julie agreed.

Charlene looked up from her menu, "I think I'll have the French toast with a side of bacon. Oh, and coffee too." She handed the menu to Julie, hoping she could stop the conversation regarding their girls' night out. Alice smiled, grateful for Charlene stepping in.

"I'll have the three-egg ham and cheese omelet with hashbrowns and coffee." Alice looked over at Walter. "How about you, Dear?"

Walter smiled, "I'll have my usual, Joe's Double Decker Burger with all the fixings, a side of fries, and a large chocolate malt." He smiled and handed the menu to Julie. "I can't find a good burger down in the city. Not like Joe's anyway," Walter remarked.

Joe walked up and shook Walter's hand. "Good to hear. That's how I know you'll bring my girl back to me from time to time! Congratulations on your engagement!"

Walter smiled, "Thanks Joe, and yes, I'll bring Alice back whenever I crave the best burgers around!"

Joe grinned from ear to ear, "You'd better. We're going to miss this young lady." He nodded and went back into the kitchen. Twenty minutes later, Julie brought them their meal.

"So, Sweetheart, what's the game plan for our wedding? Should we set a date?" Walter questioned between bites of his fries.

Alice seemed to fairly sparkle as she said, "I was thinking

a small wedding in the city. Maybe in the spring? Do you know of a church we could use for the ceremony?"

"Well, there's Old Mariner's Church down on Jefferson. It's a historical landmark, built in 1842 for the sailors to worship. I've been inside and it's beautiful. The large stained-glass window behind the altar is truly remarkable."

"That would be amazing, don't you think, Charlene?" Alice asked.

"Yes, that sounds nice," Charlene replied as she poured maple syrup on her French toast.

"Well, we could set the date for Valentine's Day! I checked and it falls on a Wednesday so there should be no problem reserving the church and having our reception in the basement. Do you think we can get things all planned out by then?" Walter questioned.

"You're such a romantic!" Alice beamed. "We should be able to. It's a couple of months away. As long as we keep it small." Alice continued, "I haven't asked this officially, but I'm asking now." Alice took Charlene's hand, "Would you be my maid of honor?"

"Of course! I'd be delighted!" Charlene replied. Both girls' eyes went misty as Charlene hugged Alice.

"So, who will you have for your best man?" Alice asked Walter.

"That would have to be Nathan Cobb. Nate and I have been friends since we were kids. He lives down the shoreline and works for a shipping company by the Blue Water Bridge to Canada. I haven't seen him in a while but I know how to get ahold of him."

"Well, it sounds like we've got a plan!" Alice exclaimed.

"Oh, we'll have to get invitations made up. Thank goodness it's going to be a small wedding. We'll just have family and a few friends if that's all right with you."

"That'll work," Walter smiled.

"Do you want to take a quick drive along the shoreline? The fall colors are just about over, but I'm sure there will be a splash of red and orange among the maples."

"That sounds grand!" Alice exclaimed. "Want to tag along, Charlene?" Walter offered.

"Thanks, but no. You two enjoy your weekend together. I've got some things I want to take care of anyway." Charlene excused herself to the ladies' bathroom.

Walter frowned, "She seems a bit standoffish. Is everything okay?"

"Charlene's just dealing with some personal dilemmas. It will take her some time but I think she'll come around and be her normal self again. At least, I hope she will."

Alice hated keeping secrets from Walter, but she felt it was necessary this time. What happened was unthinkable, and if Walter knew, he would more than likely go off on Skip like there was no tomorrow. It could possibly lead to jail time. Walter and Skip played football together and never did see eye to eye. Charlene returned as Walter and Alice were getting up to leave. Walter picked up the tab and paid Joe at the cash register.

"Thanks for stopping by, Walter. Again, Congratulations! Let me know when you set a date. I wouldn't miss you two getting married for the world!" Joe grinned.

"Will do. Alice is planning on getting out the invitations here shortly."

Outside, Charlene gave Walter and Alice a hug goodbye.

"Have fun, you two! I'll see you when I see you." Charlene waved as they got into Walter's sedan and drove North toward Vickers Point. She watched them disappear, turned, and walked down the well-worn path to Mulberry Street. Sunflowers led the way, no longer bright and yellow but an ugly brownish black, their heads bowing down in defeat as stellar jays prodded and picked away their seeds. The scene matched Charlene's mood, dark and foreboding.

She arrived back at Alice's place, walked in and climbed the stairs to the bathroom. Turning on the faucet to the tub, she undressed and examined her bruised shoulder through the steam in the mirror. It looked worse than it was, and she was grateful that it wasn't a noticeable bruising where others could see it. She added some bubble bath and watched white foam billow and float across the water's surface. Then sinking into the blissfully warm water, she closed her eyes. Reflecting back to Skip's place, she imagined being on the stand in a courtroom, giving sworn testimony with her conscience as the prosecuting attorney.

"Ms. Strypher, in the early morning hours of October 14th, did you in any way lead on Skip Rogers, suggesting you wanted to have sex with him."

"No, I did not," Charlene answered.

"Did you do everything possible to fend off the attack by Skip Rogers?"

"Yes, I did. Skip was so strong and outweighed me by at least 75 pounds. He pulled my gown over my head. Then held me down and raped me. I caught him with a blind right cross square on the nose, sending him to the floor. Then I kicked him as hard as I could, feeling bones crack under the blow. I kicked him once more for good measure. I should have…"

"That's quite enough, Ms. Strypher. Please stick to the questioning. Yes or no answers will suffice. Now, is it true that your best friend Alice Brooks asked you if she could help when you walked Skip Rogers to the door, and you refused?"

"Yes, but I thought I could handle helping him on my own."

"Helping him what, Ms. Strypher? Are you sure you refused your friend's help, hoping you would be alone with Skip Rogers?"

"That's preposterous!" Charlene sat up in the tub, breathing heavily. She realized she had dozed off in the warmth of the bath water, and her shame sent her to the edge of a nightmare. If she had accepted Alice's help, this never would have happened.

Charlene knew Skip Rogers but had no interest in him. He was a rebel. A scrapper that thought he was cool in his rattle can painted black truck and that he was God's gift to women. A real jerk. Always dressing in a black leather jacket over a white tee shirt and ripped blue jeans. He had a greasy ball cap halfcocked on his head, a cigarette tucked behind his ear, and a toothpick hanging out of the corner of his mouth. Skip always stunk of cheap whiskey. Charlene continued to think about what had happened. It wasn't so much the sex that bothered her. She enjoyed sex. It was special, best shared with someone you were at least attracted to, if not in love with. Charlene thought of Kyle and their lovemaking. She gave herself to him completely. This time was different.

Charlene didn't give anything up. Skip took it without her consent. He turned something so beautiful into an act of sheer horror. Charlene sat in the tub for over an hour, staring at the tile wall, absentmindedly scrubbing her body. She had rubbed her legs, arms, and breasts raw red without even noticing it. Simply trying to get clean.

"That Bastard!" Charlene screamed, throwing the facecloth across the room and burying her head in her hands, crying uncontrollably. The water in the tub had gotten cold, and Charlene climbed out and toweled off. Dressing in comfortable silk pajamas, she cuddled up in bed, and soon she was engrossed in reading a historical romance novel where the knight in shining armor saves the damsel in distress.

Sometime in the middle of the night, Charlene fell asleep. Her book slipped out of her hands onto the covers. She was dreaming of another time. Swords flashed as the battle raged in the darkness. All was lost until she saw him in the glow of fires burning throughout the castle. Riding hard across the battlefield on his faithful steed, Sir Kyle crashed through the front-line barricades. He'd come to rescue her from the prison that held her captive. Then the dream changed. It became ominous and dark. The smell of cheap whiskey floated in on the breeze. Skip was coming at her through the mirror, shattering the glass. He was on top of her, pawing and tearing at her silk nightgown. She lashed out but to no avail. Skip pulled the gown over her head, holding her down. His hardness tore at her insides as he entered her. She screamed.

Alice came running into the room, "Charlene, wake up! Wake up! You're having a nightmare. Shhh, it's going to be okay." Charlene curled up in a ball, crying as Alice cradled her in her arms.

"Do you want to talk about it? Was it the man again?" Alice asked as Charlene began to calm down and breathe normally.

"No, it wasn't the man this time. It was Skip. It was so real! He was here! Inside of me! Hurting me!" Charlene bit her lip. "I don't know if I can go on like this much longer." At that moment something inside Charlene snapped, she knew she could either continue to be the victim or rise above it. She struggled as the bitterness changed her attitude. No longer would she lie down and take the crap people were dishing out to her. She would do the dishing. Her private epiphany was interrupted when Alice whispered, "Remember what I told you, the man or anyone else can't hurt you here. Only if you let them. Think happy thoughts and try not to dwell on the bad things that happen. I'm here for you."

"You won't be for long. What will I do then?" Charlene asked.

"I am just a telephone call away. I can talk you through anything. Trust me." Alice kissed Charlene on the forehead and crawled under the covers holding her and whispering that everything would be okay. She lulled Charlene back to sleep.

Sunday morning, 8 a.m. Alice rolled over to find Charlene had already gotten up. She found her in the dressing room, putting on her Sunday best.

"You're going to church? I guess it might help with what you're going through."

"Yes. I decided I would go since I haven't gone in the past couple of weeks."

Alice nodded and smiled. "Walter will be by here in about an hour. He spent the night with his cousin, Marty."

"So, how did your day go?" Charlene asked, applying makeup and fussing with her hair.

"We drove up the shoreline and the fall colors got prettier the further north we went.

After we got back, we ate dinner at Vic's, then went to the drive-in. "West Side Story" was playing. We had a wonderful weekend together."

"I'm happy for you. So, I guess I'll see you tonight?" Charlene asked.

"I'll be here."

Charlene walked to Saint Mathew's and attended Service. Pastor Mike delivered a compelling sermon regarding the evils of temptation to his usual congregation. Charlene prayed silently for forgiveness and asked for strength to help her cope with what was happening in her life. Charlene decided that she would try anything to stop the nightmares.

Chapter Seventeen

Surprisingly, the next week went by faster than either Charlene or Alice could have imagined. All of a sudden, Saturday morning was staring them in the face. Alice had already packed up most of what she wanted to take to her new home. There were just a few things left she needed from her room.

"I spoke with Mom last night, and she says she'll be here at 8 a.m. I talked with Walter also, and he said he be here around the same time with his father's pickup. I'm not sure why they're making such a fuss since I only have about ten boxes and a couple of duffle bags of clothes I want to take."

"They probably want to make sure you have everything you need, and of course, your mother will want to check on the place and instruct me how to take care of everything."

Charlene sincerely thanked her friend, "I really appreciate you speaking with Florence on my behalf."

"Mom understands and agrees it will probably be better having someone here taking care of the place, give it a lived-in feel, so no one thinks it's abandoned."

Alice walked back up the stairs for one last look at her room and Charlene followed.

"This is kind of sad, I mean, I grew up here, and now I'm moving out. I'm going to miss this place. I'm going to miss you." Alice tried hard not to cry as she hugged Charlene.

"I'm going to miss you too," Charlene choked back tears. Then both girls let go, and the tears flowed freely. Hugging one more time, they heard the doorbell ring. They ran downstairs and opened the door. Walter and Florence stood there expectantly.

"Are you all packed up?" Florence asked as they walked into the kitchen.

"Yes, everything I want to take is over there in the corner. Just ten boxes, a couple of blankets, and my duffle bags with clothes." Alice remarked. Walter kissed her, and they began carrying the boxes to his truck.

"Are you going to be okay, Charlene? Alice moving out is a big step in both of your lives." Florence asked, genuinely concerned.

Charlene nodded, "I'm really going to miss Alice, but we're just a phone call away. We both knew this would happen someday and I wish her the very best."

Then Florence surprised her. She walked over and hugged her. "You'll be fine. Thank you for always being such a good friend to Alice."

Charlene smiled, "Thank you for letting me stay here. It means the world to me."

"Stay as long as you like. Keep me posted on how things go. Let me know if you need anything. Do you have my number? Of course, you do. What am I thinking?" Florence laughed.

Walter walked in with Alice, "Well, that's about it, we're all loaded up."

One last hug all around, and Charlene watched them leave. Florence sped down the highway in her Jag. Alice was cuddled up next to Walter in the truck. She yelled out the window as they pulled out of the drive, "Call you later, Alligator!" She was laughing and waving.

"In a while, Crocodile!" Charlene hollered back, tears streaming down her face as she waved goodbye and, at the same time, said hello, to a new beginning in her uncertain life.

Charlene decided that she needed to go for a long walk. It was early in the morning and the sun shone brightly, glistening off Lake Huron's white caps and the deep blue water.

She had wanted to go to Vic's to speak with John all week. His conversation was so cryptic. With each day that passed, the questions gave birth to new fears in her heart and mind. After all, John left her hanging and puzzled last Saturday night. As she walked along the highway to Vickers Point, a car slowed and pulled up beside her.

"Charlene, is that you?" Ruth McGuire called out.

"Yes, it's me," Charlene answered.

"What are you doing out here walking along the highway?" Ruth questioned.

"Just walking, heading up to Vickers Point. Maybe I'll take a stroll along the beach." Charlene replied, shading her eyes from the sun.

"Well, hop in. I'll save you a few steps." Charlene got in, and Ruth pulled back onto the highway. "I'm heading up the shoreline a few miles to see Mable Parks. She's a shut-in and

I've been visiting her. I've got a bag of groceries I'm dropping off this morning. I'm glad I bumped into you. I've been meaning to ask, are you available to help with childcare for my girls now and then? My husband, Harold, has encouraged me to get out of the house more and maybe find a part-time job. I wanted to wait until our girls were a bit older, at least Ellen, so that she could watch her sister after school, but she's only eleven and her birthday isn't till April."

Charlene shook her head, "I'm afraid not. I'm working at JoAnn's taking care of Mildred and Suzzanne. But, if something changes, I'd be happy to speak with you about it more."

"I figured you were, but it doesn't hurt to ask. If you are ever looking, please let me know." Ruth turned onto Vickers Point Road, "Here you are, Dear. I'll be coming back through in about an hour if you need a lift back."

"Thanks, Ruth. I appreciate the ride." Charlene got out and waved as Ruth drove away.

Vic's looked quiet, and the parking lot was empty. The front door was unlocked so, she went inside, her eyes adjusting to the dimly lit room. John looked up from behind the bar.

"There you are, young lady. I was wondering if I'd see you this week." John offered up his trademark grin.

Charlene sat down at the bar, "I'll have the usual cherry cola with a splash of lime. Best if I remain alcohol-free." Charlene whispered, then added, with her hand tucked up to her mouth, "I wouldn't want people to get the wrong idea and start to talk." She giggled.

John smiled wryly, "Too late, Sweetheart, they're already talking."

"Not that I give a rat's ass, but you might as well spill the beans, go on." Charlene pressed.

"Okay, don't get me wrong. What you do is your business. Same question as before, do you know what you're doing with this Kyle character?"

"I think so. He's a really nice guy and we have a lot of fun together. Why do you ask?"

John sighed, "Well, what do you know about him?"

"All I need to, for now, anyway. Why don't you enlighten me? What do you know?"

"Well, I bet you didn't know he's married, and his wife lives in Washington D.C."

"Yes, he told me. Her name is Ava."

"And you're okay with him being married to another woman and having you as his mistress?

It doesn't look good, Charlene. Some of my patrons are already speculating. They're saying some unflattering things about you."

"As I said, John, I really don't give a rat's ass about the rumors in Harbor Cove or at your establishment. People need to mind their own business and not that it's any of yours but, Kyle told me that it's a passionless marriage. I believe that it's only a matter of time before he divorces her.

"I agree. Folks need to mind their own business. This is a small town. I'm just looking out for you, Charlene. That doesn't change the facts."

"You're not telling me everything you know, are you?" Charlene asked.

"Well, no, there's more. Kyle isn't whom he seems to be." John grimaced. "We have a past. Served together in the War.

Lost track of him when it was over. Then about 13 years ago, back in January of 49', he walked through the front door with Ava on his arm and they'd just gotten married over New Year's Eve. I think they were on their honeymoon. Anyway, some guy got in his face, catcalled Ava, and a fight broke out. All hell broke loose. I've never seen anyone with the moves he has. He was brutal and unforgiving if you know what I mean. He took a pool cue to the guy and almost killed him." John's voice trailed off.

"How is that relevant? What are you trying to say, John, that Kyle is violent? It sounds like the guy got what he deserved. He was just standing up for his wife's honor. I respect that."

John nodded, "I agree in part. Just be careful, Charlene. I don't think you know what you're getting yourself into."

"Come on, John, what's there to worry about? So, people are talking! What are they calling me, his little slut? It's just talk, sticks and stones..." Charlene sipped her drink.

John shrugged, "Okay, I won't worry about it. It seems you know everything you want to know about him."

Charlene muttered under her breath, "More than you think, John. More than you think."

John's eyes narrowed. "It's your turn, what else do you know?"

Charlene sighed, "I promised him I wouldn't tell anyone, so my lips are sealed." Charlene motioned, holding an invisible key, locking her lips, and then tossing it away.

Joe grinned cynically, "Well, I didn't make any promises, so, I'm going to tell you something that's gonna shock you. Kyle Edwards is a fake name. He isn't whom he says he is. I bet you didn't know that."

Charlene remained unfazed, "Okay, but as I said, I promised I wouldn't tell anyone. You're doing all the telling."

John looked surprised, wondering exactly what she knew and how much. Charlene reveled in the moment as she watched John try unsuccessfully to get her to talk.

"Okay, do you know that he doesn't work at Detroit Motors or commute from Flint?"

Charlene remained stoic, sipping her drink and watching him.

John continued his interrogation, "Well then, can I assume you know his real name and what he actually does for a living?"

Charlene smiled, setting down her drink, "Let's assume I do, so what."

John shook his head. He leaned in closer to Charlene, making direct eye contact, his voice cutting as he clipped his words. Charlene felt a tingling along her spine. He sounded like Kyle when she first discovered his fake identity.

"Be forewarned, with all you know or think you know, you need to be extremely careful! Charlene, this isn't a game. You might get more than you bargained for." John paused, then continued, "Don't get in too deep. You might not be able to dig yourself out. If you do, you'll regret ever knowing him."

Charlene held her ground, not allowing him to intimidate her. "I'm a big girl John. I can take care of myself, and if Kyle had told me anything, why do you think I'd be telling you? And, by the way, why are you telling me?" Charlene questioned. "One other thing, there's something else you're not telling, isn't there?"

John shrugged as he idly cleaned a bar glass, "What's that?"

"I noticed Kyle's convertible covered up under a gray tarp behind one of your outer storage buildings. Kyle flew out of Willow Run last Sunday. That's a good hour south of here. It would have made more sense to park it at Willow Run or his place forty minutes down the road from here and then, take a cab all the way there." John stared at her hard, then began to laugh. He slapped his hand on the bar.

"What's so damned funny?" Charlene asked.

John grinned, shaking his finger at her, "Kyle told me that you were smart. You're clever and quite the little detective too."

"What the hell, John? Is this some kind of test?"

"Yes, and you passed with flying colors. Good girl, you didn't give him up. Now, about his car. He loves that damn thing so much that he was afraid to park it at Willow Run Airfield. Crime is high, and him being gone for at least a month, well, the car would probably be stolen or stripped when he got back. The same goes for the Refuge, Kyle's place down by the Blue Water Bridge. There's no one around there to keep an eye on it. So, he parked it here and I drove him to the airfield in my truck. I'm not happy keeping it here under a tarp but there's nothing I can do with no other place around here to store it."

"Well, since I passed your little test, you both now know you can trust me. I have access to a garage at Alice's place. It's empty and clean. Alice's mother, Florence, lives in the city, and Alice will be living with her until she gets married to her beau, Walter, in February. They came up this morning and helped her move, and left about an hour ago. I have the place to myself and we can park the car in the garage out of the weather until Kyle gets back." Charlene stopped for a second, watching John's reaction, then continued. "Of course, I'd like to use it from time to time. Nothing major, just to cruise here and there and maybe pick up Kyle from Willow Run when he flies back in."

John laughed, "What the hell, why not? Wait a minute. You can drive, right? I've never seen you driving…, anything, come to think of it. Except, maybe driving men crazy."

"Yes, of course, I can drive." Charlene spat back, not appreciating his condescending tone. "I don't have a car because I really don't need one. I can't afford it anyway."

John reached beneath the bar and retrieved a ring of car keys. Tossing them to Charlene, he smiled, "Drive safe. I'll be in touch after I speak with Kyle about all this."

"Wait, you have a way to speak with Kyle?" Charlene questioned excitedly.

"Of course. When he calls, I have a secure line. We had it put in a while back and there is no one else attached to our phones. No party line here. What did you think, Charlene? That I was just a bartender and owner of this club?" John laughed and winked. "That's all I am, nothing more."

Stepping away from the bar and walking backward with her hands tucked into the back pockets of her jeans, she nodded, "Understood."

Charlene walked out the back of Vic's along the boardwalk and across the driveway. She lifted the gray tarp off one corner of Kyle's convertible. A sudden breeze sent the tarp billowing skyward. Charlene laughed as she opened the door and got behind the wheel. Keys in hand, she turned the ignition, and the engine roared to life. "I could get used to this," Charlene said gleefully. She pushed a little too hard on the gas pedal. The car fishtailed, spraying gravel across the driveway. The tires squealed as she pulled onto the pavement. It had been a while since she'd had the opportunity to drive, as there was no real need for her to have a car in her little area of Harbor Cove. Everything she needed was within walking distance. Still, she somehow felt so completely alive driving Kyle's convertible. Charlene couldn't resist opening her up, remembering the first time she sat beside him. Accelerating up past 70 mph along the shoreline highway, her heart raced as she felt the power pulse through her. Charlene braked and slowed as she entered Harbor Cove city limits. Turning onto Mulberry Street she pulled into the driveway and got out. In the house, she walked through the kitchen, unlocked the entrance door to the attached garage and turned on the light. Charlene slid the interior lock bar and the barn-style garage doors swung open. She got back into the car and drove it into place with a few feet to spare, enough to pull the doors closed behind her. Getting out, she admired the convertible's shine under the warm light. Then, noticing the dusty interior inside the car, Charlene rummaged through the overhead cabinets above a bench, finding some clean rags and a bottle of window cleaner. She went about lovingly wiping down the interior. Across the dash and instrument panel, she emptied the ashtray, then pushed the button on the glove box. Kyle had locked it. Charlene checked the key ring. There were three keys. She tried the ignition key and it unlocked the glove box. She pushed the button and it opened. A handgun in a worn brown leather holster lay on top of miscellaneous maps and paperwork. Charlene had never handled a gun before. She'd seen enough detective movies and with her uncle being a cop, she knew not to touch this particular gun with her fingers. Grabbing a clean cloth, she picked up the gun, removed it from its holster and examined it closely. .38 S&W SPL. was factory stamped on the barrel, which was only a couple of inches long. A snub nose 38 Special, it appeared to be loaded. Charlene holstered the gun and sat it down on the seat. Curiosity spurred her on as she continued to go through the glove box. Among detailed maps of Port Huron, Detroit, Sarnia, and Windsor, Ontario, Canada, she also found a map of the United States. As she rifled around, an unsealed envelope slipped out of the glove box, falling onto the floorboard. She peeked inside, discovering the registration. The car was registered to Jacob Lawrence MacDonald, 2301 Holland Avenue, Port Huron, Michigan. Under the maps and registration, she found an open pack of cigarettes and a shiny gold lighter engraved with the letters J.L.M on one side, a black spearhead insignia embossed on the other. Lastly, a single key that looked no different than an ordinary front door key. The key matched the third one on the ring. Charlene pondered, possibly a spare key to the house where Kyle said he was staying, about forty minutes away. John had called it the Refuge. Charlene smiled, "I'm getting pretty good at playing detective." Deciding this treasure trove would be safer hidden in her room, Charlene gathered everything up and put the items in a cardboard box she found in the cabinet with the rags. The box was just the right size.

Walking around back, she opened the trunk. Kyle's golf

clubs, shoes and a black duffle bag were inside. She opened it, finding a change of clothes, a travel case with a straight-edge razor, shaving cream, a bottle of cologne, a toothbrush, toothpaste and a bar of soap. The clothes appeared to be worn maybe once. She pulled the shirt out of the bag and held it up to her face. Closing her eyes, she breathed in the scent of her Kyle. It was intoxicating, making her warm all over. After a few minutes of self-indulgence, she reluctantly put the shirt back in the duffle bag. Charlene closed the trunk and locked the car. Rechecking the lock bar, making sure it was secure, she walked around the car and through the back door into the kitchen.

Glancing at the clock above the sink she read 5:45 p.m. Charlene's stomach growled reminding her that she hadn't eaten all day. She ran upstairs with the box in hand and shoved it under her bed. Then, went back downstairs and opened the fridge to see what she could find for dinner. "Damn, there isn't much in here to eat. I need to go grocery shopping," Charlene stated. Grabbing the grape jelly and the jar of peanut butter from the pantry, she made a PBJ sandwich, washing it down with the last of the milk. At 6, the telephone rang. Charlene's heart jumped. Hoping it was Kyle, she answered excitedly.

"Hello, Brooks residence. This is Charlene."

"Hey Charlene, it's Alice! How has your day been going?"

"What, do you miss me already? You haven't even been gone a day!" Charlene joked.

"Of course, I miss you. That's why I called and to see how you are doing."

"I'm doing okay. How about you, are you all settled in?"

"Yes, but this does seem strange coming downstairs to see Mom and not you standing in the kitchen. It will take some getting used to but I'll only be here for a couple of months."

"Where will you two be living once you're married?"

"Walter has an apartment not far from The Guardian Building where he works. We'll probably stay there until we can save enough money to purchase a house."

"That sounds smart. It's going to take some adjusting to life in the big city. All that traffic would drive me bonkers." Charlene laughed.

"Yes, but I'm sure I'll get used to it. So, what did you do today?"

"Not much. I walked over to Vickers Point, well actually starting walking to Vickers Point when Ruth McGuire pulled up and offered me a ride. She was on her way up north to visit a friend. So, I pretty much just spent the day on the point. I visited with John at Vic's and then came back here. I was thinking about going to Stan's Market for some groceries. The fridge is getting pretty much empty."

"Oh, I knew we should have gone grocery shopping before I left. I'm sorry. There should be some money left in the cookie jar. Have a look-see and let me know."

Charlene removed the cookie jar lid. "Yeah, there's a twenty. I should be able to stock up a bit. I've also saved some money, so I'll be okay."

"Sounds good. Oh, did John say anything about last Saturday night?"

"Not much, only that people are gossiping about Kyle and me. I told John I didn't give a "rat's ass" about what they were saying and that everyone needed to mind their business. He agreed."

"Well, you know how it is in Harbor Cove. The town folk have nothing better to do than gossip about their neighbors."

"Ain't that the truth?" Charlene laughed sarcastically.

"I guess I'll let you go for now. Walter is dropping by, and I need to check on dinner. Miss you."

"Miss you, too. I'll call you sometime tomorrow. Have a good night."

Charlene hung up the phone. She wasn't looking forward to spending the night alone. Casting aside her fears, Charlene fetched the twenty from the cookie jar. She grabbed her jacket and the cart they used to help carry the groceries and walked to Stan's Market. Perusing the aisles, she struggled with what to buy. It was just herself she was shopping for. Bread, cheese, lunchmeat, T.V. Dinners and frozen pizza would cover her nights and weekends. She could eat at JoAnn's in the mornings like she had been when she got the girls up and ready for school.

Charlene was always welcome to join JoAnn, Sam and the girls for dinner and spend the night. When needed, she could stay in her room upstairs just across the hall from Mildred and Suzanne. She thought she might do that more often now that Alice had moved out. The fact was, Charlene, didn't like the thought of living alone. She had become dependent on Alice. Also, Alice's house was a place for her to go where there were no rules and no one to judge or tell her how to live. Caught between the freedom to live by her own rules and the need to be around people, she couldn't have both at JoAnn's. Charlene felt she was always under JoAnn and Sam's scrutiny. She was sure they disapproved of how she chose to live although she did her best not to let it concern her. As it was, things had been working nicely, allowing her to take care of Mildred and Suzanne in the mornings and be there when the girls got off the bus. Once JoAnn got home, Charlene would spend most of her nights and weekends with Alice. The only thing that changed was now, there was no Alice. Just an empty house where her voice would echo off the walls as she would walk from room to room, alone with her thoughts.

Charlene loaded her groceries into her cart and walked back to the house. After putting them away, she walked upstairs and pulled out the cardboard box from beneath her bed. The gun, still wrapped in the rag, she sat on the nightstand. Opening the map of Port Huron, she followed the highway along the shoreline south from Harbor Cove with her finger. She stopped on a black dot, marked next to the St. Clair River, just down from the Blue Water Bridge to Canada. Charlene tapped her finger on the dot. Taking out the registration, she read the address, 2301 Holland Avenue. The street name matched the dot on the map. Her heartbeat quickened. She'd found the Refuge! Not understanding the other dots and lines on the Sarnia and Windsor, Ontario, Canada maps, Charlene set them aside and opened the map of the United States. Dots marked locations in major cities from Los Angles to Washington, DC. Lines intersected lines. Charlene couldn't make heads or tails out of what she saw. It became overwhelming. She had a funny feeling she WAS in over her head. Charlene could hear Kyle in her subconscious, "You went through my billfold! Now you're going through my glove box?"

A guilty blush rose on her neck and the heat was almost unbearable. She felt like a kid who got caught with her hand in the cookie jar. Her heart was racing. She needed something to calm her nerves. Charlene eyed the pack of cigarettes. Not being a smoker, she hesitated. Then, her hand shaking, she removed a cigarette from the pack and put it between her lips. She flicked open the lighter, striking the flint, and a bright bluish-orange flame erupted. Charlene inhaled and blew out a cloud of smoke. The acrid smell of lighter fluid mingling with the cigarette smoke made her eyes water. Her throat burned, and she coughed. Waiting for a second, she took another drag and blew the smoke to the ceiling. Her nerves calmed down and she felt light-headed from the nicotine. Deciding it felt good, she took one last puff, crushed the butt on the heel of her shoe and then flushed it down the toilet. Charlene found it intriguing that she was torn between looking and not looking further at the paperwork. Her desire was just enough to make her want more. At the same time, fear's bony fingers held her tightly in its grasp. John's words resounded in her soul, "Don't get in too deep. You might not be able to dig yourself out. If you do, you'll regret ever knowing him." Charlene believed the part about getting in too deep. It was unsettling. Regretting ever knowing Kyle, she doubted it. Deciding to do whatever it took to become Charlene Elizabeth MacDonald, she gathered the items and put them back into the cardboard box.

Pacing her room, Charlene fought the overwhelming urge to grab the keys to Kyle's convertible and go for a drive. It was dark outside and no one would see her driving along the shoreline highway. The evening was too chilly to take the top down but that was no big deal. She could drive and listen to music on the radio. "Drive where?" She thought to herself. I could go up to Vickers Point, park the car behind the outer storage building and ask John when he thinks he might hear from Kyle. Acting on impulse, she grabbed the keys and the cardboard box. Pulling on her jacket, she checked her look in the mirror. It would do. Then, she went downstairs and into the garage.

She undid the lockbolt, and the garage doors opened into the cool night air. Charlene unlocked the car and got it and put the items back in the glove box. Soon she was cruising along the shoreline highway, tapping her fingers on the steering wheel to Buddy Holly's "That'll Be The Day."

She turned onto Vickers Point Road. Driving around the back of Vic's, Charlene eased the convertible behind the outer storage building. She parked and got out, locked it, then walked through the back door into Vic's.

Charlene surveyed the crowd, not looking for anyone in particular. There were a few people she recognized. Julie was there with Bud but she didn't see Charlene.

Then, leaning against the jukebox in the corner, she saw Skip sneaking a swig from his flask. His nose was bandaged and swollen, and he looked like hell.

Charlene cringed. Anger and hate boiled up inside of her. Skip hadn't noticed her. She turned and walked up to the bar. John was just finishing serving a couple of beers.

"Hi, Charlene. What brings you out tonight? What can I get you to drink?" John asked.

"The usual cherry cola with a splash of line. I was bored alone at the house, so I thought I'd come out and see what's shaking."

John grinned, "Did you drive?" He questioned.

"Yes, I did. I parked behind the outer storage building. Hope that's okay?"

"Sure, probably better anyway. We wouldn't want to risk someone hitting it with their car door in the parking lot."

Looking around to make sure no one was eavesdropping, Charlene leaned in and asked, "When do you think Kyle will call?"

John looked around, "Not sure. He usually touches base after I close for the night late Saturday or early Sunday mornings. I got a feeling he'll be calling early tomorrow morning, maybe around 7. You'd be taking a chance, I mean, it's no guarantee that he'll call, but you're welcome to drop by. Actually, I tell you what, when he gets a hold of me, we'll set up a time for him to call back so you two can talk. I'll let you know when you should come by."

"You'll need my phone number."

"I'm sure Kyle will give it to me. I don't want any numbers written down for nosey folks to see if you catch my drift."

"Understood. Well, let me know. I can break away anytime."

"Will do. I'd better get back to work. You enjoy your evening." John excused himself.

Claudia walked up behind Charlene and sat down on the stool beside her.

"Hey, how's your evening going?" She asked.

Charlene tensed, "Okay, I guess. How about you? How's your head?"

"I'm doing good. My head is better. I'm glad I didn't need stitches. I still have to repair the back window in my car, but it's just cracked, so I might not worry about it."

"Well, that's something, I guess." Charlene offered up one of her fake plastic smiles.

Claudia nodded in the direction of Skip. "Him, on the other hand, he's really messed up. He says he doesn't remember what happened. Just that he woke up on the floor hurting so bad that he thought he would die. Bud drove him to the doctor and got him all fixed up. Doc says he has a broken nose and a lot of bruising on his sides with three cracked ribs. He'll take a while to heal up. Skip thinks he must've pissed someone off, and they broke into his place. They might have taken a baseball bat or something and beat the shit out of him. Lord knows that's a good chance as any. Skip's always shooting off his mouth and getting into trouble."

Charlene half smiled, "Yes, that's probably what happened. I hope he learned something from what looks like a hell of a beating."

"Skip Rogers, learn something? Claudia snorted. "Not likely."

"Well, I'm glad you're okay," Charlene remarked.

"Thanks. Drop by the salon sometime, and I'll give you a makeover." Claudia offered.

"I will, thank you," Charlene replied.

She watched as Claudia made her way across the room to Skip. Julie and Bud had joined them in laughing about something.

Amazed and grateful that Claudia didn't seem to remember anything, Charlene decided she had enough of Vic's. Driving back to Alice's, she noticed the gas gauge had fallen below a quarter of a tank. It was late, so she figured she'd plan to fill up the next time she was out.

It was another sleepless night. Charlene tossed and turned. Getting up at 5 a.m., she made some tea, crawled into bed and tried to get back into her book. After reading a few chapters, Charlene closed her book and attempted to get comfortable. Sleep evaded her and she lay away thinking about Kyle. Her alarm clock read 6:30 a.m. She decided she would take John up on his offer to meet him at Vic's to wait for Kyle's phone call. She brushed her hair and applied makeup, dressed hurriedly in jeans and a blue blouse.

She drove up to Vickers Point and pulled around back. Even though it was early and the parking lot was empty, she didn't want to draw attention to her being there at that time. If someone saw her there at that time of day, it would set the rumor mill ablaze.

She walked across the boardwalk to the back door. It was locked. She cupped her hands and peered into Vic's. Just the neon tubular bulbs from the jukebox lit the dance floor with an eerie glow. Then she saw John standing behind the bar talking on the phone. Charlene knocked on the door. John noticed her, and after about a minute, he unlocked it.

"Is that Kyle on the phone?" Charlene asked excitedly.

"Yes, you can talk to him in a minute. I'll let him know you're here," John said as he picked up the receiver off the bar.

"Okay, understood. Yes, I will. Yes, she's here." John handed Charlene the receiver.

"Hi Kyle, how are you? I've missed you so much!" She exclaimed.

"Hi Charlene, I'm all right. I can't talk long. Things are really crazy out here. John tells me that you are storing my car in your garage. That's good, it will be safer there. I need you to do something for me."

"Yes, anything, just ask." She was excited that he was allowing her to help him somehow.

"I need you to drive to my place. John will give you the address and details. Follow them closely. Understand? The house key is on the ring with the car keys."

"Okay, I will. By the way, your car is below a quarter of a tank of gas. I'll need to fill the tank and I'm a little short on cash."

"Okay, why are you short on cash? Aren't you working two jobs?" Kyle questioned.

"Well, I had to help Alice with her move to the city. It drained my funds."

The warning bells began to ring in Kyle's head. He deduced that if Alice did need money to move, she would have asked for it from her finance' or her mother, Florence. Things didn't add up. He dismissed the thought, for now. There would be a time down the road for that discussion.

"Okay, I'll ask John to give you a draw from the till for gas. Go down this morning to my place. Remember, don't deviate from what John tells you. Got it?"

"Understood, I'll stick to the plan. Kyle, I really miss you. Any chance you are coming back before Thanksgiving? I want to see you."

"As I said, I don't know. I'll keep John posted. Miss you too. Put John back on the line." Charlene felt dismissed, hesitating she handed the receiver back to John.

"Yes?" John listened and looked at Charlene. "How much? Is there anything else? Okay, I will. I'll get it done." John hung up the receiver. He turned and removed five twenties from the till and handed them to Charlene.

"It's more than you need to fill up, but Kyle told me to give you a hundred since you're short on cash and for helping him out." He found a pen and pad of paper. "Here's the address for the Refuge. It's down by the Blue Water Bridge just off Holland Avenue. You'll drive along the shoreline on M-25 for about 40 minutes. Take Lakeshore Road, which will blend into Gratiot Avenue. It intersects with Holland. I'd go myself, but Kyle has me busy with something else." John handed her the address, keeping hold of it as he spoke, "Pay careful attention to what I'm saying. When you get to the Refuge, park around the back. Go inside. You'll see a bookcase against the far wall. Find the novel, "To Kill A Mockingbird." Pull it towards you but don't remove it completely from the shelf. Step back and the shelf will pivot, exposing an inner room. Walk over to the desk and open the top right drawer. It will appear almost empty with a couple of pens and scraps of paper inside. Remove the contents and the drawer. Turn it over and tap it with your finger. A fake bottom will appear. Inside you will find a thin black book. Retrieve it. Replace the bottom of the drawer with its contents and put it back. Next to the desk, you'll find a brown leather briefcase. Bring the briefcase and the book back here to me. Don't touch anything else. When you exit the room, push the book "To Kill A Mockingbird" back into place, and the bookcase will close. Any questions?"

Charlene couldn't believe what she was hearing. It sounded crazy, like something from a spy novel. A covert operation? She stared blankly for a moment and John snapped his fingers, "Earth to Charlene. Do you have any questions?"

Charlene swallowed, "No, I've got it. What's in the briefcase?"

"That is none of your concern." Your mission is to do the pick-up and deliver the briefcase and the book back here to me. Drive the speed limit and try to remain inconspicuous. Remember, you're just out for a Sunday morning drive along the shoreline, got it? Now go. I'll see you back here before noon."

Charlene nodded and walked out the back door. She could hear her heart pounding in her ears. So many questions rattled around in her head.

One question stood out above the rest, "What have I gotten myself into?"

Charlene filled the tank on the way out of town and proceeded along the shoreline on I-25. Watching her speed, she followed John's directions, and 40 minutes later, she found Holland Avenue and the address. The house was rundown and appeared vacant. Charlene looked around. The neighborhood also looked rundown. An uneasiness fell over her. "Get in and get out," Charlene told herself. She unlocked the door and entered the house.

Over on the far wall stood the floor-to-ceiling bookcase. Dusty books clung to its shelves. She found the book "To Kill A Mockingbird" and tipped it back. Charlene heard an audible click from somewhere within the bookcase. She watched as it moved inward roughly two feet, allowing passage into an inner sanctum. Before her, she saw a plush office. Old paintings, inside ornate frames, graced its burgundy walls. Marble and bronze statues including expensive vases positioned on pillars added a stateliness to the room. Five black leather chairs formed a half circle in front of a large mahogany desk. On the wall directly behind was a large oblong gold seal overlaid with a black obsidian spearhead. Underneath in gold print, Office of Strategic Services. Next to that hung a marble circular seal in navy blue, with white bold lettering, Central Intelligence Agency arced over the head of an eagle. Under the eagle, also in bold white letters, United States of America. Charlene walked around the desk and opened the top right drawer. Removing its contents, she turned the drawer over and tapped it with her finger, hoping she was doing it right. A false bottom sprung open, exposing a thin black leatherbound book. Charlene picked up the book and closed the false bottom. Then, returned the contents to the drawer. Charlene couldn't resist the urge to open the thin black leatherbound book. She saw rows of numbers, and words, although written in English, they made no sense whatsoever. Then it dawned on her. The writing must be complex code. Charlene closed the book and put it in her jacket pocket. Looking down under the desk, she found the brown leather briefcase. Gold monogrammed letters, J.L.M., graced the front. She picked it up and discovered it was heavier than she imagined. Setting in on the desk Charlene attempted to open the hasps and found they were locked. Taking one last look around the room she exited back through the bookcase, and pushed the book into place. The bookcase slide closed so perfectly that no one would ever know there was another room hidden behind it.

Charline arrived at Vic's by 11:30. John met her around back. "How did it go?" He asked.

"No problems. Here's the book and the briefcase." She handed them to John.

"Very good, you did well. Now skedaddle. I'll keep you posted when I hear from Kyle again."

Chapter Eighteen

It seemed like a whole day had passed, being up so early and making the run to the Refuge. Charlene got back to Alice's and put the car in the garage. She fixed herself a ham and cheese sandwich for lunch in the kitchen. Being a bright sunny Sunday afternoon, Charlene went for a walk to clear her head. Missing Sunday service wasn't her intention, but she decided it was okay. Charlene planned to be at the church Wednesday night for the youth group. The Harvest party was next Sunday afternoon, and the kids would be very excited to plan the event.

Charlene walked down to the city park, just passing the time and enjoying the sunshine. She sat down on a swing. From behind her, Suzanne called, "Hi, Charlene! Did you come out to play with us?" She looked over her shoulder. Suzanne and Mildred were climbing the monkey bars, laughing.

"Where did you two come from? Are you enjoying your afternoon?"

"Very much so," Mildred replied.

"Mommy brought us down so we could play. She's sitting over there by the fountain." Suzanne pointed.

"It looks like you're having fun. Be careful on those monkey bars so you don't fall and crack your head," Charlene warned, waving at JoAnn from her swing.

JoAnn walked over.

"Hello Charlene. Isn't this a beautiful Sunday afternoon?" She exclaimed.

"Yes, it is. The girls look like they're enjoying the playground. It was so nice of you to bring them down."

"Well, Sam is sleeping. He worked the late shift down at the plant and I didn't want the girls to wake him. He's usually off on Saturdays, but the boss offered overtime, and you know how Sam is. He signs up for all the overtime he can get."

Charlene nodded, "Can't turn down that extra money. I get it."

"I was wondering if you'd like to join us for dinner this evening. Maybe play some board games with the girls afterward? You could spend the night. That way, you wouldn't have to walk on over first thing in the morning. The girls miss playing with you. You don't always have to leave and go to your friend Alice's after I get home."

"I guess I could come over for dinner. I don't have anything else going on this evening."

"That sounds good. Let's shoot for 6" JoAnn smiled, happy that Charlene had accepted her invitation.

"Okay, I'll see you then. That goes for you two girls, also!" Suzanne squealed in excitement, running to Charlene for a hug. Mildred continued to hang upside down from the monkey bars, giggling.

Upon arriving back at Alice's, she decided to give her a

call, half thinking she might not be home. Alice answered on the third ring.

"Brooks residence, Alice speaking."

"Hi Alice, it's Charlene. I didn't think you'd be home."

"I'm here. I'm feeling a little under the weather. I'm about to start my period, but I think some kind of bug is going around here in the city. Walter isn't feeling all that well either, so, everyone is just chilling out. How are things with you?"

"Come to think of it, I should start any day now. Anyway, it's been a busy weekend. I ran into JoAnn and the girls at the park this afternoon. JoAnn invited me to dinner and asked me to play board games with the girls and spend the night."

"Are you going to? You might as well." Alice urged.

"Yes, I guess I will. For a change, it might be fun spending quality time with the girls."

"Best of all, you won't be alone. I worry about you, Charlene. I think you should take advantage of being able to live with JoAnn, Sam, and the girls."

"We've been over this. You know how Sam can get. He's mentally draining and always looking for something that doesn't meet his standards and principles. I feel like I'm being judged whenever I'm there."

"I know it's hard, but look at the bright side. You can always leave if it gets to be too much. JoAnn understands how he is."

"I know, but that gets tricky making an excuse for an exit, and I think JoAnn is scared of him. She never says much when he gets going on one of his rants."

"I know. So, what else is new? You said it's been a busy weekend?" Alice asked.

"Well, I went to Vic's last night."

"Oh my God, Charlene, why? I mean, after what happened?" Alice questioned with concern in her voice.

"Well, I can't just crawl in a hole, Alice. Life goes on. Besides, I was so bored alone at the house."

"Wait, how did you get there? It's not a short walk, especially at night." Alice exclaimed.

"Oh, I got a ride from a cute guy I met at the library," Charlene teased.

"What guy?" Alice asked. "Is Kyle back in town?"

"No, he will be gone until at least Thanksgiving."

"So, who?" Alice was becoming impatient.

Charlene didn't want to tell Alice anything that transpired during her visit with John. She couldn't. Better to keep her in the dark.

"It's just an old friend of mine. Anyway, guess who was at Vic's?" Alice sensed disgust in her voice.

"No way, Claudia? Skip? Oh my God, what happened?"

"I saw Skip leaning against the jukebox drinking his hooch. He looked awful. His nose was all taped up. You should have seen his face. It was a nasty purple, black and blue."

"I can imagine. Did Skip see you?"

"No, but Claudia came up to the bar and sat beside me. We had a "nice" little conversation. She acted like everything was fine and said her head was okay."

"Did Claudia mention anything about how she hit her head?"

"Nope, she did, however, tell me that Skip was pretty messed up. He has no memory of what happened, just that he woke up on the floor hurting so bad he thought he was going to die. Claudia even told me he pissed himself. Bud took him to the doctor. The Doc told him he had a broken nose and three busted ribs. Guess he's lucky I didn't stomp his nuts, too," Charlene laughed bitterly.

Alice tried not to laugh, "Now, now, Charlene. I think you did enough damage, even if he did deserve it. The Bastard."

"Well, I just wanted to call and catch you up on the latest, nothing much else is new."

"Thanks for calling, and have fun tonight." Alice encouraged.

"I will. Talk to you later. Miss you."

"Talk to you later. Miss you, too."

Charlene hung up the phone and got ready for her dinner date with JoAnn and her family. Arriving at 5:50, Charlene rang the doorbell and Mildred answered.

"JoAnn, it's Charlene," she said, walking into the kitchen. Charlene closed the door behind her. Glancing into the living room, she saw Sam sitting in his easy chair. Cigarette smoke curled above him as he sipped amber liquid from his rock glass. He was reading the Sunday paper.

"Well, Well, Well. If it ain't Charlene. How goes it, Kid?" Sam called out, not looking up from his paper.

"I'm fine, Sam. How are you?"

"Same old thing, different day. It's that way when you're a working man taking care of a family." Sam turned the page of his paper, unconcerned if Charlene answered or not.

"Charlene, come to the kitchen and help me mash the potatoes. You girls go wash up. Dinner is almost ready," she called out as the girls ran by to the bathroom. JoAnn prepared a delicious meal, meatloaf with mashed potatoes and gravy, homemade bread and green bean casserole. There was a fresh cherry pie for dessert.

"Okay, time for dinner. Let's get seated at the table," JoAnn urged. Sam sat at the head of the table. The girls sat next to each other and JoAnn sat at the other end. Charlene sat across from the girls. Even though Sam, JoAnn, and the girls weren't churchgoers, they did give thanks.

Everyone bowed their heads and gave thanks with a very brief prayer. The same prayer was said at all meals. As the servings were passed around, JoAnn asked Charlene, "How is school going?"

"It's going well, thank you. I will have my secretarial certificate by the end of the year. Then someday, I hope to find employment at a prestigious firm in Detroit." Charlene replied proudly.

"Find employment, what? Bringing coffee to some stiff in a suit? Then sit on his lap and take dick-tation?" Sam laughed sarcastically.

"Sam, please don't start." JoAnn gave her husband a stern look that could turn water into ice.

"What? I was just making a joke." Sam shrugged and went about cutting his meatloaf.

Charlene thought, "Great, another wonderful evening of degrading conversation."

Suzanne looked at Charlene and smiled. "We're going trick-or-treating this coming weekend. I'm going to be a princess! Millie is going to be a little devil. Can you take us? You can dress up, too." Suzanne commented excitedly.

"I guess I could take you along the downtown trick-or-treat trail." Charlene smiled, looking at JoAnn.

"Yes, that would be nice, and maybe after school this week, you can get some pumpkins carved to put out on the front porch," JoAnn suggested.

"If you're coming trick-or-treating with us, you gotta dress up! What are you going to be, Charlene?" Millie asked.

"I could dress us as the Wicked Witch of the West from the "Wizard of Oz," Charlene suggested.

"That would be scary!" Suzanne shook in her chair.

"Or maybe a Vampire, with those hideous eye teeth of yours." Sam laughed.

Charlene glared at Sam, staring him down to the point where they both looked away.

"Something is different about you, Charlene. You seem more defiant and argumentative, there will be none of that in my house!" Sam bellowed.

"Calm down, Dear," JoAnn suggested, "You know what the doctor said about raising your blood pressure."

"Daddy, please don't get mad at Charlene." Suzanne cried.

"It's okay, Suzi Q. He didn't mean it. I'm sure he was only joking." Charlene soothed Suzanne and shot a look at Sam. If the look had a word, it would have been, Asshole.

The girls finished eating and asked if they could be excused.

"Are you finished, Charlene? Let's play a game of Sorry," Mildred suggested.

"I want to play Candy Land," Suzanne demanded.

"Sorry first," Mildred argued.

"Now, quit you two. We can play both," Charlene commented, getting up and taking her plate to the sink.

"After the games, it's bath time, girls. There's school tomorrow morning." JoAnn reminded them. After an hour of board games, Charlene drew bath water for the girls, lathered them up and allowed them to play in the bubble bath for a few minutes.

"Are you staying the night, Charlene?" Suzanne asked as Charlene towel-dried her hair.

"Do you want me to?" Charlene asked, smiling.

"Yes, you can read us a bedtime story!" She giggled.

All three girls snuggled up in Charlene's bed with Charlene in the middle. The girls picked Cinderella. It was one of their favorite bedtime stories. The trip to the park that afternoon must have worn Suzanne and Mildred out, as they were fast asleep by the end of the story. Charlene snuggled down and drifted off between them, sleeping peacefully until JoAnn knocked on the bedroom door at 7 the next morning. "Rise and shine, girls. Time to get ready for school."

JoAnn had fixed a full breakfast; waffles, eggs and bacon. She had it waiting for the girls when they came downstairs.

"Girls! Did you enjoy your night with Charlene?" JoAnn asked, kissing Suzanne and Mildred on the foreheads.

"Yes, I wish Charlene would be here every night." Suzanne insisted.

"Well, you heard it, Charlene. The girls would like you to stay the night more often." JoAnn smiled.

"We'll see how it goes. Thank you for dinner and breakfast. I'll get the girls off to school." Charlene offered.

"Oh, by the way, what are your plans for Thanksgiving dinner? We'd love to have you over to celebrate with us." JoAnn asked.

"Thank you but, I'm sorry, I can't. I've already accepted an invitation to spend the holiday with Alice, Walter and Florence in the city."

"Oh... Well, I..., I wanted to ask. That's okay, you have a wonderful time. How is Alice doing? Is she still working for Joe?" She asked.

"Alice is doing well." Charlene wasn't sure how much information she wanted to share. After all, Alice and Walter had just gotten engaged.

"I'm not sure if I should tell you. I mean, I haven't seen an announcement in the paper yet. Alice and Walter are talking about marriage. When they do get married, she asked me to be her Maid of Honor. I'll know more when we get back from the city.

"That's wonderful! Keep me posted, I've always liked Alice. I hope this Walter guy will be a good match for her."

"Oh, he is. We all went to school together. He's a standup guy."

"Nice to hear. Well, Dear, I need to get to work. It was nice having you spend the night. I'll see you later this afternoon."

Chapter Nineteen

Halloween came and went, and the girls enjoyed Charlene, the Wicked Witch of the West, taking them along the trick-or-treat trail. The youth group had their party and the kids dressed up as their favorite characters from the bible. It reminded Charlene of a Christmas play, but the kids had fun and Pastor Mike was elated.

November ushered in colder weather. Dark ominous clouds hung low over the lake. Charlene hadn't heard anything from John regarding Kyle. Fear visited her daily, infringing upon and destroying all hope. Charlene called John, asking if he had heard anything.

"I'm as puzzled as you are, Charlene. I know it's hard not to worry, but there is nothing we can do. Kyle's mission is obviously making it impossible for him to make contact again. I will keep you posted if and when I hear from him."

"Thank you, John. That's all I can ask." Charlene would pace by the phone at 8:30 every morning. John told her he would contact her at that time so she wouldn't miss the call. The phone never rang.

Charlene bided her time by studying for her final exam

in shorthand. Her drive to someday be employed as an executive secretary was the only thing she was sure of. Whenever Charlene set her mind to succeed in something, she would do precisely that, succeed.

Otherwise, Charlene lived day to day in her seemly mundane life. She called Alice on the first Thursday of November, the second day of the month.

"Hi Charlene, how are you? How was Halloween?" Alice asked.

"It was good. I enjoyed playing the Wicked Witch of the West with my Princess Suzanne and Little Devil, Mildred. We collected bags of candy along the trick-or-treat trail. The youth group party was also fun. I've been spending more time at JoAnn's but I don't stay every night. Sam is the same. He's so vile. I can't stand to be around him. Anyway, how have you been?"

"Life's been busy here. Walter reserved the church for our wedding on Valentine's Day at 2:30 in the afternoon! We just finished sending out invitations! You should have yours any day. Mom helped me pick out my dress. You should see it. It's stunning. It has white lace with gold trim and a long train. She plans to redesign it and sew miniature red roses all throughout the trailing fabric. It will be beautiful, and unique. Oh! I called and asked Joe to walk me down the aisle. He started crying when I asked him. He's so sweet. You and I have to set up a time to pick out your dress. Can we do that when you come down here for Thanksgiving dinner?" Alice asked.

Charlene hesitated, "Sure can. It sounds like you've been busy."

"You sound a little off, Charlene. What's going on?" Alice asked, with concern in her voice.

"Um, Alice… I'm late."

"Late? Oh no! How late?"

"Almost two whole weeks."

"Well, don't freak out. You have been pretty stressed lately. An awful lot has happened in the past month."

Charlene tried to hide the fear in her voice but failed, "I'm scared, Alice. What if I'm pregnant? If I am, I'm sure it's Kyle's. What is he going to think? Will he be happy? He's still out of town on business and I haven't heard much from him. What if something happened? What if he doesn't come back?" Charlene's voice began to shake.

"Hey, calm down, breathe. We'll figure this out. How are you feeling?"

"My breasts seem swollen and feel a little tender. That's about it."

"Well, let's wait another week or two. Like I said, it might just be the stress of everything. That alone could cause you to miss."

"Okay, I hope you're right."

"Has anything else been going on?"

"No, not really. I have been studying hard for my secretary skills exam."

"When do you take it?"

"Friday, December 1st.

"I'm sure you'll ace the exam," Alice said confidently.

"Thanks, Alice. I wish you were here." Charlene sniffled.

"I wish I was there, too. You know I'm just a phone call away, right?"

"I know. Please don't say anything to your mother. I don't want her to think badly of me."

"Don't worry. It's our secret."

"Thank you. I've got to go. I'll call you later."

Charlene sank to the floor, tears streaming down her cheeks. She thought to herself if only I could talk to Kyle. Charlene lost all track of time, and she had no idea how long she'd been sitting on the floor. It was dark outside and the house was cold. Getting up, she flipped the light switch on and turned up the furnace. The smell of burning dust filtered through the vents. It was the first time the furnace had been fired since early spring.

Charlene went upstairs and drew a hot bath. Undressing, she looked down at her stomach and caressed it with her hands, wondering. She sank into the tub, laid her head back, and tried to relax in the warm water. Charlene felt her breasts. They were indeed tender. For a second, fear overwhelmed her. What if the baby was… Charlene refused to say his name and banished the thought. In her heart, she knew that if she was pregnant, it was Kyle's baby.

The water in the bathtub cooled. Charlene got out and dried off. She wrapped herself in her robe hanging above the heater vent. It was warm and welcoming. Downstairs she boiled water and made a cup of tea. The clock above the sink read 11:15 p.m. Sipping, Charlene struggled with what could soon change her life forever. A baby. She shook her head slowly. Looking over at the calendar, Charlene recounted the days again. Just 12 days late, she decided Alice was right. Maybe it was just the stress of everything that had happened in the past month.

"I'm not pregnant," Charlene told herself, "I can't be." Satisfied with her self-reassurance, she turned in for the night.

The next morning, in the kitchen, she x'd out the days on the calendar with a red marker. Willing herself daily to start but to no avail. Her fear became a reality when twelve days late became twenty-eight. She called Alice on Saturday morning, November 18th.

"Hello? Hi, Charlene," Alice answered.

"Hello. Well, brace yourself." Charlene broke down, "I'm pregnant. I'm now 28 days late."

Alice could hear the distress in Charlene's voice.

"How are you feeling?"

"A little nauseous in the mornings."

"I guess that's to be expected. Mom and I have been talking. Don't worry, not about you, but me, when I become pregnant. She's been filling me in on symptoms."

"Are you planning to have a baby?" Charlene asked.

"Walter and I have talked about it. Both of us want children. Hey, have you calculated when you'll have your baby? It shouldn't be too hard to do. When was the last time you were with Kyle?"

"The weekend of October 7th, that's the last time I saw him, and we spent the night together."

"Okay, that makes you six weeks pregnant right now. Let me get my calendar book. It has next year in it too. Mom says it takes 40 weeks from conception." Together they counted off the weeks and months over the phone. They came up with delivery around the end of June.

"By then, Kyle and I will be married," Charlene exclaimed.

Alice bit her lip, "When do you think you'll see him next?"

"I'm hoping shortly after Thanksgiving. He's supposed to get back around December 2nd. I plan to tell him we're pregnant the minute he gets here!" Charlene exclaimed excitedly.

"That's wonderful. I hope it all goes well. I'm sure it will," Alice replied, a little uneasy and a lot worried about Charlene.

"I know in my heart everything will be fine! So, when are you picking me up for Thanksgiving?"

"Oh! Walter and I will drive down to get you on the 22nd. We figured about noon. Will that work?"

"Yes, that would be great."

"Cool, we'll see you then. Well, I guess I'd better let you go, Charlene. Walter and I are shopping for wedding decorations for the church and reception downstairs this afternoon."

"Okay, it was good talking to you. I'm feeling better now, thank you."

"That's good. You know I'm always here for you."

"I know, just a phone call away. I'll talk to you soon, have fun shopping. I miss you!"

"Thanks, yes, we'll talk soon. Miss you, too."

Walter and Alice arrived to pick up Charlene for Thanksgiving dinner at noon on the 22nd just as planned. Hugs all around, and only spending a short time in the house, they opted for lunch at Smilin' Joes.

Joe grinned when he saw the three of them. "There you are! My favorite trio of young adults, coming to visit old Joe. It is so nice to see you!"

He embraced Alice, lifting her off the floor. Then he hugged Charlene and shook Walter's hand.

"You are here for lunch I hope?" Joe asked.

"Yes, of course, and to see you, Joe!" Alice answered.

After a meal of hamburgers, fries and shakes, Joe joined them at their table. "I am so honored that you asked me to walk you down the aisle for your wedding. It just means the world to me!" Joe exclaimed.

"I wouldn't want anyone else! I sent you an invitation with all the particulars including the address of The Old Mariners Church and when you need to be there. You should be getting the invitation any day. It will be a small ceremony. Afterward, we'll have our reception dinner in the basement of the church." Alice explained.

"That sounds good. I will be there ready to give my girl away to this fine young man." Joe beamed nodding at Walter.

An hour later they arrived. On the way up the walk, Florence opened the door greeting them. "Happy Thanksgiving!" As they entered the house Florence gave each of them a hug, "So good to see all of you again, come on in. Make yourselves comfortable. I've made some eggnog, my own special recipe. I'll get everyone a glass."

Alice got up and followed Florence into the kitchen. "Mom, remember? Charlene is lactose intolerant. I'll grab her a glass of juice."

"Oh! I keep forgetting that's a thing now." Florence rolled her eyes.

The festivities continued as the four of them enjoyed the rest of the day and on into the evening. Alice played the piano and everyone joined in singing holiday favorites. After the eggnog was gone, Florence opened a bottle of sweet California wine, toasting Alice and Walter's engagement.

Florence raised her glass, "A toast to you my lovely daughter and your handsome finance' Walter! May you have a wonderful life together and bless me with many, many, grandchildren!"

Alice blushed looking over at Walter, who grinned from ear to ear, and raised his glass with Charlene, "Here, here!"

"In the kitchen, I have cheese fondu almost ready. I'll set it up in the dining room for all of us to enjoy!" Florence exclaimed.

After the appetizer and a light dinner, exhaustion began to set in from an afternoon and evening of entertaining, reminiscing and sharing stories. Both yawning, Alice and Walter looked up as the grandfather clock chimed the eleventh hour.

"I think it's time to call it a night," Alice suggested.

"I agree, I'm pooped." Charlene stood up and stretched.

"Come on, my Love. Charlene and I are bunking in together in my room, you can sleep across the hall from us. Mom, we're all turning in for the night. We have a big day tomorrow."

Florence had been dozing off and on, relaxed from the wine and after the excitement of the day.

"Oh yes, I agree, I'll be getting up before six to put the turkey in the oven. I love the holidays but they sure are a lot of work," Florence laughed and followed everyone up the stairs.

Charlene rolled over in bed, something had woken her. She heard Florence open her bedroom door and head downstairs. Dawn was starting to chase away the night and she could see the alarm clock in the faint light, it read 5:45 a.m.

Getting up, she barely made it to the bathroom and nausea overtook her. Alice felt her get up and heard her heaving in the bathroom. Grabbing her robe, she put it on and knocked on the bathroom door, opening it.

"Are you all right Charlene?" Alice asked.

"Too much rich food last night I guess," Charlene groaned as Alice held the hair back from her face.

"No, my Dear. I believe it's called morning sickness," Alice replied patiently.

Charlene smiled faintly, "I believe you are right. I'm going back to bed." Alice helped her dearest friend back into bed.

"Well, since I'm up, I'm heading downstairs to help Mom start getting things ready for Thanksgiving Dinner. You just take it easy and rest." With that, Alice quietly left the room.

"Good morning, Alice, how did you sleep?" Florence asked, giving her daughter a hug.

"Slept like a baby. Speaking of which, exactly how many grandchildren are we talking?" She laughed, remembering her mother's toast.

"Oh, at least two or three, maybe more," Florence replied with a big smile.

"I see. And you'll be happy to assist when the two, three or maybe more are under foot and getting into everything?" Alice asked with raised eyebrows.

"Of course! I will love coming over to help out and spoil my grandbabies!" Florence laughed.

"I'll bet you change your tune when I stop by your boutique needing a babysitter so I can have a day off at the spa." Alice giggled at the look on Florence's face when she pictured her grandchildren running around the boutique. Together they laughed.

Alice helped Florence with the turkey; stuffing, basting and putting it in the oven. Florence rinsed her hands off in the sink, dried them and handed the towel to Alice.

"Did I hear Charlene upstairs in the bathroom this morning? Is she not feeling well?" Florence asked.

"I think her stomach is just a bit upset from the richness of the food last night. She went back to bed, she'll be okay."

Walter had gotten up, dressed and come downstairs.

"Anything I can help with ladies?" He offered.

"Well, since we're up, maybe we should fix a little breakfast. You can set the table while I make some coffee." Florence suggested.

"I'm going to get dressed and check on Charlene." Alice gave Walter a quick kiss and headed back upstairs.

"What's going on with Charlene?" Walter asked.

"Alice said she's feeling a bit under the weather, upset stomach from last's night's festivities. I didn't think the food was too rich, did you?" Florence questioned.

"Tasted great to me, but then I have an iron stomach and I can pretty much eat anything," Walter grinned.

Upstairs, Alice heard Charlene in the bathroom, again. She went to her aide, holding her hair back from her face.

"Thanks for the assist," Charlene sighed. Getting up she rinsed her mouth out with water.

"I hope this isn't a preview of what's to come." Charlene groaned.

"Well, Sorry to tell you, my Dear, it might very well be. Morning sickness can last six to eight weeks from what Mom told me. Let's get you dressed and eat a little something, drink some water and keep yourself hydrated." Florence smiled when Charlene came down the staircase with Alice.

"How are you feeling?" She asked, a concerned tone in her voice.

"I'm just a bit under the weather. It must have been something I ate last night. I'm feeling a little better," Charlene replied.

"Would you like some coffee or juice? I've fixed Walter and myself ham and cheese omelets. Let me prepare a couple for you and Alice. Maybe a cup of warm tea, Charlene?"

"How about just some toast and maybe water, for now anyway."

"Thanks. I'll take a small omelet, Mom," Alice answered, eyeing Charlene. "Well, hopefully, you'll feel better this afternoon so you can enjoy our Thanksgiving Dinner, turkey and all the trimmings!" Florence exclaimed.

"I hope so too. Anything I can help with?" Charlene asked.

"No, you're our guest and besides, if you have a little stomach bug, it's probably better that you just rest up. We don't want any of us to catch something you might have."

Alice hid a smile behind her coffee cup, thinking, "I doubt what Charlene has is contagious. At least I hope not." Looking down at her belly...

By 1:00 in the afternoon the turkey was fully cooked. Florence retrieved her mother's fine china from the cabinet and instructed Walter on how to set a formal table, helping him lay the tablecloth in place. Afterward, she and Alice finish preparing the rest of the meal.

"There's enough food to feed an army," Alice said as they set the last dish, sweet potatoes with perfectly roasted marshmallows on top.

"Oh, you hush! It won't go to waste. I'll send a plate or two home with Walter and the same for Charlene. You and I will have leftovers to munch on for a couple of days." Florence remarked.

"More like a week or maybe even longer." Alice teased.

Florence shook her head, "Keep it up and you and Walter will end up doing the dishes by yourselves."

"Hey now, how'd I get drug into his?" Walter asked, laughing.

"Well, we're a team, right? Where I go, you go. What I get us into, well, you get to suffer the consequences with me." Alice proclaimed.

"Now, do you still want to get married to my daughter?" Florence grinned

"Most definitely!" Walter heartily agreed.

"Good answer!" Charlene chimed in, watching the playful banter going on between them.

They sat down for the feast. After saying grace, everyone filled their plates. Charlene took smaller portions in hopes that she would be able to keep them down. Everyone enjoyed the meal, as it was one of the best Thanksgiving dinners Florence had ever prepared.

"That was amazing Mrs. Brooks, I'm stuffed!" Walter exclaimed holding his belly.

"Who's Mrs. Brooks? No Mrs. Brooks here," she playfully shot back. "Stuffed? No way! We still have dessert! There are four pies waiting in the kitchen! Pumpkin, Apple, Cherry, and my favorite, French silk." Florence declared.

"Well, maybe I have room for one piece," Walter smiled.

"You mean one piece of each, right?" Alice teased.

Finishing at least one piece of pie, each, for dessert, everyone pitched in and cleared the table. Alice and Charlene washed the china, as Walter carefully dried them. Florence returned them to the cabinet until the next special event.

After the clean-up was complete everyone retired to the formal living room. Alice snuggled up next to Walter on the sofa while Charlene drifted off to sleep in a comfortable chair, her feet elevated. Florence soon followed suit, snoring softly.

Friday morning, first thing, Charlene found herself on her knees again with morning sickness. She had braided her hair before she went to bed, anticipating praying to the porcelain Gods. When the queasiness passed, Charlene went back to bed, grateful that no one was up to hear her.

Early in the afternoon, Florence drove Alice and Charlene to her boutique. Walter opted to stay behind and watch T.V.

"What are your wedding colors?" Florence asked.

"Since it's Valentine's Day, I was thinking that a pastel pink and white would be lovely. What do you think, Charlene?" Alice asked.

"Pastel pink and white it is. What color suit will Walter's best man be in?" Charlene asked.

Florence responded, "Walter should be in a black suit, white shirt and black tie. His best man, I'm thinking, a gray suit with a pastel pink shirt and gray tie. I have the perfect dress for you Charlene and it comes in pastel pink!" Florence exclaimed, leading her to the other side of the boutique. A mannequin, modeled after Jackie Kennedy, stood on a platform looking across the room with a blank stare. A pastel blush pink dress, interwoven with pink lace and a full circle skirt, graced the First Lady.

"This dress is beautiful!" Charlene called out excitedly.

"Well then, let's try it on. I love the way it's designed. It will make the perfect dress for my maid of honor." Alice remarked.

Charlene stepped from the dressing room a few minutes later.

"It fits like it was made for me!" Charlene wondered.

"It actually looks better on you, too!" Alice laughed.

Florence smiled, "That was almost too easy." She had Charlene turn around to inspect the fit.

"We might have to do a nip here and a tuck there, but this will do nicely. I'll hang it in the back and the next time you are here, we'll fit it properly."

The rest of the weekend, Florence, Alice, Walter and Charlene spent shopping, dining and sightseeing around the city. Sunday after brunch, Florence packed up leftovers for Charlene.

"I'm so happy you could spend the holiday with us."

"Thank you for having me. I'm sorry I was a bit of a bother."

"You weren't a bother. I hope you continue to feel better, Sweetie," Florence gave Charlene a warm hug, then embraced Walter and Alice, as well.

"Drive safe back to Harbor Cove, watch the traffic. Folks will be traveling up and down M-25 coming back to the city from their holiday travels."

"Will do. See you when we get back," Alice waved.

Arriving home around 4 o'clock in the afternoon, they dropped Charlene off at the house, helping her take her overnight bag and leftovers inside.

"Thank you so much for a wonderful Thanksgiving weekend!" Charlene said as they again shared hugs all the way around.

"You are so very welcome. Please, call me if you need anything. Call me even if you don't! You know I'm just a phone call away." Alice reminded her.

Charlene smiled, "I will and thank you again. We'll talk soon."

Chapter Twenty

Exhausted from the long weekend, Charlene put the leftovers in the fridge and collapsed on the sofa with every intention of catching a little shut-eye. The phone rang, jolting her awake.

"Hello?" Charlene answered sleepily.

"There you are, I've been trying to call you all weekend."

"Who is this?" Charlene asked groggily.

"It's John! You don't sound like your chipper self. Are you okay?"

"Oh, it's you. John. Sorry. I've had a long couple of days down in the city and I'm plum worn out. Have you heard from Kyle?"

"I thought that's where you were since you didn't answer. Yes, I heard from Kyle, that's why I'm calling. He made it back. Flew into Langley this past Wednesday afternoon. After debriefing, he went home and spent the long weekend there. Kyle has some further debriefing and things to wrap up in D.C., and says it will take a couple of weeks. He'll be back here on Saturday, the 9th. Do you still want to drive down and pick him up at Willow Run Airfield? He'll be landing at 1600 hours."

"Definitely! I'll be there, I'm so excited!"

"Yes, he told me everything went well. He apologized for not getting back to us sooner. I was right, he wasn't able to make the call. He sends his thanks for making the run down to the Refuge for him."

"Did he say anything else?"

"Not really. Kyle doesn't say much over the phone. Keeps the chit-chat to a minimum. I'm sure he'll catch us up to speed when he gets here. Well, I have to let you go for now."

"Thanks for calling John and please, let me know if he calls you before I go to pick him up."

"I'll do that, talk to you later."

Charlene's heart flip-flopped at the thought that she would be back in Kyle's arms, even though it was later than she'd hoped. Her mind raced as there was so much planning to do. How would she break the news to him that he was going to be a Daddy? She'd be two months along. Then, they needed to have a serious talk about when he would be leaving Ava. No more passionless marriage. Charlene knew how to take care of her man, satisfy him in every way he needed. The thought made her warm all over. She closed her eyes and fantasized about how much fun they would have when they would finally be together.

Monday brought with it morning sickness. Charlene learned to keep hydrated, by doing so, she avoided the dry heaves. Forcing herself to go about her day she walked over to JoAnn's promptly at 7 a.m.

"Good morning, Charlene," JoAnn said cheerfully.

"Good morning."

"You look a little peaked. Aren't you feeling well?"

"I'm just a little tired from the holiday weekend with Alice. We always have a wonderful time when we go down there. Florence spoils us with all her new fashion designs at her boutique."

"I'm happy you enjoyed yourself. I know there's a lot to do in the city but it's never been my cup of tea. There are so many people, always in a hurry, and Florence, well, she's so fancy-schmancy with her lifestyle I don't know how she keeps up with it all. No thank you, I'll take living in Harbor Cove any day," JoAnn stated.

Charlene smiled, thought to respond, and decided not to. JoAnn was content with her simple life in Harbor Cove. She'd never understand or desire anything different.

The rest of the week and the next seemed to drag by. Time almost appeared to come to a standstill. Charlene couldn't wait to see Kyle.

On Friday Charlene took her final secretarial skills exam. It was a two-part exam, the first was typing, strongly graded on speed and accuracy. The second part; tested shorthand, dictation and basic clerical duties. Charlene's confidence was at its peak as she had studied hard in spite of the stress of planning her great escape from her life in that small town. Two hours later, her studying and diligence paid off. She scored at the top of her class typing 60 wpm and in shorthand, she achieved 70 wpm. Both with outstanding accuracy. Charlene accepted her certificate of excellence with pride knowing she was one step closer to her dream.

Early Saturday morning Charlene went to Betty's Salon for her scheduled makeover. She paid for it, using the rest of the $100.00 that John withdrew from the till when she drove to the Refuge for him. Charlene wanted to look her best for her beau. Retrieving the map of Detroit from the glove box. She located Willow Run Airfield and arrived in time to watch Kyle's airplane land and taxi down the tarmac. Charlene stood at the gate, heart beating wildly in anticipation. Near the end of the line of passengers exiting the plane, she saw him! Charlene waved, thinking to herself, Kyle never looked so good. Charlene couldn't contain her excitement and rushed over to him. He caught her in his embrace.

"Easy now!" Kyle exclaimed, laughing.

"I've missed you so! It's good to see you again!"

"It's good to see you too," Kyle met her kiss feeling the desire rise up within him.

"Did you miss me? Did you think about me?" Charlene asked, and looked up into his blue-gray eyes.

"Yes, I did, I'd be lying if I said I hadn't missed you. The fun we have together is what got me through being gone so long." He smiled hugging her again. Truth be known, Kyle really didn't have time to think about anything except the mission. Everything that had transpired in the past couple of months had begun to cloud his judgment and he forced himself to stay focused. Now, he had the time to decompress and further assess the overall situation. He'd spoken with John a number of times in regard to his relationship with Charlene as it had progressed. Over their secure line, he asked John about her.

"Well, I really don't know much about Charlene. She hangs out a lot with her best friend, Alice, who is a great influence on her. She lives with Alice from what I gather. I will say Charlene is a bit more on the wild and carefree side, seems you're finding that out yourself." John laughed.

"Yes, we're having fun together. I've never met anyone that totally gives 100% of herself, it's such a turn-on, and it's made it really challenging to concentrate on what needs to be done when it comes to business." Kyle admitted.

"What about Ava?" John questioned. Dark concern shadowed his voice.

"What about her? I've told you about how things are with us. Ava understands. I have needs. She doesn't want to know about or even care what I do. Out of sight, out of mind. She knows that in the end I will always be there for her."

"You have a strange outlook on relationships, my friend. Just be careful. Things could get a little dicey. From what I see, Charlene has her sights on more than just a good time."

"Well, that's about all I can offer her. When she discovered my real name and that I was married, of course, we had a pretty big blowout. We worked through it all. That's why I had you run her through the gauntlet and interrogation to see if she could be trusted. You told me she passed with flying colors and didn't give me up."

"That's true. She didn't give you up. It showed she could be trusted. I know it's not my business but it seems this girl, well, how do I put it? This girl is both good and bad for you. On one hand, she makes you feel alive, I get it. On the other hand, she's a dangerous liability to our operation. She could really muddy the waters."

"I can keep her under control. Don't worry about it. We can use her to our advantage."

"Okay, you're the boss. Just keep your head in the game, there's a lot at stake."

Walking hand in hand to Kyle's convertible, Charlene was on cloud nine. She wanted so badly to share her news but was waiting for the right time. Kyle walked her around to the passenger's side and Charlene handed him the keys.

"So, did you enjoy driving my convertible?" Kyle asked.

"Very much so. She handles quite nicely," Charlene replied.

"Thank you for taking good care of her. It was good thinking securing her in Alice's garage."

"It seemed the right thing to do. I'd have hated it if someone would have broken into her behind Vic's or vandalized it."

Kyle nodded and smiled as he exited the highway. "I need to stop by the Refuge and pick something up. By the way, what did you think of the place?"

"It's amazing! A bit overwhelming, but amazing. I can see you use it for meetings but I'm not really sure why here. I mean, you're in Washington, D.C., why Detroit?"

"Think of where the Refuge is. Close, easy access to the Blue Water Bridge and Canada. We have allies in Canada. The C.I.A. isn't like the F.B.I. We operate on foreign soil. Not so, here in the United States. Have you ever been to Canada?" Kyle inquired.

"No. Never really had a reason to."

"Well, I'll have to take you next time I have a meeting. Going over the bridge is cool. It offers a beautiful view."

"Sounds like fun!"

Pulling onto Holland Avenue they parked and entered through the back door of the Refuge.

"Even though you've been inside once already, let me give you a tour." Walking through the house he pointed out the kitchen, living room and the bathroom just off the bedroom.

"It appears to be the perfect little house. Just the right size for a couple," Charlene commented.

"When we acquired the place, we converted the second larger bedroom into our office for meetings. We built the wall with the bookcase to create the hidden room." Kyle walked over to the bookcase and pulled "To Kill a Mockingbird" outward. The bookcase swung in and he pulled her through. Kyle reached under the desk and removed a brown leather briefcase, which looked exactly like the one that Charlene had retrieved earlier. She almost asked about its contents but thought better of it, remembering John told her it was none of her concern.

"Okay, I've got what I came for. Let's go." Kyle urged, as they exited through the bookcase. Kyle went through closing it back up.

"Before we leave, I need to use the restroom. Too much coffee on the plane." Kyle set the briefcase down and went through the bedroom into the bathroom, closing the door behind him.

Charlene stood in the doorway looking at the bed. On impulse, she unbuttoned her blouse, exposing her breasts seductively and walked across the room, waiting for Kyle to come out. When he did, she surprised him with a full-on kiss, grabbing his tie and pulling him onto the bed.

Kyle followed her lead and soon they hastily removed

each other's clothing. He started out kissing her, down her neck and lightly across her perk nipples. Fingers trailed down her body, exploring. Charlene moaned, arching her back, in a feline gesture. She could feel his excitement. Then unexpectedly Charlene rolled on top of Kyle, kissing along his neck, her hair teasingly caressing his chest as she further explored his body. Kissing further she gently took him into her mouth almost driving Kyle over the edge. He fought to hold back as long as he could, then he rolled her over and entered her. They made love with no inhabitations, rediscovering each other, physically, after being apart. The stress, fear and suspicions faded away.

Later, wrapped in each other's arms, and after their breathing steadied, Kyle smiled. "That was pleasantly unexpected. One of the things I love about you is you're spontaneous and you make me feel so alive.

Charlene snuggled in closer kissing him lightly on the cheek. "It can be that way all the time, Lover. I adore giving myself to you, completely. I love you. And, I know you feel the same way about me."

Kyle, still sated from their lovemaking, looked into her eyes. "My life is so complicated, but when I'm gone, I can't stop thinking about you. You've become a beautiful distraction."

Kissing her he whispered, "What have you done to me?"

"I haven't done anything that you didn't want me to. Unless I'm missing something. Is there something else you'd like to try?" she teased.

"You are such a naughty girl. Maybe I should spank you!" Kyle played along.

"You'd better not!" She laughed, "I might have to hurt you." For a second Charlene thought he might go through with it as he turned her over on her stomach. Expecting the sting of a playful smack, she was met instead with a *new* kind of erotic pleasure.

The sun was going down when they finished. Still entwined, Charlene broke the silence and whispered, "I have a surprise for you."

Kyle gave a strained smile, "I don't think I have the energy, Sweetheart, let me rest.

"Not that kind of surprise." Charlene laughed.

"Darn, I was hoping. So, what surprise do you have for me?"

"Well..., we're having a baby! You're going to be a Daddy!" Charlene exclaimed.

Kyle sat up, stunned by the news, not sure he heard her right. "Did you say we're..,"

Charlene shook her head, "Yes! We're having a baby! I'm pregnant!"

A million thoughts came racing into Kyle's mind. He could feel the panic start welling up. First and foremost, "A baby? I'm going to be a father?" Lost in thought he stared into the past. Sadness blindsided him as Ava came to mind. They always wanted a child but Ava was unable to get pregnant due to her condition. A child, he hoped, would have added new life to their relationship.

"Say something Kyle! Aren't you excited? Aren't you happy for us?" Charlene asked. A sudden twinge of fear echoed through the corridors of her heart.

Kyle's trance broke as he stammered, "Yes... Yes, I'm

happy and excited! Talk about something totally unexpected. You are full of surprises! Are you sure you're pregnant? How do you know?

"Yes, I'm sure. I'm late and I've been having morning sickness for almost two weeks now. And, before you ask, yes! It sucks."

"When are you due?" Kyle asked.

"Alice and I counted the weeks since the last time you and I were together. We've come up with sometime around the end of June."

Kyle's thoughts were still racing when doubt entered his mind. "I've been away for eight weeks. Who else has she been with?" He pondered.

"We need to get you into a doctor to make sure that everything is okay," Kyle suggested.

"Not here in Harbor Cove. People talk. It will have to be somewhere down in the city," Charlene reasoned.

"Okay, I think I have a connection that can help us locate a baby doctor. We can go in next week."

"Sounds good, things are really changing around here. I mean, there's no way I can continue being a nanny. JoAnn and Sam are such fanatics, they would never allow an unwed mother to take care of their children. With this town being such a rumor mill, I won't be able to even work or be in public without people talking behind my back." Charlene's own panic began to rise.

"Well, my mother, Carla, lives in Florida, just out of Orlando. How would you like to spend the winter in a warmer climate? I could fly you down there. You two will get along great and she will be so excited. Mom always wanted a grandchild."

"Okay, but I'd have to give a notice that I'd be leaving so JoAnn can line up someone else to take care of the children. Do you think you could get a flight right before Christmas? That way JoAnn wouldn't be too inconvenienced, and she'd have some time to locate another nanny. Also, I would be able to give proper notice to the church I do bookkeeping for."

"Then it's settled. We'll go down to the city this week to have you checked out by a doctor. Then, I'll get a flight booked for us. The two weeks will give me time to fly back to D.C. and finish paperwork and speak with the director about upcoming business. Finally, I'll fly back to Willow Run Airfield and pick you up for our flight to Florida."

Charlene was ecstatic. Her plans were falling into place nicely. It was just a matter of time before she would become the next Mrs. Jacob MacDonald a.k.a., Mrs. Kyle Edwards.

Kyle made a few telephone calls from John's and set up an appointment for Charlene with a doctor for Tuesday at 11 a.m. Charlene called JoAnn early Tuesday morning letting her know she wasn't feeling well and wouldn't be there. Then, she called the school, asking the receptionist to let her teachers know that she wasn't feeling well and wouldn't make it in.

Kyle and Charlene drove to the doctor and Kyle sat in the waiting room. Almost an hour later, the Doctor came out.

"Mr. MacDonald, we're done with the exam. Would you like to come with me to my office?"

"Yes, thank you." Kyle got up and followed the doctor down the hall.

In the doctor's office, Charlene smiled, stood and gave

Kyle a hug. The doctor cleared his throat, "Well, I've got good news. You're definitely with child. I've heard the baby's heartbeat and you're around eight weeks pregnant. Your due date will be in the last week of June. Congratulations! We'll set up an appointment in March to see how you're coming along. Get lots of rest, eat right, lots of fluids and take your vitamins. Drink herbal tea for nausea and call me with any other concerns."

On the drive back to Harbor Cove, Kyle pondered how his life was changing. Still trying to get his head around it all. What a predicament he found himself in. He had a wife in D.C. and a mistress in the little tourist town of Harbor Cove, that was having his baby.

Charlene spoke with Pastor Mike at the next Wednesday's youth group.

"I'll be spending the Christmas holiday with Alice. She's getting married to Walter Greensboro on Valentine's Day. Her mother plans to alter my bridesmaid dress while I'm there."

Pastor Mike nodded, "That sounds lovely. You have a wonderful time." The past couple of months he'd sensed that Charlene was struggling with life. He believed that she would eventually speak with him more on the subject when she was ready. So, he kept his conversation to a minimum, waiting patiently for her to come around.

In the past three months, she had stepped away from the church, ashamed of her lifestyle. Charlene wanted to apologize but couldn't find the words.

During the two weeks before their flight to Orlando, Charlene got ready for her escape from Harbor Cove. The time was fast approaching. Kyle flew back to D.C. for meetings with Director Marshall and his team. Charlene bided her time.

The day before her flight she spoke with JoAnn and dropped off presents for Mildred and Suzanne.

"While I'm down in the city with Alice over Christmas break, we'll have fun getting things in order for her wedding. Florence plans to alter my dress."

"I was hoping you would be here for part of the holiday," JoAnn stated.

"I spoke with Julie down at the diner and she offered to help out with Mildred and Suzanne if you need her to."

"Thank you, Charlene. Well, you have a Merry Christmas," JoAnn struggled to hide her sadness, "and I hope you have a nice time with Alice. The girls will miss having you here."

"Merry Christmas to you, also. Give the girls a hug from me." Charlene walked out the front door as big snowflakes began to fall. She looked back over her shoulder at the front door as JoAnn closed it behind her. This was goodbye, she'd made her great escape. However, Charlene was bound and determined not to let dark clouds darken her day. Destination Florida, a new life awaited her.

The telephone rang at Alice's place at 9 p.m.

"Hello, Brooks residence, this is Charlene."

"Hey Charlene, this is John. I received a call from Kyle. He's tied up in D.C. and won't be able to join you on your flight to Florida. Don't worry. He'll try to join you sometime next week. I'll drive you down for your flight out tomorrow. Kyle had me draw some money from the till to purchase your ticket. You'll fly out of Detroit Metropolitan Wayne

County Airport at 11 a.m. on Pan Am. Carla will meet you in Orlando when you land. She'll have a sign with your name on it."

"I've never flown before. I really didn't want to do this alone. What should I expect?"

"It's a breeze, you'll love it. Try to get a window seat so you can see out over the land, the view is spectacular! Anyway, drive Kyle's convertible here in the morning around 8 a.m. and park it behind the outer storage building. We'll take my truck."

"I'll be there." Charlene hung up the receiver. She felt an uneasiness surge at the thought of flying alone and did the breathing exercises Alice taught her. They always worked; breathe in, hold it, breathe out. Thinking happy thoughts, she relaxed. After she finished packing her luggage, Charlene went out to the garage and put them in the back seat. She was going to miss driving the convertible and wondered if she would ever do so again.

Back inside the house, Charlene called Alice.

"Merry Christmas, Alice! How are things going?"

"Things are great. Are you still planning to come to the city? Mom needs to alter your dress and we're planning to spend Christmas Day together."

"Well, I've been busy with Kyle. I told him we we're pregnant. We drove to the city this past week and had a doctor give me an exam. He says I'm definitely pregnant and the due date will be the end of June, just like we figured!"

"Oh my God! What was Kyle's reaction?"

"He's excited he's going to be a Daddy!"

"Wow, that's great."

"Would you be all right if we postponed coming back to the city until the new year? I'm spending some time with Kyle before he has to go back to work."

"I guess that's okay, Mom is flying out for a show in New York so she won't be here after Christmas. I'll be spending quality time with Walter at his place," she giggled.

"Okay. Do me a favor. If anyone calls just tell them I'm not there and you'll have me call them back as soon as you see me."

"I can do that. So, you're spending quality time with Kyle, eh? Well, have fun. I'd tell you to be careful but I guess it's a little late for that," Alice laughed.

"Ha, Ha, maybe you need to be careful," Charlene teased.

"Oh, we are. Hey, I've gotta go. I'll talk to you soon. Have a Merry Christmas!"

"You, too!"

Chapter Twenty-One

John dropped Charlene off at the Pan American Airlines terminal at 10:30 a.m.

"Here's $500.00. That should cover the plane ticket and any other expenses you might incur. Have a safe flight."

"Thank you, John, for everything." She hugged him goodbye and walked through the doors into the terminal. At the counter, Charlene asked the agent if there was a reservation for Charlene Strypher.

"Yes, I have it here. I see you'll be flying first class."

"Yes, is there a chance I could get a window seat? This is my first time flying."

"Most certainly, Miss Strypher. The view is breathtaking." The agent said as she tagged Charlene's luggage. Your total will be $239.00. Flight time is three hours, which should put you in around 2 p.m. We're boarding at gate 3."

"Would you like anything to drink," the stewardess asked as the jet settled in at its cruising altitude of 35,000 feet.

"I'll take a cola with a twist of lime," Charlene requested.

"Would you care for any alcohol in it, whiskey or rum?" The stewardess inquired.

"No thank you, I recently found out I'm pregnant." Charlene smiled, happy to say the words out loud to a total stranger.

"Well, Congratulations!"

"Thank you. I'm meeting my mother-in-law in Orlando for the first time. She'll be so excited." Charlene gushed.

"I bet she will. Enjoy the rest of your flight and I'll bring you back your cola." The stewardess excused herself.

Two hours into the flight the intercom clicked.

"Ladies and gentlemen, this is your captain speaking. Please take your seats as we are encountering a little turbulence. We're going to climb a bit to see if we can fly our way above the storm that's settled in over Atlanta."

The plane dipped and shuddered and Charlene gasped, gripping the seat handle. She felt nausea begin to overcome her. Seems her little one wasn't enjoying the flight. Grabbing the air-sickness bag tucked into the seat, Charlene vomited. The plane leveled out and the stewardess who noticed Charlene go pale white got up to assist.

"I'm sorry, I've made such a mess." Charlene cried.

"It's no trouble, my Dear. This happens more than you know. Let's get you cleaned up. We'll be landing soon."

In Orlando, Charlene deboarded the plane, happy to be safe on solid ground. She wasn't quite sure how she felt about air travel. In the crowd, she saw a woman with short, curly, blue-gray hair and an elegant, ivory pantsuit, holding a cardboard sign, "Welcome Charlene," written in red marker.

"You must be Mrs. MacDonald," Charlene called out as she approached the woman.

"Yes, and you must be Charlene. Mrs. MacDonald was

my mother, please, call me Carla. I'm so happy to meet you. You're as pretty as Jacob told me. The two of you will have a beautiful child together. Jacob mentioned he hoped it was a boy. I'm happy with either. As long as it's healthy and I get to be a grandma."

Charlene received a call on Christmas Day.

"Merry Christmas." I'm sorry. I'm not going to be able to make it anytime soon. Looks like I have another couple of weeks here in D.C. planning another assignment. The Director insists this is top priority. It's a matter of national security."

"When will I see you again?" Charlene stammered.

"I'm not sure, but I will keep you posted. I take it your flight went well and everything is okay with my mother?"

"Yes, I'm fine. I like your mother and we're getting along great."

"Good to hear. I'd better go for now."

"Okay, I love you! Please be safe! I'll be missing you."

"Me, too."

Charlene hung up the receiver, smiling. He loves me! Life is going to be great. It's just a matter of time.

Charlene found that Carla was vibrant and fun to be around, reminding her of a much older Alice. When Charlene got up the nerve to ask her about Ava, Carla obliged.

"Ava is a sweet woman. She is ten years older than my Jacob. He stepped up and honored a promise and I respect him for that. But, it's not the marriage I'd hoped for. However, it's his business, not mine. You two will have to figure this out together. He's gotten himself into quite the predicament, this time. Whatever he does about all this, I'm sure he will make honorable decisions. Jacob is a good man. That being said, I will say no more, except, sometimes one has to look at the big picture from all angles to decide what is best for everyone involved, including my unborn grandchild."

"Happy New Year! We're welcoming in 1962," the announcer called out as the ball dropped in Times Square in New York City. Carla got up from her rocking chair and turned off the television. "Well, Charlene, Happy New Year! It's 1962 and past my bedtime so I'm going to turn in and get some sleep."

"Happy New Year to you, too, Carla. I'm right behind you. It's been a long day and I could use some sleep."

In Harbor Cove, Julie had been helping JoAnn with the children during the Christmas holiday. JoAnn hadn't heard from Charlene. She figured she was busy with Alice and was happy that Julie was there to help with the children while JoAnn worked. Tuesday morning JoAnn called Julie asking her to come over. Charlene hadn't shown up.

"Have you heard from Charlene?" JoAnn asked Julie when she arrived to help get Mildred and Suzanne ready for school.

"No, I haven't," Julie replied.

"Thanks for being here. I'll be home this evening, usual time." JoAnn grabbed her coat and walked out the door.

At lunch, JoAnn called Alice's number again but there was still no answer. When she got off work, she called the operator for Florence Brook's telephone number. There was no answer at the residence. The operator was kind enough to also give her the telephone number to Florence's Fashion Boutique. She called it and a receptionist answered.

"Hello, is Florence there?" JoAnn questioned.

"No, I'm sorry, Florence is in New York at a fashion show. She's releasing her new Spring line. May I help you?"

"Perhaps. Do you know where her daughter, Alice, might be?"

"I assume she is with her fiancé, Walter. May I ask what this is about and who are you?"

"I'm JoAnn Strypher. I'm hoping Alice might know where Charlene, my daughter, is. They're best friends. Hopefully, she's with her. Charlene never returned home after the Christmas holiday."

"I met Charlene over Thanksgiving; a charming girl. When I see Alice, I'll have her call you. Let me write down your phone number in case she doesn't have it."

JoAnn left her phone number and thanked her.

By mid-week, JoAnn was becoming seriously worried. She spoke with Sam about it.

"She's probably just having too much fun with Alice. Give it another day or two. She'll turn up." Sam said.

JoAnn called Pastor Mike at St. Mathew's Church. "Pastor Mike this is JoAnn Styphe

r, Charlene's mother. Have you seen her lately?"

"She was here to help with youth group the Wednesday night before Christmas break. She was all excited about going and spending it with her friend, Alice. What's going on?" He questioned.

"I was expecting her back by New Year's Day and she hasn't shown up yet. She hasn't called either."

"That is strange. Have you been able to get ahold of Alice?"

“No, but I’ll keep trying. Please let me know if you hear anything.”

“I will. I’ll be praying for you and your family and for Charlene’s safe return.”

By Friday, JoAnn was frantic. She called her brother Frank at the Harbor Cove Police Station.

“Hello Frank, it’s JoAnn. I think something has happened to Charlene. She’s been gone for over a week, maybe longer. I expected her back New Year’s Day.”

“When was the last time you saw or heard from her?”

“Right before Christmas break, on the 22nd.

“Have you talked with Alice?”

“I’ve called a number of times but there’s no one home. I tried to call her mother, Florence, but she’s in New York City at a fashion show. I left a message at her boutique for Alice to call me when they see her.”

“I’ll put out an all-points bulletin here at the station to see what we turn up. I’ll also do some checking around town and drop by Alice’s house to see what I can find. If it comes down to it, we’ll put her picture in the Harbor Cove Daily, listing her as missing. We can also put it in the big city newspapers. Don’t worry. We’ll find her.”

“Thank you, Frank. Please keep me posted.”

“I will and call me if you hear anything.”

Frank got in his patrol car and drove over to Florence Brook’s house on Mulberry Street. The house was locked up. No one was around. He shone his flashlight in the windows, finding nothing amiss. By the next Monday, there was still no word from Alice or Charlene. JoAnn found the most recent picture she had of Charlene. It was taken a month before with Mildred and Suzanne. Frank took the picture over to the local paper. After cropping it and enlarging the head-shot they posted her picture on the front page of Tuesday's newspaper.

> *Missing person, Charlene Elizabeth Strypher. Last seen in Harbor Cove on December 22nd, 1961. 5'6" tall, 120 lbs, blonde hair, hazel eyes, fair complexion. Please call Chief Frank Odimier, at the Harbor Cove Police Department or, contact her parents Sam and JoAnn Strypher at 1324 Sycamore Street, Harbor Cove with any information.*

There were a few calls to the police station in the next week with reports of seeing Charlene around town but it was before the 22nd.

On Wednesday morning, January 10th, John Vickers was cleaning up his bar. After taking out the trash, he retrieved his mail from the front box. He rarely read the newspaper and almost discarded three of the papers that were mixed in with the bills and other correspondences. Randomly he opened one of the newspapers, it was the Tuesday edition.

He drew in a deep, sharp breath when he saw Charlene's picture and read the missing person's report. From under the bar, he retrieved a thin black leatherbound book. Kyle told him to never call unless it was an emergency, even on the secure line. This qualified as an emergency.

"A gruff voice answered, "Code phrase?"

John responded, "With the red dawn, night's curtain falls."

"State your business."

"I need to speak with Agent MacDonald. It's urgent."

"One moment."

The line crackled, "He's off base."

"Have him call Haven42, a.s.a.p. its top priority."

The line went dead. All John could do was wait. Wednesday turned into Thursday. The phone under John's bar rang at 9 a.m., Friday morning.

"John, what the hell is going on?"

"We've got a problem, Kyle. Charlene's picture is in the paper with a missing person report. Seems she left some loose ends leaving Harbor Cove… Her parents, are looking for her."

"Damn! What the fuck? She told me her parents were dead! Who lies about something like that? She mentioned something about her uncle being the Chief of the Harbor Cove P.D."

"Looks like the uncle is heading up the investigation."

"What a fucking mess. Pick me up from the airfield. I'll fly out tonight on the red eye. Should be there around 3 a.m. I have to fix this."

"Will do, I'll be there."

Saturday morning, John handed him the newspaper. "What are you going to do?"

"What can I do? I'll simply go over to the parent's house and let them know their daughter is okay. Hopefully, once they know she's all right, they'll settle down."

John shook his head, "I told you she was a liability to our operation. If she talks…"

"She won't talk. That's the least of my worries."

John pushed the envelope. "Have you told Ava?"

"What the fuck, John? What do you think? No, I haven't told Ava. Not yet anyway. Give me the keys to my car, I'm driving over to talk to the parents."

John tossed him his keys, "Good luck. Call me if you need me."

Kyle drove his convertible out of the driveway, spinning gravel across the pavement as he pulled onto the highway. He pulled along the curb at 1324 Sycamore, checked his mirror to make sure he was presentable and walked up to the door. He knocked. JoAnn Strypher and her husband, Sam, opened the door and stepped out onto the porch.

"Hello, I'm Jacob MacDonald. I wanted you to know that your daughter Charlene is safe. She's currently staying with my mother in Florida." Jacob explained carefully. "I have something else to tell you. I am the father of her baby."

The Stryphers stood in stunned silence. JoAnn's jaw hung slack. "Baby…? She's barely seventeen years old!?!"

He felt sick. The blood drained from Jacob's face. Reeling, he thought he might pass out and leaned against the porch railing for support. "That can't be… I mean, she looks and acts like she's in her mid-twenties."

Running back into the house, JoAnn returned with Charlene's birth certificate and handed it to him. Reading the birth date, December 27, 1945, he shook his head in disbelief and handed the birth certificate back. "I'm sorry. I didn't know…" Sam tensed, eyes blazing. "You Fucking Prick!" With fists clenched, he lunged forward but, Jacob was too fast. He dodged to the left and ran to his car. In no time he was racing down the highway. Cursing aloud,

"How could I have been so fucking stupid! Seventeen? No fucking way!"

Thinking fast he decided to drive down to the Refuge, get far away from Harbor Cove as possible. There, he would gather his thoughts, call Charlene and get her to explain why she lied to him about her parents. And, although he never asked, why didn't she tell him her age!? He wondered what other lies she'd been telling him. Driving too fast, he was ten miles out of Harbor Cove when he saw the red and blue lights of a roadblock. He slammed on his brakes, coming to a squealing stop. Three police cars blocked the highway. Officers, with pistols drawn, motioned for him to get out of the car. Thinking he'd put it in reverse and speed off in the direction he came from, he stopped abruptly when two more police cars pulled in behind him. The officers got out with guns drawn. Chief Frank Odimier pulled Jacob from the car and roughly took him to the ground, cuffing him. "Jacob MacDonald, you're under arrest for the kidnapping and rape of a minor." He escorted Jacob to his police car. On the way back to Harbor Cove, Chief Frank Odimier spoke low and precise. "Boy, you are in a heap of trouble! Charlene is my favorite niece. Your license says you're 38 years old. I'm gonna see that they throw the book at you, lock you up and throw away the key!"

Jacob didn't respond. At the station, after processing, they locked him in an interrogation room. The chief, along with a deputy, stepped in and began questioning him. The good cop, bad cop routine didn't faze Jacob. He remained silent. After an hour they gave up and locked him in a cell. The next morning, an officer escorted Jacob to a pay phone. "You get one call. Make it good."

The telephone rang under John's bar. He answered it. "Collect call from Jacob MacDonald. Do you accept the charges?"

"I accept the charges."

Jacob came on the line. "John, I'm in jail. Call my lawyer, Miles Carter. Meet me at the courthouse downtown. I'll explain what happened later."

"Will do. Be there in a jiff."

John hung up the receiver and shook his head in disbelief, grabbed the brown leather briefcase and drove down to the courthouse.

"Hear ye, Hear ye! All rise for the Honorable Judge Morris Brown.

The prosecuting attorney stepped forward. "The defendant, Jacob MacDonald, is charged with one count of Kidnapping and one count of Statutory Rape."

Judge Brown asked, "How do you plead, Mr. MacDonald?"

Jacob's defense lawyer answered for him, "Not guilty, Your Honor."

The prosecuting attorney responded, "Considering that Jacob MacDonald is not a member of this community and the seriousness of the charges against him, this office recommends that he be detained with no bail."

Miles Carter stood up, "Your Honor, Jacob MacDonald, although he is not a member of this community, is an upstanding citizen. With no priors, he has a full-time job at Detroit Motors and on his own accord, informed the parents in person that their daughter was safe in Florida with his mother. He has taken responsibility for his actions and there is no flight risk. I request bail be set at $1,000.00."

Judge Brown glanced at Chief Frank Odimier and the Chief nodded ever so slightly. Expecting the judge to deny bail, he was taken off guard by his response.

"After careful consideration, this Court sets bail at $5,000.00. And, the defendant must surrender his passport. Further, Jacob MacDonald must remain in Harbor Cove, while awaiting trial."

Defense Lawyer Miles Carter stood, "We are able to make bail at this time, Your Honor."

Judge Brown looked down at his calendar. "Good. A closed trial will commence in my chambers on Monday, February 5th at 9:00 a.m., sharp." As the Judge brought down his gavel, he made it a point to make direct eye contact first, with the Chief of Police, then, Jacob MacDonald. "Next case."

The bailiff escorted Jacob down the hall and his lawyer followed with the brown leather briefcase in hand. At the front office window, paperwork was drafted and signed and Miles Carter counted out $5,000.00 in hundreds. "Let's go to my office and discuss everything," Miles suggested. He closed the briefcase and they walked out the door.

At his downtown law office, Jacob and John sat across from Miles.

"So, Jacob, tell me everything that led up to this."

Jacob recounted his and Charlene's relationship.

"You never asked her age?" Miles questioned, incredulously.

"No! My mistake, why would I? She acts and looks like she's in her mid-twenties. How was I supposed to know? God! I can't believe that she was only 16 when we met." Jacob shook his head in disbelief.

"Well, let's get down to the nitty-gritty. I'm sure when I meet with the District Attorney, I can get the kidnapping charges dropped if you get Charlene on a plane back here pronto. As for the statutory rape charge, that might be a bit tricky. A lot will depend on Charlene. You're sure she's really pregnant and that it's your child?"

Jacob nodded, "Yes, she's pregnant and I'm pretty sure the child is mine. I took her to a doctor in the city. He did an exam and the time frame is right."

"You're positive she hasn't been screwing some other guy? You were gone for eight weeks." Miles reminded.

"I doubt it. She's crazy about me! I didn't ask but the date lines up with when we last had sex. I'd like to say I trust her but, after all that's happened, well, I don't know anymore." Jacob replied.

"Big question. What are your intentions when the child arrives? If it is your child, that could get complicated. There's child support and a possible custody battle, just for starters."

"I haven't given that much thought, to be honest, but I think I'd like to be part of the child's life, if at all possible."

"Does Charlene know about Ava?"

"Yes."

"And she's okay with that? You being married, and her being your mistress? You're in quite an awkward situation, my friend. In a perfect world, it would be every man's dream. Unfortunately for you, this is a nightmare."

"No shit! Charlene wants me to leave Ava, and that's not happening!"

Miles looked straight at Jacob, "Have you told Ava what's going on?"

Jacob shook his head no.

"Well, you better make the call. It's best she hears it from you instead of the press. If they get a hold of this and it all goes south, it could get messy, real fast." Miles sighed, then continued.

"Talk to Charlene, get your ducks in a row. It'll take some luck but we might get the rape charge thrown out of court. It will depend on the Judge and what Charlene says. Make the call to your mother and get Charlene back her A.S.A.P. Then, call your wife. I'll cut the deal with the Prosecutor to get the kidnapping charge dropped and see you in court Monday the 5th." Miles handed the briefcase back to Jacob.

John drove Jacob back to the bar. "We'll have to go pick up your car from the impound lot."

"We'll get it later. I need to call my mother now."

"Hello, Mom? Yes, it's Jacob. Hey, we've got a problem. You need to get Charlene on the next flight back to Detroit."

"Why? We're having such a good time getting to know one another," Carla said.

"Well, if you're getting to know one another, why don't you ask her how old she is? No, let me tell you. She just turned seventeen in December! She's a damn minor!"

"What, are you kidding? How did you not know? Didn't you ask?"

"No, I didn't and she didn't tell me either." He spoke through gritted teeth. "Look at her, she looks and acts like she's in her mid-twenties! I went to talk to her parents when they reported her missing. By the way, her dead parents. When we met, she told me her parents were dead! I was arrested for kidnapping and statutory rape! My lawyer assures me the kidnapping charge will be dropped if I get Charlene back here to her parents, immediately."

"Well, that's something. What about the rape charge?"

"That will all depend on Charlene and then the Judge's decision. Just get her on the plane back to Detroit."

"I'll get her packed and on the first flight out that has a seat available."

"Thanks. Call me and let me know what airline and arrival time."

Carla cradled the receiver, "Charlene, I need to talk to you."

"I'm in the living room, what's up?"

Carla stalked into the room and towering over Charlene she demanded, "First, how old are you? and don't you dare lie to me!"

Charlene knew the game was up. She looked down at the floor, "I'm seventeen."

"Charlene, you told my son your parents were dead! What is the matter with you? They are very much alive and put out a missing person's report on you. Jacob went to their house to let them know you were okay and here in Florida with me. He explained that he is the father of your baby. Now, Jacob's been arrested and charged with kidnapping and statutory rape! You're on the first plane out of here to Detroit! Hopefully, they'll drop the kidnapping charges when you're back home with your parents. As for the rape charge, you need to really think about how this will all go down! If he's convicted and goes to prison, you'll never see him again. Is that what you want!? And that won't be the end of it either. Trust me!" Her eyes flashed and Charlene could feel the disdain and wrath boiling within Carla. The tingling down her spine she felt when Kyle and John swore her to secrecy, was nothing compared to what she was feeling now.

"I'm sorry," That was all Charlene could say, fighting back hot burning tears.

"You're sorry? Pack your bags we're heading to the airport. I am so disappointed in you!"

At the airport, Carla watched Charlene board the Pan Am flight to Detroit. From a pay phone, Carla called Jacob.

"Charlene is on the last flight out, 2351 nonstop to Detroit, it's taxiing down the runway now. She should be in there in about three hours. Sorry, it took me longer to get her a flight than I thought it would. Seating was limited. She should land around 1 a.m."

"Thanks, Mom, I'm so sorry about all this."

"I don't know what to think Jacob. I hope it all works out. Keep me posted. I love you, son."

"I love you too, Mom, and I will call with whatever news I find out."

Jacob hung up the phone as John filled a rock glass to the top with scotch and handed it to him.

"Now, I call Ava." Jacob's hand began to shake as he dialed his home number in D.C.

Ava answered on the second ring, "Hello?"

"Ava? It's me, Jacob."

"Hey, I wasn't expecting your call today. Is everything okay? Where are you?" Ava questioned, slight concern in her voice.

"Well, I'm in Harbor Cove at Vic's, John is here with me. Ava, there's no easy way to put this. I'm in trouble."

"Trouble?" What kind of trouble? Has something gone wrong with the mission? Are you okay? Do I need to call the Director?" Alarm rose in her voice.

"No, no. It's not that kind of trouble, I'm okay." Jacob hesitated then continued, "Ava, I really fucked up this time. I've had an affair and just found out the girl is only seventeen years old. And, she's pregnant. I'd have flown back to D.C. to tell you in person but I can't leave Harbor Cove. I've been arrested and charged with kidnapping and statutory rape. The court date is on the 5th of next month. I sent the girl to stay with Mom in Florida before this all started. I'm not in jail. My attorney, Miles Carter, got me out on bail and he's sure he can get the D.A. to drop the kidnapping charge once she gets back here. Ava, I'm so sorry." Jacob waited for her response as he listened through the silence. He braced himself expecting a major tongue-lashing.

"Oh, Jacob. How could you not know she was only seventeen? You, of all people, didn't you have her checked out? Jacob, I know that you fool around, I've always known. I look the other way, out of sight out of mind. Funny thing is, it really doesn't bother me that much. I know you have needs and our intimacy is lacking due to my condition. Circumstances beyond our control brought us together. You've always been there for me and I believe you always will be. You're my best friend, my soulmate. And no matter what happens, I love you for it. We can talk more about this later. Let me know what happens as soon as the court case is over."

Jacob thought her heard her voice crack. His mind rushed trying to further explain but she was gone. The dial tone rang in his ears.

When Charlene stepped off the Pan Am flight in Detroit, Jacob and John met her at the gate.

"I'm so sorry, Kyle," Charlene cried.

He held her at arm's length, shaking his head, eyes blazing, "First off, there is no Kyle! Charlene, you need to stop using my fake name. I can't have my cover blown. Here and from now on everything is real, my name is Jacob MacDonald. Do you understand?"

She nodded her head, avoiding eye contact.

"Say it! Say, 'I un-der-stand.'" His voice, hard as steel, jaw set, eyes dead serious.

"I understand Jacob," She replied.

"You need to think long and hard about how you are going to testify when this goes to court," John scolded.

Charlene recoiled, "I'll handle this John, just chill." Jacob remarked.

"Okay, calm down. Yes, we're pissed. We need to figure all this out."

Charlene continued to sob. "Why did you go to my parents? This could have all been avoided."

"Well, if you would have been more straightforward with me, none of this would have happened at all! Why didn't you tell me you were only 16 when we met? Why lie about your parents being dead?" Jacob asked in utter disgust.

"Well, I really liked you when we first met and I knew in my heart you were the one, my Mr. Right. You never asked me my age and so I never offered. Age has never meant a thing to me. Love knows no boundaries. As for lying about my parents being dead, I wish they were! I have such a shitty life living at home with them. Sam is a bully. He's mean and abusive. JoAnn won't do a thing about it. She won't stand up for me. When I try to tell her what Sam does to me, she says I'm lying. JoAnn just wants to keep peace in the house. It's easier for her to look the other way. I live at Alice's as much as possible and now that's changing since she's getting married next month."

Jacob held Charlene while she cried uncontrollably. "All right, all right. Calm down, I get it. This has all gone too far. Let's get you home."

"I don't want to go home, please let me stay at Alice's tonight. Can't we do this in the morning? Sam will call me a slut. He'll probably beat me with his belt." Charlene shook with fear, her eyes red and bloodshot from crying.

Jacob looked at John who shook his head no and then looked away. Jacob didn't have the heart to throw her to the wolves.

"Do you have any ideas, John?" He sighed, "Well, she can't stay at Alice's. You can bet the cops are watching that place like a hawk. I guess she can stay out at one of the cabins on the point. Number 10 has two bedrooms. Charlene can take one of them, you can have the other and I'll crash on the sofa. It will give us time to plan. No one knows she's back, yet. Once we get it all worked out, we can take Charlene to the station and turn her over to the police Chief, her Uncle Frank. Will that work?" John directed his question to Charlene and then Jacob.

Charlene relaxed a little, "Yes, that would be better. Sam won't talk down to him. I'm Uncle Frank's favorite niece."

"So he told me," Jacob said curtly.

John drove them back to Vickers Point, arriving at 2:30

a.m. He stopped in the bar and retrieved the keys to Cabin 10.

Before everyone turned in, John put a large oak log in the fireplace. It was still burning when they awoke. He added some kindling and another log. Soon the cabin was toasty warm as the fire crackled. Jacob looked in on Charlene, she was sleeping peacefully. She stirred in her bed, stretched and yawned. "Good morning, Jacob, John. Would one of you please get me a glass of water? I think I'm going to be sick."

Charlene ran to the bathroom and emptied the contents of her stomach.

"Are you okay?" Jacob called out. John handed him the glass of water.

After a few more seconds of heaving, Charlene replied, "I will be, in a couple of months when this morning sickness goes away. Can you bring me that glass of water?"

That day, the three of them sat around the fire and talked, planned and discussed how they were going to get through the February 5th court date. Charlene came up with a plan and Jacob and John agreed it just might work.

By noon, they got in John's truck and drove to the police station. Chief Frank Odimier greeted his niece with open arms, glaring at Jacob over her shoulder. Miles Carter showed up and spoke with the D.A. The kidnapping charge was dropped but the statutory rape charge was still to be tried as scheduled.

After a lengthy discussion with the Chief in regards to her home situation, Charlene convinced him to let her stay at Alice's until this was over, with the agreement that Jacob would not go near her.

"I'll be watching you, Jacob MacDonald. You, stay away from my niece."

"Understood," Jacob replied.

Monday, February 5th, 1962.

"This will be a closed hearing. Because our victim is a minor, there will be no public access. No reporters, no cameras and no chaos." Judge Brown sat down in his chambers. A makeshift stand was placed next to his desk with a chair to the right of him. In attendance were; the prosecuting attorney, the defense attorney, the bailiff, court clerk, arresting officer, Chief Odimier, Charlene, her parents, JoAnn and Sam, and lastly, Jacob MacDonald.

The prosecuting attorney called Jacob to the stand and after being sworn in, he began his line of questioning. Jacob answered his questions honestly when it came to meeting Charlene. Accusations were made and objections were rebutted. He denied everything else except knowing her and feeling sorry for her situation with her parents. Jacob admitted to sending her down to Florida to stay with his mother. Judge Brown sat quietly listening. When Charlene was called to the stand, the tension in the room became palpable.

"Please state your full name."

"Charlene Elizabeth Strypher."

"Do you know Jacob Lawrence MacDonald?"

"Yes, I do."

"I'm going to get right to the point, Ms. Stryper. Are you pregnant?

"Yes, I am."

"Is Jacob Lawrence MacDonald the father of your baby?"

Jacob could hear his heartbeat racing.

"No. He is not the father of my baby," Charlene carefully replied. There was a noticeable murmur of disagreement from Sam and JoAnn. In her mind, she was telling the truth. Jacob MacDonald *wasn't* the father of her baby. Kyle Edwards, the man she fell in love with, *was*.

"Remember Charlene, you are under oath. Jacob MacDonald told your parents he was the father. How do you explain that and if he isn't the father of your baby, who is?"

"I will not disclose the father. I will say that Jacob MacDonald is a very kind man that offered his help in my time of need by sending me to Florida to stay with his mother. He only said he was the father of my baby to protect me. He is not the father. I feared for my life when I became pregnant so, I ran away," Charlene looked hard at Sam, then added. "Jacob gave me a way out. He provided a refuge from the severe consequences I feared I would surely receive at home. He was being the kind of gentleman I could only hope to marry someday."

Sam began to say something but JoAnn gripped his arm, so hard her fingernails bit into his flesh. He winced and remained quiet.

The prosecuting attorney tried to rally but, in the end, he sat down, "No further questions Your Honor."

Judge Morris Brown sat staring. First at Jacob… then at Charlene… You could've heard a pin drop. He cleared his throat.

"Upon hearing the testimonies, I believe there isn't enough evidence to render a sentence against Jacob MacDonald.

Case dismissed." He banged his gavel and the Bailiff escorted everyone out of the chambers.

In the front of the courthouse, Sam yelled obscenities at Charlene. "You are a slut and you're not ever coming back into my house again! Take your bastard child and disappear for all I care!" Charlene flipped him off as she got in her uncle's police cruiser. Jacob and John suggested to her that after the case, whatever the verdict, she shouldn't be seen with either of them.

Uncle Frank dropped Charlene off at Alice's house.

"Call me if you need me, Sweetheart. I'll be here for you and I'll be watching."

Charlene thanked him and walked into the house. She called Vic's. "We did it!" Charlene exclaimed.

"Yes, we did. Correction, you did," John replied. "Let me get Jacob."

Jacob picked up the receiver, "Thank you, Charlene, you really came through for me."

"I couldn't just let you hang for it. After all, I wanted you as bad as you wanted me. There was no rape. Besides, now we can leave Harbor Cove and be together in some other place. Maybe in Florida, or even Canada. After you divorce Ava, we can get married and raise our son. I want to name him Jacob Kyle MacDonald, Jr. What do you think?"

There was a long silence on the line. Finally, Jacob spoke, his voice was precise and to the point. "Wake up Charlene! I'm. Not. Leaving. Ava. Listen to me. I made a promise to an old friend during the war. His name was William Gray and he died in my arms during the shelling of our camp. Ava was his wife. Before he died, he asked me to promise that I would take care of her. I'm an honorable man, Charlene. I've kept that promise and will continue to do so. I married Ava thirteen years ago. She's become my best friend. Although it's an unusual marriage, Ava understands I have needs. You fulfilled those needs and I love you for it. I love Ava. The only way this will work is if everything stays as is. I'll take care of you as I take care of Ava. You and I can enjoy raising our child, here. I'll continue my life as it has been, sharing time between Washington D.C. and Harbor Cove. We can have a happy life, the four of us."

"I don't care about some stupid promise! Call me when you leave Ava because I won't be your little piece of ass on the side! So, man up Jacob. You cannot have us both. Pick! It's me or Ava."

Charlene slammed down the receiver. She sank to the floor and buried her head in her hands. Hot tears welled up in her eyes and streamed down her face.

Chapter Twenty-Two

Charlene became so worked up from the day's events that she hadn't eaten or drank water. The room began to whirl and she passed out on the kitchen floor from sheer exhaustion and dehydration. In her unconscious state, a blurred vision quickly came sharply into focus. She was standing at the edge of a precipice, staring into the chasm between love and heartache. The golden key to her hope chest slipped out of her hand and disappeared into the black abyss where her heart once beat wildly. Next, she was standing in front of her two-story house and watching in horror as the paint peeled off the white picket fence and disintegrated into ash. With it, her hopes of financial stability and dreams of a better life blew away. Charlene could see herself falling, spinning out of control, disappearing into the blackness as her golden key had done. Then, Charlene hit rock bottom, clinging tightly to self-pity and wandering aimlessly along the plains of self-destruction. She was lost in a seemingly endless maze. In time, she found the passage that led her in a new direction, finally realizing that the only way to go was up. Charlene rose from the ashes of a burning heartache with a new attitude and enlightened spirit. Although not healed, her heart had been tempered and hardened by the fires, which still burned deep within her soul.

Charlene came to and stood shakily, catching her balance, and resting on a kitchen chair. She weighed her options, looking at the bridges she hadn't yet burned, purposely or accidentally. Her friendship with Alice, first and foremost, was timeless. She had no doubt she would always be there, her saving grace. Among all the negativities, at least she had a place to stay. Charlene got up, went upstairs to her bedroom, and retrieved a coffee can from the top shelf of her closet. Throughout the summer, she pinched pennies, saving whatever money she could. Inside, Charlene counted the wad of bills acquired. It was a weekly allowance her mother had given her.

Early on, Charlene stopped calling her parents, Mom and Dad, referring to them by their first names, JoAnn and Sam. At first, they found it unnerving, but in the months to come, they decided fighting with her wasn't worth the stress. For a moment, Charlene felt the guilt of leaving her sisters. She swallowed hard and shook off the sadness. Counting the bills, she came up with almost $100.00. Knowing it wouldn't last long, she was still comforted that she wasn't broke. Scrounging around her room through pants pockets and dresser drawers, she found an additional seventeen dollars and .83 cents. Returning the coffee can to the top shelf, satisfied with her findings, she glanced around the room one last time. A soft golden glint reflected on the floor near the edge of her nightstand. Charlene walked across the room and bent down for a closer look. A single key lay against the wood, hidden by the carpet. She picked it up, and a chill ran across her arms. It was the spare key to the Refuge. Charlene thought, "It must have slipped out of the cardboard box she'd stored the items in from the glove compartment." Holding it tightly, she felt lightheaded. She fought hard not to reminisce on the last time she and "her" Kyle shared their love at the Refuge. She was unsure when or even if she would ever return to the Refuge, but still, she took comfort in its seemingly unlimited possibilities.

Downstairs Alice walked in frantically calling. "Charlene, where are you?"

"Oh, Alice, I'm so glad you are here!" Charlene cried, running down the stairs and almost falling into her arms. They clung to each other for a second.

"I've been so worried about you! At Mom's fashion boutique, the receptionist got a hold of me saying your mother was looking for you. I tried to call but you didn't answer. I saw your picture in the Detroit paper! The Harbor Cove Daily shared the missing person's report with them. Oh my God! Are you okay?" Alice was barely keeping her emotions in check.

"I'm okay. Still shaken up a bit, but I'm fine. Come and sit down with me and I'll fill you in on everything that's happened." Charlene took Alice's hand and they sat down on the sofa.

"You've got to pinky swear that you'll never repeat to anyone what I'm about to tell you." Charlene held out her pinky, "This is serious. You can't tell anyone, promise."

Alice looked at her inquisitively, then linked her pinky in Charlene's, hesitating, "I promise."

After all that happened, with Jacob, John and even Carla trying to scare her into keeping silent, Charlene no longer felt any loyalty. A twinge of fear poked at her subconscious but she was tired of looking over her shoulder and feeling all alone. Sharing with Alice would make life bearable. They talked on into the night as Alice sat wide-eyed in stunned silence.

"I always felt something wasn't right with Kyle, but John being involved is a shocker. I'm so sorry you've gotten caught up in all this and now you're having Kyle's…, I mean Jacob's baby. How do you keep it straight? It's amazing you aren't more of a mess. I'd be crying all the time. What are you going to do?" Alice asked, shaking her head still trying to understand it all.

"About what, which part? My life is in shambles, Sam and JoAnn kicked me out of the house, not that I lived there much anyway, but I won't be able to see my little sisters. I'm pregnant and, soon, when they see my baby bump, I won't be able to go to school. I won't graduate either, at least not with my class. As for my not being more of a mess, you missed how I was earlier. I'm all cried out, for now anyway. There are no tears left." Charlene sighed, feeling every bit as old as she ever pretended to be.

"Well, you can continue to live here, although, brace yourself, I heard Mom talking about maybe selling the house this next summer since Walter and I will be getting married soon. What about money? Maybe you could work at Smilin' Joe's."

"I told you about the money I have, but I know it won't last forever. Especially, if I can't figure out a way to add income to it. Remember Ruth McGuire? She asked me a while back if I could watch her girls, Ellen and Louise. Ruth said something about wanting to get a job. Maybe I can get a Nanny position with her?" Hope began to shine, chasing away the darkness haunting her immediate concerns. Charlene's face lit up.

"That's what you should do! I hear Ruth is an amazing cook so you'd be eating right. And, the closer you get to your due date, well, she would be there to help you."

"As long as Ruth doesn't freak out when she learns that I'm pregnant. I'm sure her husband, Harold, won't be impressed."

"It can't hurt to ask. Just be honest, never say never. They might surprise you."

Alice thought to herself, "This is far from over. So much turmoil. I hope Charlene has learned something from this. The pattern was daunting. Always dating older men. They just use her and throw her away after they've had their fun. Although Jacob doesn't seem that way, after all, he did offer to help her…"

"Can I ask you something, Charlene, without you getting angry with me?" Alice asked, her face was serious but her eyes shone with love and concern.

"How do you honestly feel about Jacob? I mean, since you've been burned so badly this time? I worry about you."

Charlene replied, "he says he won't leave Ava. He made that very clear. Right now, to be honest, I hate Jacob and I don't care if I ever see him again. Then, on the other hand, I know I can't just forget about him. I'm having his baby. He told me he'd be there to take care of me and our child but I just can't get my head around him staying married to Ava. The three of us; Jacob, Me and the baby, that's how it should be. Four is one too many. Even if I never saw Ava, I know she'd be there, a ghost."

"Will you try to find someone else to take Jacob's place?"

"Oh, hell no! I've learned my lesson. I'm done with men! It doesn't matter how old or young they are. All they want is one thing and the woman pays the consequences."

"I hope you'll be able to make it. You know I'll always be there for you. You're family." Alice smiled and pulled Charlene in for a hug.

"On a brighter note, my wedding is next week! Walter and I have everything ready. I just need to get you down to Mom for your fitting. Are you still planning to come back with us and spend the next week with me through the wedding? Walter is with Nathan tonight. They're having a few beers at Vic's and he'll come by and pick us up tomorrow around noon."

"Well, there's no reason for me to stay here. Everything is out in the open, no more having to worry about how I'm going to handle things with JoAnn and Sam. Sounds like a great idea to me. Let me grab some clean clothes and repack my suitcase."

And, just like that, Charlene had a plan… once again.

Back in the city at Florence's Fashion Boutique, Charlene stood in the pink chiffon gown as Florence directed her seamstress in the fitting.

"Try not to move, Darling, so my seamstress doesn't poke

you with one of her little silver pins." Florence reminded Charlene in her sing-song voice.

In an hour, with a nip here and a tuck there, Charlene looked like a princess ready for the ball. The women had outdone themselves.

The sun rose on Valentine's Day, brilliant in a cloudless blue sky. Alice awoke with butterflies in her stomach, "It's my wedding day! I'm going to be Mrs. Walter Greensboro!"

Florence called up the staircase, "Rise and shine ladies. We're burning daylight and we have a wedding to get ready for!"

After a quick breakfast of croissants and coffee, the girls drove to Old Mariner's Church. Florence had her crew from the boutique already there decorating the pews with red, white, and pink bouquets. By noon, the team, under Florence's direction, transformed the church into a masterwork of art to be rivaled only by top wedding professionals. Next, the hairdressers and makeup stylists worked their magic. Upon completion, Alice found herself nervous about the final result. She took a deep breath to steady herself and turned toward the mirror. The vision that greeted her there took her breath away.

"There she is, our blushing Bride to be!" Florence declared clapping her hands.

Charlene joined in, "You are stunning!" Alice had never felt more beautiful. Gratitude threatened to overwhelm her.

Standing in her wedding dress, white with gold trim, Alice glowed with radiance. She turned and admired the train her mother skillfully embellished as Charlene helped to fan it out behind her. Florence had interwoven tiny red rose buds throughout as she said she would. Behind the scene, the photographer captured the moment and the picture would become one of Alice and Walter's favorites. Soon after the hairdressers and makeup artists finished with Charlene and Florence. Dressed in her pink chiffon gown, her hair done up with tiny white and red roses Charlene, looked like a model stepping from the cover of one of her glamor magazines. Florence, dressed in a rich burgundy gown, stood proud next to her daughter as the photographer snapped more photographs.

In the basement Walter, Nathan and Joe were dressed in their wedding suits. Walter in black, Nathan and Joe in light gray. They watched the clock tick away the final half hour.

"So, are you nervous?" Nathan asked smoothing out Walter's lapels.

"Maybe just a little. More anxious than anything. I am one lucky guy!" Walter grinned.

"Well, I'm a nervous wreck," Joe exclaimed. "I can't seem to get my tie right!" Joe struggled, and Walter took over.

"There's nothing to it, Joe, just relax. We'll get through this."

Nathan pulled a flask from his inner suit coat pocket. "A little nip to calm our nerves gentlemen!" He handed it to Joe. "Looks like you need this more than Walter or I do." The guys laughed, all taking a healthy swig.

Joe pulled out three, fine Cuban cigars from his vest. "I'm saving these for later."

"You're a good man, Joe!" Walter slapped him on the back.

The organ music began to play and that was their cue

to go upstairs. Walter trailed the minister up to the altar. Charlene and Nathan followed, walking side by side. Florence came next, beaming with pride. The ushers then pulled the white runner down the aisle as the organist began to play. "Here comes the bride," filled the church. With the familiar notes, everyone stood.

Joe escorted Alice down the aisle. Tears of joy flowed freely down his cheeks as he smiled his signature toothy grin. Alice was on cloud nice and felt like she was floating on air. Walter couldn't stop smiling when he saw his bride in her wedding dress for the first time.

"Welcome, family and friends. We are gathered here today to join Alice Marie Brooks and Walter Lyndon Greensboro in holy matrimony. Who gives this woman to this man?"

Joe cleared his throat, "Her Mother and I." Then, he walked Alice up to Walter and nodded, with a big smile on his face. Charlene tended to Alice's train as she moved, fanning it out behind her. Handing Charlene her bouquet, Alice took Walters's hands.

"Very good," The minister smiled looking first at Alice and then at Walter. "I have to ask this before we go any further. If anyone can show just cause why these two beautiful young people should not be lawfully joined together in holy matrimony, let them speak now or forever hold their peace." He looked out over the guests, smiled, then nodded. "Very well. Let us pray." After the prayer, he read from 1 Corinthians 13 beginning with verse 4.

Charlene barely heard the rest of the ceremony. She was lost in thought. "It should be Kyle and I up here getting married. After all, I am carrying his baby. We should be a family!

Together. Looking forward to OUR happy future."Then the realization hit her. Echoing from a not-so-distant memory, she heard him, "There is no Kyle." Jealousy reared its ugly head and Charlene blinked back hot tears. And not happy ones for her best friend as they should have been. The next thing she heard was when the minister said. "...the power vested in me by The Old Mariner's Church and the State of Michigan, I now pronounce you Man and Wife. You may kiss your bride!"

Walter looked into Alice's eyes, her beautiful brown eyes. "I love you," he whispered.

"I love you!" Alice fairly shouted, and they shared their first kiss of many as husband and wife.

"Ladies and Gentlemen let me be the first to introduce you to Mr. & Mrs. Walter Greensboro!"

The guests cheered their congratulations as Mr. & Mrs. Walter Greensboro walked down the aisle. Alice's train flowed out behind her. Charlene painted on her plastic smile and walked down the aisle with Nathan. Florence followed Joe, and Walter's parents, Jeremy and Elaine. Over fifty guests were in attendance. Fortunately, the basement was large enough to accommodate the reception. Toasts were made from glasses of fine champagne provided by Florence and Walter's parents. Joe stole Walter and Nathan away to enjoy his fine Cuban cigars on the steps in the back of the church. Afterward, Alice and Walter opened their presents as Charlene kept track of who gave what gift by writing them down in the back of the guest book. At the end of the reception, Alice and Walter cut their wedding cake and made sure everyone received a piece to take home with them.

The guests gathered out front, hands filled with rice, waiting to send the newlyweds on their way. On the steps of the church, Alice tossed her bouquet over her shoulder. It spun through the air, and as Charlene reached skyward, it grazed the tips of her fingers. The bouquet landed in the snow, entangled behind the rose bush briers that grew alongside the church. The rice fell like rain as Walter and Alice ran to his car. Nathan and Joe tied beer cans to the bumper along with a "Just Married" sign attached to the trunk. Driving away, Walter and Alice waved, honked the horn, then sped off into a beautiful future together. Charlene watched in envy and then looked back at the bouquet, longingly. It was just out of reach. As unattainable as her Kyle. She thought to herself, "Destined to be a bridesmaid, never a bride."

The next morning Florence drove Charlene back to Harbor Cove. On the way, Florene broke the silence.

"You gave folks quite a scare over Christmas. My receptionist told me your mother called looking for you. I know it's none of my business, Charlene, but it seems there are people that care about you. Don't be too hasty to turn your back on them. Someday you may need their help."

"Hell will freeze over before I ask for help from JoAnn and Sam. I can take care of myself!" Charlene replied angrily.

"So, how far along are you?" Florence asked.

Charlene's jaw dropped. "How did you know, Alice promised she wouldn't say anything!"

"Alice didn't say anything. I could see that you gained a little weight when we fitted your gown. Your breasts are a bit larger too, and you have that "glow" about you. It didn't take long for me to figure it out. Besides, you had a pretty good bout of morning sickness over Thanksgiving. Are things calming down a bit?"

"Yes, thank you. I'm about 16 weeks along. I had an exam and the doctor gave me a due date around the last week in June."

Florence nodded, "What about the father? Is it that Kyle fellow you were tagging around with at the end of September?"

"Yes, Kyle is the father. I know what you're going to say so please don't say it. Yes, he is older. I believe that age doesn't matter and it's my business whom I see."

"Okay, I was just asking. I assume he knows. Is he going to take responsibility?"

"Of course, he knows. And yes, he offered to take care of me, but..," Charlene broke down, she couldn't handle the stress of it all any longer.

"There, there, no need to cry. You've gotten yourself in trouble with, let me guess, a married man and now there's a baby on the way? It's not the end of the world, it's actually the beginning of a new life for you. Even if it ends up just you and your little one, simply put your mind to it and you'll make it somehow. Never give up. You are welcome to continue to stay at my house in Harbor Cove. I am considering selling it later this coming summer, but until then I'd be happy knowing you're keeping an eye on it for me."

Charlene dried her eyes, "Thank you, Florence. That means the world to me."

"I know Dear, and remember. There are people in your life who care and are willing to help out, just ask."

They arrived at Florence's in Harbor Cove. "Would

you like to come in? I'd love to have you spend the night." Charlene asked.

"No, I need to get going. There are a lot of orders to fill from my last show in New York. You take care and call if you need anything." Florence smiled and gave Charlene a hug and sped back to the city.

Chapter Twenty-Three

Thursday, Charlene walked to the high school and went to the office.

"Well, hello, Charlene. You should be in class. What can I help you with?" Mrs. Warner glared.

"I need to speak with Principal Logan."

Mrs. Warner, a busybody who loved gossip, inquired with the utmost interest. "May I ask what this is in regards to?"

"No. Is he in? If not, I'll come back later."

Mrs. Warner picked up the phone, not impressed that Charlene wouldn't share the reason why she needed to speak with Principal Logan. "Principal Logan, student Charlene Strypher is here to see you."

A few seconds later, the office door opened and Principal Gary Logan ushered Charlene in.

A heavy-set, balding man, always sweating profusly, with black plastic-framed glasses perched on the end of his nose, sat down in his black office chair across from her. He began munching on a bag of pork rinds.

"What can I do for you, Miss Strypher?" He asked, tipping the bag toward her, offering the snack.

With a look of utter disdain, her nostrils flared. "I'll get right to the point, Mr. Logan. I'm quitting school."

"What? You're in your senior year! You graduate in three months!" Mr. Logan remarked.

"I know, I don't really want to quit but I have to, I'm pregnant. Unless you'll allow me to continue to attend classes? Might be a bit awkward. I'm due at the end of June." Charlene smiled wickedly as she caressed her baby bump.

"Oh! Oh my... I'm, I'm sorry to hear that." Mr. Logan stammered.

Just out of spite, Charlene asked. "What? Sorry to hear I'm quitting school. Or sorry that I'm pregnant?" Charlene didn't try to hide her smile and enjoyed Mr. Logan's uneasiness as he tried to respond professionally.

"Um, sorry to hear you're having to quit school of course." He opened his desk drawer and handed Charlene a form. "Take this home to your parents and have them fill it out. Then, bring it back to me."

"Sam and JoAnn kicked me out of the house, my being pregnant and all, so I guess I'll be filling this form out myself. Gotta pen?" Charlene asked as she reached across the desk.

"Oh! This is most unusual. We need an adult of legal age to sign off on your withdrawal." He pulled at his collar and adjusted his tie. Charlene reveled in his discomfort.

She smiled and leaned forward, "Come on Gary, you're an adult, why don't you sign off on it for me? You might as well, because when I leave here, I won't be coming back."

Charlene picked a pen from his pencil holder and signed her name on the bottom of the form.

"Have a nice day."

Mrs. Warner looked up from her desk as Charlene walked out of the office. In defiance, Charlene leaned down and whispered, "It's none of your damn business why I had to talk to Gary." She rubbed her baby bump, smiled, and walked out the door, slamming it behind her. Charlene thought to herself, "That should fire up the rumor mill at Harbor Cove High."

From there, she walked back to Mulberry Street to Ruth McGuire's house. She knocked on the door and Ruth appeared.

"Hello Charlene! It's so good to see you. Come on in! I'll make some tea. What can I do for you?" Excitedly she added, "Are you here to take up my offer to be my nanny?"

"Well, actually, that is why I'm here," Charlene replied.

"Oh, that's great news, Harold will be thrilled! I've heard that they might be needing some help at the hospital. I've been wanting to get back into nursing, I stopped when the girls were born." Ruth smiled and Charlene could tell in her face that she missed it.

"I didn't know you were a nurse," Charlene commented.

"Yes, back before I met Harold. Let's see, we've been married going on 12 years. I received my training during the war effort. When it was over, I continued schooling down in the city and got a job at Mercy General. That's where I met Harold. Back then, he was just starting out as a Postman delivering mail. He had a delivery to the front office, and I just happened to be there filing some daily reports on my patients. I'll tell you, when our eyes met, it was love at first sight! We were married later that year. Harold's parents had this house here in town and when they passed away, he moved us here.

It's so nice not living in a big city. Our Louise was born a year later and then Ellen came along. With the responsibility of raising children, I've stayed home. Harold continues to work as a Postman." Ruth continued as she filled the teacups. "Tell me more about yourself, Charlene. How is it that you're available to nanny? I thought you were already employed. What happened?"

"Well, that fell through. I want to be honest with you so I'm just going to come out and say it. I'm pregnant. JoAnn and Sam frown on having an unwed mother working for them. I enjoyed taking care of the girls, but they let me go." Charlene watched Ruth's facial expressions, expecting her to see through her half-truth. Instead, Ruth replied excitedly.

"I sure can use your help around here. Even if I only go back to work part-time, you will make life so much easier. When are you due?"

"My doctor says the end of June."

"Okay. Well, I'll be able to help you along through the rest of your pregnancy. May I ask if the father is in the picture?"

"No, I'm afraid he's not available to help out. He lives back east and has a life of his own."

"I'm sorry to hear that. We'll be here to help out. Are you still living with Alice Brooks just down the street?"

"It's Alice Greensboro now. She just got married on Valentine's Day. I'll be staying at her house as I have been for the past couple of years."

"That works but, we do have room for you if you need to spend the nights as you get closer to your due date. I'll discuss this all with Harold tonight when he gets home and let you know tomorrow."

"Thank you, Mrs. McGuire. I really appreciate it."

"Call me Ruth and my husband is Harold. We're not that formal here." She laughed.

Charlene began nannying for Ruth and Harold on March 1st. The hospital scheduled Ruth to work the 7 a.m. to 3 p.m. shift, Monday through Thursday. Although the hours she nannied were about the same as she had at JoAnn's, things were much more relaxed. The stress was out of the equation, for now. Alice was right, Ruth was an amazing cook and Charlene spent the evenings dining with the McGuires. The atmosphere was joyous and Harold was very kind, and in no way judgmental. Charlene enjoyed taking care of Louise and Ellen. When walking them to the bus stop, she would see her sisters Mildred and Suzanne. Even if it was just for a few moments, she treasured their hugs. JoAnn hired Julie as their full-time nanny.

In the weeks to come, Charlene became anxious about her new arrival. She had felt the first flutter and kick from within. From fear to joy and back to fear again she rode the roller-coaster of emotions. Rubbing her baby bump and speaking to the little one growing inside of her, she couldn't wait to meet this little person. Alice checked in from time to time to see how she was doing. She and Walter were enjoying married life together. He continued climbing the corporate ladder while Alice became Florence's assistant in her design business.

"So, what are you hoping for, a boy or a girl?" Ruth asked her.

"I'm thinking my baby is a boy, I'm not sure why, maybe that's what I'm hoping for. I've picked the name, Jacob Kyle, after his father." She smiled.

"What if he's a she?" Ruth questioned, laughing.

"Well, then I just name her Kylie Jay. Regardless I will be overjoyed as long as he or she is healthy."

The Winter gave way to Spring and Charlene continued walking Louise and Ellen to and from the school bus. Her sisters would come running when they saw Charlene. They would ask how she was doing, hinting they wanted to feel her belly.

"Come on then, feel right here," Charlene would take their little hands and guide them so they might feel a kick or possibly her infant turning. Mildred and Suzanne would giggle when they did. Julie continued being Charlene's friend, keeping her updated on how the girls were doing.

"JoAnn asks me about you. She sends good wishes," Julie remarked one morning.

Charlene pursed her lips, "Well, tell her I'm fine." Thinking to herself, "I'm fine. Fine without them!" She vowed to her unborn child that JoAnn and Sam would never be a part of their lives.

The school was let out for the summer in the first week of June, and Charlene officially moved in with Ruth and Harold. They insisted she stay with them in her last month of pregnancy. Louise and Ellen shared a room, leaving a small bedroom downstairs for Charlene. She would get up from bed and waddle to the bathroom, grateful it was close. Braxton Hicks contractions would come and go and her back ached to the point of tears.

It was late afternoon on June 28th when Charlene was getting up from her chair and her water broke.

"It's time!" She called out to Ruth who was in the kitchen. She had just gotten off her shift.

"Okay! Let me grab your overnight bag and we'll be out the door to the hospital." Ruth rushed over and grabbed the bag that they packed a week earlier. She helped Charlene up and they made their way to the car. In the 20-minute drive to Harbor Cover Memorial Hospital, Charlene went into hard labor. Ruth called out, "Breath in through your nose, exhale through your mouth. Slow down a bit, not so fast, we don't want you to hyperventilate. We're almost there."

In the hospital room, the doctor examined Charlene, "You are about four centimeters dilated. How much pain are you in?"

"It hurts!" Charlene screamed.

"Would you like something to ease the pain?" He asked.

"Yes!"

The doctor patted her leg, "I'll get you something."

In the hall, he spoke with the nurse on duty and she returned shortly with a glass of water and a small white pill. "Take this and you should start feeling some relief in a half hour or so."

Charlene never experienced something so physically draining to her system. The pain came in waves and at times, it was unforgiving. Her room was just off the nursing station. The doctor continued to monitor her throughout the night. "Things are coming along nicely. We'll be moving you to the delivery room soon."

Her mind raced as she stared at the ceiling. "I wish your father was here for this." Tears of mixed emotions and pain rolled down her cheeks as the contractions increased. Charlene saw the clock in the hall above the nurse's station. It read 4 o'clock, "It must be the morning of June 29th." She thought to herself. The doctor and a nurse rolled Charlene down to the delivery room as the overhead fluorescent lights blurred her vision. The experience was surreal.

"It's time Charlene, I need you to push." Charlene heard the doctor call out.

She pushed and the pain threatened to cut her in half, she grabbed the rail on the side of the bed.

"Again, push! We're almost there, I can see the head." The doctor urged her.

Lost in the excruciating pain, Charlene bit her lip clean through. Blood ran down the corner of her mouth on the heels of the last push. "It's a boy! The doctor exclaimed as he cut the umbilical cord and cleared the airway. The seconds ticked away as Charlene listened through her exhaustion, anxiously waiting for the cry of her son. She heard the smack of the doctor's hand on her son's backside. Then, came his cry, lusty, vibrant, and loud, echoing down the halls. Tired smiles touched the corner of the nurse's mouths as they went about their tasks at their stations. Another successful birth.

After the delivery nurse cleaned up the baby, she weighed him, calling out to the doctor, 5 pounds 5 ounces. The doctor nodded, "That 5 ounces will hopefully be enough to keep him out of the incubator. He appears healthy and has quite the set of lungs on him." The doctor laughed as the nurse handed Charlene her son. So tiny. So precious. Charlene smiled through now happy tears, counting ten little fingers and ten little toes. She eased her son's mouth to her breast as he began to suckle, then caressed his head, "Hello Jacob Kyle Strypher, my little Kyle. I love you."

At the nurse's station across the hall the telephone rang. Charlene's door was open and she could hear the conversation.

"Yes, this is the maternity ward. Charlene Strypher, yes, she had her baby, a boy. Okay, her father, calling from California? I'll let her know you called."

The nurse cradled the receiver and walked over to Charlene's room. "Your father called from California. He wanted me to offer his congratulations."

Charlene knew it wasn't her father, but her little Kyle's father, Jacob. She wondered how Jacob knew she was in the hospital giving birth to his son. Then it dawned on her. John must be keeping tabs on her and passing the information on to Jacob. Charlene had mixed feelings, not quite sure how she felt about it all. On one hand, she was happy that Jacob still cared enough to call. On the other hand, it was unnerving. She knew in his line of work, that if Jacob tried hard enough, he would be able to find her, almost anywhere.

Charlene closed her eyes, just for a moment but, the exhaustion overwhelmed her.

"Hey, you! Congratulations!" Alice and Walter walked into her room. Alice set a large bouquet of daisies, with a brown teddy bear hugging the vase, on the dresser.

"Hi!" Charlene replied, a bit sleepily. Her little Kyle lay nuzzled against her breast, full and content, sleeping soundly.

"He's beautiful! Look at him Walter, he's so tiny!"

Walter nodded, "He is a small little tyke. Kind of cute though, all wrinkled up there sleeping."

"Would you like to hold him, Alice?" Charlene offered.

"I don't want to wake him. He looks so peaceful."

"My little Kyle will probably sleep right through. We're both exhausted."

Alice reached in and picked Kyle up, cradling him in her arms. "Oh my, he's so tiny he can't weigh much more than five pounds. He looks like you!"

Charlene smiled, "5 pounds, 5 ounces. The 5 ounces have kept him out of the incubator, and look again, he looks like Kyle, I mean… Jacob. Right down to the devil's dimple on his chin. Has his blue-gray eyes too."

"Well, I can see both of you in this little guy," Alice commented, rocking him in her arms. A half hour went by and Alice could see that Charlene needed rest. She tucked little Kyle back in Charlene's arms where she nuzzled him back alongside her breast. Alice bent down and kissed Charlene on the forehead, then Jacob Kyle.

"Nice job, and again, congratulations!" She whispered.

After keeping Charlene and Jacob Kyle overnight for observation, the doctor released them Saturday morning. Ruth picked them up in her car, taking them back to her house. There, her husband Harold, along with their daughters had decorated the house with blue balloons and a banner strung across the porch that read, "Welcome home Charlene… and baby!"

In the months to come, under the guidance of Ruth, Charlene learned how to take care of her little Kyle. She became confident and fell into a routine, going for walks in the warm sunshine. One sunny afternoon in early September, while she was pushing her baby carriage past Smilin' Joes, she noticed the baby blue and white convertible. Her heart skipped a beat when Jacob stepped out on the sidewalk.

"Hello Charlene. This must be my son, Jacob Kyle?" He knelt down looking into the pram. Blue-gray eyes stared back at him and then a smile from his son.

"Hi Jacob. You're here in Harbor Cove? Where have you been?" Charlene asked, stifling her desire to give him a hug.

"I'm just getting back from a mission, a long one this time. I've spent the past three months abroad. Did you get my phone message at the hospital?"

"Yes, John must have been keeping tabs on me and letting you know I was having little Kyle."

Jacob smiled, "Smart girl. I've been very concerned about you since our last phone call so I asked John to keep me posted on how things were going." He looked back down at his son.

"You've done a wonderful job, and we've made a beautiful boy together."

"Thank you, Jacob, and yes, we did make a beautiful baby. Since you are here, I'm going to have little Kyle baptized this Sunday at the Old Mariners Church, where Alice and Walter got married. Would you care to drive to the city and join us?" Charlene asked.

"Yes, I would, Thank you." Jacob stood, proudly smiling at his son, then at Charlene. He reached for her. Charlene stared at Jacob, and for a second she almost let her guard down. She wanted him, even after all that had happened. Then, she stopped, shying away from his touch.

"Have you left Ava?" Charlene asked the only question she wanted an answer to.

Jacob replied, "We talked about this, it's complicated."

"Until you do, nothing can happen between us, understand?

You're my son's father and I'm not going to deny you seeing him, but that's all." Charlene stood her ground and Jacob nodded, "Understood."

It was a private gathering Sunday afternoon at the Old Mariners Church. Charlene felt a touch of sadness standing next to Jacob at the altar. She always pictured they would be standing together as husband and wife. Alice, chosen by Charlene to be little Kyles's Godmother, held him in her arms at the baptismal fountain. Charlene dressed Kyle in a white baptismal gown and had his already growing, curly blonde hair styled handsomely. At the fountain, little Kyle studied Alice intently. Pastor Burg sprinkled the holy water on Jacob's head. Surprised at the coolness of the water, Jacob Kyle wrinkled up his face and expressed his dissatisfaction. With his thumb, Pastor Burg made the sign of the cross on his forehead and said a prayer welcoming the child into God's graces.

Afterward, Pastor Burg gave Charlene the baptismal certificate and the white handkerchief, embroidered with a gold cross, that he had used during the baptism to dry little Kyle's hair. Upon exiting the church, Charlene paused at the bottom of the steps and glanced at the rose bushes growing alongside the wall. She remembered Alice's bouquet that had grazed her fingertips, and how they landed behind the rose bushes. Charlene thought to herself, "Still unattainable."

To save Alice and Walter the drive back to Harbor Cove, Jacob offered to take Charlene and little Kyle with him. Charlene accepted, and on the way back Jacob started a conversation.

"So, what are your plans now, Charlene?" He asked.

"Plans? For what?"

"Well, for raising our son. Are you working? What about your income? How long do you plan to live at Ruth's?" Jacob waited for her response.

"I am employed, as a Nanny for Ruth. For now, it's working nicely. As for how long I plan to stay with Ruth and her family, I'm in no real hurry to move on, but you never know. Things change."

"I've been thinking, I know all this has been overwhelming, but you could go back down to Florida and live with my mom. Carla would love to meet her grandson, and she's been asking about the two of you. Would you please send her a picture of Jacob Kyle?"

"I guess I could send her a picture, but I wouldn't want to live with her, maybe just visit."

"Okay, how about over Christmas? I could fly down after I wrap up the year-end business in D.C. with The Director."

"It seems that you were supposed to do that last year and you weren't able to get away."

"I know, and I'm sorry. Things kind of went haywire in so many different ways. It's time to get past all of that, for Jacob Kyle's sake. I want to be in his life, be there financially, at the very least."

"That's very honorable of you Jacob, but the fact remains, I won't play second fiddle to Ava. We've gone over this and I don't want to fight about it!" Charlene exclaimed.

"Okay, I'm sorry. Please, just give it all some thought. At least go and visit Carla. I'll buy you a round-trip plane ticket." Jacob pleaded.

"I'm not too keen on flying. Maybe a bus ticket would be better, although that's like a 24-hour ride. Regardless, I'll think about it." Charlene replied as they pulled into the driveway at Ruth and Harold's home in Harbor Cove.

Chapter Twenty-Four

With summer gone, school started back up in Harbor Cove. Charlene put little Kyle in his stroller and walked with Louise and Ellen to and from the bus stop every morning and afternoon. Mildred and Suzanne looked forward to each day when they would see Charlene and their nephew.

"He's so tiny. Just like a little doll!" Mildred would say.

"When can we play with him? I wish you would bring him by the house. Mommy would love to meet little Kyle!" Suzanne begged.

Charlene would respond the same as always, "Maybe someday. I'm so very busy so you'll just have to be happy seeing him here at the bus stop."

One sunny September afternoon, Charlene sat on the bench at the school bus stop waiting for the girls. Instead of Julie sitting down beside her, it was JoAnn.

"Hello, Charlene," JoAnn struggled to begin, "I have a little something for your son." She handed her a wrapped present.

"May I?" JoAnn asked as she looked over longingly at the carriage.

Taken aback, Charlene hesitated, "Yes, you may have a look, but he's sleeping so please don't wake him."

JoAnn looked down into the carriage. Little Kyle was, indeed, sleeping. Charlene learned early on that her son loved riding in his carriage and it was the perfect way to get him to sleep.

"He's so beautiful!" JoAnn exclaimed quietly. "You know, I'm so sorry things worked out the way they have."

"Don't worry about it. We're doing fine." Charlene paused, seeming to gather her thoughts, "I am curious though, why was Sam always so mean to me and why didn't you ever believe me when I told you things he'd done?" With each word, Charlene seemed to punctuate every traumatic experience inflicted upon her by *the man.*

JoAnn sighed. "Sam wasn't always the way he is. When we met, he was kind and loving. When he came back from the war, he wasn't the same man I married. The war did something to Sam. He wouldn't talk to anyone, and he was withdrawn, a changed man. I loved him anyways. You came along nine months after he got home. My husband wasn't ready for a child. He even hinted that he thought he wasn't your father. Sam accused me of having an affair. I never stepped out on him. I mean, look at you! You are his daughter. You have the same eyes and facial features as all you girls do."

Charlene glared at her, "That's no excuse! You have no idea what he's put me through, what both of you put me through!" She ground out.

The school bus pulled up irrupting their conversation. Charlene got up and placed the gift from JoAnn in the basket, under the carriage. She gathered up Louise and Ellen and left. Mildred and Suzanne watched her go then looked up to their mother, questioning. "Is Charlene mad at us?"

"No, she's not mad at you. She's mad at me and your dad. Come on girls let's go home."

Charlene was still furious when she got back to Ruth's. Louise and Ellen played in the backyard while Charlene went inside with little Kyle. She opened the present, bitterly pulling out a one-piece pajama set and a pair of little jeans with a light blue shirt. She put them back in the box shoving them under the bed. Charlene already decided she wouldn't use the clothing but would return them with a note saying they didn't fit.

That evening, Charlene's day went from bad to worse. Upon returning from her stroll with little Kyle in attempt to get him to fall asleep, she overheard the last part of a conversation between Ruth and Harold as she walked in.

"…It would be in the best interest of the boy," Ruth said.

"I agree. When should we discuss it with her?"

Ruth smiled, "We'll know when the time is right, maybe over Thanksgiving. It will be so nice having a little boy around to grow up with our girls."

Charlene's mind kicked into overdrive and her paranoia consumed her. "They're trying to take my son away from me! Like hell they'll take my son away from me! Over my dead body!"

In the months to come, she maintained her composure, but she became standoffish as she, once again, planned her escape.

In actuality, Ruth and Harold adored Charlene and little Kyle, so much so, that they were considering speaking with her about becoming a McGuire. They entertained the idea of adopting her and making all of them one big happy family. Charlene had jumped to the wrong conclusion and became less communitive. She kept to herself and stayed over at Alice's house more. The McGuires didn't understand why Charlene was acting the way she was and the opportunity to speak with her never arose.

The phone rang under the bar at Vic's and John answered.

"Good afternoon, Vic's. John speaking."

"Hi John, it's Charlene. Have you heard from Jacob lately? Any idea when he'll be back in the area?"

"You just missed him. Jacob was here yesterday. He mentioned something about taking his car down to the Refuge and then across the bridge into Canada for some government business. Why do you want to know?"

"He asked if I was interested in taking little Kyle to visit his mother in Florida over the holidays so she could meet her grandson. I was just calling to talk to him more about it."

"I'll let him know the next time I hear from him. By the way, how is your baby doing?

You know Jacob is one proud father."

"Little Kyle is doing great, growing like a weed. He'll be six months old on the 29th of December."

"Wow! Time sure does fly. Well, I'm sure I'll talk with Jacob soon. One good thing, if you go down to Florida it will be a lot warmer than it is in Harbor Cove. I hear there's a winter storm brewing up north that's supposed to be a doozie. We could be in for a hard, cold winter this year. After I speak with him, how do you want me to get ahold of you?"

"Just like we used to. Call me at Alice's. I can be there in the morning around 9 a.m. Pick a day of the week."

"Let's make it Monday. With any luck he'll check in this weekend."

"Okay, Thanks, John."

Whenever Charlene got something in her mind there was no changing it, she often acted before looking at the big picture. This time she honed in on the one thing she knew how to do, run. Run from the problems she created for herself, not paying attention to the catastrophic consequences of her decisions.

Monday morning the phone rang at Alice's preciously at 9 a.m.

"Hey, it's John. I spoke with Jacob. He'll be back here tomorrow afternoon. Says that he'll pick you up at Alice's around 6. From there he'll drive you down to the city where he'll get you and Jacob Kyle plane tickets. Looks like you'll spend the holiday in sunny Florida!"

"Sounds good, we'll be ready. Thank you."

In the past couple of weeks, Charlene had been packing things she knew she'd need for her and little Kyle. In her room under the bed, she found the package JoAnn gave her. The next morning, she walked over and left the package on JoAnn's front step with a note stating the clothes were too small. Charlene returned to Ruth and Harold's deciding to leave them a note thanking them for the opportunity to work as their Nanny. She made up a story that she had a sick relative and had to leave unexpectedly to help out. She apologized that she wasn't able to give notice and hoped they would understand. When she got back to Harbor Cove, she would contact them.

While Charlene was gathering up the bags for their flight, she eyed the last remaining bottle of chardonnay under the liquor cabinet. "Why not? I could use a glass to take the edge off. I can't believe that bastard is putting me on a plane… Again!"

Jacob arrived at 6 to pick up Charlene and little Kyle.

"I checked the bus schedule and it would take 25 hours to get to my mom's. If you thought flying wasn't your cup of tea, trust me, after riding on a bus that long you'd be cussing me more than you ever have. You'll land in Orlando in three hours. Mom is very excited. She'll be waiting to pick you two up at the airport."

"Thanks for booking our flight instead of a bus ticket. Yes, 25 hours would have been an excruciating nightmare and I'm sure little Kyle would have had a lot to say about it," Charlene laughed.

"I'm planning to join you right around Christmas Day if all goes as planned," Jacob assured her.

At the airport, after he checked them in at the ticker counter, Jacob walked them to the gate. Kneeling down he smiled at his son, who smiled back. "He really does look like me, doesn't he?" Jacob smiled up at Charlene.

"Yes, he does. Right down to that devil's dimple in his chin."

"Looks like it's time for you two to board, so. I'll let you go, for now." Jacob watched as they walked to the gate. Charlene handed her tickets to the flight attendant. Little Kyle looked over her shoulder at his father, waving as they boarded the plane.

As expected, Carla waited anxiously as the plane from

Detroit disembarked. She waved from the gate when she saw Charlene holding her grandson.

"Hello Charlene! Welcome back. Thank you for bringing me my grandson." Carla reached out taking little Kyle from her. "Hello Jacob Kyle. I'm your grandma! You sure are a cute little thing, aren't you?" Carla exclaimed.

Kyle just smiled, as he did whenever he received attention from anyone. At the house, Carla added a crib to the spare bedroom. Hanging above the crib, a mobile turned freely with blue airplanes, hot air balloons, white fluffy clouds and cream-colored stars. Charlene laid little Kyle down in the crib. He watched the mobile turn, smiling and reaching upward.

"It's so nice to see you again," Carla said as she helped Charlene get her luggage into the spare bedroom.

"I was a little concerned that you might not want to see me considering how things went down the last time I was here," Charlene confessed.

"All is forgiven and forgotten. Everything worked out okay. I have waited so long for Jacob to give me a grandchild and you've brought my beautiful grandson to me! I am so happy!"

"Well, it's been a long day. I hope you don't mind us turning in right away?" Charlene asked.

"That's fine, my Dear. I'll bring a tray with some refreshments," Carla replied, smiling.

Charlene checked on little Kyle in the crib. He had already fallen to sleep, holding onto his little stuffed teddy bear that was attached to the bouquet of daisies Alice and Walter had given her at the hospital.

From the Thanksgiving holiday through December, Charlene relaxed in the Florida sun with her little Kyle. Carla enjoyed her grandson, holding him whenever she had the chance. Two weeks before Christmas, they put up an aluminum tree with blue ornaments. Kyle smiled and laughed at the shiny branches. Charlene laid him down on his back under the tree.

"The perfect present!' Carla exclaimed and ran for the camera.

A week before Christmas the tree was overflowing with gifts. Charlene purchased a gold money clip for Jacob and wrapped it in a small box with a red bow. She believed things were finally going to end up okay and Harbor Cove would be a distant memory.

On Christmas Eve, the phone rang and Carla answered it. Charlene was holding Kyle and listened intently as Carla spoke.

"Hello Jacob! Merry Christmas!" Carla listened and her expression became ashen. "I see. I understand. I'll tell her. I hope she gets feeling better soon. Keep me posted. Love you too."

Carla hung up the receiver and let out a long sigh.

"He's not coming, is he?" Charlene questioned, tears already welling up in her eyes.

"Charlene, Ava is very ill. She's in the hospital. Jacob can't make it but he hopes you can understand. He'll try to get here after the new year. I'm so sorry, Charlene. I know this must be incredibly hard for you."

Charlene swallowed past the lump in her throat then, thinking to herself, "Ava has come between us once again. It's obvious where little Kyle and I stand."

"Please say something Charlene," Carla pleaded.

"I understand. I'll be fine." She soothed little Kyle in the rocking chair, staving off hot tears, wheels turning in her mind as she planned her next move.

"I think we're going to turn in for the night. Little Kyle and I need our sleep." Charlene explained offering a fake smile. She got up and went into the bedroom, packed her luggage and all that she brought with her, then waited. The house was quiet and the clock read 11:15 p.m. Carla was lightly snoring, asleep in her room. Charlene went into the kitchen and called a cab. Fifteen minutes later she climbed in with her son.

"Where to?" The cabby asked.

"Is there an all-night diner somewhere around here?" Charlene asked.

"There's Darcy's Diner just up the road about five minutes."

"That will work, drop me off there, please."

Five minutes later the cab stopped in front of Darcy's Diner. Charlene paid the fare and went inside. Kyle lay soundly asleep on her shoulder. The waitress smiled at her and brought a menu, seating her in a booth by the door.

"Just coffee please. Do you have a pay phone?" She asked.

"Sure Hon, right around the corner next to the restrooms," The waitress pointed.

Charlene held Kyle and picked up the receiver. Not wanting to go back to Harbor Cove, she remembered her Aunt Lotus Odimier. She lived in Houston, Texas. Aunt Lotus, JoAnn and Frank's sister, was 10 years younger than Frank and was estranged from the family due to her unacceptable behavior and lifestyle. Charlene remembered JoAnn and Sam mentioned something about Lotus being a burlesque fan dancer in Houston's classy nightclubs. Charlene dialed the operator requesting to be connected with Lotus Odimier in Houston, Texas. The phone rang once, twice, three times. On the fourth ring, a woman's voice with a southern drawl answered, "Hello?" Charlene deposited two quarters to make the connection.

"Hello, Aunt Lotus? This is Charlene. I'm JoAnn Strypher's daughter, your niece, from Harbor Cove, Michigan."

A second of silence, then, "Well, Merry Christmas Charlene! How are y'all doing up there in the Great Lake State? It's been a coon's age since I saw you last, it's been at least, what, 8 years?"

"Yes, it has, Aunt Lotus. Hey, I hate to ask but I'm in trouble. I was wondering if I could come to stay with you for a while. I have money for the bus ticket."

"In trouble, are you pregnant Charlene?"

"No, not now. I do have a baby. His name is Jacob Kyle, my little Kyle. He's six months old. I'm in Orlando, Florida. The father of my child is supposed to be here with me but I found out that he's married and won't leave his wife. I just need a place to stay and get things sorted out."

"Oh my! Yes, of course, you can stay with me. Call me when you get to the Houston Bus Station and I'll come to get you. Before you make the long trip, what about your parents? Won't they help?"

"My parents kicked me out of the house when they found out I was pregnant, so that answer would be, no."

"I'm not surprised, considering how the family treated me. So narrow-minded! You just hop on that ole bus and come see me. Auntie Lotus will take good care of you!"

"Thank you, Aunt Lotus, you're a lifesaver. See you soon!"

Charlene hung up the receiver and felt a surge of confidence. Kyle had woken up hungry and she stepped into the restroom, nursing him. After he had suckled his fill, Charlene called the Orlando bus station discovering there was one bus leaving for Houston at midnight. She called a cab and drank her coffee while she waited. Ten minutes later, the cab pulled out front. Charlene paid for the coffee and the cabby rushed her to the bus station. Jacob had given Charlene some money to purchase Christmas presents for little Kyle and Carla. Fortunately, she hadn't spent it all. There was enough to cover the cost of the bus ticket.

Sleeping off and on through the next 24 hours, Charlene and little Kyle made it to the Houston Bus Station. Charlene had the chance to eat along the way to keep up her energy and keep little Kyle content. She called her Aunt Lotus from the bus station payphone and 30 minutes later she arrived, pulling up in a black t-bird.

"Charlene!! This must be my nephew, Jacob Kyle. *Your* little Kyle. He is just adorable! Welcome to Houston!" Aunt Lotus smiled, "Let's get you two back to my place, get you fed and off to bed. You're gonna need some sleep, that was a long trip!"

Back in Orlando, Jacob called Carla's house on Christmas morning.

"She's gone? What do you mean gone, Mom?" Jacob asked, stunned at what he heard.

"I woke up in the morning and Charlene had taken little Jacob Kyle and left sometime during the night. She's gone, Jacob! And, I don't know where! No note, no nothing!" Carla cried.

"I'll call John and Alice, maybe they know something. Gone…?" Jacob just couldn't get his head around it.

"That's not our only crisis at the moment. How is Ava doing?" Carla asked, carefully.

"She's doing much better. I'm bringing her home from the hospital later today. The doctors say her new medication caused a delayed reaction that made her deathly ill. They've given her a different drug and she seems to be adjusting."

"Well, that's some good news. Let me know as soon as you find anything out about Charlene and my grandson!" Carla hung up the receiver, finding herself frantic with concern.

Jacob was in shock. He knew Charlene would be angry that he couldn't make it to spend Christmas with her and Jacob Kyle, but he thought she would understand. Too late, he realized how very wrong he was. He called John and then Alice, but neither had heard anything from Charlene. She had simply vanished, taking his son with her.

Chapter Twenty-Five

Two days had passed since Charlene took her little Kyle and disappeared from the lives of Jacob and his mother Carla. Although still somewhat exhausted, Charlene was adjusting. In short order, she managed to regain her confidence and control with her Aunt Lotus in Houston. The retreat to this, a metropolis, large enough that one could literally disappear without a trace, was preciously what Charlene thought she needed.

"I see you're back with the living. I thought you two were going to sleep forever! You must be famished. Get dressed. I'm taking you two out to breakfast. By the way, Happy 18th Birthday!" Lotus gave her a hug and smiled. "You're officially no longer a minor! We are going to celebrate tonight!" A single birthday had never passed for Charlene or her sisters without receiving a card from Aunt Lotus. Charlene's eyes lit up at the realization. With her life being so crazy, she'd forgotten it was the 27th of December, her 18th birthday. Thinking to herself, "I'm of legal age! No one can take my baby from me now!" That epiphany filled Charlene with a sense of purpose and power she desperately needed.

After breakfast, Charlene told Aunt Lotus about her crazy life. Lotus listened intently, asking questions here and there throughout the conversation. She shook her head in amazement, "I thought I had a crazy life starting out here in Houston. Sweetheart, you take the cake! It sounds like you've learned so many lessons the hard way, especially about men in general. You're right, they only want one thing. I wish you would have shown up on my doorstep a year ago. You might not have had to go through so much heartache."

"Well, I'm here now."

"That you are and, it's never too late to teach you new lessons in life so you don't have to continue learning them the hard way."

Charlene found her Aunt Lotus's carefree lifestyle refreshing. She was nothing like JoAnn, besides a slight resemblance, Charlene couldn't believe they were sisters.

Lotus Odimier, at 35, was as vibrant and feisty as ever. She learned early on that if women were going to make it in the world, they had to work twice as hard as men. Lotus made a name for herself and enjoyed a very profitable career as a burlesque fan dancer. She was frowned upon by the upper-class women whose husbands paid to watch her dance in the upscale nightclubs throughout the bustling downtown district. Lotus lived up to her namesake. She was as intoxicating as the fruit from the Greek mythological flower. With her long curly red hair, dark brown bedroom eyes, mischievous smile and body most women would die for, she could lure even the most devoted man. They would lose all sense of space and time, mesmerized, as she danced in the spotlight, naked behind her fans.

That evening, there was a knock at the front door. Lotus opened it and a young woman entered.

"Charlene, this is my friend, Nancy. She's great with kids and has offered to babysit little Kyle while you and I go paint the town for your birthday." Lotus grinned.

"Pleasure to meet you." Nancy held out her hand and Charlene shook it, a little uncertain about leaving her little Kyle with a stranger.

Lotus saw the concern in Charlene's eyes. "Don't worry Charlene, Nancy here works with me. She's a dancer, too, and a damn good one, I might add. I can vouch for her. She's done her share of babysitting for our dance company."

"Yes, I have. A few of the dancers have children. There were five of us in my family and since I was the eldest, I pretty much raised my siblings." Nancy took Kyle from Charlene and he instantly took to her, laughing as she tickled him. "Aren't you the little heartbreaker!" Nancy exclaimed.

"Okay then, I guess we'll get going," Charlene conceded, "I love you Kyle, Mommy will be back soon. You be good for Nancy."

In her T-bird, Lotus lit a cigarette and she offered one to Charlene.

"Oh, thank you but I don't smoke." Charlene smiled.

Lotus took a drag, "Nasty habit so, don't go starting." She laughed.

"So, where are we going?" Charlene asked.

"I think we'll go to the Paradise Club. I dance there now and then. It's a high-class joint with some nice clientele." Lotus remarked.

Twenty minutes later, the ladies walked into the front entrance of the club.

"We're here to celebrate my niece, Charlene! It's her 18th birthday!" Lotus exclaimed.

Drinks were purchased and the party ran into the night. Lotus noticed a good-looking cowboy had been eyeing Charlene all night and that she had been flirting with him also.

"Let's go powder our noses." Lotus got up, took Charlene's arm and went into the bathroom.

"I see some sparks flying between you and that cowboy leaning against the bar," Lotus remarked touching up her lipstick.

"He is cute. It's been a while since I've had any interest in anyone. It must be the drinks affecting my judgment, I do feel a bit tipsy." She giggled.

"Oh, there's nothing wrong with your judgment, Hon! He is defiantly cute and interested in you. How long has it been since you've been with a man?"

"Not since I found out I was pregnant with little Kyle."

Lotus smiled, "You're way overdue then. It sounds like you need some "special" attention. Charlene, it's up to you, but let me tell you something. As you know, men are after one thing. Most of them are looking for experience, notches on their gun, check marks in their little black books. Call it whatever you want. They're just sowing their wild oats. Here's something to think about. They want experience. You don't just have to give it away. If the opportunity arises, make them pay for it. It's a win, win, especially if you enjoy the sex. I'm not saying you should be a whore. I'm just saying that we have what they want. If you can find a way, take advantage of it. Keep that in mind." Lotus dug through her purse and gave

Charlene, a handful of condoms. "I wish someone would have given you these a long time ago. You probably wouldn't have little Kyle, not that he isn't beautiful, you just don't need another one, right now." Lotus held up the condom waving it. "Make that cowboy put this on before things get going too far; that way you can have fun and not pay the consequences. Oh, and you don't have to fall in love with him, even if the sex is amazing. It's just sex. A little something to get you through the night."

Charlene nodded and smiled. "It's been way too long and I miss the feeling of being loved, even if it's just for the night."

"Then go get him! There's a romp room upstairs. I'm in no hurry to leave. Hell! I might just get a little myself."

Two hours later both, Charlene and Lotus left the club, smiling. Charlene's hair was a mess and she was totally relaxed. "I so needed that!" She purred.

"You enjoyed your birthday and had fun with your cowboy? What's his name?"

"Who cares. I just called him Cowboy!" Charlene giggled.

"Exactly, you're learning. Oh, and you used the protection I gave you, yes?" Lotus asked.

"Yes, we did. How about you, did you have fun?" Charlene asked, hinting.

Lotus smiled wickedly, "Yes, of course, I always do."

Charlene settled in with Lotus with no intentions of ever going back to Michigan. She'd found someone who actually understood her. Lotus validated that how she was living, was fine. Two weeks had passed when Lotus asked while they were lounging on the back deck.

"Does anyone know that you're here?"

"No, no one knows. I believe it's for the best, at least until things settle down a bit. I'd like to let my best friend Alice know. She's probably going out of her mind wondering what happened to me."

"From what you've told me, it's probably best you don't let anyone know your location. You could call Alice and let her know you and Kyle are all right, just don't tell her where you are. That way, if Jacob does contact her, she can say honestly, she doesn't know." Lotus suggested.

Charlene agreed and dialed Alice's number.

"Greensboro residence, this is Alice speaking."

Charlene paused and let out the breath she'd been holding. "Hi Alice, it's me."

"Oh my God! Charlene, are you all right? Where are you? Mom went down to check on the house and you weren't anywhere around. She checked with Ruth McGuire and she's also very worried since she hasn't heard from you. Ruth said something about you leaving a note saying you were taking care of a sick relative?" Alice questioned worriedly.

"Little Kyle and I are okay. I can't tell you where I am in case Jacob is looking for me. I'll explain someday. Try not to worry about us."

"Jacob has already called me, twice. I've been honest, I haven't heard from you and I don't have any idea where you are."

"Trust me, it's better this way. I'm not sure when I'll be able to call again."

"Well, at least write me a note now and then. Send me pictures of my Godson, I bet little Kyle's growing."

"I'll try. Again, don't worry about us, we're in good hands. I've got to go, Love you."

"Love you, too. Please be careful."

Charlene hung up the receiver, "There. I feel better, I was right, she was worried about us."

Lotus nodded, "I've got an idea, maybe we should dye your hair. Pick a color, any color!"

"I've been a blonde all my life. How about black? Maybe cut my hair short?" Charlene questioned as she ran her fingers through her long hair.

"Wow, a whole new look, I like it. Let's get to work!"

Lotus got out her scissors and a bottle of black hair dye. An hour later, she handed Charlene a mirror. Staring back at her was a completely different woman. Lotus cut her hair into a pixie and dyed it jet black. Her long blonde locks were gone. Charlene teased what was left of her hair. Charlene decided she could handle having her hair short for a while and that it would be easier to take care of, knowing it would be a lot cooler in the Houston heat.

"I love it!" She exclaimed.

"This hairstyle really looks good on you!" Lotus beamed.

"Can we take some pictures with little Kyle and me?"

"Sure. What are you thinking?"

"Well, how about across the street and down the block? The grounds are so well groomed."

"What, the cemetery? That's creepy!"

"We could use the gravestones as a backdrop. I really like that large tall oak tree that sits in the middle. I could lean against it with little Kyle playing in front of me. Let me get into some nicer clothes."

Charlene went and changed into a black dress that fanned out around her. She picked up her little Kyle and the three of them walked to the cemetery. Lotus took several pictures with her 35mm camera. She agreed. By having Charlene sit on the ground with her back against the oak tree and little Kyle in front of her, the gravestones made for a unique backdrop.

On Monday, Charlene took the film in to be developed and picked it up the following Thursday. She chose her favorite photo; she turned it over and started writing a note on the back to Alice. She stopped. Then, taking a page out of Jacob's playbook, Charlene thought, "Charlene Elizabeth Strypher." She stared at her middle name, Elizabeth. Breaking it down, she came up with possibilities for a new name; Liz, Liza and Beth. Deciding on Liz, she wrote a note on the back of the picture to Alice. *The New Me! Love, Liz and your godson, Little Kyle. 1/20/63.* She addressed an envelope to Alice and Walter with the picture enclosed, then stamped and mailed it.

Charlene discussed her idea for a new name with Lotus.

"It would make it harder for Jacob to find you." Lotus had connections in Houston that helped her create a fake I.D. She snapped close-up facial shots of Charlene, and in two weeks, Charlene Elizabeth Stryper became Elizabeth Marie Baker, birthdate 3/22/38, age 24, with a Houston, Texas address.

"Hello, Liz Baker. Welcome home," Lotus played along. She smiled and handed her the driver's license. "Get used to using your new name so you don't slip up."

Charlene smiled, speaking her name aloud, "Elizabeth Marie Baker. Hello, I'm Liz Baker, a pleasure to meet you, and this is my son…" She thought for a second, "Edward? Eddie." Charlene grinned, "Liz Baker is a rather simple name but I can get used to it. Thank you, Aunt Lotus!" Charlene gave her a hug and put her new I.D. in her purse.

In the months to come, Charlene watched little Kyle develop. After mastering crawling, he began to pull himself up to stand, wabbling then falling down on his butt, crying at his failure. Then, he would pull himself back up and try again. The first week of April, Kyle took his first steps at the coaxing of Charlene and Lotus.

From January through June, Charlene sent pictures of her and little Kyle to Alice, writing notes on the back. Short correspondences to let her friend know they were all right, and, so she would have pictures of her godson.

Lotus and Charlene celebrated little Kyle's 1st birthday with a party at The Paradise Club. All of the dancers, with their families, attended. Colorful balloons decorated the bar and everyone wore little pointed birthday hats. They sang "Happy Birthday" as Kyle smashed his first birthday cake. He received more presents than he could play with.

Life was good for Charlene and little Kyle. Lotus loved having her niece and nephew living with her and thought of Charlene as her younger sister. She convinced Charlene to settle down with her permanently in Houston. The next two years slipped by; celebrating holidays and birthdays together, including living it up in the Houston nightlife. Nancy would babysit little Kyle now and then when Lotus and Charlene had the itch to go out on the town. Their night would often end up at the Paradise Club, upstairs in the Romp Room, sharing partners and faking love. Some nights Charlene would watch Lotus dance naked behind her fans. It truly was an art form all its own, and she could see why men couldn't resist the power Lotus had over them.

Monday, May 18th, 1964

Charlene braved the Houston heat and drove down to her favorite bakery to get morning doughnuts for Lotus, herself and little Kyle. She walked in and noticed a businessman dressed in a black suit and tie. Seated next to the window, he pulled his fedora down appearing to be reading the morning newspaper. As Charlene walked past, he looked up and spoke in a questioning tone, "Charlene? Is that you?" Not knowing the man, she acted like she hadn't heard him and proceeded to the counter. She placed her order and paid for it. Charlene's hands began to shake as she attempted to calm her nerves. Looking straight forward, she turned and the man rose from his chair, "Let me get the door for you, Miss." He commented, staring at her inquisitively.

Charlene faked a smile and nodded, "Thank you, Sir," and walked out the door. She was unnerved and rattled as she got into Lotus's T-Bird. Letting out a breath, she started the engine and pulled onto the road. Charlene noticed the man walk out and stand on the sidewalk, watching her as she drove by. In one hand, he held an 8x10 photograph. In the other, a brown leather briefcase. Charlene drove past Lotus's house, around the block then to the next block, checking her rearview mirrors. After circling the area for ten minutes, and satisfied she didn't have a tail, Charlene parked across the street and two houses down from Lotus. She walked into the kitchen, panicking as she closed the door behind her. Peeking through the blinds one last time at the street, Charlene found Lotus holding Kyle.

"I think they've found me!" Lotus could hear the distress in her voice. Charlene was gripping the bag of donuts so hard, that they were most certainly squished.

"Try to calm down. Who found you? What's going on?" Lotus asked.

"At the bakery. There was this man dressed in a black business suit. When I walked by, he called out, "Charlene is that you?" I didn't know him so I acted like I hadn't heard him. I walked past him and placed my order. On the way out he got up and opened the door for me. It was unnerving, Lotus! When I left, he was standing on the sidewalk watching me drive by. He had a picture in one hand and a brown leather briefcase in the other. How did they find me and why now?! It's been years. I was sure Jacob had given up!" Charlene began to hyperventilate, and shake uncontrollably.

"Here, sit down Charlene, slow your breathing, you'll be okay." Lotus set little Kyle down on the table and pulled out a kitchen chair. She guided Charlene into it, concerned that she might pass out.

"Okay, let's put our plan into action." Lotus retrieved an envelope from her secretary's desk in the living room. Inside the envelope, they had stashed five one-hundred-dollar bills. She called the airline to make sure there was a seat available.

"Yes, I need to secure a seat on the first flight out to Detroit. Yes, today. Flight 2281, flying out at 1:00 p.m.? Yes, thank you, she'll be there." She hung up the receiver. Lotus and Charlene had a plan in place. If there the threat arose that Jacob had found her in Houston, she would fly to Detroit under her fake I.D. and stay with Florence until things cooled off. The thought of Charlene flying back to Detroit wouldn't make sense and they hoped to throw Jacob off. Detroit was the last place Charlene would turn up. Hiding in plain sight, where she was least expected to be, just might work. Lotus devised a plan to further throw Jacob off if he ever contacted her or the crew at the Paradise Club, by telling him that Charlene went to Los Angles for work. If by chance Jacob was watching Alice's mail, Lotus had a friend postmark a letter to Alice from Los Angles. She wrote Charlene's name with a fake address in the return-to-sender spot.

"Okay Charlene, let's get you and Kyle to the airport. I'll call Florence once you're on the plane so she can pick you up." Lotus coaxed, shaking Charlene out of her panicked state.

At the airport Charlene fought back tears, "I'm going to miss you, Aunt Lotus!" She cried.

"Now, now. It won't be forever, just for now. I'll miss you, too. Everyone down at the Paradise Club will miss you. Take care of yourself and my nephew." Lotus knelt down and kissed Kyle. Then she stood and hugged Charlene. Tears rolled down her cheeks.

"Be careful and call me when you get settled in with Florence. Remember, there are a lot of people who love you and are watching out for you. You're not alone. I love you. Oh, and remember to stay protected," Lotus winked, smiled, and kissed Charlene on the cheek.

"Thank you for everything, Aunt Lotus. I'll call you

soon. Love you." She picked up Kyle, and walked to boarding gate 3, handing her ticket to the agent. Over the airport intercom, the speakers crackled, "Paging, Charlene Strypher. Please come to Gate 26. Your flight to Los Angles is boarding." Looking over her shoulder, Liz Baker smiled and waved to Lotus Odimier as she and her son, Eddie, boarded the flight to Detroit.

Lotus watched as the jumbo jet rose into the air under a hazy and hot Houston afternoon. From her house, she called Florence.

"Hi Florence, It's Lotus. We've had to initiate our exit plan. She'll be landing in about three hours making it 4 p.m. your time."

"Okay, I'll be waiting to pick her up, Thank you."

Lotus hung up the receiver, smiling to herself. "I think we've got all the bases covered. Let's hope they take the bait, at least it will throw a monkey wrench into their pursuit." When she was at the airport with Charlene and little Kyle, as they were checking in, she walked down to the far end of the terminal where the flight to LAX was preparing to board. Pulling a $20.00 bill out of her purse she spoke briefly to the gate attendant. The announcement was simple and the gate attendant appreciated the tip.

Chapter Twenty-Six

Back in Harbor Cove, Jacob paced behind the bar at Vic's. Joe sat on a barstool watching him.

"You're gonna wear out my mat behind the bar if you keep pacing."

Jacob nodded, "Okay, I just can't get my head around all of this. Agent, #4 in Houston thought he had her. All he had to do was identify her and bring her in. He said that it wasn't a positive I.D. The woman drove off in a black T-Bird, he lost her in traffic and didn't get the license plate. Damn! She could be anywhere by now!" Jacob cursed.

"You had agents watching the bus terminal and the airport, did they turn anything up?" John asked.

"Maybe. Agent #6 said he thought he heard her name being called over the intercom at the airport. Something about boarding a flight to LAX. By the time he got to the gate the plane was taxing down the runway. It will be a pain in the ass to get ahold of the flight manifest to see if she made the flight. You know how much red tape our friends at the bureau like to wrap us up in. I'm starting to think this fucking game of cat and mouse is becoming more than it's worth! I'm running out of patience and manpower. Getting short on funds also. There's Ava's treatment program in D.C. and that isn't cheap. On top of everything, Director Marshall is hinting toward another mission for the crew. I don't know how much more of all this I can take." Jacob ran his hands through his hair and let out a long sigh.

"If this is becoming so unbearable, why continue? I mean look at yourself! Man, you're a fucking wreck! Maybe it's not worth all the effort after all?" John questioned.

"Oh, it's worth the effort. Charlene's taken our son and is keeping me from him. All I want is to see Jacob Kyle and be part of his life. He's the son that Ava and I could never have and I know having him in our lives would help her feel complete. I won't give up."

"How is Ava doing?" John asked.

"She hanging in there. The treatments seem to be helping. It's all experimental, but if it works as planned, the doctor says Ava should live a healthy life. Much longer than then he originally projected."

"Well, that's a plus. See? Just put a positive spin on it, things will work out."

"Nice try John. I appreciate your candor."

"So, what's the plan?" John asked.

Jacob shrugged, "Same as always. Keep our ears open, ask a few questions to see if anyone has heard from her. I'll keep leaning on her friend, Alice. If she knows anything, I'll get her to crack, eventually. Right now, she's not speaking and she might not know where Charlene is. I underestimated Charlene, she's a smart girl. Anyway, I'm due back in D.C. this afternoon. Drive me to the airfield. I have a flight to catch."

Florence arrived at Detroit Metropolitan Airport shortly before 4 p.m. She scanned through the passengers deboarding the plane, twice. Then, she spotted her. Charlene had a black scarf tied around her hair and wore a pair of dark sunglasses. She held her son on her hip. Spotting Florence, she gave a little wave.

"Oh, my goodness! I would not have recognized you if you hadn't waved at me." She gave Charlene a hug. "So, this is your little one. Hello Kyle, you sure are a handsome young man." Kyle grinned, then played shy, looking down at his teddy bear.

Charlene picked up her luggage and they drove to Florence's.

"I've got you set up in my bedroom downstairs. That way we won't have to be worrying about Kyle and the steps," Florence commented.

"Good thinking. Thank you for letting us stay with you on such short notice."

"It's no problem. Like I've said, Charlene, you'll always be family." Florence smiled.

Alice and Walter came by that evening to welcome Charlene and little Kyle back to Detroit.

"Oh, my goodness, you look so different! Love your hairstyle and that dark tan you have going on. It looks amazing. I have missed you!" Alice hugged Charlene.

"I've missed you, too. It's been so long!" Charlene exclaimed.

Florence walked into the formal living room with Kyle in her arms. "Check out this little man. Isn't he the handsome one?"

"Yes, he is!" Alice reached out taking Kyle from Florence. "We need to get reacquainted, little man. I'm your Godmother and it's been a long time since I held you. Wow, you've grown, and look at this curly blonde hair!" Alice ran her hand through Kyle's ringlets and curls, then tickled him. He giggled and squirmed in her arms.

"My little Kyle will be three-years-old next month! He is such a joy, and really good-natured. A little shy around men, so don't feel bad Walter. He's just been around women more. Give him time and he'll warm up to you."

They spent the evening catching up on each other's lives. Alice and Walter purchased a home in Plymouth, a suburb of Detroit.

"It's a thirty-minute drive to the office but traffic usually flows smoothly," Walter commented. Little Kyle had been eyeing Walter and started to warm up to him by playing peek-a-boo around the corner of the sofa.

Alice smiled, "I'm still helping Mom with her fashion company. We moved her boutique to a larger location in Midtown, off Woodward Avenue. You'll need to come by and check it out sometime. "

"Most definitely." Charlene recounted the past couple of years in Houston with her Aunt Lotus. "I really like it in Houston. It gets a bit hot in the summer months but everyone has air conditioning so it's not unbearable. Once all this with Jacob calms down, I plan to move back."

"What are you going to do until then?" Alice asked.

Charlene smiled, "Well I've been thinking a lot lately. First off, I want to go back to school and get my diploma. Then, go find that secretary position I've always wanted. I need to start making it on my own. It will give me a sense of purpose in life."

"Good for you, Charlene!" Alice, Walter, and Florence praised her decision.

Florence thought for a moment, "I have a girl down at my boutique that helps me set up my fashion shows. Her name is Maureen. She had to quit school when she got pregnant in her senior year, also. Maureen told me that she took a night school program and had her diploma in a matter of months. I'll ask her how it works if you'd like."

Charlene answered excitedly, "Yes, please. If the program only lasts a couple of months, I could be working by as early as September!"

The next day, Florence got all the information from Maureen and passed it on to Charlene. The classes were to start on Monday, June 15th. Charlene would have to take the intercity bus to and from the school. Florence agreed to watch little Kyle while Charlene attended class.

From her first class on June 15th to her last class on August 15th Charlene devoted every spare moment to studying and polishing up her secretarial skills. It had been two years since she worked diligently on her typing and although she was out of practice, it didn't take long to get it back up to speed. Once she received her diploma, she began searching through the help wanted ads and going on interviews. In September, she noticed an ad for a legal secretary/ personal assistant at the law firm of Stevens, Corman and Woodworth in downtown Detroit. She called the law office and set up a 9 a.m. interview with Mr. Dan Corman, the second partner in the firm. Charlene perused through

Florence's extensive wardrobe, selecting a professional-looking black dress that accentuated her hips and breasts. Not too much but, enough to catch the eye. She had kept her pixie haircut and continued to keep it black, mainly because she liked the look and it was easy to style. Charlene finished applying her makeup and stood back from the mirror, smiling approvingly. Florence allowed her to take the car to the interview so she didn't have to walk far.

Arriving 15 minutes early, Charlene walked through the oversized brass and glass doors at the law firm. She introduced herself to the petite, professionally dressed, blonde front desk receptionist. "Charlene Strypher to see Mr. Corman, I have an interview."

"Welcome Miss Strypher, I'll page Mr. Corman to let him know you are here."

Twenty minutes ticked away on the clock. The door opened to an inner office and Mr. Dan Corman stepped out. Larger than life, he towered over Charlene, bulky and aging. More gray than black hair was slicked back over his balding crown. Tired blue eyes with crow's feet permanently etched at the corners, wrinkled when he smiled through coffee/tobacco-stained teeth under a pencil-thin mustache.

He cleared his throat. "Hello Charlene. I'm Dan Corman, the second partner in this firm. Come on into my office."

Charlene stood and nodded, "Thank you for the opportunity to speak with you regarding the position."

Dan Corman nodded giving her body an appreciative look, "Certainly, please have a seat."

Charlene sat across the ornate black walnut desk. Stacks of paperwork, files, cigarette butts overflowing in the ashtray and rock glasses half-filled with week-old whiskey, covered the desk surface.

"Pardon the mess. I lost my personal assistant a couple of weeks back," Mr. Corman stated.

"No problem," Charlene replied, uncertain what to think.

Mr. Corman leaned back in his chair. "Our firm works mostly with personal injury law and I travel a lot, sometimes with my personal assistant, and sometimes not. I need someone that can keep up in the courtroom with shorthand and be able to type with speed and accuracy. Help with filing and keep me ready for the courtroom. Think you can handle that?"

Charlene nodded, "I average 60 words per minute typing and 70 words per minute in shorthand with outstanding accuracy. I was top of my class in both. I have experience in bookkeeping and filing, as well."

"Impressive. How are you at making coffee?" He laughed, loudly.

Charlene responded with a smile, "I make an awesome cup. Do you take your coffee black or with cream and sugar?"

Dan Corman slapped his big hand down on the top of the desk and let out a laugh, startling Charlene. "I think you'll do nicely. We can discuss pay and benefits after you fill out some paperwork. When can you start?"

"I can start whenever you want me to!" Charlene exclaimed excitedly.

"Great, let's get the paperwork done. Donna, our receptionist, will take you through the orientation and you can start tomorrow at 8 a.m." Mr. Corman raised up from his seat, offering his hand, "Congratulations and welcome to Stevens, Corman and Woodworth."

Charlene stood, his hand engulfed hers as she shook it. "Thank you, Mr. Corman. I'll see you tomorrow morning at 8 a.m., sharp."

At the front desk, Donna smiled and handed her a packet containing an in-depth application, code of conduct booklet, benefits information and government tax forms.

"Please, fill these out completely and bring the packet back with you tomorrow morning. By the way, I'm Donna. Welcome to the team."

"Nice to meet you. I'm Charlene and thank you!"

The next day, Mr. Corman reviewed Charlene's paperwork before he set her to work cleaning his office. "After reviewing your skills and experience, I've decided to start you at $4,600.00 a year. There are quarterly bonuses you can earn that hinge on your performance reviews. We offer health insurance and retirement should you choose to take advantage of them. Any questions?"

"Yes. You mentioned that you take your personal assistant with you out of town for court cases. How often do we go out of town? I have a three-year-old, my son Kyle. I do have childcare lined up, however, a schedule would be helpful, if at all possible, so I can be prepared."

"That won't be an issue. I can give you a monthly schedule. I won't take you out of town for a couple of months. You need to be trained in our filing system, transposing notes, clerical duties and in general, how things work around here."

"Okay. That sounds good. Thank you!" Charlene replied.

"Today, I'd like you to file this stack of paperwork and clean things up a bit. You'll find I have issues with keeping my office tidy..." Mr. Corman gave a hearty laugh as he worked on a case file.

Charlene set to work cleaning Mr. Corman's office, doing her best not to disturb him while he was working. She filed away the stack of paperwork on his desk and began rearranging its overall contents. There was a 5x7 frame that was lying face down on the desk that was under the stack of paperwork. Charlene wiped it down with her dust cloth and gave it a brief look. The picture was of Dan smiling with a captain's hat on his head. A woman was tucked in between Dan and another man that looked like he might be his brother. The woman was holding out a bottle of champagne and they stood in front of a sleek red and white sailboat. Dan glanced up from his case file.

"That's my Catamaran, *Due Process*." He chuckled and grinned proudly, "I purchased her a couple of years back."

"Very nice. Who's standing with you?"

"My brother, Gerald, and his wife, Meredith. They were visiting the day I had the boat delivered. We smashed the bottle of champagne across the bow. Good times!" He smiled and went back to reading his case file.

Charlene set the picture aside and wiped down the rest of the desktop. Dusting the bookcase behind the desk, she admired the leather-bound law books. By the end of the day, the office was spotless and Charlene was proud of her accomplishments. She rode the intercity transit bus to Florence's house. Florence had enjoyed the day, babysitting Kyle.

"There's my little guy!" Charlene smiled, picking him up. Kyle grinned back and squealed with excitement, happy that his mother had arrived home.

"How was he with me being gone?" Charlene asked.

"Kyle was an angel. A little cranky at first but, it didn't take long and he was happily playing with his toys. He ate his breakfast and lunch and then took a nap. So, how did your first day go?" Florence inquired.

"First day went well. Mostly I cleaned and filed. There's a lot to learn but I'm sure I'll be able to handle the job. My boss, Mr. Corman, set me up with a starting salary of $4,600.00 a year plus a quarterly bonus, insurance and retirement plan. I'm going to start looking for an apartment and a nanny to take care of little Kyle. I really appreciate your helping out but I understand you have your own life and a business to run." Charlene remarked.

"I don't mind helping out, Dear. But, you're right. I do have a business to run. The wage he set you up with should be enough for you to get an apartment and someone to watch Kyle. If you're lucky, you might find a place close enough to work so you wouldn't have to ride the bus."

"Let's hope. The bus is okay but there are some pretty shady characters that hop on and off along the route."

Charlene found an apartment a week later within walking distance from the firm. Upstairs, with her hands full of groceries and little Kyle at her side, she fumbled with her keys trying to open her door, when a neighbor stepped out into the hall.

"Hello. You must be the new tenant in our building. Here, let me help you with that." A woman, looking to be in her late 60s, walked over and caught the bag of groceries just as it was about to fall out of Charlene's hands.

"Thank you! Yes, my son Kyle and I just moved in. I'm Charlene Strypher."

"Pleasure to meet you. I'm Wanda Blake. I live at the end of the hall, apartment 327.

Is it just you and your son? Is there a Mister Strypher?"

Charlene laughed, "No mister here. Just me and little Kyle. I just started working for the Stevens, Corman, and Woodworth law firm, down the block on the corner."

"Yes, I know where that is. You're lucky to have found a place so close to your job. Who watches your son while you're at work?" Wanda asked.

"Well, actually, I'm looking for someone to help with that. Florence, my best friend's mother, has been helping me but she has her business to run and it's become a real inconvenience for her. Any chance you know someone who be interested?"

"I might. My husband passed away a few months back. I pretty much just spend my time reading and watching T.V. I'd love to take care of your little one for you. He'd give me something better to do with my time. Come on down to my apartment after you get settled. We'll have some tea and talk more about it." Wanda smiled.

They spent the evening in Wanda's apartment. While little Kyle played with his teddy bear and little toy cars, Wanda and Charlene drank tea and shared stories. Mostly, Wanda shared stories with Charlene. She was quite the talker, admitting she was lonely since her Myron passed away. "He had been sick for quite some time; the cancer finally took him. We were married for almost 40 years."

"Did you have any children?"

"Yes, a son." Wanda let out a long sigh, "We lost him in the war...," her voice trailed off.

"I'm so sorry for your loss."

"Thank you. Sometimes, you just have to accept the hand that life deals you and play it the best you can."

"So, would you be available to watch my little Kyle while I work? You'd really be helping me out." Charlene pleaded.

"I'd be delighted!" Wanda agreed.

Things were really looking up for Charlene; a new job with a good wage, child care for little Kyle and an apartment close enough to walk to work. She slowly but surely let her guard down and began to breathe.

Chapter Twenty-Seven

"That's the last bag," Ava called.

Jacob closed the trunk, walked around and opened the door for her. "Well, I guess it's time we head to the airport."

"Yes, I'm grateful that Director Marshall gave you some time off, a month will do you some good. Us some good."

"The Fall colors will be brilliant from Harbor Cove all the way up the shoreline. It will be nice to get away from the craziness of Washington D.C."

Ava's doctor suggested that she and Jacob take a vacation together. A place where there was fresh air and a less stressful environment. Ava was in remission. There had been a breakthrough in the experimental treatment for her condition. Although she was not completely out of the woods, Ava was feeling stronger than she had in years. There was color in her cheeks and she began to gain some of her weight back.

"I actually feel like my old self again and I'm looking forward to this time together," Ava exclaimed.

They had worked through Jacobs's affair, emotions and feelings of betrayal. Ava was able to forgive his indiscretions.

She wondered what Jacob's son looked like and had a genuine concern for the boy. A young mother trying to raise a child on her own? To Ava, that was unheard of. It had been over three years since Jacob told her about Kyle. Driving through the fog of emotions, she pushed away the anger that would normally wreck any chance of reconciliation. Instead, Ava made one request. "Get the child. Do whatever it takes. We'll raise him as our own. He'll look like you and we'll have a son. It will make our life complete and we can give him the future that his teenage mother will never be able to." Ava's request drove Jacob on a relentless search for Charlene and his son.

They landed at Detroit Metropolitan Airport and John was waiting for them at the gate.

"Good to see both of you together. It's been too long!" John gave Ava a hug and a kiss on the cheek.

"Yes, it has. You're looking good. How have you been, John?" Ava asked.

"I'm doing well, thank you. As for my looking good, you should have your eyes checked. You're the one that is looking good." John smiled.

"Thank you, John, that's very kind. I am feeling better and hope this getaway is just what I need to continue to do so."

"Well, I've got a cozy little cabin located at the end of the point, waiting for the both of you. The sunsets are amazing and the maple trees are all ablaze." John opened the door for Ava as Jacob fired the engine in his convertible.

As they drove along the shoreline, Jacob considered stopping at the Refuge and decided to make the stop towards the end of their trip to confirm all was in order.

At Vic's, John poured top-shelf scotch into a couple of rock glasses for Jacob and himself. He knew better than to offer alcohol to Ava with all her medications. John poured a glass of chilled cranberry juice and added fresh-cut orange slices. He handed it to her, then raised his glass. "Cheers to good health, good friends and good scotch. May you enjoy your journey as much as your destination, wherever that may be."

Fall had descended upon Harbor Cove, bringing with it cooler weather. Frost warnings urged farmers to bring in the last of their crops. Aspens and birch trees turned golden along the point, intermingling among the red and orange leaves of the maples, all set against a backdrop of cedar and evergreen trees. They spent the majority of their vacation reconnecting and enjoying the Michigan shoreline, following it north, all the way to Mackinaw bridge. The color blazed along the highway offering a breathtaking view in all directions. In Mackinaw, they strolled along the street, enjoying the famous local fudge and other convections from little curio shops. They took the ferry over to Mackinaw Island and spent a night at the Grand Hotel. The next day, they rode around the island in a horse-drawn carriage under a bright blue, northern Michigan sky. From there they drove into the upper peninsula, taking in the sights at Sault Ste. Marie. At the Soo Locks, they watched long iron ore freighters negotiate the channels on their way from Lake Superior into Lake Huron. The last attraction was Tahquamenon State Park. The majestic Upper and Lower Tahquamenon Falls roared, sending amber-colored water down the Tahquamenon River. The views left Ava and Jacob speechless lost in the serenity.

"What causes the water to look so amber?" Ava questioned.

Jacob read from the brochure he'd picked up at the park station. "The amber color is tannic acid from cedar and hemlock swamp areas that feed into the river water. It is rather beautiful." Jacob commented, and Ava agreed.

While they were traveling, Jacob checked in a couple of times with John.

"Everything is quiet here and in D.C. Enjoy your vacation and don't rush to get back. I know how you are!" John playfully scolded.

They arrived back in Harbor Cove the third week of October.

"How was your vacation?" John questioned.

"It was amazing!" Ava answered. "We so needed to get away. The Fall colors along the way were stunning!

"You look a little tired Ava. Maybe we should go back to the cabin and relax," Jacob suggested.

"Yes, maybe we should. This trip has been a bit taxing. It's taken a lot out of me. Luckily, we still have a week left. I promise I won't take too much time to rest up. There are still some things I'd like to see in the city." Ava remarked. Jacob drove her to their cabin overlooking Vickers Point Lighthouse. Setting in a chair in front of the crackling fireplace, Ava sipped a hot cup of tea.

"If it's okay with you, I'm going back to Vic's to catch up on things with John."

"That works, I'll do some reading and take a little nap cozied up here in front of the fire. I'll see you soon. Maybe tomorrow we can drive down into the city."

John looked up from the bar when Jacob entered, "How's Ava feeling?"

"She's worn down, but this trip has been so good for her, for us. After she naps, she'll be doing better. She wants to drive down to the city tomorrow. I know I'm not supposed to worry about work, but I'll stop by the Refuge and see what, if any, correspondence has come across from our Canadian contacts."

"You know, if you call in, Director Marshall will rip your ass for it." John laughed.

Jacob shrugged, "I'm at the end of my vacation so he won't get too ruffled. Especially if there's any important intel to share. Have you heard anything in regard to Charlene?"

John shook his head. "Not a peep. If you ask me, there's a good chance she is in L.A. You mentioned something about catching a glance at a letter from Charlene in Alice's mailbox. The return address was in Los Angles, right?

"Yes, but the trail's gone cold. It was over a month ago and the address was a post office box.

I guess what's nerve-racking, is how well she's been able to hide from me. I mean, we're operatives that carry out successful missions on foreign soil, with outcomes beyond comprehension and I can't find one girl with a child here in the good ole U.S.A?" Jacob shook his head. "It's fucking embarrassing!"

"Looks like the fox has been outfoxed." John laughed. "I'm sure she'll turn up somewhere, someday when you least expect it. And if she does, then what? Charlene's like twenty years old now, no longer a minor. There's no way you could take Kyle from her. Hell, she's probably married and living it up in suburbia, soaking up that California sun." John remarked sarcastically.

"All I want is to be able to see my son and be some small part of his life. Anything would be better than nothing. Even Ava wants that. I can't understand why that's too much to ask." Jacob looked defeated.

"Well, my friend, hopefully, it will all work out someday."

It was 7 p.m. when Jacob got back to the cabin. Ava was still asleep in the chair under a quilt she'd gotten off the bed. The fire had turned to ashes and only a few glowing embers remained.

Sunday morning, Ava awoke well rested. They ate breakfast at Vic's and started their last week of vacation. The weather had been better than they hoped for. They traveled under clear sunny skies.

On the way to the city, Jacob stopped by the Refuge. Ava waited in the car as she knew he wouldn't be long. Within minutes, Jacob locked the door behind him. In his hand, he held the brown leather briefcase.

In the city, Ava suggested they check out the Detroit Institute of Arts Museum in Midtown.

"Before we do, let's find a deli somewhere close. I'm hungry. So glad my appetite is back."

Jacob drove around the back of the museum and parked.

"I'm sure we can find a place to grab a bite near here. I'm going to bring my briefcase with me, there's a file I need to read."

Walking along Woodard Avenue, Ava and Jacob passed numerous boutiques, bookstores and shops. Ava spied a deli across from a small park. "How about there?" She pointed.

"Looks good to me," Jacob replied.

Dimitri's Deli was filled with patrons enjoying their

Sunday afternoon in Midtown. Ava took a number from the stand and stood waiting for it to be called. Jacob noticed a couple leaving and secured their table. It was next to the window that overlooked the park.

It just so happened that on that particular Sunday afternoon, Charlene and little Kyle were visiting Florence at her boutique

"I'm sorry. Alice won't be in today. She hasn't been feeling well the past week. I think she might be pregnant but Alice assures me she's not. As we know, time will tell," Florence laughed, and leaned into Charlene.

Charlene grinned, "Cute. You're right, time will tell. And, might I add, your boutique is beautiful!"

"Thank you, Dear! I love the location and business is much better here in Midtown."

There was a steady flow of customers and Florence made it a point to greet each one.

"It's a busy Sunday afternoon," Charlene remarked.

"Yes, it is. It's busier than I expected. Hey, Dimitri's Deli is just down the street, across from the park. Be a Dear and go get us lunch. I'd go with you but I can't break away, get whatever looks good, I'm not picky." Florence handed her a twenty.

As Charlene walked through the door at Dimitri's Deli, she noticed little Kyle was becoming restless. "Do you have to potty?" Charlene asked. Kyle nodded.

"Okay. I've got a number, come with me to the restroom." She took Kyles's hand and they walked to the back of the deli. In the lady's restroom, Charlene attended to Kyle. The door opened and a tall, thin woman with gray hair, tied back in a ponytail, walked up to the sink and washed her hands.

"What an adorable little girl you have!" She exclaimed.

"Thank you. Actually, he's a boy, I'm planning to get his hair cut this afternoon. He's long overdue for one." Charlene smiled and ran her fingers through Kyles's curls and ringlets that were almost touching his shoulders.

"Oh my! I'm sorry. My mistake. He's a cutie. My husband and I always wanted a child." She touched up her lipstick in the mirror.

"Why didn't you?" Charlene asked, making conversation.

"I found out years ago I couldn't have children."

Charlene felt terrible, "I'm so sorry."

Ava shrugged, "Life goes on and we make the best of things. I do love children, though."

Charlene nodded. "Well, we'd better get back to waiting for our number to be called. This place is really busy today."

"Why don't you join my husband and me? We're seated at a table with four chairs and it looks like it will be a while before they call either of our numbers."

"Are you sure? I wouldn't impose long. I'm planning to take my order to go."

"No problem at all. My husband won't mind and I'll enjoy your company.

As they walked up to the table, the woman smiled at her husband. "I met this young lady with her son in the restroom and invited her to sit with us since we have two empty chairs. I didn't catch your name, Dear."

Charlene replied, "I'm...," at the last second, she froze. Seated across the table from where she was standing, looking down at a file folder and taking a sip of water, sat Jacob.

"I'm Liz Baker, and you are?" She recovered.

"I'm Ava MacDonald and this is my husband, Jacob. It's a pleasure to meet you." Ava smiled.

Jacob looked up and the color drained from his face. He choked on his water as he recognized Charlene.

"Are you okay, Jacob? You look like you've seen a ghost," Ava asked, concerned.

Regaining control, after almost drowning himself, he tensed. In a hoarse whisper, he asked unbelieving, "Charlene?" Her response was clipped and cutting. "There is no Charlene. I am Liz Baker." Charlene glared. For a second their eyes locked and there was an audible silence as tempers rose.

Ava looked at Jacob and then Charlene, and back again. "You two know each other!" Instantly she put two and two together. She knelt down, eyes tearing up. "You must be little Kyle. Jacob has told me all about you. My goodness! You're the spitting image of your Daddy."

In his pure innocence, he replied smiling, "I'm Kyle."

Charlene cursed. "Damn!"

Ava could see emotions were beginning to escalate as the situation began to deteriorate, "This is a delicate matter. Jacob, Charlene, let's try to remain calm."

As Jacob tried to come out of his chair, Ava grabbed his arm, "Jacob, STOP! Charlene, please, sit down. We can all talk like civilized adults!"

Charlene wanted to bolt. Instead, she sat down across from Ava.

"Fine!" Charlene remarked with pure contempt in her voice, glaring at Jacob. She turned and smiled sweetly at Ava, "So, what would you like to talk about? How's this? I'm sorry, Ava. I didn't know he was married when we first met. He must have forgotten to mention it while he was fucking me. By the way, Jacob, do you even know how many children you have out there?" Charlene questioned sarcastically as she continued to glare.

"Listen here," Jacob snarled as he began to get up out of his chair, once again wanting to choke Charlene.

"Quit! Both of you! Jacob, sit back down! We need to stop this, now! From what I gather, you were both very much at fault back then. And now, here we are. Fighting will do no good!" Changing the direction of the conversation, doing her best to alleviate any further disagreement, Ava asked, "So, Charlene, do you live in the Detroit area?"

"No. I'm just visiting friends and family. I live in L.A. and am going back in a couple of days. I hear you live in Washington D.C." Charlene recovered quickly as she delivered her well-rehearsed ruse.

What brings you to Detroit?" Charlene asked, pulling Kyle onto her lap, protectively.

"Well, we decided to take the Fall Color Tour along the shoreline to reconnect. Due to Jacob's demanding profession, we haven't taken a trip together in years. The Director was kind enough to give us a month away from the hustle and bustle of D.C."

"Yes, the fall colors are breathtaking. Especially along Harbor Cove and Vickers Point where I grew up." Charlene agreed.

Jacob was struggling with the niceties. He ached from the palpable tension racking his mind and body. Trying to sort through the hundreds of scenarios in his head, he made a final attempt to be civilized and join the conversation. "Kyle sure has grown to be a handsome boy. Although, his hair is a little long. I barely recognized either of you."

Charlene offered a weak smile, "Yes, Kyle is growing up fast. Seems like only yesterday that I was holding our tiny baby. Now he's three years old."

Ava listened cautiously to their brief exchange and seized the opportunity. "Charlene, you mentioned that you were going to take Kyle to the barber shop this afternoon. I noticed the one on the corner. Is there any chance you might let Jacob take him? He'd so like to have a little time with his son. You and I could take our lunches and get to know one another better in the park across the street." Ava suggested, waiting patiently for her response.

Charlene looked at Jacob and saw the hint of hope in his eyes. Somehow, Ava had broken down her defenses. She wasn't the wicked, jealous other woman Charlene expected. Under other circumstances, they might even be friends. She sighed, "Well, Kyle is your son and I guess it would be okay. Just to the barbershop. Oh! Save one of his long curly ringlets for me. I want to put it in his baby book."

They ordered their sandwiches and walked across the street to the park. Jacob handed Ava his briefcase. Charlene hesitated as he took little Kyles's hand and they walked down the sidewalk to the barbershop.

"Let's go to that picnic table in the shade," Ava suggested.

They sat down across from each other. Charlene sat so she could keep the sidewalk in view and watch the barbershop.

Ava began, "Charlene, I know this has been overwhelming for you, for all of us. We don't have to be enemies."

Charlene replied curtly, "We'll, I can't see us being friends the way things are. I mean, with everything Jacob has put me through. His relentless pursuit has made me fear for my and Kyle's life. I've done everything I could think of. I changed my name, my appearance, my address, and my life and he's still found me. When does it stop?"

"Jacob has always been, and always will be, good at tracking. That's his specialty when it comes to his missions. However, this was pure happenstance that the two of you wound up in the same place, on the same day. He wasn't searching for you here in Detroit. In Houston, yes. Only because you created this game of cat and mouse. Please, try to understand, he only wants to see his son and somehow be part of his life. Despite his indiscretions, Jacob is a good and honorable man. He simply wants the best for Kyle."

"We are doing fine without him in our lives. He needs to understand that Kyle is mine. Maybe, if he would back off, I might see to it that he gets to visit now and then. I find it hard to believe he means me no harm."

"I'll tell you what. Here's my address and telephone number in Washington D.C. Feel free to call me anytime you feel threatened by Jacob and I'll handle it. In return, please keep in touch so we can set up a time for Jacob to see Kyle. He travels all over the country so, no matter where you are, I'm sure we can plan a visit. What do you think? Is that doable?" Ava asked, holding out the piece of paper she had written her address and telephone number on.

Charlene took the piece of paper and looked down at it. "Okay, I'll consider it but, no promises."

"Thank you, Charlene."

In the barbershop, Jacob set little Kyle in the chair. "This little man needs a haircut. His mother asked that you save a long curly ringlet of his blonde hair for his baby book. Make it two of them." Jacob smiled. Kyle sat still as his hair fell around him. The barber finished snipping and combed Kyle's hair. Then he turned the chair so it would face the wall mirror, and Kyle smiled, blue-gray eyes sparkling beneath his little boy's haircut. Jacob put one of the long curly locks in Kyle's blue jean pocket, "A little gift for Mommy." Kyle smiled, patting his pocket. Jacob put the other lock of hair in his own pocket then paid the barber.

On the walk back to the park, Jacob asked Kyle, "So little man, is there someone that your Mommy is living with? Maybe a man you call Daddy?"

Kyle shook his head no, "Wanda watches me while Mommy works."

"Who is Wanda, is she your babysitter?" Jacob questioned.

Kyle shook his head, yes, smiling.

Jacob asked, "So does Mommy work far from here?"

"She walks to work, it's hot," Kyle replied.

Jacob thought to himself, "Hot? In Houston, L.A.? How could he get Kyle to tell him what city?" Deciding Kyle probably didn't know, Jacob stopped questioning as they walked up to the park. Kyle saw the swing set and playground. "Swing!" He exclaimed running towards the play area. Jacob followed after him, glancing over to where Charlene and Ava were sitting. He waved. Jacob followed Kyle to the playground and pushed his son on the swing.

"Higher!" Kyle shouted. From the swing, they went over to the slide. Jacob carried him up with him and they slid down together. Father and son smiling and laughing. It was one of the best days. How could it not be? Jacob was finally spending time with his son.

Twenty minutes passed. Jacob picked up Kyle, lifted him on his shoulders and walked back to where Charlene and Ava were sitting.

Ava and Charlene smiled, both thinking to themselves, "If only this could be a real family picture, Jacob walking back with *their* son."

Ava longed for little Kyle as much as Charlene longed for Jacob. Ava pulled a camera out of her bag, "Do you mind? I'd like a picture of Jacob and little Kyle." She snapped the shot before Charlene could protest.

"Thank you, Charlene!" Jacob smiled as he handed Kyle back to her. The three of them sat down together. A calm silence came over them, each lost in the moment.

"I've been thinking, Charlene," Jacob commented as he reached for the brown leather briefcase. He snapped the hasps and began to open it. Charlene saw the stacks of $100 bills inside and her mind raced. Her desire battled against her conscience.

"Swallow your pride. Go ahead. Take the money. You know you could use it." She heard Lotus say, "I agree. Take the money. Make him pay!"

"You can't take the money. You'll be indebted to him. He'll have power over you! Never surrender!" She heard Pastor Mike, "Money, my child, is the root of all evil. Stand fast."

Charlene gathered her wits and stopped Jacob before he could go any further. "Don't even think I would accept any money from you! I don't want or need your money! Kyle and I are doing fine on our own!"

"I just want to help out. I don't understand. You never had a problem taking my money before?" Jacob glared.

Charlene acted before giving it any thought and slapped him hard across the face. "How dare you!" She screamed.

Ava tried to calm her down but was unsuccessful. Charlene put Kyle on her hip, grabbed Florence's lunch, and walked away, not looking back. Jacob sat in stunned silence while Ava just shook her head in disbelief and dismay. The bridge she worked so hard to build crumbled into a pile of rubble. It was all for naught.

Back at Florence's boutique, Charlene slammed the door behind her, tears streaming down her face. She sat Kyle down and handed Florence her lunch.

"What the hell happened? Why are you so shaken up?" Florence questioned.

"They were there at Dimitris! Jacob and his wife, Ava! They've found me! What am I going to do?"

"Calm down. Tell me everything that happened."

Charlene took a deep breath and recounted their chance meeting.

"So, this was all by chance? Same place, same time? What are the odds? Why, they're incalculable!" Florence mused. "God! Could they have set the meeting up?" She questioned. Charlene panicked. Her paranoia fed her fears and she bit her lip, "Oh, no?!" She cried.

"Wait a minute, you told them you lived in L.A.? That you were flying back in a couple of days, right?" Florence asked.

"Yes, I did."

"Then, there's nothing to worry about. If Jacob continues

to look for you, he'll search in L.A., not here in Detroit. Just lay low for a bit. They'll fly back to Washington D.C. and everything will go back to normal for you."

"I hope you're right," Charlene murmured, unsure of Florence's conviction.

Later that evening, she undressed Kyle and put him in his pajamas. He had fallen asleep on the floor playing with his toys as he was worn out from the day.

"Night, night, my little prince. Mommy love's you." Charlene gave him hugs and kisses as she laid him on his bed. While putting his shirt and blue jeans in the laundry, she noticed a tuff of hair sticking out of the front pocket. She pulled on it and a 6" long, curly blonde ringlet unfurled, bouncing up and down at the end of her fingertips.

Chapter Twenty-Eight

By mid-November, Charlene had her duties down at Stevens, Corman and Woodworth. Her speed and accuracy impressed all three partners. Stevens and Woodworth agreed that Corman had the best assistant. It was time to put Charlene's skills to work in the courtroom.

"We have a case that could last two, three days down in Cleveland starting next Monday. We'll drive down in my Lincoln. I'll get us hotel rooms at the Garden Suites. During the day, we'll be in court and in the evening, after dinner, we'll work on the case. This will be a good one to get your feet wet and see how you do under pressure."

Charlene made sure everything was okay with Wanda watching Kyle for the three days she'd be gone. "I'll call you every evening," Charlene told Wanda. "Kyle, you be a good boy for Wanda while Mommy's gone. I'll be back before you know it." Charlene hugged him. "I love you, bunches!"

Kyle smiled, "Love you, bunches!"

Monday morning at 6 a.m., Dan Corman and Charlene drove down to Cleveland and secured their rooms at the Garden Suites. In the courtroom by 9 a.m. with opening arguments, Charlene took shorthand, keeping up with the court proceedings. After dinner, Charlene transposed her notes and typed them up. Dan studied the case file, directing questions at Charlene. She scanned through the notes answering quickly and precisely as he planned his strategy for the following day.

Tuesday brought about more deliberation and the trial heated up. By the end of the day, Dan Corman was grasping at straws. Dinner led to drinks to help him relax. They went back to going over the case files as he strategically planned out his moves for the last day of the trial.

Wednesday morning Dan Corman woke with a major headache, possibly from overindulging in scotch. Charlene knocked on his hotel room door. "Are we about ready to get going?" She asked.

"Yes, just about. I'm almost ready." He was standing by the bed smoking a cigarette. Charlene sat down in a chair next to the nightstand to adjust her heels. He stepped closer.

"Help old Dan relieve some stress." He unzipped his pants and pulled out his hardening shaft. Taken aback, Charlene looked up, eyes wide in disbelief. She could hear Lotus, "We've got what they want. Why give it away for free? If the opportunity arises, make them pay for it." Charlene had been in this place before back at the Paradise Club. It was nothing new, except the fact, that this was her boss. Not some guy she probably wouldn't see again.

Charlene smiled up at him and took a gamble, "So, what's in it for me?"

Dan grinned cynically, "Pleasing your boss and getting on my good side of course."

Charlene countered, "Well, I'm thinking I should get a little extra something." She slowly began to stroke him, smiling devilishly.

Dan looked up to the ceiling and let out a long, disgusting moan, "Okay, the quarterly bonus is coming up, Old Dan will make it worth your while. Now do it!"

Satisfied and no longer stressed, Dan zipped his pants, grinning, "Let's go win us a case!"

With his shark-like tactics, Dan Corman rallied and won the case with his closing argument. Thinking to himself and smiling, "I have my personal assistant to thank for her skills."

During the next month at the law firm, Dan made frequent passes at Charlene. Flirtation was at an all-time high. The code of conduct book got lost in the shuffle and they discussed many cases behind the closed doors of his office. Dan enjoyed his stress-free environment and pampered Charlene by setting her up with her own expense account. He gave her the keys to a company car so she could run errands. These included makeovers and going shopping for clothes that Dan insisted she needed for her position. At first, Charlene was hesitant, but it didn't take long for her to fall into place as Dan Corman's new arm candy. At 54, Dan used to feel like every day of 70. It had taken him 20 years to make full partner at the firm and those years had taken their toll. With Charlene on his arm, he felt young again. With a boost in confidence, he began winning more cases and the partners couldn't be happier.

A week before Christmas, on Friday, December 18th, Stevens, Corman and Woodworth held their annual Christmas party at the firm. An elegant dinner was catered and they had an open bar. The partners handed out the quarterly bonus checks as their employees enjoyed cocktails before dinner. Charlene opened her envelope and smiled when she saw the check. Dan Corman had written it for $500.00 instead of the customary $100.00 bonus most employees received. It was like getting an extra month's paycheck. Thinking to herself, "Lotus was right. Why give it away for free? If the opportunity arises, take advantage of it. Make him pay."

A band was hired for dancing in the upstairs conference room that was large enough to accommodate every party they'd ever thrown. Lawyers, secretaries, receptionists, personal assistants and clients enjoyed the evening to the fullest extent, drinking and partying. Dan and Charlene found their way back into his office with a bottle of champagne. They drank it laughing, kissing and tugging at each other's clothes. The alcohol loosened what was left of any inhibitions and poor judgment soon became no judgment at all. Charlene unbuttoned Dan's shirt and then unzipped his pants, removing them. She performed her "stress-relieving exercises," something he could never get enough of. When Dan could take no more and thought he was about to burst, he cleared everything off his black walnut desk with one swipe. Paperwork and files flew about the room landing on the floor. He lifted Charlene on top and ripped her off her skirt, pulling her ass off the edge of the desk. In the sexual frenzy, Charlene very briefly remembered Lotus handing her condoms but, in her acholic haze, she cast the memory aside as quickly as it came to her. Tearing the rest of her clothes off, he kissed her bare breasts and then slid himself inside of her. Her eyes widened as he did. Gipping the edge of the desk, "You're huge!" Charlene cried out, feeling like he was stretching her beyond imagination with every thrust. Soon, the pain gave way to pleasure. Pure unadulterated sex filled their senses. Charlene felt Dan swell inside of her and almost passed out as together they reached a new level of climax. Dan collapsed on top of her, spent. His seed slipped down her inner thigh. Afterward, they cleaned up in the office bathroom and then staggered out into the hall. Charlene put on Dan's long overcoat as there was little to nothing left of her clothes, she pulled on her heels and walked to the front doors.

"I hope you have a Merry little Christmas, and a Happy New Year!" Dan slurred his speech, "Let me drive you home."

Charlene laughed, "You're so funny when your drunk! I live just down the block. I can walk home. Just let me try to sober up first." She poured a cup of day-old coffee from the cold craft in the entrance and drank it, making a face of utter disgust as she swallowed.

Back in her apartment, she shed the overcoat and went to shower. Thankful that she'd left Kyle with Wanda, telling her she'd be out late and would pick him up in the morning. In the bathroom, she glanced in the mirror, thinking she looked twenty years older than her day. Her makeup was smuggled, her hair all a mess and she smelled of raw sex. In her reflection, he appeared out of nowhere, looking over her shoulder. He stared at her from the other side of the mirror, grinning sadistically.

"You dirty little slut. At it again I see. Or, should I call you a whore? Now that you're making money at it. At least you're not giving it away. I always knew you'd be

good at taking dick-tation. Enjoy it while it lasts, cuz, when you think you're at the top the only way left to go, is down! Down, get it! Down on your knees. Doing those stress-relieving exercises for the boss, just so you can stay on top."

Standing there naked, Charlene began to shake as shame overwhelmed her. She smashed the medicine cabinet mirror with a bottle of foundation, cutting her hand in the process. Wrapping her hand in a towel, cussing and crying, she slid to the floor.

In the morning, Charlene had come to terms with what had happened, writing it off as a crazy night. The week before Christmas, she went shopping for little Kyle in Midtown, stuffing the company car with presents, justifying her actions.

Christmas morning, in Wanda's apartment; Charlene, Kyle and Wanda opened the presents that spilled out in every direction beneath the tree. After little Kyle finished with his last gift, Charlene handed Wanda an envelope.

"Here's a little extra something for Christmas. A thank you for all you do."

Wanda shook her head, "I can't take this. You work long hours to make a living for you and little Kyle. Besides, you've already paid me for babysitting."

"Please take it. I'm making good money and can finally afford what I want and what I want is for you to have this."

Wanda nodded with tears in her eyes. "You are too good to me."

On New Year's Eve, Charlene went out with Alice, Walter and Florence for dinner at a beautiful restaurant in

Midtown. Wanda watched little Kyle for the evening. In the restaurant bar, on the color television, they watched the ball drop at the Times Square celebration and counted down the last seconds of 1964.

Chapter Twenty-Nine

It was a dreary and cold Monday morning on January 4th when Charlene walked to the firm. Everyone returned to work and attended the monthly meeting in the conference room.

Mr. Stevens stood up in front and walked to the podium. "Thank you for attending our first meeting of the New Year. I trust each and every one of you had a wonderful Holiday." Mr. Stevens continued, discussing the goals for the new year.

Charlene sat bewildered. The seat for the firm's second partner, Dan Corman, was empty. She checked her calendar and there was nothing in it to explain his absence. Charlene looked around the room and a feeling of self-consciousness swept over her. She thought everyone was looking at her, whispering behind their hands. Charlene began to feel uncomfortably warm as she sank down in her chair, wishing she was invisible. In her subconscious, *the man* laughed. He held her in contempt, his voice taunting,

> *"Now what are you going to do? No more sugar daddy. Maybe old Stevens is looking for a little stress relief..."*

Charlene jumped as Mr. Stevens spoke, "On another note, our second partner, Mr. Corman is not in attendance today and will be out the rest of the week. He has taken an extended vacation with family over the holiday. His employees will work with me and Mr. Woodworth to file and help prepare for upcoming cases."

The meeting came to a close and Mr. Stevens approached her, "Charlene, you look a little flushed. Are you feeling all right?"

Charlene avoided looking into his eyes, "I um, feel a little warm. Maybe I just need some air."

Mr. Stevens nodded, "When you regain your composure, check with Donna. She'll get you situated with some cases that need to be worked on. Nothing too trying, general arranging and transposing notes. I might use you later this week on a case. Mr. Corman really talks you up when it comes to your skills in the courtroom."

The rest of the week, Charlene concentrated on her work and continued to impress Mr. Stevens and Mr. Woodworth. On the following Monday, Dan Corman was seated in his office when Charlene arrived for work.

"Hello Charlene. Are you ready for another week of exciting cases?" Dan questioned, smiling.

Charlene smiled back, "Yes, I am."

"Good. Bring me the Kent Davis personal injury file. Let's get to work."

Charlene found it hard to read Dan. He seemed a bit reserved acting like nothing happened between them.

"Here are the files you requested, Mr. Corman," Charlene said, walking back into the office and placing them on the black walnut desk.

Charlene asked, "Did you enjoy your vacation?"

Dan looked up from the Kent Davis file, "Yes, very much so. I spent it with my family. How about you? How was your holiday?"

"It was nice. I spent Christmas with my son, Kyle. Then, went out with friends for New Year's Eve."

"That sounds like it was fun. Now, about the Kent Davis case. It was supposed to be tried in Ann Arbor but the defense attorney has requested a change of venue to Grand Rapids. Something about where the accident happened. So, it looks like we're going on another road trip. It's almost a three-hour drive so we'll head out early next Monday morning."

"How long do you think we'll be gone?" Charlene asked.

"This might take the week and will depend on varying factors. It will be hard to prove that the C.E.O. of Oakenstone Enterprises was intoxicated behind the wheel the night of the accident. Kent is suing them for $750,000, for personal injury. He may never walk again. We'll do what we can for him. Let's just hope, when the dust settles, there's enough evidence for a win."

Charlene couldn't get her head around the fact that Dan was so businesslike. Maybe things would change when they were away from the office.

As the week progressed, Dan took Charlene out on business lunches to meet with clients. She maintained her professional look with her tight skirts and business dress that Dan had insisted she needed to wear, continuing to be his arm candy.

At home, Charlene made sure Wanda would be able to watch Kyle the next week. She purchased plenty of groceries and supplies for them. With Wanda watching Kyle more and more she worked with him daily on his alphabet and numbers. Charlene had introduced Kyle to picture books but had little time to actually teach him. Wanda was a godsend when it came to teaching and Kyle was catching on quickly, excited when he was able to recite the alphabet and count to ten without many mistakes. Sunday evening, after Charlene tucked Kyle into bed, she kissed him, thanked Wanda and went back to her apartment. All day, she had been feeling off. She felt swelling in her breasts and her nipples were tender. She counted the days back in her mind. She was almost three weeks late. Charlene panicked, "Not again. Oh, hell no!"

Monday morning, they drove to Grand Rapids and made their court appearance at 9 a.m. As usual, the opening arguments were presented and court proceedings continued throughout the day. Charlene took her shorthand, keeping up nicely.

Dan drove to the 29th Street Inn and purchased two adjacent rooms. By mid-week, both Dan and Charlene were feeling the stress of the lengthy trial. After dinner, they went back to the room and began going over the case for what seemed like the hundredth time. Dan, paced smoking cigarettes and pouring scotch into his rock glass. Charlene, sipped a glass of chardonnay while reviewing notes and answering questions. While pacing, Dan's shoe caught the corner of the desk sending files onto the floor. Charlene bent down to pick them up and Dan towered over her.

"Did you enjoy your bonus?" he asked.

Charlene looked up smiling. "Yes, very much so. Thank

you. We had a wonderful Christmas. It was nice to have extra presents under the tree."

Dan grinned as he unzipped his pants. "I told you Old Dan would make it worth your while!"

"Will you continue to do so?" Charlene asked as she stroked him to hardness.

"You know it," Dan assured her.

Charlene performed her stress relief but didn't finish. Instead, she leaned over the bed and Dan lifted her skirt pulling her panties aside. "I see you want some stress relief, too," Laughing as he plunged into her, riding her until he pushed Charlene over the edge, she screamed in ecstasy.

The last night before closing arguments, they shared a bed together for the first time and slept through the night. Well rested, they enjoyed breakfast and cruised through the final court proceedings.

"Have you reached a verdict?" The judge asked the head juror.

"Yes, we have Your Honor." A hush fell over the courtroom.

"The jury rules for the plaintiff, awarding Kent Davis damages totaling $675,000."

Kent let out a sigh shaking Dan Corman's hand. "It's not what we asked for but, it's close enough, Thank you!"

"Payday!" Dan grinned at Charlene as they exited the courtroom.

On the way back to Detroit, Charlene considered sharing her concerns about the possibility of her being pregnant but thought better of it. After all, she wasn't sure she was pregnant. There had been a lot of stress lately. Maybe she'd have her period soon. Deep down Charlene knew that was wishful thinking.

Monday, February 1st

Charlene woke up with morning sickness. After she cleaned herself up, she got Kyle out of bed and took him over to Wanda's. At the firm, she sat through the monthly morning meeting. Dan smiled at her as she followed him into his office. He closed the door and came up from behind, grabbing her ass. "Wanna have a little morning fun?" He teased. Knowing what he wanted she led him to his office chair, got on her knees, and unzipped his pants. As she stroked his shaft hard, Charlene decided the time had come to tell him.

"Dan, I'm pregnant." She watched the look on his face fearing the worst.

He stiffened holding her at arm's length, "Pregnant?"

"Yes, pregnant. And yes, I'm sure. And, yes, it is yours. I haven't been with anyone else since you hired me."

Dan stood and zipped his pants, no longer in the mood for a little morning fun. He ran his hand through what was left of his graying hair.

"How far along are you?" He questioned, stepping into lawyer mode.

"I figure it happened the night of the Christmas party. That was the 18th of December. Do the math, that makes it six weeks since you came inside me. Remember?" Charlene questioned, dryly.

"We were trashed. I don't remember much of anything from that night."

"Remember or not, I'm pregnant and you're the father."

"Well, what do you want me to do about it?" Dan questioned defensively.

Charlene stood up crossing her arms, "What do I want you to do about it? Well first off, I want you to step up and take responsibility. We should get married."

"Get married? You've got to be kidding! We were just having fun! I don't even love you!" Dan exclaimed.

"What's love got to do with it? We need to get married to avoid scandal. It would really suck if your partners find out! What would become of your career?" Charlene questioned innocently.

Thinking to himself, he cursed, "You conniving little bitch."

Blinded by the sex, too late, he discovered that Charlene Strypher was a formidable adversary, always one move ahead with her eyes on the prize.

"Okay. You win, you're right. If we do this, things will continue as they have and I mean no changes whatsoever. You'll work here until you start to show. Then, you'll resign from your position. We'll be married by the Justice of Peace and you'll move into my place."

Charlene smiled, "Sounds good, with a few changes."

"Like what?" Dan questioned.

"We go to the Justice of the Peace and get married this month, on Friday, February 12th. As close to Valentine's Day as we can legally get. I'll move in with you and in exchange, I'll keep my mouth shut. Your partners will never know." Shamelessly leveraging her demands against him, Charlene could see her white picket fence rising out of the ash. Financial stability was within reach and to Hell with her husband's approval.

Dan sighed. "Deal." He knew that he'd been beaten.

The rest of the day they worked on case files. Charlene acted as if nothing had happened. Dan was still reeling, calculating his next move. He realized he had none and submitted to what he thought was defeat. Charlene noticed he was tense around her.

"Don't fret Dan. We can still have fun. I agree, no changes whatsoever." Charlene grinned as she grabbed his ass.

"To the victor go the spoils then?" Dan questioned, with an uncertain smile.

"Something like that. I get what I want and you continue to get what you want," Charlene coaxed seductively.

They stayed late and waited until everyone had gone home. Charlene picked up where she left off, on her knees. Dan would have let her finish but, he picked her up and took her against the wall. The feeling of sex at this new level of commitment was intoxicating. They climaxed together in a gray area, somewhere between right and wrong.

Charlene spent the next week planning and re-planning. She was excited that she was about to secure a solid future for herself, Kyle and her unborn child. The caseloads slowed, allowing time for Dan and Charlene to get their blood tests, pick up their marriage license and schedule a time with the Justice of Peace.

At 1 p.m. on Friday, February 12th, Dan and Charlene walked up the steps in front of the Wayne County Courthouse. Charlene was dressed in a white skirt and blouse with a white lace cape draped around her shoulders. She had let her hair grow and had styled it in a bob, dying it back to her original strawberry blonde color. Dan wore a black custom-fit suit and tie with black slacks and wingtips. They resembled a couple on a cake topper, standing there in front of the Justice of the Peace. The witnesses were the court stenographer and a bailiff that signed the marriage certificate. The paperwork took longer to get together and processed than it did for the actual ceremony. It may have not been the wedding that Charlene dreamed of, but it was a wedding just the same. Her wedding. On her terms. Charlene held the key to their two-story mansion in the upscale city of Grosse Pointe. Her white picket fence was freshly painted and it shone brightly in the afternoon sun.

On March 1st, Charlene packed up her apartment and picked up Kyle from Wanda, thanking her for babysitting. Wanda made Charlene promise that she would keep in touch and bring her family by whenever she was in the neighborhood. Charlene resigned from her position at Stevens, Corman, and Woodworth the following week.

The mansion in Grosse Pointe sat on a ½ acre of land nestled against a private beach on Lake St. Clair. The front portico, with its marbled pillars, led to the dark walnut front door with a half-moon-stained glass window. On a brass plaque the name, Corman, gleamed beneath the matching door knocker. Inside, the formal living room with its white carpet and white leather furniture trimmed in gold, looked like it belonged in a museum. The formal dining room, with the highly polished mahogany table and buffet, appeared to have never been used and the gourmet kitchen would make any culinary chef drool at its design and high-end appliances. Upstairs the master bedroom was adorned with plush cream-colored carpeting and a king-sized deep mahogany canopy bed. It was complimented by matching nightstands and dressers with ornate mirrors. The closet was a room all its own with storage and space enough for even Florence's wardrobe of a thousand outfits. The master bath sported a sunk-in tub, walk-in tiled shower and a marble-topped two-sink vanity. All with gold hardware. Off the master bedroom, was another suite with a turret overlooking Lake St. Clair. Charlene decided it would make the perfect nursery. The third bedroom, with a half bath, was located downstairs just off the formal dining room. Dan converted that room into an office that housed his floor-to-ceiling bookcases, filled with law books and ledgers. The black walnut leather top executive desk brought a smile to Charlene's face. Out back, the pool waited patiently for the summer to come back around, as did the catamaran winterized and tucked away in the boathouse. This was an estate that would be pictured in magazines, advertising Grosse Pointe to those who could afford a life of luxury. Charlene was in seventh heaven. "So, this is how it feels to be at the top. I could get used to this!" She exclaimed, falling back onto the king-sized canopy bed.

Within the week Dan fitted the nursery with a customized car-shaped bed for Kyle and a crib that Charlene positioned in front of the turret window.

"I'm hoping for a girl!" Charlene told Dan one evening. "We could paint the nursery pink. What do you think?" Charlene asked.

Dan just rolled his eyes, "Don't go buying dolls or painting the nursery pink until after the baby is born. What if it's a boy? That could scar him for life."

Charlene gave it some thought and laughed, "Let's agree to disagree on that one."

At the firm, Dan hired a new personal assistant as he could no longer use Charlene at the office or on the road. Charlene did help out in the home office as her skills far exceeded any personal assistant he'd ever had. In the office, they would work on case files behind a locked door so there would be no chance of an interruption, by Kyle, just in case the stress levels became too intense. Throughout the rest of her pregnancy, Charlene enjoyed her life of luxury. Basking in the summer sun as Kyle played in the shallow end of the pool with swim floaties attached to his arms. On weekends, Dan would take them on boat rides in their catamaran. The white sails billowed against a deep blue, southern Michigan sky.

The life of luxury, as it does with many that haven't been born into it, went to Charlene's head and encased her heart in a layer of ice. Months went by and she never made an attempt to reconnect with Alice, Florence, or Lotus. She barely noticed her, "past life," as she referred to it, slip away into a distant memory.

The doctor set Charlene's due date for September 16th. Fortunately for Dan, being the second pregnancy, Charlene had a better idea of what to expect. As the date approached, a high-profile personal injury case that require all three partners to get involved, took Dan to Chicago. Each partner had their own special expertise. In cases of this magnitude, when all three partners worked together, it was a thing of beauty. Like a well-oiled machine, they were usually unstoppable. Usually was the keyword. In this particular case, a group of 50 people signed on to test a new product designed to streamline the weight-loss industry. The company guaranteed their product to be safe but, in the end, sickness with severe consequences resulted in long-term effects. Over half filed suit against the company, five of whom lost loved ones. The high-profile case began on Tuesday, September 7th. The partners predicted that they could wrap it up for the win within the week. They were wrong. The company that initiated the test had the people sign waivers, so technically, there was no case from the company's viewpoint. However, the wording in those documents was vague, misleading and not properly written. The trial became lengthy and expensive. The jury was sequestered after the defendant claimed possible media influence. Deliberation continued. In the midst of the chaos, Charlene went into hard labor on the evening of September 14th and was admitted to the hospital. The partners wouldn't let Dan leave early as the case was so close to being decided and a sum of money thought to be astronomical was up for grabs. Dan was needed for closing arguments that should have happened days ago. The jury was deadlocked and, in the end, there was a mistrial. The partners flew back to Detroit empty-handed on September 17th. Dan arrived at the hospital and Charlene looked up from the bed. She gave a weak smile. In her arms, wrapped in a light blue baby blanket, sleeping peacefully, lay their son.

"Let me introduce you. This is Daniel David Corman. He's a big fella. Weighs almost ten pounds. I was in labor for 16 hours and it was excruciating! Where were you? You missed your firstborn son's birth!"

"That wasn't my fault! I couldn't get away," Dan insisted.

"Your partners have families and I bet they would have made it a point to break away for *their* first child's birth!" Charlene became combative.

"You know how they can be! The case took longer than anticipated. I was needed for the closing arguments."

Charlene scoffed, "I needed you here, with me. So, did you at least win the damn case?"

Dan shook his head, "No, it was a hung jury that ended up in a mistrial. We'll regroup and decide what to do after talking with our clients."

In the months to come, Dan's stress, both in and out of the office, began to escalate. He was losing more cases than he won and the partners were becoming financially concerned. Charlene did her best to keep things going smoothly on the home front, to no avail. Her stress relief tactics began to lose their charm for Dan and she wondered if his new personal assistant had taken her place. Feeling rejected and less attractive on the inside, Charlene struggled to at least maintain her outward appearance. She painted a smile on and dressed the part of the good wife. In public, when they were together, they continued the façade. If it was a newspaper headline it would read, "Country Club Elite maintains their status and continues to mingle with the beautiful people." The game continued, as did their downward spiral. Drinking and partying seemed the only way to keep their sanity in check. It spilled over into the home where Dan drank extensively. His fuse was short and he often exploded, going off on the children when their toys were underfoot. He would lock them in the nursery as punishment. Charlene and Dan would fight behind closed doors. At first, when they were worn out from yelling and arguing, they would end up having angry makeup sex. Eventually, there was no makeup sex at all. Just arguing and the bitterness remained. Verbal abuse was at an all-time high as her white picket fence morphed into a prison wall. Charlene's only solace and reprieve was when Dan, "The Warden," wasn't around.

Charlene went all out for little Danny's first birthday party by having an outdoor feast catered and inviting the neighborhood. All Dan could do was fret about the cost of the event. As cases became less frequent, it wasn't just the firm whose finances were in peril. Charlene had no idea their bank accounts were dwindling and Dan's credit was maxed to the hilt. The sharks began to circle his Catamaran, anchored just off the beach.

Still attempting to maintain their status, Dan and Charlene attended the New Year's Eve party at the Arrowhead Country Club. Dressed to the nine's, they enjoyed dinner and danced to Glen Miller's band, which was the highlight of their evening. In between dances, while Dan went to visit with some of his golfing buddies, a familiar voice from long ago called out her name. Charlene turned around to find none other than Jacob MacDonald, standing in front of her. Stunned by his presence, she struggled to maintain her composure. So many feelings hit her all at once. Half of her wanted to slap him and the other half wanted to embrace him as she secretly still held him in the deepest recesses of her heart.

"Jacob? What are you doing here?"

"Ava and I are members of Arrowhead. I was in town on business, Ava flew in and we're here to ring in 1967."

Charlene wanted to tell him he looked good all dressed

up, instead, she held out her hand to show him her one-carat diamond ring. "I'm married now."

"I heard you got married, Congratulations. So how is…?"

Before he could continue, Charlene interrupted, "You've heard? How so? We never even announced our engagement, let alone our marriage!"

Jacob just looked at her, thinking to himself, "It's what I do. How could I not know? Did you really think I would just disappear from Kyle's life? Not a chance. He's my son." Jacob continued to stare at her, then asked, "How's Kyle? I'll bet he's growing."

Charlene answered, "Yes, he is growing. He loves his little brother, Danny. We celebrated Danny's first birthday on September 16th. They are the cutest pair, always getting into things. I swear, sometimes I can barely keep up." She smiled and Jacob noticed a tell-tale sign in her eyes. She was tired. Charlene's confidence and composure began to wane.

"It's been almost two years since I last saw my son." Jacob hesitated, "I'll be flying out next month to Japan on business. I'd like to take Kyle with me. Before you say no, please, hear me out. Japan has an amazing culture. Kyle would have the best schooling and I believe it would do him a world of good to have this opportunity. I have a contact that would give him the best care imaginable while I'm at work. I'd be home every evening so we'd spend quality time together." Jacob waited and Charlene could see the hope in his eyes, the same hope she saw in Midtown.

Charlene shook her head slowly, thinking to herself, "Japan? It had to be a mission. It could be dangerous. What if something went wrong?"

Then her eyes flashed angrily, "First, you have the audacity to offer me money, saying you just want to help out. We both know your real intentions, to get Kyle for your own. Maybe you thought you could somehow buy him from me with your brown leather briefcase stuffed full of cash. Fat chance! Now, you want to take him away from me, all the way across the world? Are you out of your fucking mind? Not just no but hell no! Kyle is mine!" Charlene struggled to maintain control.

"I'm flying out in two weeks. I'd like to at least see Kyle. Maybe we can meet at that deli in Midtown?" Jacob asked. He snapped his fingers, "Dimitri's? We could have lunch. Or if you'd like we can meet at Wanda's place."

"Wanda's place? How do you know about Wanda? Jacob, you know too much, you've been keeping tabs on me!"

Jacob became tired of the game and he tipped his hand. "Of course, I have been keeping tabs. I saw right through your lie when you told us you were visiting from Los Angles. You arrived from Houston and never left after you got here. I just had to watch Alice and Florence's place, including her boutique in Midtown. I knew you'd show up sooner or later. The fake letter addressed to Alice from you with a Los Angles address? Now that, *that* was a clever ruse. I almost fell for it but I knew it wasn't your handwriting. As for Wanda, it wasn't hard for me to figure that out either. Once you took that job at the firm, I just sat back and waited for you to find an apartment. When you married your boss, Ava suggested I step back and let you live your life and now we're here. I don't want to cause problems, Charlene. I just want to see my son. Why can't you understand that?"

"Oh, I understand it. That's not the problem! The

problem is that I don't trust *You*, Jacob MacDonald! Stay away from us!" Charlene cried.

Not to further cause a scene, Jacob called out just as she turned her back on him to leave, "Okay, I'll stay away. For now. But know this, I can find you anywhere and someday I'll be back when Kyle is old enough to decide for himself."

Charlene whirled back around but, before she could respond, Jacob was gone. He'd disappeared into the crowd of New Year's Eve guests as they counted down to 1967.

On New Year's Day, Dan and Charlene picked the boys up from Wanda's. Hungover, they went back to their mansion and lazed the day away. Dan continued to libate and Charlene watched the children as they played in their suite. She sipped chardonnay, pondering her dilemma. The walls of her prison had begun to close in on her months ago. She felt like she was in a round room searching for a corner. Depression ate away at her lust for life. Every day was the same, an endless game of trying to maintain the status that faded away long ago. It became tiresome and all that remained was a shell of a relationship built on lies and deceit. Still, she soldiered on, lost in an endless maze.

On Saturday evening, February 11th, the day before their anniversary, Charlene was upstairs doing anything she could to distance herself from Dan who was in his office when the telephone rang. She answered it.

"Hello? Corman residence."

"Hello, this is Meredith."

"Oh Hi, you're Dan's sister, right? I saw a picture in his office of you and your husband christening his Catamaran, *Due Process.* I've looked forward to meeting you."

"Sister? Is that what he told you? Really? Let me guess. You're his personal assistant."

"No, I'm Charlene. His wife!"

"You're his what? Wife? Since when?" She asked incredulously.

"Well, two years now. We married right after I got pregnant with our son Danny. Tomorrow happens to be our anniversary.'

There was a long pause. "Happy Anniversary, Bitch! I've been his wife for over 20 years. We have three sons together down here in North Carolina. Our oldest just turned 19 last week!"

What was left of Charlene's world shattered and all she could say was, "Un-fucking-believable," she slammed down the receiver. Her mind racing, she dressed the boys in their winter jackets. She put on her coat and grabbed her bag from the nursery. They walked downstairs. Dan came out of his office holding a half bottle of scotch slurring his speech, "Who was that on the phone and where the hell are you going?"

Standing by the door, Charlene pulled off her wedding ring and threw it at him, "It was your sister, oh! I mean your wife, Meredith!" Charlene shook her head in disgust, "You Fucking Bastard!"

Dan crossed the room in seconds. He slapped her across the face and pushed her against the wall. Bracing for another strike, Charlene shielded her children. Then, bringing her knee upward and solidly connecting with his groin, she screamed, "This is for all you fucking assholes who have screwed me over!" Dan buckled to his knees, groaning in agony, holding his crotch. "We're leaving and you'll never see us again!" Charlene picked up Danny and set him on her hip then opened the door. In one swift movement, she pulled Kyle through. They heard a bottle shatter against an interior wall as Dan bellowed incoherently in primal rage.

Chapter Thirty

Outside a winter storm was building, the wind howled relentlessly and falling ice crystals stung their faces as the bitter cold cut through their clothes. Danny and Kyle began to cry as Charlene knelt down in the snow and pulled the hood up around Kyle's head.

"Don't cry. Everything will be okay. We've got to be strong." Charlene did her best to reassure her sons. She feared her words, like her life, were being blown away by the perpetual hurricane of her twisted reality.

Trudging through the snow, along the street, she pushed on and took shelter from the unforgiving storm in an inner-city bus enclosure. She pulled her children close and then realized they weren't alone. A hollow-eyed drifter, huddled in one corner, was conserving what remained of his body heat. From inside his coat, he pulled out a bottle of brandy, took a swig and with a weak, broken smile that crunched up under a full beard, he offered it to Charlene. In other circumstances, she would have turned up her nose in utter disgust. This time, she discovered a strange rapport. Almost a kinship with this lost soul. She took the bottle, thinking for a second she should wipe off the mouth. Instead, casting away her last shred of dignity, she nodded a thank you and sipped the deep purple liquid. It burned down her throat, warming her inners. Handing the bottle back to the drifter, she noticed the headlights of a taxi cab. Knowing her children couldn't take the bitter cold any longer, she waved him down. They got in and the driver looked at her in his rearview mirror.

"Where to, Lady?" He questioned.

"Anywhere warm. The closest motel will do." Charlene dug through her bag. In a small inner pocket, she found a twenty-dollar bill tucked away in case she ever needed a little extra cash.

"Closest one is the Shady Pine Motel, about a mile from here." The cabby commented.

"That works," Charlene replied, holding Danny and rubbing Kyle's hands in hers, trying to get his little fingers warm.

The cabby pulled into the driveway at the motel. Charlene paid him and took her boys inside to the front desk. The room was ten dollars for the night. Inside, Charlene cuddled up with her sons in the double bed. Worn out from enduring the cold, they fell fast asleep. Sunday morning, Charlene got up and pulled the curtain aside. The snow continued to fall. Old Man Winter held Detroit tightly in his grasp. The boys were still asleep at 10 a.m. and checkout time was at eleven. Charlene went through her bag, searching in vain for more money. She found none. After the cab fare and the motel, she had eight dollars left. In bed, the children stirred. Kyle sat up and rubbed his eyes.

"I'm hungry, Mommy."

"I know. Me, too. Let's see if we can find a restaurant

somewhere close." She attempted to sound cheery. Danny woke up crying. Charlene had gotten used to this over the past 17 months, as he was not a morning child. She held Danny, comforting him.

"I know, shh, it's okay. Let's find you something to eat." Charlene dug through her bag and found his bottle and formula. She made it with warm water from the bathroom sink. After Danny had his fill, she changed him. Charlene bundled the boys up in their coats, put hers on as well, grabbed her bag and the three of them stepped out into another snowy day. Across the street, a corner diner, despite the weather, was filled with Sunday after-churchgoers. While Kyle finished a breakfast of pancakes and sausage links, Charlene had a cup of coffee and nibbled on a Danish. She paid for their breakfast and was left with just six dollars and 92 cents. She noticed, on the bulletin board, a poster advertising a local mission. It read, "Come in out of the cold. Join us for dinner at the Labre Rescue Mission, 77 Saint Benedict Avenue, every Sunday evening." Outside, the snow continued to fall and the wind had picked up. Charlene used the payphone and called a cab.

Blank stares and odd smells from the homeless welcomed Charlene and her little family into their midst when they entered the mission. As she stood in the long soup line with her children, she was overcome with trepidation. The sheer magnitude of her situation was overwhelming and the room began to spin. Charlene felt like the kid back in school.

Caught in the middle of a group of playground bullies. They were all there, circling around her, the nameless faces urging them on. Then, Dan was raising his hand to slap her, Jacob was reaching out, trying to grab Kyle and Skip was unbuttoning his pants, sneering. The man stepped forth, his belt hissing as it cleared the belt loops, taunting her with his degrading accusations.

Charlene cowered and thought she would pass out. Then, she heard... "Breathe in, hold it. Let it out slowly. And, again," Alice was there. She reached out and hugged Charlene but the response was stiff and emotionless. As Charlene looked up, there was a vacancy in her eyes. It was blank, cold and unyielding. Taken aback, shaking her head in disbelief and embarrassment, she stammered, "What...? Why? What are you doing here?"

"I volunteer to help out in the soup kitchen every Sunday here at the mission. Oh my God, Charlene! What's happened to you?" Alice questioned.

"We're fine. Just a little down and out at the moment," Charlene managed.

"Fine?! You're in a soup line at Labre Rescue Mission! This is far from fine! Charlene, please let me help you and your boys. Come live with Walter and me or you can stay with Mom. We'll get you back on your feet again.

Charlene just shook her head, "I've got this. Just let it go. I don't want your sympathy. I've got a lead on a new job that I'll check out in the morning."

"At least let me take the boys until you can get back on your feet. Walter and I can raise them for a while. I'm Kyle's Godmother for Pete's sake!" Alice pleaded.

"Raise my boys? Not on your life. Besides, Jacob and Dan

would find them and take them from you. That is not going to happen! If I can't have them, no one can! Do you understand me? No one! Just leave us alone!" Charlene raged.

Alice was at a total loss. As she stared, unbelieving, her heart ached.

She sighed, "The storm is getting worse and if I don't leave now, I won't make it home. There are wool blankets for you and the boys. After you eat you can get some sleep. Stay warm. I'll be back in the morning to check on you. We'll fix breakfast and talk things through. I love you, Charlene." Alice turned as tears ran down her cheeks. She got into her car and banged her hands on the steering wheel in anger at Charlene's stubbornness and foolish pride.

In the morning, the storm subsided and Alice made her way to the mission. She searched among the remaining homeless. Charlene, Kyle and Danny were gone. They'd left before Alice could get back.

Charlene took her boys and boarded the inner-city transit to Saint Christopher's Recovery Mission in south Detroit. Inside, the volunteers prepared breakfast and furnished Charlene with baby formula for Danny's bottle. After they ate their fill, a short, heavier-set, curly-haired, black woman approached them offering a warm smile through perfect bright white teeth. Her blue, thick-framed glasses made her eyes larger than they actually were.

"Hello! Such a beautiful little family, welcome to Saint Christopher's! My name is Luanne Braden." She shook Charlene's hand, gave a quick tickle to Kyle and tousled Danny's dark brown hair. "Handsome boys!" Her pleasant, unjudging demeanor won Charlene over immediately.

"Nice to meet you, I'm Charlene Strypher and these are my sons, Kyle and Danny."

"Charlene. What brings you to Saint Christopher's? Isn't there anyone that you and your boys can stay with that is willing to help out? Family or friends?" Luanne questioned.

Charlene hesitated, "There's no one. My parents are dead and I found out my alcoholic husband, Dan is married to another woman. He's gotten so abusive, that I fear for our lives. We left with just the clothes on our backs. I have nowhere else to turn." Charlene replied.

"I'm so sorry to hear that. Is Dan the father of these two strapping young lads?" Luanne smiled at the boys.

"Just Danny, my youngest. Kyle's father, Ky… Ja… Jacob, is out of the picture."

Luanne sighed, "I see this happen so many times to young women just starting out. It's so sad. Charlene, this is no life for you and especially your sons. If there is no one for you to stay with, you are welcome here at our mission. We can help." Luanne continued, "You might consider giving your boys to families that are financially stable. Families who will love and raise them as their own. I'm not saying you are a bad mother, because I know you love these two with all your heart. I'm just saying that you can share that love by giving them both better lives. You could start over someday, knowing that your boys are loved and safe with their new families."

Charlene wrestled with her thoughts, then conceding, not to defeat, but to hope and reason that Luanne was right. "So, how does it work?" Charlene questioned.

"We'll go over to our adoption agency and fill out the paperwork. I promise. This is the best thing for your children.

We'll foster them until we can find a suitable family. You have nothing to worry about." Luanne assured her.

At the agency, Luanne took Kyle's hand in hers and an assistant picked up Danny.

"Come with me. We have a fun playroom down the hall with lots of toys and other children to play with," Luanne told them.

Charlene knelt down and gave Kyle a hug. "You go with Miss Luanne. Mommy is going to stay here in the front office and fill out some paperwork. I love you." Charlene watched, choking back tears, as they turned and walked down the hall. In the room, there were other children happily playing with toys and Kyle excitedly joined them.

Back in the office, Luanne produced the paperwork. "Once your sons are adopted, their last names will change to the adoptive parents. Their birth certificates will be changed, also. No one will ever be able to find them. As for your alcoholic husband, with him being married to another woman, your marriage will be annulled. He will have no rights to Danny whatsoever. What about Kyle's father, Jacob? Do you know where he is?"

Charlene shook her head, "I have no idea. He's never been a part of our lives."

"Well then, that won't be a problem either. Just sign at the bottom of these documents and we'll get the boys into the system." Luanne handed her a pen.

Charlene hesitated. Her hand shook, barely able to hold the penpoint on the dotted line.

"I really don't want to do this to Kyle, he's my life and I love him so much." Charlene broke down crying.

"You're not doing this *to* Kyle. You're doing this *for* Kyle. I know this is hard for you, Charlene, but it's best for your sons, both of them. They will have better lives. I promise I will make it so Kyle can find you someday. You can check in here at the agency regularly and I'll keep you posted as to how the boys are doing. There will be limits, of course, to what I can share."

Charlene reasoned with her conscience, steadied herself and signed the documents. A strange peace came over her as she did so. Charlene believed she was making the right choice. She got up, turned and walked towards the front door. As she opened it and stepped outside, Charlene heard Kyle behind her, yelling down the hall, "Mommmeee…!"

She was gone in an instant. Gone from her son's life. Gone forever.

In the office, Luanne spoke to the director. "We've got to get him placed, now! The trauma will be devastating, is devastating, not to mention the abandonment issues that await him. That poor child hasn't stopped crying since his mother left."

The Director replied. "The foster family will be here soon. He'll be… Fine."

Caught in the game
of don't ask, don't tell
Lies and deceit
soon take their toll
It feels like heaven,
then hurts like hell
to gamble your heart
and lose your soul...

Dear Reader,

We hope you enjoyed, "Justified?" by Rob Piotter.

The journey is far from over. Please enjoy this teaser to his upcoming novel, Unhinged!

"Mommy? Mommy?! "Mommmeee…!"" Kyle watched in horror, tears streaming down his face as the front door closed in front of him. Luanne rushed to his side. Kneeling down, she held him. "Shh… Everything is going to be okay. Your brother needs you to be strong. Let's go find little Danny," she coaxed gently, methodically, slowly. Quietly even. Luanne led him back down to the nursery. Danny was crying, as well. He was sitting with his back against the wall, baby toys strewn across the floor. As soon as he saw his big bother, Kyle, Danny's tears began to abate. His sobs dwindled to hiccupping gasps. Walking over to him, in his best, well beyond his age, with his five-year-old voice, he spoke, "Just breathe, everything will be okay, we've got to be strong, we can do this."

Luanne could see the weight on Kyle's shoulders, it was unfathomable and it broke her heart. Thinking to herself, "This little boy is far from *fine*."

The rest of the day, they played with toys. At dinner, the boys picked at their meal with little to no appetite. Luanne was at a loss. All she could do was care for them and pray. As long as they were here, she would prepare them for the traumatic aftermath that was sure to come. The emotional roller coaster ride of foster care placement, interviews and meeting prospective adoptive parents and the like were enough to cripple any adult, let alone a small child. Luanne thought to herself, "What would cause a young mother to abandon her two beautiful boys?

Was she... Justified?"

Watch for Rob's next novel
Unhinged!
The saga continues...

CPSIA information can be obtained
at www.ICGtesting.com
Printed in the USA
BVHW050332271222
654921BV00002B/2

9 781977 258267